PENGUIN BOOKS

An Orphan's Wish

Beryl Matthews grew up in a family of avid readers. Amongst other jobs, she has worked at an aircraft factory and as a credit controller. She published her first book at the age of 71 after joining a writers' group and has since written over twenty novels. Her hobbies include travelling, swimming and golf, but writing is her first and foremost joy.

An Orphan's Wish

BERYL MATTHEWS

PENGUIN BOOKS

PENGUIN BOOKS

UK | USA | Canada | Ireland | Australia
India | New Zealand | South Africa

Penguin Books, Penguin Random House UK,
One Embassy Gardens, 8 Viaduct Gardens, London SW11 7BW

penguin.co.uk
global.penguinrandomhouse.com

First published as *Fighting with Shadows* by Penguin Books 2005
This edition published 2023
001

Set in Monotype Garamond by
Palimpsest Book Production Limited, Polmont, Stirlingshire
Printed and bound in Great Britain by Clays Ltd, Elcograf S.p.A.

The authorized representative in the EEA is Penguin Random House Ireland,
Morrison Chambers, 32 Nassau Street, Dublin D02 YH68

A CIP catalogue record for this book is available from the British Library

ISBN: 978-1-405-94063-4

www.greenpenguin.co.uk

Dear Reader,

An Orphan's Wish is my fifth book with Penguin and I very much hope you enjoy it. When I had the idea for this story, I couldn't wait to start writing and see it take shape and form. I loved it so much that it seemed to be finished in no time at all.

That isn't always the case, but whether the story comes slowly or tumbles out, I find the process of transferring an idea into words on a page exciting. I consider myself very fortunate to be doing something as enjoyable as writing.

While I am in the process of creating a story, the characters are with me all the time, whatever I'm doing. Angie and the little boy Danny were my constant companions for several months. I felt their pain, sorrow, laughter and joy.

One of the biggest rewards is knowing that my books have brought pleasure; that for a few hours you have left behind the problems of everyday life, as I do when I am writing. I would love to hear what you think of *An Orphan's Wish*. Do you remember this period just after the end of the Second World War? You can write to me c/o Penguin at any time, and you can sign up for my regular newsletter telling you what I am up to!

Many thanks for reading my books,

Love,

Beryl Matthews

To sign up for Beryl's regular newsletter, please visit www.penguin.co.uk/berylmatthews to register your details; alternatively, please send your details and any correspondence to Beryl Matthews c/o Abbie Sampson, Penguin General Publicity, 80 Strand, London, WC2R 0RL.

I

Stepney, London, 27 May 1949

Danny Harris ran into the front room, giggling, and threw himself on the floor next to his mother. She was always playing games with him and they had such fun. It was his birthday today. He was three!

With a squeal of delight he leant across his mother. He'd tickle her. She liked that.

When she didn't move, he sat back on his heels, his bottom lip trembling with disappointment and fair hair falling in his eyes. 'Mummy?' She wasn't laughing. Why wasn't she laughing? She always laughed and kicked in delight.

Danny started to cry. Now he was frightened. 'I don't like this game,' he sobbed. 'Mummy! Mummy!'

Terror took hold and he scrambled to his feet, eyes fixed on the silent form of his mother as he backed away. 'Auntie Angel,' he cried. 'Must find Auntie.'

He hurtled to the front door, standing on tiptoe to open the latch. It was a struggle; he could only just reach it. Once outside he started to run, tripped and fell on the path with a crash. He was immediately back on his feet and tearing along the pavement.

Auntie lived close. He knew that. He pounded along,

sobbing. Where was her house? He'd only been there with his mummy or auntie. On reaching the end of the road, he spun round in confusion, then began running back, sobbing in great wrenching cries. He was lost; he didn't know where he was! This shouldn't be happening today. It was his birthday! Mummy had made a great big cake and bought him lots of lovely presents. 'Mummy, Mummy, I'm frightened.'

Out of breath with running and crying at the same time, he stopped, stood where he was and started to scream. 'Auntie Angel! Auntie Angel! Where are you? I want you. Please, Auntie!'

Suddenly he was swept up and a familiar voice was saying, 'I'm here, Danny. Shush, be quiet. Whatever is the matter?'

He threw his arms around her neck and held on with all his might. His auntie was here. He was safe. She'd talk to Mummy about frightening him so much. That was not a nice game. He hadn't liked it.

He felt the comfort of her hand running over his hair and he whimpered on her shoulder. 'Mummy won't play! Mummy won't play.'

Angie Westwood held Danny close, speaking gently in an effort to calm him. The boy was distraught, and had even wet himself. His little trousers were sopping. Her heart was hammering at an alarming rate. Dear God, what had happened? He was always such a happy child.

Several of the neighbours had rushed out to see what the commotion was all about, but Angie told them everything was all right. Danny had got out and become frightened, that was all. They had always looked down on her cousin Jane for becoming pregnant at the age of seventeen and not marrying. Jane had never told anyone who Danny's father was, but she adored her son and was a marvellous mother. She would never let her darling son be frightened like this!

'Mummy won't play,' Danny moaned, his head tucked on to her shoulder.

'All right, my lovely,' she soothed, returning to her house as quickly as possible. She wasn't going to be able to put the boy down because he was hanging on in desperation. Hitching her handbag on her arm, she left the house. 'We'll go and see her now, shall we?'

The only reply was a sob that shook right through him. He was shaking badly and still whimpering. It was a heart-rending sound.

Angie slammed the front door of her house and hurried to Jane's, just six houses down the road. She hoisted Danny to a more comfortable position, ignoring the wet seeping through her jumper. Poor little thing, she thought, dropping a kiss on the top of his head. He must have sneaked out to find her and Jane hadn't seen him go. It had to be something like that. What else could it be? Jane would be frantic. Angie loved Danny, and often envied her cousin for having such an adorable child. She hoped to have children of her own when she married Alan. They had been going out for six months, and she was sure he was about to propose soon.

She was surprised to see Jane's front door wide open and she hurried inside. 'Jane!'

'Mummy's in the front room.' Danny lifted his head, his face smeared with tears. 'She won't play!'

Now she was thoroughly alarmed. Why did he keep saying that she wouldn't play? Her anxiety had been building all the way here and now she felt ill with worry. A quick glance in the front room made panic rip through her. Jane was on the floor, unmoving. She must have fainted; she did sometimes but always recovered quickly. It had never been anything to worry about, at least, that's what she had always been told.

'Mummy . . .' Danny was gazing at his mother. 'Why won't she get up?'

'I expect she's fainted.' Angie took Danny into the kitchen. 'I want you to stay here while I go and help your mummy.'

His arms relaxed their tight grip and he allowed Angie to sit him on a chair. 'Is Mummy sick?'

'Yes, darling.' She fought to keep her voice steady. 'I want you to be really brave. I'll be right back.'

He agreed not to move from the chair and she ran to her cousin. It looked as if she had just collapsed. Kneeling beside her, she took hold of her limp hand, rubbing it gently. 'Jane, darling, wake up, please. Danny's very frightened.'

When her cousin didn't move or respond, Angie's breath caught in her throat, making it painful to breathe. 'Jane,' she called again, her voice thick with distress. She was so still, as if there was no life there. No, it couldn't be. It was impossible. What should she do? Think! Think!

Check for a pulse. Placing her fingers on Jane's wrist, concentrating hard to feel some movement. Nothing – there was nothing there. Oh, dear God, what had happened? She couldn't be dead – she just couldn't. Tears flowed down her face. Jane wasn't even twenty-one until next month. But through her shock came the certainty that her cousin was dead. That something special about Jane was no longer there. She had to get help.

Scrambling to her feet, Angie ran out of the house to the phone box on the corner and dialled 999. After explaining what she had found and giving their doctor's name, she was told to go back to the house and wait.

Danny was still sitting where she had left him, quiet and withdrawn now. He looked up, his beautiful grey eyes dark with worry.

Angie bent down in front of him. 'Someone will be here soon to see to your mummy.'

He scrambled off the chair. 'I'll go and see her. Make her better.'

'No!' Angie caught hold of him as he trotted towards the door. 'We mustn't disturb her until the doctor gets here.'

He stopped, holding her hand tightly and looking down at his trousers. 'I've been a naughty boy and weed my drawers. Mummy said I mustn't do that now I'm a big boy.'

'You're not naughty, darling.' Angie gathered him into

her arms. 'You were frightened and couldn't help it. Mummy understands that. Shall we go upstairs and change your clothes?'

He nodded. 'Mummy's made me new trousers for my birthday. Can I wear those?'

Angie felt as if her heart were going to break, but she had to keep control for Danny's sake. He didn't understand what had happened. 'Of course.'

She had closed the front-room door so he couldn't see in, and, when he hesitated outside, she firmly steered him upstairs to the bathroom. After stripping off his wet things, she gave him a quick wash, listening all the time for the doctor.

'There, that's better. Where are your new clothes?'

'In my bedroom.'

Angie followed as he ran to his room. The bed was littered with wrapping paper, clothes and a couple of toy cars – Danny's favourite things.

'Here they are.' He held up a pair of long trousers in dark blue, with red cars embroidered on the front pockets. There was also a pair of red braces to go with them. Angie knew that Jane had been sewing these trousers at night once Danny was in bed. She had made a lovely job of them.

She found a clean pair of pants in his chest of drawers, and then helped him on with the trousers. He was quite able to dress himself, but she needed to be doing something. She knew what she had seen downstairs, but her mind was having difficulty accepting it. Jane couldn't be dead! She couldn't . . .

6

Danny was gazing proudly at himself in the mirror, admiring his first pair of long trousers. He conjured up a devastating smile, and two dimples were in evidence. 'Mummy's made a big cake. She's put it in the larder. I know, 'cos I've seen it.' He headed for the stairs. 'I'll show Mummy how nice my trousers look.'

This was a nightmare! She caught Danny and took him back to the bedroom. Please come. Somebody – anyone! She spoke as calmly as she could. 'Show me the rest of your presents.'

He began to show her how the cars ran along the lino floor, and then he stopped and gazed up at her, the worry back in his eyes. 'Why doesn't Mummy come up and play with us? She always plays with me.'

The plaintive question was nearly her undoing, and Angie had to use every ounce of her strength to stop herself from sobbing like a child. She mustn't do that; it would frighten Danny. She would have to tell him something. 'When the doctor comes, they will take your mummy away. I'm so sorry, darling, but you can stay with me tonight.' She watched his bottom lip tremble. 'I've got some presents for you, and we'll take your cake with us.'

Danny chewed his lip. 'Are they going to make her better?'

She desperately wanted to wait until tomorrow before telling him the truth, and she struggled to find something he would accept. 'They are going to look after her.'

At that moment, much to her relief, there was a

knock on the door. She kissed Danny and stood up. 'Collect your things together.' Then she hurried downstairs, relieved to see their own doctor standing there.

'Dr James, I'm so pleased you're here.' Angie was shaking as she reached out to him for help. 'Something terrible has happened. I think Jane's dead.'

He nodded grimly. 'An ambulance is on its way. Where is she?'

She opened the front room door and watched the Doctor kneel beside Jane. It only took a few moments before he stood up again.

'I'm so sorry. You're right. She is dead.' He made her sit on a chair by the door.

She'd known that, of course, but to have it confirmed was heartbreaking. The tears she'd been holding back began to flow. 'Why? What happened?'

'I can't be certain yet, but it looks as if her heart finally gave out.'

'Heart? But she was only twenty.'

'She was born with a heart defect.' He frowned. 'Didn't you know?'

'No, Jane never said a word, nor did her parents or mine when they were alive.'

'When your cousin came to see me, I warned her that the birth would put her life at risk. She said the doctor in Somerset had already told her that, but she was determined to have the child. It weakened her heart further.'

Angie rested her head in her hands. 'Dear brave

8

Jane. How she must have wanted the child to take such a risk.'

'Do you know who the father is? She never would tell me.'

'No, I'm sorry, Doctor.' She looked up. 'But you needn't worry about Danny. I'll bring him up.'

'I was hoping you'd say that, or else he would have had to go to an orphanage. I'm sure your cousin would have wanted you to look after him.'

'I'll never let anyone put him in a children's home!'

The ambulance arrived then, and two men came in with a stretcher. After a quick word with the Doctor, they went over to the body. Angie couldn't bear to watch as they set about moving Jane. They had been more like sisters than cousins. They even had the same colouring: deep chestnut hair and hazel eyes. Angie had been around two when Jane had been born, and from that moment they had been constant companions. Neither had grown to more than five feet three inches, although they had both longed to be taller.

The pain of loss gripped her viciously. What silly things to remember at a time like this.

The men were just coming out when Danny tumbled down the stairs. After a quick glance into the now empty room, he ran towards the stretcher. 'Is that my mummy?'

'Danny.' Angie tried to catch hold of him, but he fought free.

'Why have you covered her right up? Stop it! She can't breathe like that. She can't see me in my new trousers. It's my birthday. We're going to have a party.' He grabbed hold of the stretcher. 'Stop them, Auntie! Stop them.'

With a cry of distress Angie knelt on the floor and put her arms around the frantic boy. She would have to tell him now. 'Danny, you must let the men go. I'm so sorry, my darling, but your mummy was very sick. She's had to go to heaven and the angels will take care of her now.'

He went very still and whimpered, 'Mummy.'

'I'm so sorry, darling. You'll come and live with me and I'll look after you now.'

He gazed up at Angie, eyes dry, fists clenched. 'Isn't she coming back? Doesn't she love me any more?'

'She loves you very, very much, Danny, but she was ill and has gone to heaven to be looked after properly. She didn't want to leave you, but she couldn't help it.'

A single tear trickled down his cheek and came to rest in his dimple. 'They'll look after her?'

'Yes, they will, and I'll look after you. I love you and will take good care of you. You know that, don't you?'

He wrapped his arms around her, and Angie stroked his silky hair, both silent in their grief. She hoped he understood because he'd had a cat that had been run over, and Jane had explained to him that Dinky had gone to heaven. He knew the cat never came back, but had this really sunk in?

The birthday cake was on the table, untouched. They just hadn't been able to slice into it. Jane had even drawn a car on the top in red icing with the number 3 underneath. Her cousin must have been gathering the ingredients for some time, because four years after the end of the war they still had rationing.

Angie watched Danny curled up on the settee, asleep at last, his face wet with tears. He had refused to leave her and go upstairs to bed, so she had let him settle down here. He was clutching a battered teddy bear in his arms. He had abandoned this a few months ago, declaring that he was too old for the toy, but tonight he was a grief-stricken little boy who needed the comfort of something loved and familiar. He would be her responsibility now, and one she would take on gladly. How she wished he had some grandparents who would love and spoil him, but the war had put an end to that pleasure for him.

Damn the war! She didn't think she would ever be able to forgive the Germans, who had bombed London night after night. It had been a clear Friday night in December 1940 when their parents had been killed. They had gone to the pub in the next street: a bomb flattened the place, killing all inside. Angie relived that time in her mind. They had been heartbroken and frightened at being left on their own. Jane had been twelve and she fourteen. After the death of their parents they had been evacuated to Bridgewater in Somerset. The Sawyers had taken the two distressed and grieving girls into their home and hearts. The beauty of the farm and the love given to them by John and Hetty Sawyer had helped them to heal. Jane had eventually settled down, but Angie had been restless, missing her home. After six months she had returned to Stepney and her parents' house, which was still standing, as was Jane's a few doors away. She had gone to work in a factory, making small metal things, though she never did find out what they were for. Something vital for aircraft, she had been told. The work had been repetitious and boring, but she'd stuck it out, and looked after their two houses until the end of the war and Jane's return home.

Angie ran a hand over her eyes and sighed. And what a shock that had been. It was Christmas 1945 before Jane had returned home, seventeen years old and four months pregnant. She had stubbornly refused to say who the father was.

Now she was dead.

The tears began to flow again as she remembered how Jane had involved her in every day of Danny's life. As he'd started to toddle, Jane had even let him stay with her overnight when she had time off from her job as a typist. Her cousin had always been unselfish, and it hadn't seemed strange. It was just Jane wanting to share the joy her son had brought to both of them. Danny may not have a father, Jane had told her, but he's got two mothers who love him. And it was true. Angie had loved the little boy from the moment he had been born.

Since the Doctor had told her about the state of Jane's heart, Angie was beginning to wonder if this had been a reason for sharing Danny. She must have known how ill she was. Had she been preparing Angie to take on the job of bringing up her son? Had she known she was going to die young?

She dried her tears and gazed at the sleeping child, a feeling of certainty filling her thought. Yes, Jane had known!

How sad she must have been, aware that she might not live to see her son grow up. Jane had done everything in her power to make these early years as happy as possible for her son . . .

Angie stood up, a determined look on her face as she gently scooped up Danny to take him upstairs with her. She wouldn't let Jane down. Danny would have a happy life with her.

2

Two days after the funeral and Angie knew she was going to have to tackle the painful task of going through Jane's personal papers. She had been putting it off, telling herself that there was too much to do: arranging the funeral and looking after a sad little boy. But it couldn't be avoided any longer. There was so much to sort out. After their parents were killed, Angie and Jane inherited the two houses they lived in. When Jane returned home, Angie suggested they live together and sell one of the houses, but Jane insisted that she wanted to keep it to pass on to her child. The houses were close enough for them to look after each other, so they lived separately. They came to an arrangement that worked very well for them. Angie had a good job as a typist, and, as Jane wasn't able to work, she kept them all. There wasn't any money to spare, but they managed and were very happy.

Jane had often said that there was a biscuit tin in the bottom of her wardrobe that contained all her important papers. It was time to collect it and find out what was to be done with the house. Her cousin was a sensible girl and, knowing she was ill, would almost certainly have left a will. Then she must see about legally adopting Danny. She didn't want his father to turn up one day and take him away from her. That was something she was never going to allow anyone to do! Danny was hers now, and she was sure that's what Jane would have wanted.

Angie gazed at Danny having a nap on the settee. He had abandoned the teddy bear immediately after the funeral, but he still wouldn't let her out of his sight. She gave a sad smile as she remembered how brave he had been at his mother's funeral. His little face serious, lips tightly pressed together in dogged determination not to cry. And he hadn't. She had been so proud of him, and his courage had enabled her to hang on to her own composure.

Seeing he was fast asleep, she made up her mind. Moving quietly, she left the house and ran to Jane's, opened the door, hurtled up the stairs and found the tin. It had taken her less than five minutes. Danny was still asleep.

Once she'd got her breath back, she sat at the table and removed the lid. Right on the top was the thing she'd been hoping for – a will. Quickly scanning it, she breathed a sigh of relief. Everything had been left to Danny, and there was a request that Angie adopt her son and manage his affairs until he was old enough to do this for himself. The document had been drawn up by a solicitor and was irrefutable proof of her cousin's wishes.

'Bless you, Jane,' Angie murmured. Her cousin had left everything in good order.

'Auntie Angel!'

'I'm here, darling.' Danny, half awake, was calling for her, as he often did since his mother had died.

Rubbing his eyes, he slipped off the settee and clambered on the chair next to her. 'What you doing?'

'I'm going through your mummy's papers. We've still got a lot of sorting out to do.' He couldn't read it, but she spread the will out in front of him. 'She's left the house and everything to you, and has asked that I adopt you. Would you like that?'

'What does that mean?' He looked slightly alarmed.

'It means you will be my son and I'll look after you.'

He knelt on the chair and leant across the table to peer at the document, then turned his head and gave a dimpled smile. 'I'd like that.'

'Good, that's settled, then.'

'What else is in the tin?'

'I don't know. Let's have a look.' Angie removed a bundle of letters and saw that they were the ones she had written to Jane during the war when they had been apart. Next was Danny's birth certificate, and Angie read it eagerly to see if there was any mention of the father, but there wasn't.

'My goodness! I didn't know your mummy had given you another name.' She grinned at the child. 'Your full name is Daniel Cramer Harris.'

'That's a funny name.' He didn't look impressed.

'It's unusual, but I think it's nice.'

He shrugged, more interested in the contents of the tin. Shoving more papers out of the way, he gave a cry of triumph and dived in his hand. 'Look what I've found.'

Danny was holding up a small wooden truck, obviously hand carved and painted in bright blue. He jumped down and began to push it along the floor. 'Look, Auntie, the wheels go round. Isn't it good?'

'Yes, it's very nice.' Angie frowned. What on earth was that doing in Jane's box of special things?

Danny stood up and ran back to her, his eyes bright with pleasure. 'I 'spect Mummy bought it for my birthday and forgot to wrap it up.'

'Yes, that's what must have happened.' Angie knew that couldn't be true. It had been put away, and must have been something very special to Jane. But why would a cheap toy be that precious to her?

He clambered back on the chair and put the toy on the table in front of him, gazing at it with such a sad expression. 'Do you think it's all right if I have it now?'

'Of course you can.'

His face brightened and the dimples flashed again. 'What else is in the box?'

'Some photographs.' She pushed two towards him. 'That's your mummy and me when we were children. And these were your grandparents.'

He moved his truck out of the way so he could look closely. 'That really you and Mummy? You're very little, aren't you?'

'We were small like you once.' She couldn't help smiling when he looked at her in disbelief.

He turned his attention to the picture with four adults sitting by the sea. 'Mummy said my grandparents were dead.'

'They are, darling. They were killed in the war by a bomb.'

'Nasty war. Shouldn't drop bombs. They look nice.'

'They were.' Angie felt her throat close with emotion. Even after nine years it still hurt.

'What's in that?' He was pointing to a small white envelope.

Angie opened it and removed another photo.

'That's Mummy,' Danny declared; his bottom lip trembled but was quickly brought under control. 'Who's that with her?'

'I don't know.' She looked closely, but the picture wasn't very clear. All she could make out from the bad black and white print was that the man was tall. It looked as if the light had got in the camera, almost obliterating the image of the man, though Jane was quite clear. Was that some kind of uniform he was wearing? She shook her head. Jane was looking up at him and laughing, obviously happy. Was it Danny's father?

'It's a nice picture of Mummy. Can I have it beside my bed?' Danny was running his finger over the image of his mother.

'I'll find a frame for it.' The request gave her hope. Danny had refused to sleep in his own room, but if he had this picture by his bed perhaps he would do so now. The sooner he got back to a routine the better it would be for him.

He flashed her a smile of thanks and got down to play with his new toy again.

*

The next morning Angie and Danny headed for the solicitor Jane had named as executor of her will. Mr Simpson's office was only a ten-minute bus ride away, and on the second floor of a rather smart building. Jane had obviously taken the trouble and expense to engage a reputable solicitor.

The secretary looked up when they entered and immediately smiled at Danny. 'Hello.'

'Hello.' The boy returned the greeting politely.

'We'd like to see Mr Simpson, please.' Angie glanced at Danny standing quietly beside her and was so proud of him. There was never any problem taking him anywhere. He always behaved impeccably, and not because of any badgering from his mother. It seemed as if he had been born a gentleman, and even his young age couldn't hide the innate quality.

'Do you have an appointment?'

Angie looked up. 'No, I'm afraid not, but it's most important I see him at once. My name's Angie Westwood, and I'm Jane Harris's cousin.' She explained briefly about Jane, and the will she had found.

'Oh, I'm so sorry.' The secretary was on her feet and heading for the solicitor's office. 'Please take a seat.'

She had hardly disappeared before a man of around forty strode out. 'Miss Westwood, this is sad news indeed. Please come in.'

There were two chairs in front of his desk and Angie settled Danny on one of them and then sat down as well.

Mr Simpson took his seat behind his desk and shook his head. 'When did this happen?'

Angie explained, and told him she had only found the will yesterday.

The secretary came in with a tray of tea and a glass of milk. She gave the glass to Danny and was rewarded with his best smile. She then handed Mr Simpson an envelope. 'Miss Harris's papers, sir.' After pouring them both a cup of tea, she left the room.

The solicitor removed the papers and spread them out on his desk, then sighed and sat back. 'I must ask you for some identification before we proceed.'

Angie fished in her bag and pulled out her identity card. 'Will this do?'

He checked the details with the ones on the will and returned it to her. 'That's fine, Miss Westwood.'

'And this is Jane's son, Danny.'

Mr Simpson smiled at the boy. 'I know. We've already met, haven't we, Danny?'

He smiled politely at the solicitor and wriggled his feet about. It was obvious from his face that he didn't remember.

Mr Simpson turned his attention back to Angie. 'You know the contents of the will, of course.'

'Yes, I read it yesterday. Everything goes to Danny.'

'Your cousin left this with me for safe keeping.' He held out a sealed envelope with her name on it.

Angie slit it open, fighting back the emotion as she read Jane's words.

Dearest Angie,

If you are reading this, then I have died. The Doctor has warned me that my heart is not too good. I might live for many years if I'm careful, and I pray that I do, but if the worst should happen I want to be sure Danny will stay with you until he is old enough to make his own way in life.

I am so sorry I didn't have the courage to prepare you for this, but I didn't want to worry you. It was selfish of me, but the three of us have been so happy and I didn't want to spoil that.

I have left the house and contents to Danny, but if he is too young, I appoint you as his guardian and trustee. Adopt him, please, Angie, and give him a secure home with someone who loves him as much as I do. I give you authority to sell my house and put the money in a savings account for him, if you think that is the best thing to do.

The next part made Angie gasp.

I never told Danny's father I was expecting. He had great problems and had to return home. He wanted to stay in touch, but, knowing the state of my health and the risk that the baby would never be born, I thought it best if we parted. I loved him too much to cause him more pain. As I've watched his son grow more like him every day,

I'm not sure I've done the right thing, but I have no idea where he is now. It has worried me that I have deprived my son of his father, and the father of his son. I only did what I felt was right at the time. I beg your forgiveness, and the forgiveness of his father, should he ever find out.

I know you love Danny. Look after him for me.

My eternal love to you both,
Jane

Angie blew her nose, fighting the tears. Then she handed the letter to Mr Simpson.

He read it quickly, nodded and asked, 'Do you want me to handle the adoption for you?'

'Please, and as quickly as possible.'

'Miss Harris has made her wishes very clear. When she came to me and explained the situation, I advised her to have a legal paper drawn up stating the supportive role you have played in the child's life from the moment he was born, and that it would be in his best interests to be adopted by you. This has been done and I have it here.' He glanced up. 'Is there any prospect of your marrying in the near future?'

'Well, I have a steady boyfriend. We've been going out for about six months, but he hasn't proposed or said anything about marriage.' She clenched her hands with tension. 'Is being single going to be against me?'

'It isn't usual for a single person to be allowed to adopt.'

Angie felt the blood drain from her face.

'But this situation is unusual,' he continued. 'We don't know who the father is, or where he can be found. And, even though your cousin had doubts, she still has not named him. He has never been a part of Danny's life, and you are, therefore, his only known relative.'

'That isn't strictly true.' She was twisting the strap on her handbag in agitation. 'We do have an uncle, but we've never met him because the family refused to have anything to do with him. I don't know why. Only that they had a big row over twenty years ago and never spoke to him again.'

'That shouldn't be a problem, then. Now I will explain what will happen. We will put in the application straight away. Someone will come to your house and talk to you and Danny. If they are satisfied, there will be a hearing at the Magistrates Court. Once the adoption has been agreed, you will receive a new birth certificate showing Danny as your child.' He smiled. 'Please don't look so worried, Miss Westwood; I'm sure everything will be all right. You have a lot of advantages. You own your house and have supported the child from birth. Now, what are you going to do about the house?'

Having composed herself with difficulty, Angie glanced at Danny, who was sitting quietly on the chair with the wooden toy in his hands. Because it had been found in his mother's special tin, he kept it with him all the time. She was determined to talk to him about everything. Great changes were taking place in his life

– in both their lives – and she wanted him to understand.

'Danny, your mummy has left the house to you. Do you want us to live there or would you rather stay in my house?'

He thought about it for a while, then said, 'We'll live in your house.'

Angie was relieved by his decision. It would have been so painful for them if they had moved into Jane's house – a house full of memories. She turned back to the solicitor. 'What do you think we should do? Sell?'

'Why don't you rent it out? That way you would keep Danny's inheritance and also get an income from it.'

'Oh, that might be just the thing to do. I could put the rent money away for him.'

Mr Simpson pursed his lips. 'Have you thought about your own financial situation? I know you have supported Miss Harris and Danny, but how are you going to be able to work with a young boy to care for?'

That had been worrying Angie as well, but she'd decided to sort everything out before she tackled that problem. She had a small amount of savings, but she was going to have to hang on to it until she knew how much the solicitor's costs would be. After Jane's death she had taken a week off work, and that was stretching into two. Her boss wasn't going to stand for much more and she expected to be sacked at any moment. She wouldn't leave Danny in anyone else's care when he was so vulnerable.

That had also been a cause of friction between her

and Alan. He'd made it clear that having the boy around all the time was not to his liking. Still, she thought, shrugging away her unease, he'd come around to it in time. Danny was such a lovely boy; everyone loved him.

Sensing her confusion, Mr Simpson leant forward. 'I would recommend that you rent out the house, and use the income so that you can stay at home with Danny. These coming months are going to be very hard for him.'

Angie frowned. 'Jane said the money must be put aside for her son.'

'Only if you sold the house. She said nothing about renting. I see no reason why you can't use the rental to bring up Miss Harris's son.'

It felt as if a weight had been lifted from her shoulders. 'I'll do that until I've sorted myself out. As soon as Danny goes to school I'll be able to work, and then I'll save the money for him.'

'Very sensible, Miss Westwood.' Mr Simpson nodded and smiled. 'I'll have all the necessary papers drawn up. Would you like me to deal with the renting as well?'

'Would you?'

'Of course. There are a few papers to sign now, and if you could come back in two days I'll have everything else ready for you.'

Danny ran his fingers over the truck and waved his legs about. This was taking a long time and he wanted a wee. He looked anxiously at his auntie. Mummy had always said he mustn't butt in when grown-ups were talking. He had his long trousers on and he wasn't going to make them wet. His mouth set in a determined line.

'Would you like some more milk?'

The nice lady who'd smiled at him was back in the room and bending down in front of him. He seized the chance and whispered in her ear, 'I need the bathroom.'

She held her hand out and he took hold, slipping off the chair. He was really bursting! His auntie was busy writing, so he walked as quietly as he could out of the room.

'Do you need help?' the lady asked when they reached the small room.

'No, thank you,' he said politely. As a measure of his trust in her he gave her the truck to hold, then pushed the door to.

When he finished, he collected the toy just as his auntie and the man came out of the other room. Much more comfy now he'd had a wee, Danny took his auntie's hand and they went down the stairs.

Later that evening, when Danny was in bed, Alan arrived. Angie kissed him and was pleased to see he looked in a better mood than the last time she'd seen him. He hadn't come to Jane's funeral, because he'd said he couldn't take the time off work. It had upset her, as she could have done with his support at this distressing time.

'What did the solicitor say?' he asked as soon as he was in. 'Jane must have left everything to you.'

That, and the gleam in his eyes, jolted Angie. She hadn't told him what was in her cousin's will, wanting to get it all sorted out before she said anything. For the first time since she had met him she wanted to know what was behind that polite smile. It suddenly looked rather false.

'No, she's left everything to Danny.'

'But he's only a kid!' A scowl appeared and disappeared almost at once. 'But of course you'll have control of the house.'

Angie narrowed her eyes at his enthusiasm. 'We're going to rent it out.'

'Ah, that will bring in a nice income.' He kissed her playfully on the nose. 'We could get married soon. I've done my National Service, so that's out of the way, and it's not as if we've got to find somewhere to live; you've got this house and will soon have money from the rent of your cousin's.'

It was as if she were seeing him properly for the first time. How had she ever believed she loved him? The greed was obvious. She felt all her illusions about him melt away. He was quite good-looking, with his dark hair and blue eyes, his manner relaxed and affable. She had enjoyed going out with him and hadn't looked closer than that. Now she saw clearly that he had only latched on to her because she owned a house. What a blasted idiot you are, Angie Westwood, she silently berated herself.

'What a charming proposal!' Her laugh was scathing. 'The money will be put aside for Danny.'

Irritation flashed through his eyes. 'I'm not getting down on my knees, if that's what you're hoping! I thought we had an understanding.'

'Really?' Angie raised her eyebrows. 'I wonder where you got that idea from?'

'Stop messing about. You know I want to marry you.'

'Marry me – or the house?'

'Oh, come on, darling.' Alan draped his arms around her shoulders. 'What are you going to do with the kid? Put him in an orphanage?'

'I'm going to adopt him.' She shook off his arm. 'The solicitor is arranging that for me.' She was thoroughly disgusted with him now and wanted him out of her house.

Alan surged to his feet. 'Don't be daft! I'm not going to take on someone else's bastard.'

'I'm not asking you to, because I'm not going to marry you.' She spoke calmly but felt like hitting the selfish man. She rose slowly to her feet and faced him. 'Don't you dare call him names. Jane loved Danny's father, and she had a good – unselfish – reason for not marrying him.'

The easy smile was back. 'Don't get so het up. Let's talk about it.'

He reached out and she slapped his hands away. 'There's nothing to talk about. Get out, and don't come back!'

He shrugged and sauntered past her. 'You're an idiot, Angie. You'll be sorry. No man will take you on with that burden.'

'If the rest are anything like you, then they can keep out of my way.' She was shaking with rage when she slammed the door behind him. That was the end of that!

'Auntie.'

The cry had her tearing upstairs. 'I'm here, darling.'

'I heard a big bang.' Danny wiped a hand over his eyes, heavy with sleep.

'One of the doors slammed, that's all.'

'Oh.' His eyes were already closing again.

Angie stayed until she was sure he was fast asleep, and then bent over to kiss his cheek, her heart full of love. Nothing in this world would make her give him into the hands of strangers.

3

It was the end of July and the weather was glorious, so they had come to Green Park for the day. Angie was feeling buoyant. The last two months had been difficult. They had filled in lots of forms, been visited by the adoption people and had their lives thoroughly scrutinized, but it looked as if everything was going to be all right. And Danny had told them quite firmly that he was with his Auntie Angel because she was his second mummy and she loved him. All they were waiting for now was the hearing at the Magistrates Court. The solicitor had been wonderful, supporting and guiding her each step of the way. He was certain the adoption would go through without any problems.

Angie laughed as she watched Danny tearing along, trying to get his kite in the air. They had spent all yesterday afternoon gluing it together and she was pleased to see it was holding up to the rough treatment. He still had times when he cried for his mother, and that was only to be expected, but things were improving. Their lives were settling down to a happy routine, and that was what Danny needed. To feel secure and loved was the way to adjust to life without his mother.

The house had been let almost immediately, and that had meant Angie had had to tackle the painful job of clearing out Jane's things. She was glad that was over. A middle-aged couple, bombed out during the war, had taken the house, and the adoption process was under way.

She grinned when Danny squealed in delight as he tore along and made the kite rise about six feet off the ground.

He rushed back, a broad smile on his face, the kite fluttering behind him. 'Look, Auntie, you have a go.'

Taking the string from him, she kicked off her shoes and started to run. A gust of wind lifted the kite high in the air and she felt light with hope for the future. She tipped her head back as she ran, her long wavy hair streaming behind her as she watched the kite dance and cavort. Such a liberating sight!

She turned and ran back to Danny, who was hopping about in glee.

'It's gone a mile high,' he yelled.

And that was how high her spirits were, she realized. On this beautiful summer day, the problems of the past and concern for the future seemed as nothing. The money from the rent was enough for them to live on, if they were careful, so there was no need to go out to work at the moment; she could stay and make a proper home for Danny. There hadn't been a sign of Alan since their row, and that was a relief. She'd had a lucky escape there.

Out of breath now, she skidded to a halt in front of Danny and collapsed on the grass, the kite fluttering down gracefully beside her. Danny jumped on her and they rolled around, laughing.

'Wish I could fly that high.' Danny scrambled to his feet and began to gather up the kite. The dimpled smile flashed at her. 'This is a smashing day. What are we having for tea?'

'Hungry?' Angie grinned as she thought of the jelly in the larder. It had been made last night after Danny had gone to bed and was nicely set by morning.

'Starving!' He began to roll up the string on the kite and picked it up very carefully. He didn't want to break it.

'Come on, then.' Angie stood up and took the kite from him. They headed for the bus stop, with Danny chatting away, still excited about making the kite fly.

They got off the bus at the top of their road, and, as they walked towards the house, Angie frowned. A man and woman were waiting on her doorstep. Or at least the woman was waiting; the man was pacing up and down the path. She could feel his irritation from where she was.

When she was close enough to see them clearly, she felt a jolt of recognition. The man resembled Jane's father. She stopped suddenly as realization dawned. Jane's father and Angie's mother had been brother and sister, so this must be their brother. The family resemblance was unmistakable. She could remember her parents talking and saying that he was a bad lot and they wouldn't have anything to do with him.

Danny tugged at her hand. 'Why have you stopped?'

'It looks as if we've got visitors.' She carried on walking again, holding firmly to Danny's hand. Worry gnawed at her insides. What on earth were they doing here?

'Are you Angelina?' the man demanded as soon as she opened the gate.

'I'm Angie, yes. And who are you?'

'I'm your Uncle Malcolm. We've only just heard that my brother's daughter is dead. If we hadn't met someone from round here who knew us, we would never have known.' He glowered at Danny. 'And that's her kid, I suppose.'

She felt Danny press close to her legs. Placing her hand on his shoulder, she held him. He was easily upset at the moment and they'd had such a lovely day. Now this disagreeable man had turned up, raising his voice. She could see why the rest of the family had cut him out of their lives.

'What are you doing here?' She spoke sharply but kept her voice down.

'I've come to sort out my brother's affairs,' he snapped.

Angie couldn't believe she was hearing this. 'Your brother *and* sister died nine years ago. Why didn't you come then?'

'We weren't coming to London with bombs dropping.' He looked at her as if she were an imbecile to think such a thing.

'Aren't you going to let us in?' The woman spoke for the first time. 'It was a bleedin' long journey from Cornwall.'

So that's where they lived. Angie studied her carefully. Brassy blonde hair, obviously dyed and in need of touching up; too much make-up; very high heels and nylon stockings. Wonder where she got those, Angie thought waspishly, taking an instant dislike to the woman. 'And who are you?'

'I'm Malcolm's wife, of course.'

'Really?' If her uncle had married her, he was a bigger fool than their parents had said. She looked more like a woman of the night – one past her prime.

'Let us in, Angelina,' her uncle snarled. 'We can't discuss business on the doorstep.'

'Business?' Angie glared at him. 'There isn't anything to discuss. Our family hasn't seen you for over twenty years.'

'I'm a blood relation.' He smirked now. 'If you won't let us in, then give us the keys to my brother's house.'

Angie was furious. So that was what this was all about. Well, they'd had a wasted journey. It amazed her what crawled out of the shadows when greed took over. He had completely ignored them for years, but, as soon as he thought there might be something in it for him, he'd come running. She silently thanked Jane for tying up everything legally. It was going to give her great satisfaction to put him right.

'Jane left everything she owned to her son, and that includes the house.' She glanced down at Danny and smiled reassuringly. He was looking worried by these people he didn't know.

Her uncle swore.

'Watch your language!'

He ignored her reprimand and turned to his wife. 'We'll have to take over the kid, then.'

'You can forget that idea!' His wife looked at the child with open disgust on her face. 'I'm not tying myself down with someone else's brat!'

Angie's heart was hammering in her chest, and, although the final papers had not yet been signed, she lied. 'You can't anyway. He's my son. I've adopted him.'

Danny whimpered now, alarmed by the raised voices. Angie dropped the kite and swept him up in her arms. 'How dare you turn up here and try to take what you have no right to? Jane left a will. It's all legal. Danny is mine and everything she owned is his. Now leave. There's nothing here for you, and you're not wanted.'

'I don't believe you. She used a solicitor, I take it, so what's his name? I'll go and see for myself.'

Angie knew she wasn't going to get rid of him unless he was able to check the facts. She told him where the solicitor was and watched him storm up the road. His wife, tottering along on her heels, complained all the way.

'I don't like them,' Danny muttered.

'Neither do I, darling, but they won't be back.' That statement was made with a fervent prayer that that was the last she saw of her uncle. She put Danny down, her arms numb from carrying him; he was getting heavy. She had lost weight since Jane had died, and with her slight build that was something she couldn't afford to do. As she watched him pick up the kite, determination surged through her. No one was going to take him away from her. No one!

'Oh, it's broken.' Danny held up the kite for her to see. One of the struts had come unglued.

'We'll soon mend it again.' She took her key out of her bag and opened the front door, feeling sick with worry. Please, Mr Simpson, don't tell my uncle that the adoption papers aren't signed yet.

They reached the kitchen and she put on the kettle at once, needing a cup of tea to calm her nerves. Just when things seemed to be improving, and she and Danny were beginning to laugh again, this came along. First thing tomorrow she would go to the solicitor and ask if the adoption process could be speeded up. She wasn't going to be able to relax until Danny was legally hers.

Danny put the kite carefully on a chair. It wasn't broken much. Auntie would soon fix it. She was smart like that.

'Go and wash your hands, darling, while I get the tea.' She grinned at him. 'I've got something special for you.'

He ran up the stairs as fast as he could. He liked special things, and wondered what it was. It was good those nasty people had gone. Auntie Angel hadn't liked them, but she'd held him tight, so he hadn't been too frightened.

After having a wee and washing his hands, he returned to the kitchen. What fun they'd had today. The kite had gone right up in the air. His mummy would have laughed and clapped her hands if she'd seen it. He wished she had been there.

He swallowed hard to stop from crying. It hurt to think of her, but Auntie said to remember the good things. So he would try.

Clambering on to his chair, he saw what was on the table. Bread, jam, a cake and . . . 'Jelly! We've got red jelly.'

His sadness was banished at the sight of the wobbling castle in the middle of the table, his smile brilliant.

'You must eat some bread first,' his auntie said.

With a nod he obediently tucked into a slice, never taking his eyes off the treat.

All through tea, Angie was expecting her uncle to return and hammer on the door. If he did, she wouldn't open it. She could hardly control the sick feeling in her stomach, but thank goodness his wife had declared that she wouldn't look after Danny. Not even for a house. It had been a small comfort, though, because her uncle had seemed determined to get what he wanted, no matter what he had to do.

She gave Danny another spoonful of jelly. He was enjoying it and, thankfully, didn't appear to be too troubled about the row. He didn't understand what it had been about, of course, but he was a sensitive boy and would have picked up on the charged atmosphere. He was such a brave little soul, trying so hard to come to terms with the loss of his mother. She didn't want him upset any more.

Once tea was over and the dishes washed, they sat at the kitchen table and mended the kite. By the time Danny was tucked up in bed and asleep, there was still no sign of her uncle returning. She knew she would have a sleepless night, wondering what had happened at the solicitor's.

By nine thirty the next morning Angie was climbing the stairs to the solicitor's office, anxious to find out if her uncle had come here yesterday, or given up and returned home.

'Hello, Miss Westwood.' The secretary smiled at both of them. 'Mr Simpson thought you would come today.'

Angie's heart missed a beat. So her uncle had come to see the solicitor.

'Ah, good, I'm glad you've arrived early.' Mr Simpson came out of his office and held the door open for her. 'My secretary will look after Danny. I'd like to see you alone.'

Now Angie was really worried. She bent down in front of Danny. 'Will you stay here while I talk to Mr Simpson?'

Danny looked a bit worried and chewed his lip. 'You won't be long, will you?'

'Only a few minutes.'

The secretary smiled again at Danny. 'My name's Pauline. Will you show me your lovely truck?'

He looked down at the toy he always carried around with him, and then trotted to the desk, holding it out for her. 'It was in my mummy's special tin.'

Pauline winked at Angie, and, seeing that Danny was all right, she slipped into the office. Mr Simpson closed the door behind her.

'Sit down please.' The solicitor didn't waste any time.

'I had a visit from your uncle, Malcolm Harris, yesterday afternoon.'

'I sent him. I'm sorry, I didn't know what else to do.' Angie sat on the edge of the chair, screwing up the handle of her handbag in agitation.

'You did the right thing —'

'He wanted to take Danny away from me. Please, where are the adoption papers? I must sign the papers —'

'Don't upset yourself, Miss Westwood. As soon as your uncle had gone, I managed to get the hearing brought forward to ten o'clock tomorrow morning.' He smiled kindly. 'They had a space and with a *little* persuasion they changed the date. I don't believe there will be any opposition to the adoption.'

Angie sighed in relief and wiped a tear away as it trickled down her cheek. She hadn't realized she was weeping. 'Oh, thank goodness. I was so frightened.'

'Your uncle demanded to know about Miss Harris's will and I explained the position. He wasn't pleased to discover that everything had been set out clearly and legally. He was obviously looking for a loophole, so that he could step in and take charge. I pointed out that if he tried to contest the will, he would most certainly lose, and costs would far exceed the value of the property.'

'And what about the adoption: did he accept that?'

'Ah.' Mr Simpson gave an amused smile. 'I didn't mention that it wasn't finalized yet. I merely told him that your cousin had left her son in your care with a request that you adopt him.'

She sat back in the chair, feeling more relaxed. 'And what was his reaction to that?'

'He stormed out without another word. I doubt you'll hear from him again. It was the house he was after, but he knows now there is no way he can get his hands on it. In the unlikely event that he does turn up again, you send him to me and I'll deal with him.'

'That makes me feel easier.' When this tragedy had first happened, she'd thought there was a chance that she would marry Alan, and have his help and support. But that hope had soon been dashed. She was on her own, and knowing the solicitor was there to help was a blessing. She stood up. 'I must tell Danny about the hearing.'

Mr Simpson also got to his feet. 'Just a moment more, Miss Westwood.'

She sat again and waited for him to do the same.

'Do you have any idea where your cousin met Danny's father?'

Angie started at that question. 'Well, yes, they met while she was still living in Somerset. We were evacuated there after our parents were killed.'

'That would be the place to start.'

Angie sighed anxiously. This wasn't something she wanted to face at the moment.

'I can only advise you.' Mr Simpson studied her, his expression understanding. 'Danny will be legally yours soon and you won't have any more trouble from your uncle, but I do believe that for your own peace of mind you should find out who Danny's father is.'

Angie wasn't at all happy about this. Her whole

concentration was on the adoption and making sure Danny was happy. 'I know Jane had doubts, but if she'd wanted him to know she would have put his name in the letter.'

'I agree, and the decision will be yours.'

'I'll think about it – sometime.'

Mr Simpson stood up. 'I'm sure you'll come to the right decision, Miss Westwood. And any time you are troubled about anything, come to me.'

Angie got to her feet and shook his hand. 'I've already taken up a lot of your time. You must tell me how much I owe you.'

He opened the door. 'My secretary will send you a bill in due course. We'll be flexible about how and when you pay.'

'Thank you.' Angie really looked at the solicitor for the first time. He was greying a little at the temples, but still had a youthful look about him. He was also a kind, understanding man. Jane had chosen well.

The hearing took only twenty minutes and an excited Angie was heading back to the solicitor with the precious certificate in her bag. Danny had come into the court with her and had behaved wonderfully. He glanced up as he trotted beside her and they grinned at each other. Her relief was immense. The solicitor had been there to support her and had left while she waited for the certificate. She was eager to show it to him now; he had been so kind, and she was sure everything had gone smoothly because of his help.

'Ah, good, you're back.' He smiled as they tumbled into the office.

She held out the certificate, too overcome to speak.

'Good, come into my office. You can leave Danny with my secretary.'

When they were seated, Angie had one pressing question on her mind. 'What would happen if Danny's father turned up someday?'

'The child is now legally your son. If the father wanted custody, he would have to go through the courts, but, as he's never played any part in his life or contributed to his upkeep, he would be unlikely to succeed. Yet, because of the unusual circumstances of the case, he would probably be granted visiting rights.'

'I understand that. Thank you for all your help and advice.'

As she stepped back into the other office, Angie laughed. Danny was sitting on Pauline's lap, while she showed him how the typewriter worked. He was absolutely fascinated: he seemed to have a curiosity about anything mechanical.

He glanced up when he heard her. 'Look, Auntie, I can type!'

'So I see.' She bent down and held her arms out to the little boy she could now call her son. 'I've got some good news for you. You know we went to that place this morning and talked to the people there?'

He nodded.

'Well, that was to agree the adoption, and you are now mine.'

He scrambled down and gave her a hug, but she doubted he understood what it meant. It would not have occurred to him that he would live with anyone but his Auntie Angel, as he called her. But if she hadn't been here, he would most likely have been put in an orphanage.

The thought upset her, and at that moment she decided that she would see if she could find his father. Danny had a right to know who he was.

And if she did track him down, he was going to be on the receiving end of her wrath for seducing a seventeen-year-old girl!

4

Two weeks later, and Angie was worried sick. Danny had been so brave and appeared to be recovering well from the death of his mother, but all of a sudden it seemed to have hit him that he was never going to see her again. He was distraught and she wasn't able to comfort him. He would burst into tears at any time, sometimes in great wrenching sobs, and sometimes in silent misery. The Doctor had told her not to worry; it was probably delayed reaction because he hadn't fully grieved at the time his mother had died. She thought that telling her not to worry was a stupid piece of advice. It was tearing her apart. The dimpled smile and animated chatter had vanished. He wasn't eating properly, and no amount of special treats could coax him into more than a couple of mouthfuls, to please her.

She had to do something!

The house was quiet now that Danny had finally drifted off to sleep. Angie rested her head in her hands, tired beyond belief. What they both needed was to get away from all the sad memories. Somewhere with green fields, open spaces and trees . . .

She sat up straight. Of course! The farm in Somerset. John and Hetty Sawyer hadn't been able to come to the funeral because John had broken his ankle, but they'd sent flowers and a letter saying that she could come to stay with them any time. Scrabbling in the drawer of the table, she found paper, envelope and pen, then began to write quickly.

Dear John and Hetty,

I am thinking of taking a holiday and would like to accept your invitation to stay with you for a few days. It would be lovely to see you and the farm again. Please let me know if sometime in the next two weeks would be convenient.

I hope John's ankle is now healed and that you are both well,

Love, Angie

She sealed the envelope ready to post in the morning. The Sawyers were kind people, and the girls had been very lucky to be billeted with them. John and Hetty had originally come from London, but they had moved to Somerset many years ago when they had been left the farm by John's uncle. They had treated two distressed girls as if they were their own children, and not all evacuees had been so fortunate.

Angie hadn't mentioned that Jane had a son, and she knew Jane hadn't either, as it would have upset them to know she had become pregnant while in their care. She would explain about Danny when she got there. And it would be an opportunity to do a little investigating. They were bound to know who Jane's friends had been. Perhaps finding his father would help Danny, for, goodness knows, nothing else was working. She was desperate enough to try anything.

Three days later the reply arrived, and it was just what Angie had been hoping for. They would love to see her; she could come as soon as she liked and must stay with them for as long as she wanted.

Danny was in the front room, gazing aimlessly out of the window and tracing the raindrops with his finger as they trickled down the glass. She walked up to him with a bright smile on her face. 'We're going on holiday tomorrow, Danny. Come and help me pack our cases.'

He got down from the armchair he'd been perched on and walked beside her. 'Where we going?'

'To a beautiful farm in the country. It's got horses, sheep, cows, dogs and cats, and lots of other animals.' She took his hand as they made their way upstairs, relieved to see a flash of interest in his eyes.

'Have they got a tractor and things?'

'Lots – you'll be able to have a ride on them.'

Once in the bedroom she pulled a suitcase off the top of the wardrobe and tossed it on the bed. 'Would you like that?'

She nearly cried with relief when the dimpled smile appeared, but she controlled herself, knowing it was important to act naturally around him while he was so troubled.

He was more of a hindrance than a help with the packing, but she couldn't stop smiling. This was the most animated she'd seen him for some days, as he trotted around bringing her things he *absolutely* must take and bombarded her with questions about the animals.

She hadn't received the bill from the solicitor yet, but she didn't care if this holiday took every penny of her savings. They were going to stay in Somerset until Danny was stronger. John and Hetty would make a great fuss of him, and that was what he needed: lots of people around him and new distractions.

The train was going ever so fast! Danny knelt on the seat so he could see out better. They whizzed past houses, and now there were green trees and fields. Green was a nice colour. Something caught his attention and he pressed his nose to the glass. There were lots of sheep all white and running and jumping about. He giggled and swivelled round to his auntie. 'There's sheep in that field. I've never seen real ones before. Oh, we've gone past now.' He was sorry about that; he'd have liked to watch them more. Houses again now; they weren't such fun.

'Will there be sheep where we're going?'

'Yes, darling, lots.'

That was good. With nothing interesting to watch outside, he sat down so he could look at all the other people. There was a sudden lurch of the train, causing the truck to slip out of his fingers and tumble on to the floor. A man opposite picked it up and examined it with a deep frown on his face; then he smiled and handed it back.

'Thank you,' Danny said politely, holding the precious toy with both hands. He'd been frightened the man was going to keep it.

'That's a lovely truck.'

The man had a nice deep voice, and Danny smiled at him, nodding.

'Where did you get it?'

'It was in my mummy's special box.' He looked down at the toy, trying not to cry. Why did his mummy go away like that? He wanted her with him.

Angie saw the change in Danny and immediately tried to steer his thoughts away from his pain. She knew that the day would come when they could both talk about Jane without breaking down, but at the moment Danny was unhappy and couldn't understand why she had left him.

She made space between them and put the basket of food on the seat. 'Are you hungry? We've still got quite a way to go.'

He peered in the basket and then looked up at Angie. 'Have we got corn sandwiches?'

'Yes, corned beef, jam, biscuits and orange drink.'

At that moment the train stopped at a station and all the passengers in their carriage got out, except the man who had picked up Danny's toy. He was a soldier and handsome in a rugged way; although his features were strong, he had gentle, very pale blue eyes. It was hard to gauge his age, but Angie put him in his late thirties. The crown on his shoulders showed him to be an officer, and a highly decorated one. She wondered what he had been doing during the war. Those awful years had changed so many lives, and many would carry the scars, physical and mental, for a long time.

When the train moved on again, she unwrapped the sandwiches and gave Danny one, pleased to see him eat it with enjoyment. The journey was bringing back his appetite. When he finished, she poured him a drink and was rewarded with a dimpled smile of thanks. That look always warmed her heart.

Before taking a sandwich for herself, she held out the packet to the soldier. 'Would you like one?'

'Thank you, I am rather hungry.' He smiled as he leant across. 'Where are you going?'

'To Bridgewater.'

'We're going on holiday,' Danny told him. 'It's a farm with lots of animals.'

'My word, what fun that will be.'

The soldier had a cultured, well-educated voice. He also had a very penetrating gaze, and she doubted if he missed anything. She had seen the swift glance at her left hand, devoid of rings. When he finished his sandwich, she held out the bag, but he shook his head.

He sat back, rested one ankle across his knee and draped a strong hand over his shoe, surveying her thoughtfully. 'I'm sorry, but I seem to have upset him by asking about the toy.' He spoke softly so as not to disturb Danny, who now had his nose pressed to the window once again.

'His mother died a short time ago and he hasn't got over it yet.'

'That's sad. She must have been very young. How did it happen?'

'She had a heart defect.' Angie didn't want to talk about this in front of Danny. The holiday was intended to get him away from the memories, if possible, and to help him heal. 'Would you like a drink? I've only got orange drink.'

He shook his head and gave a slight grimace that made her smile. It was obviously not his favourite kind of drink.

After putting both feet back on the floor, he leant forward and held out his hand. 'My name's Robert Strachan, Bob to my friends.'

She shook his hand. 'I'm Angie Westwood and I'm Danny's aunt.'

'A pleasure to meet you, Angie.' He sat back again. 'And Danny's mother had a special box she kept the toy in?'

She merely nodded, puzzled about his return to the subject of the truck.

'Do you know where she got it?'

'No idea.' She frowned at him. 'You seem very interested in a wooden toy.'

'Do I?' One eyebrow lifted. 'I have a nephew about Danny's age and thought he might like one.'

She gave him a disbelieving look. That answer had been plucked out of nowhere – not the truth. His whole demeanour was relaxed, casual, until you looked into his eyes. This was more than idle curiosity. With a smile he changed the subject.

'Are you staying in Bridgewater?'

Angie shook her head. 'We are going to the Sawyers' farm in Huntstile.'

'Really.' The smile was enticing. 'How do you come to know the Sawyers?'

'I was evacuated down here with my cousin, Jane, after our parents were killed in a raid.'

He sat up straight. 'Was your cousin Jane Harris?'

'Yes – did you meet her?' Angie's heart leapt in anticipation. Jane had mentioned in her letters that there was a camp near by and that one of the officers came to dinner now and again. But she had never gone into detail. Could this be Danny's father? She studied him carefully, but he was dark and nothing like Danny. Jane had said her son was like his father.

'Yes. I know the Sawyers well and often went there for a meal. Your cousin was a delightful girl.' He gazed at Danny for some moments, then back at Angie. 'I wouldn't have thought she was old enough to have a young son.'

'No, she was much too young.' Angie felt the rage rush through her, as it always did when she thought about some man taking advantage of her cousin. Jane had chatted away in her letters, telling her of the people she'd met, but Angie couldn't recall a Robert Strachan being mentioned. She must have known him, though, so why hadn't she mentioned him? She was beginning to realize that her outgoing cousin had been secretive about some parts of her life while at the farm.

She glanced quickly at Danny, who was still looking out of the window. He had a quick mind and sharp ears, and, as much as she would have loved to question this man more closely about Jane, she didn't want to do it in front of Danny.

He didn't pursue the subject. 'I'll have a car waiting for me at the station, so I can give you a lift. I'm just down the road in Goathurst.'

Her instinct was to refuse, but Danny was going to be very tired . . .

He picked up on her doubt and gave a wry smile. 'Don't be uneasy: there will be a military driver with us.'

It would save waiting for a bus. 'In that case I accept.'

He tipped his head back and laughed at her quick acceptance now she knew she wouldn't be alone with him.

At the sound of the laughter, Danny sat back on the seat, eyeing the soldier with interest. 'What's that?' He pointed to the row of ribbons on his chest, slipping off the seat to get a closer look. When the man held his hand out, Danny gave the truck into Angie's safe keeping and walked across to him.

He was swept up so that he could sit on the soldier's knees to examine the decorations.

'They're pretty.' Danny ran a finger over the brightly coloured ribbons. 'What's it for?'

'They are the colours of medals.'

'Hmm.' Danny turned his attention to the epaulets and pointed to the crowns. 'Why've you got those up there?'

'They show my rank. I'm a major.'

Danny stared at him in wonder. 'Is that good – like a general?'

The Major gave a deep chuckle. 'It's way off a general, but it's quite good.'

Angie watched, fascinated by the way Danny was talking to him. He looked so at ease with the big man, and it was at that moment Angie knew he ought to have a man in his life. Why had Jane cut herself off so completely from his father, not even leaving a clue as to his identity? In Jane's letter she had said that he had great problems. What could they have been?

She had been preoccupied with her thoughts and gasped when she looked across the carriage. Danny was fast asleep on the Major's lap.

'Oh, I'm so sorry.' She stood up, but he waved her down again.

'It's all right. Let the little fellow sleep.'

She tumbled back as the train clattered over points. 'Are you sure you don't mind? He's quite heavy.'

'Do I look like a weakling?' He grinned in amusement, showing a row of perfect white teeth.

Returning the smile, she shook her head. That was certainly not a description that fitted him. She hadn't seen him standing, but from the length of his legs he must have been at least six feet. An aura of strength emanated from him – mental and physical.

'Is Danny your responsibility now?'

'I've adopted him. After Jane died, I was the only one left to care for him. Not that I mind,' she added hastily in case he got the wrong impression. 'I love him very much.'

'And what about his father?' The question was asked gently.

'My cousin never told me who he was.' Now that Danny was asleep, she took the chance to ask, 'How well did you know Jane?'

His gaze narrowed as he caught the meaning behind her question. 'I am not the child's father. She was little more than a schoolgirl to me.'

Angie felt embarrassed at her suspicion but pressed the subject. 'Do you happen to know if Jane had any particular friends?'

'You mean men friends? I only saw your cousin when I went to the farm for a meal. I don't know what she did or who she went out with.' He raised an eyebrow. 'I can't help you there.'

'I'm sorry. I just thought you might know something.'

'Don't apologize. I realize what a responsibility you've taken on, but I can assure you that I'm not the one who seduced your cousin.' He looked down at the sleeping child. 'He's lucky to have you.'

'I'm the lucky one, Major Strachan.'

'Bob, the name's Bob.' He rested his head back on the seat, his gaze never leaving her face.

Why was she talking to him so freely? He was a complete stranger, and she didn't usually let personal details tumble out like this. She turned to look out of the window, effectively breaking off the conversation, and was pleased when he fell silent.

The next half an hour passed in that way until Danny suddenly cried out, 'Mummy!'

Angie shot to her feet and reached out for the child. 'It's all right, Danny. Wake up!'

His face was wet with tears as he held his arms out for her. 'Auntie Angel!'

She gathered him into her arms, and Bob stood up to help her back to her seat. Angie concentrated on calming the distressed boy, ignoring the tall man hovering over them.

'I was frightened,' Danny gulped. 'I didn't know where I was.' He sat up, rubbing his eyes with his fists. 'Are we nearly there?'

'Another ten minutes,' Bob told him, still standing with a deep frown on his face. 'Then I'll take you in my car to Mr and Mrs Sawyer.'

'Is it a big one?' Danny had soon recovered.

'Very big.' Bob smiled and sat down again.

The next stop was theirs. Bob dealt with the luggage while Angie carried Danny off the train and out of the station.

'Ooh!' Danny was immediately wide-eyed and struggling to be put down when he saw the army officer's car: very large and painted khaki. He was running as soon as his feet touched the ground. 'We going to ride in that?'

The driver, a corporal, saluted his officer smartly, and

then opened the rear door so that Danny could clamber in. Bob ushered Angie in as well, while the driver stowed away their luggage in the boot. Then Bob and the driver got in the front.

'Where to, sir?'

'The Sawyer farm in Huntstile.'

'Right, sir.' They were on their way at once.

Danny grinned in delight as they sped along and began to examine every inch of the car, leaning forward so he could see all the levers and dials in the front. Bob answered all his questions with good humour.

It seemed no time at all before they were swinging into the yard and pulling up in front of the farmhouse. A dog rushed out barking excitedly as John and Hetty came to meet them.

'Hello, Bob.' John was all smiles as the Major got out and shook hands with him. 'Good to see you again.'

'And you. I hope you've both been well?'

'We're just fine, thanks. Broke my ankle a while ago, but it's back to normal now.'

'I've given your visitors a lift from the station.'

'Angie!' Hetty rushed up and hugged her. 'How lovely to see you again.' She turned to her husband. 'Look how pretty she's grown, John.'

'She has that.' His expression sobered. 'We were dreadful upset to hear about Jane.'

'It was a terrible shock.' Angie placed a hand on Danny's shoulder as he waited patiently beside her.

'And who is this?' Hetty bent down in front of the child.

'I'm Danny, and we've been on a train and in that big car.' This information was delivered with some pride.

'My goodness, what an exciting day.' Hetty stood up and looked at Angie questioningly. "You didn't say you had a son?'

'He's Jane's.' Angie saw the shock register.

'My mummy's gone to heaven,' he told them, speaking of his mother without the usual distress. 'My Auntie Angel looks after me now.'

Angie became aware that the car hadn't yet left, so she turned. 'Thank you for the lift; it was very kind of you.'

Bob was standing motionless, watching the scene. She appreciated his help, but wished he would leave. Introducing the Sawyers to Jane's son for the first time was something she would rather do in private.

'It was my pleasure. Have a good holiday.' With a smile to everyone he went to get back in the car.

Danny had seen the driver salute at the station, and he rushed up and copied it.

Bob immediately returned the salute in true military style, making Danny giggle. Then he got in the car and they drove away.

5

By the time they'd had tea, Danny was so tired he could hardly keep his eyes open, although he had been listening intently as John told him about all the animals on the farm.

'We'll go and see them in the morning.' John smiled at Danny. 'And if you can be up at six o'clock tomorrow, you can see the cows being milked.'

'I can do that.' He looked excitedly at Angie for confirmation. 'Can't we, Auntie?'

'I'll make sure you're ready in time. But,' she said, standing up, 'as you're going to be up so early, I think you ought to go to bed now.'

He was too tired to make a fuss, and Angie could see him fighting to stay awake. He could be a very determined little boy at times, if he wanted something badly enough.

'Come on.' She held out her hand. 'Say goodnight to Mr and Mrs Sawyer, and thank them for letting us stay with them.'

He came obediently, took her hand and gave one of his most beguiling smiles. 'Night, and thank you.'

'We are so happy you came.' Hetty had tears in her eyes when she kissed him. 'We'll all have a lovely day together tomorrow.'

The kiss had produced a shy smile as he trotted beside Angie upstairs to the bathroom.

They were using the room that she had once shared with Jane because it had two single beds. She had asked if they could be in the same bedroom: she didn't want Danny waking anyone else up if he cried out in the night.

Danny was soon bathed and tucked up in bed. Angie sat beside him, and he was asleep within five minutes. It had been a long and exciting day for him. Leaving the door open so she could hear him if he called her, she went back downstairs and found John and Hetty sitting quietly in the lounge.

'Come and sit down here, Angie.' Hetty patted the empty seat next to her on the settee. 'You look fair worn out. What a difficult time you've had.'

Feeling drained, Angie couldn't hide the sigh of relief.

As soon as she was settled, John leant forward, elbows on knees. 'You must tell us about Jane and her son. We didn't ask questions in front of the lad, but we're dead worried. How old is Danny?'

'He was three in May – the day Jane died.'

Angie could almost hear their minds working, and it didn't take them long to come up with the answer.

'So that means Jane was pregnant when she left here.' Hetty appeared distressed. 'Why didn't she tell us?'

'I know why!' John exploded. 'I'd have found out who was responsible, and then I'd have broken his bloody neck. She was only a child, and under our care.' He was now pacing the room.

'Don't shout, dear,' his wife told him. 'You'll wake the boy.'

John muttered under his breath and moderated his tone. 'Who was he, Angie?'

'I don't know.' She then told them as much as she knew, and by the time she had finished John had calmed down.

'I'm so glad you came to us,' Hetty said. 'Let's hope we can help the poor little scrap get over his mother's death.'

'I'm hoping a change in scenery with plenty to occupy him will do that. Jane loved him very much, and I believe she loved his father as well, but because of her health she'd cut herself off from him.' Angie looked at them expectantly. 'I was hoping you might know who her friends were.'

'She used to go to the pictures with the two Chandler girls, but I always drove her there myself and brought her back.' John gazed into space, a deep furrow in his brow.

'Jane mentioned them in her letters, but I want to know if she had any particular boyfriend.'

'Not that we were aware of. We did have a lot of casual labour during the war . . . and just after. Bob used to come for a meal now and again and a couple of the others from the camp.'

'But, John,' Hetty interrupted, 'Jane never showed any great interest in them. She was friendly, that's all. She was friendly with everyone.'

'That's what we thought at the time, but some

blighter got past our guard.' He ran a hand over his eyes. 'I'm sorry, Angie, we should have taken better care of her. I'm furious that we never noticed her interest in some man.'

'You mustn't feel like that!' Angie was immediately on her feet, not wanting these kind people to blame themselves. But she couldn't help feeling disappointed that they didn't know the man her cousin had been friendly with. 'Jane adored her son, and so do I. Whatever happened, I know she never regretted having Danny. He's a lovely child and has brought both of us great joy.'

'Then we must be happy about that.' Hetty smiled at last. 'He really is an appealing child.'

Angie chuckled quietly. 'I hope you still think like that after he's been *helping* you with the farm for a few days.'

The atmosphere lightened and they all grinned.

Major Robert Strachan strode around the now deserted camp, allowing the memories to flood back. He wasn't usually one to dwell on the past. Most of that was best forgotten, like Dunkirk and then his time as one of the Desert Rats. But he was a professional soldier, and accepted the rigours and dangers of the battlefield. He had been away for long periods, and it was on his return from the desert that he'd found his wife had left him for someone else, without even having the decency to write to him. A 'Dear John' letter would have been preferable to the shock of finding her gone. His smile was wry.

The betrayal no longer hurt him, and he wouldn't marry again. Army life was anathema to a happy marriage, especially to someone who couldn't adapt.

He opened the door of Hut 6 and walked in; looking around, he could almost feel the hostile stares of the German prisoners that had always greeted his arrival. Strange, but he could remember only one or two faces. On a crude wooden table was a small tin that had once held bright blue paint: the colour of the little lad's wooden toy. He had been intrigued when he'd seen it, but as soon as he knew they were going to Huntstile he understood. Many such toys were made here during the war and given to the local children.

Leaving the hut and closing the door, he continued his prowl. How quiet it was now: no shouting, jeering or singing. Ah, how he remembered the singing. He had often thrown open his office window and listened to the rousing songs.

He paused to light a cigarette, watching the smoke drift into the air. After Rommel had been beaten, he'd been in the thick of D-Day. The exhilaration as they'd pushed towards Germany was something he would never forget. At last they were going to finish the war, and he was determined to go all the way to Berlin. Bob rubbed his left leg. That had been his intention anyway, until they'd come under fire from tanks hidden behind some derelict buildings. A blast threw him in the air, and the next thing he knew he was in a military hospital with his leg in a mess. He was shipped back home, where the skill of the surgeons saved his leg. He made a good recovery, and, although he had a slight limp, he was eager to get back in the fight again. The top brass had other ideas and sent him to take charge of this camp. He was furious and not in any mood to stand the truculent attitude he met when he arrived. There were two hardened Nazis trying to intimidate the rest of the prisoners. There was a grading system of white, grey and black. The Nazis were classed as black. It didn't take him long to discover that the majority of white or grey prisoners were not looking for trouble, so he had the difficult men shifted to a tougher camp. Things settled down after that. He'd come to like some of them, especially the Luftwaffe crews. Many had been real gentlemen, but they still needed to be watched carefully.

As the war drew to a close, the prisoners were shown films of the concentration camps. Some refused to believe it; others were openly distressed. He remembered one man stumbling outside; he'd followed, finding him being violently sick and tears in his eyes.

'Are you all right?' Bob asked, feeling shock as the man faced him. The look of despair on his face was something he would never forget.

'If you were me, would you be all right?' he ground out, violence just under the surface.

Bob sighed. In view of what they'd just seen, there was no answer to that. He stubbed out his cigarette and leant against a hut, looking up at the clear sky with a bright moon shining.

Repatriation of the prisoners had taken a long time, the last leaving only this year. Some had nothing to go back to Germany for and had stayed here as DPs — displaced persons.

He straightened up and continued to walk towards his office. In just two weeks he would be on his way to a posting in Germany, but before that he had the tiresome job of clearing up and shutting down this camp.

Perhaps he'd take out the girl and the child he'd met on the train. She had been quite lovely, with chestnut hair and hazel eyes. It would be a way to pass a few pleasant hours. The boy had called her Auntie Angel, and, as far as he could see, that was quite appropriate. Though if the colour of her hair was anything to go by, she was an Angel with a temper. He had watched fire flash through her eyes during the journey, when she'd thought he might be the child's father. But he had the impression that it would take a great deal to make her erupt.

'Is it time yet?'

Angie woke suddenly to find Danny kneeling on her bed and whispering in her ear. She sat up and reached for the clock on the bedside table, peering at it in the gloom. 'It's only half past four.'

'When we got to be up, then?'

Propping herself against the headboard, she smiled. That had been the best night's sleep they'd had for some time. He hadn't called out or had bad dreams. She was so glad they'd come here. The farm would heal Danny, as it had her and Jane after their parents had been killed.

64

Danny wriggled about until he was sitting beside her. She placed an arm around him and he snuggled up closely.

'Don't go to sleep again, or we'll miss the cows.'

She chuckled. 'Just another half an hour and we'll get up, have breakfast, and go to see the animals.'

They sat like that until the alarm clock went off at five. Danny was immediately tugging at her.

'It's time now, Auntie!'

As they washed and dressed, a wonderful smell of cooking wafted upstairs, making Angie realize just how hungry she was. They tumbled into the kitchen, eager to start the day.

Hetty was by the large wood-burning stove, tending to various pans on the top. She turned, a broad smile on her face. 'Good morning, my darlings. You made it on time, then.'

Angie nodded. 'Danny made sure I didn't oversleep.'

Hetty looked at them both with such love in her eyes that it brought a lump to Angie's throat. The Sawyers had thought the world of them, especially Jane, who had stayed with them the longest. What a wrench it must have been for them to see her go.

'Sit yourselves down. Egg and bacon, Angie?'

'Yes, please.'

'And what about you, young man? How about a nice boiled egg with home-made bread cut into soldiers?'

He smiled and nodded just as John came in the kitchen and sat at the table with them.

'I got up,' he told John proudly, before John had had

a chance to say even good morning. 'I don't want to miss the cows.'

'I should think not.' John dived into his huge plate of breakfast as soon as it was put in front of him. 'When we've had this, you can help me get them into the milking shed.'

Danny could hardly contain his excitement and treated everyone to a bright smile.

'Ah, he's a bonny boy,' Hetty said quietly to her husband.

John stopped eating for a moment and studied Danny, who was completely absorbed in dunking the bread soldiers in his egg. 'But he was bound to be: he's Jane's son.'

When the plates were empty, John stood up. 'Time to get the cows in.'

Danny nearly fell off the chair in his haste.

By the back door was a covered porch with all the wellingtons lined up. Angie had made sure to pack theirs, knowing how important they were around the farm. She helped Danny into his and slipped on her own. Then they were in the yard, with the excited child running after John, who was making for the field. The large cows walked towards the gate as soon as he called them.

'They're coming on their own,' Danny squealed as Angie caught up with him. 'Look, Auntie. They're whopping.'

John swung the gate open and the cows ambled towards the shed, casting them stares with velvet brown eyes.

'Ow!' Danny wriggled in awe as the large animals passed within four feet of them. 'What are the two dogs doing?'

'They're making sure that none of them stray.'

'Are they?' He looked up at her, his little face glowing. 'But they're just sitting there.'

'I know, but see how they are watching carefully. If a cow doesn't go where it's supposed to, they'll spring into action and guide it in the right direction. They do the same with sheep.' It was all coming back to Angie now. She and Jane had been as interested as Danny.

'They must be clever dogs.'

'They are, darling, but you mustn't pet them unless Mr Sawyer says so, because they are working dogs, not pets.'

The morning sped by as Danny collected eggs, saw the pigs, sheep and horses. He went into raptures about the donkey, crying out with delight when John sat him on the animal. He seemed to spend the entire morning running; not once did Angie see him walk anywhere. He was so determined not to miss anything.

By the time they finished lunch he was nearly asleep at the table and had to sleep for a couple of hours in the afternoon.

The next morning there was a fine drizzle falling, but it didn't deter Danny. He was out as soon as breakfast was over, getting in everyone's way in his eagerness to *help*. Angie kept a sharp eye on him from a distance, giving him the freedom to run and roam that he had never had at home. She chuckled when she saw him clambering on to the fence so that he could look at the huge black and white pigs in the pigsty. He didn't show any fear, no matter how big the animals were.

Bob drove up, got out of the car and, after a quick wave to her, made straight for the boy. 'You're in a fine mess, young man.'

Danny swivelled his head round and gazed up at the tall man in army uniform, and jiggled excitedly. 'Come and look at these. They're ever so big and they've got little ones – all pink! Ain't they great!'

Bob glanced into the pigsty, nodded and said drily, 'Very nice. Would you and your auntie like to come for a ride this afternoon?'

'In the big car?'

'Yes.'

This was even more exciting than the pigs. He slithered off the fence and stood in front of Bob, saluting him.

Bob sprang to attention, making Danny laugh out loud. 'Where we going?'

'For a ride through the hills, and, if we're lucky, we might find a teashop selling real cream cakes. Would you like that?'

'Yes, please.'

Danny was standing in a patch of sticky mud, so Bob lifted him up and placed him on a dry piece of ground. 'You must ask your auntie if it's all right first. She might not want to come.'

''Course she will.' Danny spun round and, seeing her close by, took off, shouting excitedly. 'Auntie Angel, can we go out with the Major? We're gonna have real cream cakes!'

When she smiled and nodded, he jumped up and down, giving a whoop of delight.

'Hello, Bob.' Hetty joined them. 'Will you stay to lunch?'

'Thanks, Hetty, I'd like that.'

'Let me get Danny cleaned up before we eat.' Angie took his hand and shook her head in disbelief. 'How on earth did you get in such a mess?'

Danny looked down at his muddy boots and clothes; wiping his hands on his shirt, he left another streak of dirt across it. 'Dunno, but it was easy.'

When everyone laughed, he beamed all round.

Angie was so happy she could have cried as she cleaned up Danny and put him in fresh clothes. He was a different boy already. The sparkle was back in his gorgeous eyes. He had slept better and eaten a good breakfast as well.

'The Major said we'd have real cream cakes,' he told her for the umpteenth time. 'And we're going in the big car again.'

'That will be lovely, won't it?'

'Yeah, he's nice.' Danny had made an effort to dress himself and was sitting on the bed and frowning at his feet.

Angie slipped off his shoes and put them back on the right feet. 'I think you'll do. Let's go and eat now.'

'I'm starving!' He jumped off the bed and dashed out of the room, making for the kitchen with all speed.

It was a pleasant lunch, and Angie watched Bob with interest as he talked. He was a likeable man, and she couldn't help wishing that he had been Danny's father. But there wasn't the slightest resemblance between them. Bob had dark hair, Danny the opposite, with fair hair and pale grey eyes. In fact Danny didn't look like Jane or anyone else in their family.

As soon as the meal was over, they were on their way. Angie was looking forward to their drive as well. She sat in the front with Bob, and Danny in the back, so he could kneel on the seat and look out. The countryside was beautiful, and Angie sighed with pleasure. This would be a much better place to bring up Danny. London was noisy, crowded and held sad memories of what had happened to Jane.

'Beautiful, isn't it?'

'Yes, I'm glad we came. I was at my wits' end trying to comfort Danny, but he's loving it here.'

Bob gave her a sympathetic glance. 'And I notice he isn't clutching that toy as if his life depended on it.'

'It's sitting on his bedside table now, which is a good sign, because he took it everywhere with him.' She changed the subject. 'How long will you be stationed here?'

'My job is to clear up, so the camp can be closed down. In two weeks I'll be in Berlin.'

'Isn't there any need for the camp now?'

'No.' He shot her a puzzled look. 'The prisoners have all been repatriated at last.'

'Prisoners?'

Bob pulled up by a café, turned off the engine and faced her. 'German prisoners. Didn't you know that was what the camp at Goathurst was?'

'No, but I was only down here for about six months, and Jane never mentioned it.'

'Is this where we're gonna have cakes?' Danny's face appeared between them.

Bob laughed, got out and opened the rear door, hoisting Danny into the air. 'Come on, let's see what they've got.'

They had cream scones – a great treat and thoroughly enjoyed by all of them. When they had eaten their fill, they walked for a while. Danny was holding Bob's hand, chatting away, and Angie's heart squeezed with emotion. He needed a father. She hung back a little, watching the two of them. It would be no hardship to marry a man like Bob: he would make a wonderful father for Danny. She clamped down on that line of thought at once. It wouldn't be right to marry someone just to provide a father for Danny. Anyway, Bob was most likely already married with a family of his own.

'Come on, Auntie,' Danny called, making Bob stop so she could catch up.

Dismissing her foolish thoughts, she ran towards them, laughing. She loved Danny so much, and was quite capable of bringing him up on her own.

6

The next afternoon, much to Danny's disappointment, the rain was torrential, confining him to indoors. After gazing out of the window for a while, he got fed up with that and curled up in an armchair to sleep.

Hetty and Angie were talking when John walked into the front room, towelling his hair dry. 'Filthy weather out there. I think I'll give myself a couple of hours off.' He grinned when he spotted Danny asleep in *his* chair. Tossing aside the towel, he sat on the settee with his wife. 'The rain will stop by evening.'

Angie didn't question this statement, as John had an uncanny knack of predicting the weather, as did many who worked on the land.

'The boy's happy here.' John gave Angie a thoughtful look. 'Why don't you come and live here?'

'That thought has already crossed my mind, but . . .' Angie shrugged. 'I don't know. London has always been my home.'

'You've got Danny to think about now, though.' Hetty's expression was eager. 'There's a good school in the village, and he'd make lots of new friends.'

Angie chewed her lip. 'I suppose I could rent out my house; I don't want to sell it. But where could we stay?'

'Here!' John and Hetty spoke at the same time.

'Oh, I couldn't do that. You'd never have a moment's peace with Danny running around all the time.'

'We wouldn't mind.' Hetty's smile was tinged with sadness. 'We loved you and Jane as daughters. Although you only stayed a few months with us, we came to know you well through Jane and your letters. You were the determined one, and we understood your need to return to London and do your bit for the war.'

'That's right,' John said. 'You and Jane were the children we never had. You've adopted Danny, so why not adopt us as his grandparents?'

'We'd love that.' There was longing in Hetty's voice, her eyes lingering on the sleeping child.

Tears burnt the back of Angie's eyes. Making their home here would bless not only Danny but Hetty and John as well. Danny would grow up with a loving family around him. It would be a wrench to leave London, but she must do what was best for her lovely boy.

She took a deep breath and made up her mind. 'It's kind of you to say we could live here, but I think it would be better if we had a small place of our own. Not far away from you, of course.'

'What about the Douglas cottage, Hetty?' John asked. 'It's on the edge of the village and only about a mile from here.'

'Oh, that might do nicely. It's been empty for some months, but it will need a good spruce up.'

'We'll soon do that. I'll take you to have a look at it tomorrow, Angie, see what you think. The rent's cheap.'

'All right.' Their enthusiasm was catching, and Angie

felt as if this was meant to be; as if someone was saying, 'This is the way, walk ye in it.' That a few words from the Bible should come to her was a surprise. They had attended Sunday School as children, but she hadn't been a regular churchgoer for some years. Still, she was happy to see where this idea might lead.

While they had been talking, they hadn't noticed Danny wake up and wander over to the piano in the corner of the room. When notes sounded, they all spun round. He was pushing down each key and listening intently to the sound, his head tipped to one side.

John grinned and put his finger to his lips to stop Angie speaking.

Danny was completely absorbed in the sounds, and after about half an hour Angie gasped when he began to pick out the tune of a nursery rhyme Jane used to sing to him.

'He's trying to play "Ba, Ba, Black Sheep",' she whispered in awe, watching his hands. He had long fingers for his age. Not a bit like Jane's or hers, she thought, looking down at her square hands and short fingers.

John and Hetty were staring at the child as he bent over the piano keys.

Hetty gave John a questioning look but said nothing.

Angie studied Danny, still experimenting with the notes and trying to make a tune. 'How can he do that? None of our family have ever been able to play an instrument. We're not that musical.'

'Well, Danny obviously is.' Hetty smiled brightly. 'Look how quickly he's sorting out the notes.'

Just then a much clearer rendition of the nursery rhyme echoed round the room.

'That's bloody marvellous,' John whispered. 'When you're settled here, you must take him along to Mrs Poulton for lessons.'

'I'll do that, but I still can't believe he's trying to play and making a tune. He's never touched a piano before.'

'The lad is musical. Haven't you noticed how intently he listens to the wireless, never moving, drinking in each sound, especially classical music?'

'Well, yes, you're right, Hetty . . .' Angie turned her attention back to Danny, who was oblivious to them. 'Jane used to play records a lot. Sometimes I would find them both listening and didn't dare make a sound until the record had ended. I'd forgotten that.'

'Ah, Jane saw it, then.' Hetty stood up rather too quickly, putting an end to the conversation. 'I'll start getting dinner now.'

After Angie had put Danny to bed that evening, she came downstairs to find Bob had arrived and was talking to John and Hetty, their expressions serious. They stopped talking as soon as she appeared.

'Hello, Angie.' Bob smiled. 'I was just hearing how Danny tried to play the piano. If he's got some talent, it would be worth nurturing.'

'I agree.' She pursed her lips and studied their faces. You couldn't tell anything from Bob's expression, but Hetty and John looked uncomfortable, as if they'd been caught doing something they shouldn't. From their strange reaction when she'd walked into the kitchen, she had a strong feeling that they didn't want her to know what they had been talking about. Had they been discussing who Danny's father might be? Did they know, or have a suspicion who it was?

'What is it? Do you know something you're not telling me?' She held her hand up when John opened his mouth to speak. 'Please don't keep anything from me. If you know anything about Danny's father, then I would rather hear the truth, because if I don't I will start imagining all sorts of things. Like did he have two heads, for goodness sake?'

They grinned at that and John shook his head. 'We really don't know, Angie. There were a great many casual workers on the farm during the war and just after. We might see some resemblance to one or two, but we couldn't say for sure if one of them was Danny's father.'

They all sat around the kitchen table and Hetty poured cups of tea. 'If we knew anything for certain, we'd tell you.'

Angie sipped her tea. Of course they would. She was becoming paranoid about finding out who the man was. She must stop asking herself if, but, or might have been. She was fighting with shadows. Whatever had happened in the past, she couldn't regret Danny's being born; nor had Jane, even though his birth had short-ened her life.

After lunch the next day John and Hetty took them to see the cottage. Angie fell in love with it immediately. The roughcast outside was whitewashed, and with the dark grey slate roof it was a picture. The tiny garden in the front had been badly neglected, and the trellis by the front door was falling apart. The only thing holding it up was a climbing rose that had run wild. The front door opened straight into a small front room.

'Oh, look at that.' Angie sighed when she saw the stone fireplace with a large wooden surround.

'Fine piece of work.' John ran his hand over the mantelpiece. 'Solid oak, that is.'

The only other room on the ground floor was the kitchen. All it contained was an electric cooker, sink and one cupboard.

'This will need some work.' Hetty examined the room carefully. 'The tiled floor will come up with a good scrub, but Angie will need more cupboards.'

'That will be easily done.' John opened a door and peered in. 'There's a larder here. And the water and electricity's already laid on, so you won't have to worry about that, Angie. Let's have a look upstairs.'

There were two bedrooms and a bathroom. The cottage was small, but Angie could see how cosy it would be for the two of them. From the back bedroom she could see a garden with open farmland as far as the eye could see.

'What do you think, Danny?' She held him up so he could look out. 'Would you like us to live here?'

He nodded vigorously. 'Could I have a swing on that big tree?'

John peered through the grubby window. 'I expect we can fix one up for you.'

Angie became serious. These plans were all very well, but was she going to be able to live here? 'How much will the rent be, John?'

'Eight shillings a week, but you'll be responsible for the rates and services.'

That didn't sound too bad. If she rented her house out as well, that would be money coming in from two houses; and if they really liked it here, she could sell her house and just keep Danny's . . .

'I've already spoken to the owner and it's yours if you want it.' John shoved his hands in his pockets and grinned at Danny. 'If you live here, you'll still be able to help me with the animals, won't you?'

Danny pulled in Angie's hand. 'Can we, Auntie?'

'Yes, I think we would like it here.'

'Yippee!' Danny danced over to Hetty and John. 'We're gonna stay here. When can you make the swing, Mr Sawyer?'

'As soon as I can get the rope. And why don't you call us Grandpa and Grandma?'

Danny thought about this for a moment, then said, 'Auntie said all my grandparents died in the war.'

'They did, darling.' Hetty held out her arms and Danny walked into them. 'But your mummy and auntie came to live with us, so we're like family.'

He glanced at Angie, seeking approval, and when she smiled and nodded, he hugged Hetty first, then John, calling them Grandma and Grandpa.

'Hello, anyone there?' someone called up the stairs.

Hetty was quite overcome but quickly recovered. 'We'll be right down, Sally.'

Standing in the front room was a girl of about Angie's age, rather plump and homely-looking, with dark hair and nice green eyes. She held out her hand. 'Hello, I'm Sally Tenant and I live next door. Hetty told me you might be moving in.'

Angie shook her hand, liking her at once. 'Yes, we will be.'

'Wonderful!' Sally bent down. 'And you must be Danny.'

He nodded shyly and pushed close to Angie.

'Well, you're going to love it here. I've got a little girl around your age. You'll be able to play together.'

This suggestion produced a dimpled smile.

Sally stood up again. 'What a lovely boy. Emma will be so excited to have someone to play with. This cottage has been empty for far too long.'

'My grandpa's gonna build me a swing,' Danny told her with some pride.

'Won't that be fun?' Being rewarded with another smile, Sally chuckled and turned to Angie. 'We run a Mothers' Relief group in the church hall on Tuesday and Thursday mornings, and Danny would be very welcome.' Sally grinned at Angie's puzzled expression. 'We call it that because it gives the mothers a chance to go out on their own for a while, and on Thursdays we even give the children a meal. That gives the mothers even more time to go shopping or whatever. We run a rota system and could do with a bit of help, if you felt you could.'

'I'd love to.'

'Wonderful! As soon as you move in, come and see me.' She looked thoughtful. 'I don't suppose you can type, can you?'

'Well, yes, I can. Why?'

'The Rector needs help with parish notices and his sermons.' Sally chortled. 'He's typing with two fingers and it takes him ages, and for a man of God the air turns an unpleasant blue around him. If you could help on the days Danny's with the group, he'd happily pay you. It won't be much, mind you.'

Angie couldn't believe this. She was being offered a job as well! 'I'd be pleased to do his typing.'

'I'll tell him. He'll be so delighted.' Sally headed for the door and looked back. 'I must dash. Mum's looking after Emma for me and she'll wreck the place if I leave her there too long.' She tore out of the door and up the road.

'You'll like Sally and Emma,' Hetty said.

John gave an amused laugh. 'You'll have to watch Emma, though. She's a real whirlwind.'

'Sounds fun.'

'You could say that.' John was laughing harder now. 'She looks docile enough, but I'm sure Danny can cope with her.'

'Meaning other children can't?' Angie was intrigued.

'She's too much for the girls, but fits in with the boys okay.'

'I can't wait to meet her,' Angie said drily.

'Talking of meeting people,' Hetty said, standing up, 'while we're here we might as well take Danny to meet Mrs Poulton and fix up his piano lessons. She's just across the road.'

They locked up behind them and knocked on the door of the cottage directly opposite. Mrs Poulton was a tall, spare woman of around sixty, with grey hair and a gleam of amusement in her eyes, as if she viewed the world with a good deal of tolerance.

'Ah, come in, my dears. I'm just finishing off a lesson with young Frank Burrows.' She led them into the kitchen. 'Wait here and we'll soon be done.'

She strode back to the front room leaving the door slightly open. The laborious efforts of Frank could be heard quite clearly and Angie was sure Danny winced when a discordant note was thumped.

Ten minutes later the student was shown out and Mrs Poulton came back to them, a broad smile on her face as she studied Danny. 'So you want to play the piano, young man?'

Danny nodded, but didn't look too sure about this imposing woman.

'Good.' Mrs Poulton glanced at Angie. 'Hetty tells me he's three and he might have some musical talent.'

'Er, he might.'

'Let's see, shall we? You and Danny come with me.'

In the front room was a beautiful grand piano and little else, apart from a few small chairs.

'Sit yourself over there, my dear, while I see what your boy can do.'

It gave Angie a thrill to hear someone call him her boy. He was now, of course, but she still thought of him as Jane's son, and always would. She straightened her shoulders. But he was her son as well.

The teacher put two cushions on the stool so Danny could reach the keys; then, after making sure he was comfortable, she glanced back at Angie. 'Hetty tells me he can play a tune. You taught him that?'

'No, he did it on his own.'

'Did he now?' Mrs Poulton's eyes gleamed even brighter. 'Will you play it for me, Danny?'

Angie could see that he couldn't wait to touch the keys. He began to pick out the tune of 'Ba, Ba, Black Sheep'. When he played a wrong note, he started again and corrected it.

Mrs Poulton listened, head on one side, studying the face of her new pupil as he concentrated. When he finished, she turned to Angie again. 'You say no one showed him how to do that?'

'No one. He was messing about with the piano and just played it.'

'Well, Angie . . . I may call you that?'

'Of course.'

'I think this boy of yours has a good ear for music and I would like to teach him to play. I charge two shillings for an hour, if you can manage that.'

'Thank you, Mrs Poulton, that will be fine.' Perhaps the money from the Rector for doing his typing would cover that.

'Good.' She smiled at Danny, who was sitting

patiently on the stool. 'We shall have fun together, you and I.' When she helped him off the seat, he whispered something to her. 'You'd like me to play you something?'

Danny nodded and smiled shyly.

'What does he like?' she asked Angie.

'He seems to enjoy classical music on the wireless, but anything will do.'

Mrs Poulton sat at the piano and started to play the Moonlight Sonata. The wonderful music brought John and Hetty to the door. Danny stood close to the piano, watching every move of her hands. The expression on his face brought a lump to Angie's throat. Oh, yes, he was musical, and she must give him every chance to develop the talent.

With all the business of the day finished they returned to the farm, and over dinner that evening they made plans.

'It will only take a few days to clean up and decorate the cottage,' John said, 'so why don't you pop back to London and sort out what you're going to bring down here? Have you got someone who'll take care of the renting of your house?'

'Yes, Mr Simpson, he's a solicitor. Some of my furniture will fit into the cottage, so I'll choose what we need and have it delivered here. I haven't got a piano, though, and we'll need one.'

'I'll find you one.' Hetty couldn't stop smiling.

'Not too expensive.'

'Don't you worry about that, Angie.' She gazed at Danny. 'My grandson must have a decent piano because he's going to be a wonderful pianist. Just like –' She stopped abruptly as John glared at his wife. 'Just like Mrs Poulton.'

Hetty hadn't been going to say that, Angie was sure, but before she could question her about the hesitation, Danny claimed their attention. The feeling that they were being secretive again was very strong.

'She played smashing.' Danny's smile was dreamy. 'I want to do that, Grandma.'

Angie couldn't believe how quickly Danny had accepted the Sawyers as his grandparents. He obviously liked having a family.

'And you shall, my angel.'

Danny giggled. 'That's not my name, it's Auntie's. I've got another name as well. Haven't I, Auntie? What is it? I can't remember.'

'Your full name is Daniel Cramer Harris.'

'Yeah, that's it.' He ginned proudly at everyone. 'Great, isn't it!'

'Very nice, darling.' Hetty stood up quickly and held out her hand. 'Want to help me get the chickens in?'

Danny leapt to his feet. 'Mustn't let the foxes get them.'

'I'll check that the gates are all closed.' John followed them out.

'Just a minute.' Angie stopped them before they could leave the room, suspicious of their hasty exit. 'Does the name mean something to you?'

Hetty kept walking, but John turned and faced her, his expression bland. 'No, should it?' Then he left the room.

Finding herself on her own, Angie closed her eyes. Had John just lied to her? Was Cramer the name of Danny's father? How dumb she had been not to think of that sooner. She had just assumed it was some fancy name Jane had heard somewhere and liked. And, from the hurried disappearance of John and Hetty, she was sure they knew as well, and yet they still denied it. Their reluctance to tell her anything about him was frustrating, but she was damned well going to get to the bottom of this once she'd sorted out everything in London. But for the moment she wasn't going to fight with shadows any more! Danny now had a family, and was happy. But she had a growing need to find out who this elusive man was, and why on earth no one would talk about him.

Surging to her feet, she went upstairs and packed her bag. She would leave for London tomorrow, see Mr Simpson about renting out her house, then make arrangements to have some of the furniture delivered to the cottage. It shouldn't take more than two days, and Danny could probably stay with Hetty and John – his new grandparents. They loved him and would take good care of him.

7

Schnell! Schnell! Dieter Cramer was half out of bed when he awoke with sweat pouring off him. Cursing, he settled back on the bed, pulled up his knees and rested his head on them, the pilot's frantic shouting still ringing in his ears. Dear God, it was some time since he'd been plagued with that nightmare. It brought back that moment so vividly.

Their target had again been London, with orders to destroy the docks this time. He had plotted their course, as he had done many times, but before they reached their target they were caught in a searchlight. Then the anti-aircraft guns opened up. The plane shuddered and lurched, and fire broke out on the starboard wing, licking its way towards the main fuselage with frightening speed. They still had a full load of bombs, yet the plane was out of control and losing height rapidly. The pilot yelled for them to get out as he wrestled with the stricken aircraft. Dieter saw that two of the crew were already dead as he hurled himself out.

As his parachute opened, he saw another member of the crew shoot past him; he watched in horror as the man sped downwards with no sign of a chute opening. Later he found out that it had been his friend Kurt, like him just twenty years old. The plane exploded in the air, killing the pilot and everyone else left on board. Dieter had been the only one to survive.

He landed in someone's back garden, and the owner, a man of around fifty, came out brandishing a kitchen knife and shouting to his wife to get the Home Guard.

Dieter was so badly shaken by what had happened and the death of his friends that he stood on trembling legs, holding his hands in the air. 'I'm not going to try to escape,' he said in English. 'May I unhook my parachute?'

The man nodded and waved the knife menacingly. 'Don't try anything.'

Dieter released the harness just as a young boy of about fourteen sidled up to the man. 'Is he German, Dad?'

'Yes, Jimmy. Speaks passable English. Looks a bit rough, though. Go and get him a drop of that brandy I've got in the cupboard.'

The boy sped off and was back almost at once with a glass in his hand. Dieter took it from him and gave a slight bow, struggling to keep his hand from shaking. The fiery liquid burnt its way to his stomach, making him gasp. He had been close to losing consciousness, but that had certainly brought him back to life.

'Good drop of stuff, that,' the man said, seeing his reaction.

Dieter couldn't argue with that, but it had settled his insides a little. Probably with shock, he'd thought wryly.

Two soldiers arrived with HOME GUARD on their uniforms. 'What you got there, Harry?'

'Fell out of the sky. Made a bleedin' mess of my spuds,' he complained. 'Speaks English, but he looks real bad so I gave him a drop of the 'ard stuff.'

'Are you hurt?' the Sergeant asked, as he searched him for weapons.

'I don't think so.'

'Hmm. Any more of you around for us to collect up?'

'I think they're all dead. The plane blew up. You'll find a body somewhere. His parachute didn't open.'

'You a pilot?' the boy asked.

Dieter shook his head – carefully, as the drink on an empty stomach was making him feel light-headed. He almost laughed. What a way to treat an enemy – giving him brandy. The raid was over, but the place was lit up like day by the raging fires. They ought to be lynching him! 'No, I'm a navigator.'

Young Jimmy still looked impressed.

The other soldier took out a packet of cigarettes and lit one, and then handed it to Dieter. He took a deep draw on it and blew the smoke out on a sigh of relief. He had some in his jacket pocket but hadn't wanted to make any unusual moves. These people appeared to be extraordinarily friendly – not at all what they had been told to expect – but he was sure that at the first indication of a threat they wouldn't hesitate to deal with him.

Much to his surprise he was taken first to a military doctor, who gave him a thorough examination. It was only then he realized that his hands were burnt, but not badly, and that there was a cut on his forehead, probably done as he'd fought his way out of the plane. The Doctor had been brisk but not unkind. Dieter was confused, but he wasn't sure if this was due to the bump on his head or to his utter amazement at the treatment he was receiving. The Luftwaffe had been coming over night after night and unloading their bombs, giving them no rest. Even now London was ablaze, with untold numbers dead or injured.

He remembered sitting on the edge of the examination table, shaking his head in disbelief as he thought about the brandy and cigarette he'd been given in the garden. The whole thing was surreal.

'The military police are here for you.' The Doctor shone a light in his eyes again. 'Do you feel well enough to walk?'

'I'm all right. Thank you, Doctor.' Dieter had hauled himself to his feet. Military police! Now things would change. He wouldn't be shown any mercy.

But he was wrong. They took him in a lorry to somewhere else in London for interrogation. On the way he'd seen the terrible damage caused by the raid. Flames were leaping in the air as buildings burnt and came crashing down. Firemen were tackling the hopeless task of trying to contain the fires; people were digging in the rubble, looking for survivors. And it wasn't only men: there were women out there, side by side with the men. Everyone was going about their job with urgency, but there was no sign of panic. They had all been told that the systematic bombing of cities would make the

British capitulate. From what he could see, Dieter doubted that very much.

'Looks a bit different from down here, don't it, mate?' His guard lit a cigarette and handed it to him. 'If your Hitler thinks he's gonna break us like this, he's very wrong. All you're doing is making us bloody mad, and that's not a good thing to do. We won't stop now until we've won this damned war.' He stared long and hard at his prisoner.

Dieter didn't say anything. The man sounded so sure, but, sitting in that truck with London in flames around him, he didn't see how this beleaguered country could possibly survive. After their losses at Dunkirk, they were completely alone, with the might of the German Army just across the Channel. The odds were stacked against them.

They arrived at their destination, and he was marched into a room containing a simple table: two army officers sat on one side and an empty chair was on the other side for him. His heart was thumping. Now he expected some brutality.

But he was wrong again! They asked, politely, for his name, number and rank; which he supplied. When he refused to name his airfield and denied knowing what the future plans were, they left it at that. They even gave him a cup of tea, for heavens sake!

Being a prisoner had come as a nasty shock, and he'd prowled the barbed-wire perimeter, struggling with despair and a longing to be free. He eventually came to accept it, but the desire for his home and family was a constant ache in his heart. Over the next three years he went from camp to camp. Some weren't too bad; others he was glad to get away from if there were hardened Nazis there. They really made life unpleasant for the more moderate Germans like himself, and he learnt very quickly to keep his mouth shut. He ended up in Somerset at Goathurst Camp. It was around March 1945 when he heard about the bombing of Dresden – his home town – and he was frantic with worry for his parents and sister. All news from them stopped, and by the time the war ended he was convinced that they were dead.

Repatriation had been a slow business, and even being billeted on a farm with a certain amount of freedom hadn't eased his worry. The Sawyers were good people, though, and treated him with great kindness; and he repaid them by seducing Jane, the young girl they were looking after. He was still ashamed of that.

Dieter groaned. He was sure she had been in love with him, and he had taken advantage of her affection. He was a young man and had been a prisoner for four years; the temptation was too great. When he looked back now, he could see that the only time he had found any peace was when he had been with her. She had been such a gentle girl, delicate, and so loving. She asked him if he would stay in England, but he couldn't do that. He had to find out what had happened to his family. She understood his need to go back to Germany, and said she must go back to her home as well. On the day she left, she hugged him with tears in her eyes and said that she hoped he would find his family. She refused to give him her address, saying that it would be better if they didn't see each other any more. Then she had gone, and he'd never seen or heard from her again. At the time he had been too desperate to get back home to let it bother him. If that was the way she wanted it, then that was all right with him!

It was the middle of 1947 before he was on his way home. What he found tore the heart out of him. His beautiful city was all but obliterated, and there was no sign of his family, not even a grave. It was as if they had never existed!

When it was evident that his family had perished, he got out of Dresden and headed for Charlottenburg in Berlin, one of the boroughs managed by the British Army. For two years he drifted aimlessly. He lived in a squalid basement room and played piano in bars for food and drink. Too much drink. But there was a terrible shortage of food, and anything he could get was a blessing. He had lost a lot of weight since his return and looked older than his twenty-nine years.

He knew this was no way to live and that he should do something to pull his life together, but he couldn't seem to rouse himself. If he stopped drinking, he might be able to sort himself out, but the drink helped to ease his pain for a while. It made him physically sick when he thought how his parents and young sister must have suffered in the horrific bombing.

Dieter dragged himself off the bed and stumbled to the sink in the corner of the room, splashing cold water on his face.

The past was too awful. He didn't want to think about it any more.

Forcing himself to move, he took his only suit out of the cupboard and laid it on the bed, tossing a clean shirt and tie beside it. A vigorous polish of his shoes hid their shabby appearance. He had found a job in the bar of a decent hotel, a big improvement on some of the seedy places he'd been playing in. He had better make himself look smart because the wages were a lot better than those he had been earning, and he might be given tips instead of drink.

Then he turned his attention to his face. God, what a mess! His fair hair was matted and standing on end; he had two days' growth of beard and dark smudges under his eyes. Picking up a towel and soap, he headed upstairs to the only bathroom in the building. The bath was too stained and unsavoury-looking to sit in, so he half filled it with tepid water and stood to wash himself and his hair. He grimaced in disgust. Conditions had been better than this in the prisoner-of-war camps.

By the time he was dressed he looked and felt more respectable. The hotel was half an hour's walk away, and he used that time to clear his head. He had to make a good impression on his first night.

When he arrived, he was shown into a large lounge. It looked even bigger than when he had come for the interview. It was already busy, with waiters rushing around serving drinks. It was a popular place with the British officers, so business was brisk.

'Ah, Herr Cramer.' The manager came up to him.

'Play quiet music, please. We wish our guests to relax and be able to talk to each other without shouting above the music.'

'I understand.' Dieter sat at the beautiful grand piano.

'Where is your music?' the man asked.

'I don't need any.' Dieter gave a wry smile when he saw the manager's doubtful expression. It had been the under manager who had interviewed him; this man had never heard him play. 'I only use music when I'm learning a new piece. After that I can play without it.'

'Very well. You are on a week's trial, so we will see how it goes. You will play from eight until midnight, with a half-hour break at ten o'clock, when you will be given a meal.'

'Thank you, sir.' Dieter opened the piano lid and ran his hands over the keys, feeling the smooth ivory under his fingers, and then he began to play.

The manager listened for a couple of minutes, nodded in satisfaction and walked away.

The lounge almost emptied out when dinner was served, but Dieter kept playing. Music was like balm to him as he lost himself in the sound. He was surprised once to hear a spattering of applause when he stopped for a moment. Turning his head, he smiled at them, then continued to play.

At ten o'clock he went to the kitchen and was given the best meal he'd had in a long time. And he could actually taste the food; he hadn't had one drink tonight. When he finished, he thanked the chef and took a small glass of beer back to the piano. He would see if he could manage with that tonight. He was sure too much alcohol had triggered the nightmare.

The lounge was crowded again now, everyone chattering after their dinner. Dieter took a mouthful of beer and began playing again. He was stone-cold sober, and when a young woman walked past with dark chestnut hair, the memories of Jane flooded back; try as he might, he couldn't stem the flow. She had been such a loving girl, and they had spent as much time together as they could without raising suspicion. Although the Sawyers had treated him with respect, he was a German, and he knew they would not approve of him spending so much time with Jane. His months at the farm had been a blessed relief from camp life, and, if it hadn't been for the worry about his family, he could have been happy. Jane had such an infectious laugh, and he had grabbed at any moments of forgetfulness in her company. Had he felt more than affection for her? He shrugged, knowing that he hadn't been capable of love at that moment, or now. He shouldn't have seduced her, though. She hadn't been much older than his sister . . .

The pain ripped through him. His darling sister hadn't had a chance to grow into a woman. Jane had gone back to her life in London, but there hadn't been a life for him to return to. Since stumbling through the ruins of his home he had been lost. Utterly lost.

He stopped playing, removed his hands from the keys and bowed his head. Today he had looked into the shadows of his life without the dulling effect of drink. So much sorrow and anger. So much regret . . .

It was only then he realized that the room was silent. He lifted his head just as the enthusiastic applause filled the room.

The manager strode up to him, all smiles. 'That was wonderful, Herr Cramer. Play like that and we will employ you on a permanent basis.'

Dieter was then inundated with requests, and he settled down to finish the last half hour of his session, with plenty of tips being put in his dish. He was a good pianist, but this was the best response he'd ever had. Of course it was obvious what had happened: he had poured his pain and anguish into his music. Well, he was sure he could do that every night, because he had plenty of raw emotions to spare.

8

Being anxious to get back to the farm, Angie rushed through what she had to do. Danny had been very brave in agreeing to stay with Hetty and John, but she had seen his worried expression as he hugged her when she left for the station.

The solicitor was a great help, immediately finding her a tenant for the house – someone he knew. The next job was to pack their personal belongings and choose enough furniture for the cottage. As she gazed around the house before leaving, she cried a little, and was rather ashamed of herself. She had lived there all her life, and the place held such happy memories of her parents. But she wasn't selling and might come back one day, so that gave her some comfort. It was still a terrible wrench to leave, and she didn't dare look back as she walked up the road.

The return journey to Somerset helped her to sort out her feelings. She had Danny to think about now. This move was right, she told herself firmly. It would give him the chance of a much better life.

The account with Mr Simpson had been settled, and he would take a small commission for looking after the houses for her. It wasn't the kind of work he usually took on, she was sure, but he genuinely seemed to want to help her. She had a feeling that Jane had made a big impression on him. He asked if she had found out anything about Danny's father, and she explained that she suspected the Sawyers knew more than they were willing to tell her. She felt that if no one would talk about him, he couldn't be a very desirable person. Yet it was hard to believe that Jane would have been in love with someone who wasn't a good man. Her cousin had been a loving girl, but Angie had never considered her to be a fool. And when she considered Danny, it was impossible to imagine that his father could have been anything but a fine man.

The train pulled into Bridgewater Station at three in the afternoon, and she was lucky enough to catch a bus almost at once. She had managed everything in two days and hoped Danny was all right.

When she walked into the yard, Danny gave a cry of delight, throwing himself at her and nearly knocking her off her feet. She was relieved to see that he looked bright and lively, and hadn't been pining while she had been away. It was very reassuring.

'Auntie, you're back! Come and see. We've got a baby cow.'

Angie allowed herself to be dragged towards the barn, laughing and waving at Hetty as she came out of the house.

The barn was warm, smelling of hay and animals. It wasn't at all unpleasant, and made Angie smile as she remembered how two young girls had believed it was a wonderland. And after the dust, noise and destruction taking place in London at that time, a magical place was how it had appeared to them. Now Jane's son was enjoying the same pleasure.

'Look,' Danny whispered, squirming with pleasure. 'She's sleeping.'

The calf lifted her head and gazed at them with velvet brown eyes, then went back to sleep again.

'She's beautiful,' Angie said quietly. 'Let's leave her in peace, shall we?'

Danny nodded, and they slipped out of the barn.

Hetty and John were in the yard waiting for them, and when Angie saw their smiles of pleasure at her return, the sadness about leaving London vanished. This was their home now. Danny was happy, and she would soon settle in.

'Come and have a cup of tea and tell us how you got on.' Hetty gave her a hug, and they all trooped into the kitchen. Danny held her hand, looking up and chattering away nineteen to the dozen. He was so pleased she was back. When they were enjoying their tea, Hetty told her that he had been a good boy but had missed her very much.

'Did you manage to make all the arrangements to move?' John asked eagerly.

Angie nodded, her mouth full of a delicious sponge cake. She was hungry after her journey. Swallowing, she said, 'The house was rented out almost immediately. There is a great shortage of houses to let in London, and the removal van will be coming the day after tomorrow.'

'That will be just right.' John stood up. 'Come and

have a look at the cottage, Angie. We've had a lot of help and you won't recognize the place.'

'I'd love to see it.' Angie steadied Danny as he slithered off the chair, in too much of a hurry as usual. 'I hope my furniture will fit all right.'

'I'm sure it will.' Hetty held Danny's hand as they clambered into John's old truck. 'And we've found a lovely piano, haven't we, Danny?'

He gave an excited dimpled smile and sat on his grandmother's lap, as that was the only way they could all fit in.

When they arrived at the cottage, Angie couldn't believe her eyes. The outside had a fresh coat of white paint; a soldier was mending the broken trellis and another digging over the front garden.

'What's going on?'

John laughed. 'That's nothing. You wait till you see the inside.'

'I don't believe this,' was all she could say. There were more soldiers working away. The kitchen had been transformed, and the rooms gleamed with fresh paint.

Danny suddenly gave a squeal of delight and shot out of the back door. Angie followed and saw Bob, jacket off and sleeves rolled up, climbing the tree with a length of rope in his hand.

'Uncle Bob's building my swing!'

'Our swing.' A little girl around Danny's age was wriggling through a gap in the hedge. 'Uncle Bob's doing it for both of us.'

'It's in my garden.' Danny looked offended.

'You can have first go.' She pulled a piece of privet out of her hair, ignoring the fresh tear in her frock.

Angie watched in amazement. Uncle Bob? And this must be Emma from next door. She fought back the laughter as the two children continued to bicker about whose swing it was. Emma was petite, with fair hair and baby blue eyes. She looked like every mother's dream of a beautiful, gentle little daughter, but that was as far as the illusion went. The determined set of her mouth showed a little girl with a strong character and a tendency to want to be in charge. Hearing a noise coming from the tree, Angie looked up and saw Bob convulsed with laughter.

He winked at her. 'You're going to have fun with those two. They've been arguing ever since they met.'

Angie decided to deal with this straight away, and in a firm voice said, 'You'd better come down, *Uncle Bob*. We won't have a swing if the children are going to fight over it.'

Suddenly there was silence as two pairs of eyes gazed at her in horror. Emma was the first to recover. 'We won't fight. We'll share it. We can push each other.'

'She knows it's my swing,' Danny protested, not willing to give way on this important point. 'But I'll let her have a go. She's just bossy.'

'I'm not!'

'Enough!' Angie could see they were about to start again. 'You must promise me not to fight or I'll have it taken down again.'

Both children clamped their lips together and

nodded. Their expressions said that if this was what it took to get their longed-for swing, then no sacrifice was too great.

'Good.' Angie looked up the tree. 'You can go ahead, Uncle Bob.'

He was fighting to look severe, and disappeared into the foliage, chortling with amusement.

Angie was sure she heard a sigh of relief from the children and, not being able to control herself any longer, went back to the kitchen and collapsed in helpless laughter.

'Ah,' said John. 'I see you've met Emma.'

After a while she managed to pull herself together and, straightening up, wiped her eyes. She wasn't sure if it was from laughing or tears. It was so wonderful to see Danny behaving like a normal boy after the trauma of losing his mother. 'What's all this *Uncle Bob* business?'

'Danny started that.' Hetty was grinning as she watched the children in the garden. 'He was trying to get the better of Emma by declaring that Bob belonged to him, so the swing he was going to put up would be his.'

'And what did Emma say about that?'

'She said he was her uncle as well, so there.' John roared with laughter. 'Don't worry, Angie, they're going to be the best of friends. Sally told us that Emma is full of excitement about Danny coming to live next door.'

'I hope you're right, otherwise I'll spend my time

prising them apart.' Angie watched Bob jump from the tree and walk towards the cottage. There were two stout pieces of rope hanging from the tree. All it needed now was the seat, which was propped up by the kitchen door.

'Oh, he's hurt himself.' Angie jumped up. 'He's limping.'

'He shouldn't be climbing trees,' Hetty told her. 'He was injured soon after D-Day and shipped back home. When his leg healed, they sent him down here to take charge of the camp in Goathurst.'

'Much to his disgust.' John watched as the two children stopped him, talking and waving their arms about. 'He wanted to get back in the fight, and when they wouldn't let him he turned up here in no mood to stand any nonsense. He soon sorted out the troublemakers and had them shipped to another camp. He's a tough man but a fair one.'

'He's got a gentle side as well.' Hetty smiled. 'Look at the way he's talking to the children.'

Tough, fair, gentle. That made him a complex man, Angie recognized. 'Is he married?'

'Not now.' Hetty's smile died. 'The poor man came home from the desert war and found his wife had left him. He says he'll never marry again, and that would be a shame.'

Angie nodded, feeling sadness for the man she was growing to like and respect. How terrible it must have been for him to find his wife had left him while he'd been away.

The children ran off, chasing each other and shrieking with laughter as Bob came into the kitchen. 'Give me a hand to fix the seat, will you, John?'

'Have a cup of tea first, Bob.'

He held up his hands in mock alarm. 'Not just yet, Hetty, my life won't be worth living if I don't get this swing finished.' He winked at Angie. 'Danny's just told Emma she can have first go, so they're the best of friends again.'

'He mustn't always give in to her.' John frowned.

'Oh, he hasn't given in.' A deep rumble of laughter ran through Bob. 'She's promised he can play with her train set tomorrow.'

'Train set?' Angie's eyes opened wide. 'What's a little girl doing with a train set?'

'She says they're more fun than dolls.' Bob picked up the wooden seat for the swing. 'Emma might look angelic, but she ain't no lady!'

The two men went back to finish the job, grinning widely.

'I think it's going to be lively living here, Hetty,' Angie said drily.

'Never a dull moment, but you'll both be happy. Danny will have children of his own age to play with, and you'll make friends. And we've gained a daughter and grandson. It will give us great joy to watch Jane's son grow up.'

Angie felt her eyes cloud with tears. 'I think Jane knew that was something she would never see her son do. How hard that must have been, but she never said a word, or complained to me about being ill. She covered it so well.'

'I know, my dear.' Hetty placed an arm around Angie's shoulder. 'But she had the comfort of knowing that Danny would have you to care for and love him.'

Angie banished the sad thoughts and smiled. 'I'm so glad we came here. Danny's gathering quite a family around him. Grandparents, and now an uncle. It looks as if Danny has adopted Bob as well.'

'And he's got Emma as a friend.'

They laughed at that prospect just as shouts of delight came from the garden. The swing was finished, so they went outside to join in the fun. Bob was trying it out to see if it would hold his weight, and, when he was sure it was safe, Emma clambered on for her turn.

Two days later the furniture arrived. Much to Angie's relief everything fitted quite well, and the only thing they had trouble with was her wardrobe. But the removal men were experts and managed to ease it up the narrow stairs.

Sally had taken Danny next door with her so he wouldn't get in the way. When Angie had peeked in, he'd been happily playing with Emma's trains and giving the orders. Allowing her first go on the swing had been a shrewd move, she thought. Her Danny was turning into a smart kid.

As soon as the cottage was in some kind of order, Hetty and John returned to the farm to tend the animals.

They were coming back the next morning to help her unpack the mountain of boxes. Angie gazed around and felt a thrill of pleasure. It was August now, and there was still a little of the summer to enjoy, then the beauty of autumn in the countryside, and when winter arrived they would be very cosy here.

Bob turned up late afternoon, gave both children a push on the swing, and then joined Angie in the kitchen. 'Something smells good.'

'It's only spam fritters, vegetables and bread and butter pudding. Would you like to stay and eat with us?'

'Have you got enough?'

'Yes, I can always do extra veg.'

'Thanks, I will, then.' Bob leant against the table, watching as she worked.

'I must thank you and your men for all their help. The cottage looks lovely now.'

'No trouble. We'd just about finished at the camp, and they were happy to do it.' He gave her a wry smile. 'I didn't have to order them. They volunteered.'

Angie laughed and glanced at him in disbelief. 'I'm not sure I believe that, but nevertheless I'm grateful. How's your leg?' She changed the subject. 'You were limping after fixing the swing.'

'I knocked it climbing down the tree, that's all.' He gave a rueful grin and rubbed his leg. 'I should be more careful, but it's fine now.'

'Good.' She turned the fritters over in the pan and looked up at him, interested in finding out how he felt about being in charge of the camp. 'Was it difficult looking after the prisoners? What were they like?'

'It wasn't a job I enjoyed, but I had been injured and was not considered fit enough to rejoin my unit. As for the prisoners, there were a few hard cases, but the majority were decent young men.' The expression on his face said that he would have preferred active duty.

'I expect they were all pleased to be repatriated.'

Bob shrugged and sighed. 'The poor devils must have had a terrible shock when they did reach their homes. Their country in ruins, with a severe shortage of housing and food – all the basic necessities of life, really. And those in the Russian sector are even worse off.'

'Would they have done better to stay here?' Angie had no love of the Germans after what they had done to her family, but she could put herself in their place and understand their plight.

'Many did.' Bob moved to allow Angie to lay the table. 'And many more must wish they had, but the need to see their families again was overwhelming.'

'I expect it was. It must have been terrible for prisoners of both sides to spend so much time behind barbed wire.' She glanced at the clock. 'I'll collect Danny and then we can eat.'

In fact she didn't have to, as Danny was scrambling through the hedge when she stepped outside. The hole was getting larger with constant use, but it might be an idea to put a proper gate there later on. It would certainly be easier on the children's clothes and knees.

Danny was excited to see Bob, telling him all about

Emma's trains while they ate their meal. After helping her to wash up, Bob returned to camp. He would be leaving in two days' time and heading for his next posting in Berlin.

She was going to miss him, and she knew Danny would. He had become fond of the big man, and so had she. He said he would write, and it was a promise she hoped he would keep.

9

With the last of his kit packed, Bob glanced around the camp office. The important papers had been shipped for storage and the rest destroyed. The buildings and huts had been cleared and securely locked. The men assigned to help him had already left, leaving only himself and his driver. The camp was now completely empty, and the army could do what they liked with it. He was pleased to see it closed down at last.

There was only one more thing left to do and that was say goodbye to John, Hetty, Angie and Danny. He'd go to the farm first.

'All done, sir?' His driver, Corporal Hunt, came into the room.

Bob nodded. 'Yes, thank God. I'd like you to drive me to the Sawyers first.'

'Yes, sir.' He hoisted Bob's kit on to his shoulder and they went out to the car, locking the office behind them. 'You won't be sorry to see the back of this place, sir.'

'No, I never wanted to come here, but the top brass had other ideas.'

'Ah, well,' Hunt said, grinning as he opened the car door for his officer, 'you're going to see Berlin at last.'

'About bloody time.' Bob slid into the back seat and wondered why he was so irritable. He was looking forward to his new posting. The army hadn't had any choice but to take him out of the fighting; his leg had been too badly injured and he would have been a liability. Nevertheless, as soon as it was healed, he had put in for a transfer, and done so time and time again, only to have each one turned down. They had been frustrating years. At the end of the war repatriation had taken ages, and he had felt sorry for the poor sods as they'd pleaded to be sent back to Germany. So many had been worried out of their minds for their families – and with good reason. What they had found when they finally arrived home must have been terrible. Bob sighed. What a mess.

It was the ordinary people who were suffering in the aftermath of this conflict. During his time at the POW camp he had come to know a lot of the prisoners. They were young homesick men yearning to see their families.

The car pulled into the yard, and John and Hetty came to meet him.

'Hello, Bob.' John smiled. 'On your way, then?'

'Yes. I've just popped in to say goodbye.'

'It's been lovely to see you again.' Hetty hesitated. 'We've been wondering if you'd do something for us.'

'If I can.'

'Would you make inquiries and see if you can find Dieter?'

'I'll try, but it will probably be hopeless.' Bob noted their concerned expressions. 'If I come across him, do you want me to tell him that he has a son?'

'No!' John spoke firmly. 'That isn't up to us. Angie

must decide about that, but if you can find him, would you try to persuade him to come back here?'

Hetty held out an envelope. 'This is for his fare and other expenses. We liked Dieter.'

'He shouldn't have made our Jane pregnant, though.' John scowled and sighed deeply. 'But Danny's a lovely boy and ought to have the chance to meet his father. Angie told us that Jane had doubts about whether she had done the right thing by not telling him.'

'I expect she thought she was doing right at the time.' Bob waved the money away. 'If I find him, I'll take care of his expenses.'

Hetty pushed the envelope into his hand. 'No, we insist you take this. If you can't find him, then you can give it back to us sometime.'

Seeing her determination, he slipped the envelope into his pocket. 'Does Angie know that Cramer is the man her cousin was in love with?'

'We haven't told her yet, and, unless he can be found, we don't see the point in her knowing. We've been avoiding her questions, because she has no love for the Germans after losing her family.' Hetty shook her head sadly. 'I'm sure she's realized that we've guessed who Danny's father is, but she's holding back from demanding an explanation. Part of her wants to find him for Danny's sake, but part of her is frightened about having a stranger come into their lives who has a claim on the child.'

'It's a dilemma, I agree,' Bob said.

'We'd be grateful if you would do what you can. He

ought to come back and sort this out with Angie.'

'All right, John, I'll write if I have any news.'

'Where to now, sir?' Hunt asked when he reached the car.

'To the village. I want to see Angie and Danny before I leave.'

'Nice kid, that.' He held the door open. 'Wonder if that little girl next door has got the better of him yet?'

Bob laughed as they drove out of the yard, remembering the man who was the boy's father. Cramer had been quiet, artistic, but no weakling. There had been a strong character under the surface. 'I doubt that very much.'

His driver nodded in agreement as he negotiated a tight corner.

As soon as they arrived, Danny came running out of the house, giving a salute; when he received one from the driver as well, he went into peals of laughter. He caught hold of Bob's hand. 'Come and give me a push on the swing. You give the bestest pushes.'

'Will you be long, sir? Only I'd like to see someone if there's time.'

Bob consulted his watch. 'I'll be about an hour. Will that suit you?'

'Plenty, sir, and thanks.'

'Sound the horn when you get back.'

'Right, sir.' Hunt hurried up the street.

Probably found himself a girl while he's been here, Bob thought as he allowed Danny to drag him indoors, through the kitchen and into the garden. He only had time to wave at Angie. As if by magic there was a rustling in the hedge and Emma appeared just as Danny sat on the swing.

'Five minutes each,' he told them. 'That's all I've got time for.'

Bob was scrupulously fair and timed the sessions so each child had exactly the same and couldn't argue about it. 'Now you push each other,' he said. 'I'm going to talk to your auntie, Danny.'

'Thanks, Uncle Bob,' they both said.

He stooped down in front of Danny. 'I won't be able to come to see you for a while, as I'm going away.'

'Oh.' The pleasure faded from Danny's face. 'Will you be long?'

'I might be, as it's a long way away, but I'll come as soon as I have leave.'

'Promise?'

'I promise.' He stood up, pleased to see the boy smiling again. It was a good job he was being posted, because he was becoming far too fond of the child – and his aunt – he had to admit.

He could see Angie watching him from the window as he strolled towards the back door. She really was quite lovely with the sun streaming in and turning her dark chestnut hair to red and gold. Not only was she attractive but she also appeared to be a sensible girl, able to cope with life's difficulties without panic or resentment. He hesitated, with his hand on the door. He was finding her very appealing, but he really didn't want any permanent commitments.

Turning the handle, he walked in, and his resolve not to get involved faded as Angie smiled at him.

'Have you told Danny you're going away?'

'Yes, he took it quite well after I promised to come to see him when I was on leave.'

'He's going to miss you.' She folded the last little shirt and put it on the top of the pile of clean clothes.

'And what about you, Angie, are you going to miss me?' He reached out and turned her to face him.

She held his gaze as she spoke. 'Yes, I shall.'

He liked the way she had responded to his question. No awkwardness or fluster, just a straight answer. Pulling her gently towards him, he lowered his head. As he felt the softness and warmth of her lips on his, he slipped his arms around her, deepening the kiss, revelling in the closeness of her body against his . . .

A shriek from the children playing in the garden cut through his aroused senses. Releasing her, he stepped back. She was flushed and staring at him, eyes wide.

'I didn't mean to do that.' He lifted his hands in an apology.

'Really?' The word came out in a croak and she cleared her throat. 'If you kiss like that when you don't mean it, then it must really be something when you do.'

The wry expression on her face made him chuckle, and he was relieved to see her smile spread. Oh, yes, she was special and he liked her. More than that he was not prepared to admit.

A car horn tooted outside, and he glanced at his

watch. 'I must go. You and Danny take care of your-selves. I'll return when I can.'

He strode out without looking back and slid into the car, sighing deeply as they drove away. He had prom-ised himself that he would never get emotionally involved with anyone again, but he hadn't reckoned on meeting someone like Angie Westwood . . .

'Here we go, then, sir. Next stop Berlin.'

Bob pushed away the thoughts of Angie. He could do without that kind of a problem. 'Glad to be going, are you, Corporal?'

'Yes, sir. The landlord's daughter at the Crown was getting too serious. Nice girl, but I'm not ready for anything permanent. If you know what I mean.'

'Ah, running away, are you? I hope you were careful?'

'Very careful, sir.'

'I'm relieved to hear it. You don't want an irate father chasing after you.' Bob had seen that happen a few times in his career as a soldier.

'Perish the thought, sir!' Hunt visibly shuddered. 'What about you, sir? Are you sorry to be leaving that nice girl and the boy?'

Bob frowned. Hunt was chatting away and looking very pleased with himself. He should be feeling the same. This was a posting he'd been longing for. He caught sight of Hunt watching him in the rear-view mirror, his eyes glinting with interest.

'You can take that look off your face. I'm too old for her.'

'Never, sir! You're not above thirty, surely?'

Bob tipped his head back and roared. 'You're fishing.'

'Who, me, sir?'

'Yes, you, but I'll satisfy your curiosity, although I'm sure you already know. I was forty last month.'

'I'd never have believed it, sir.'

'You're a liar. Stop prying into my private life and drive, or you might find yourself as a *private* again!'

He watched the driver's shoulders shaking with suppressed laughter. They had been together for almost five years, and he was pleased Hunt was coming to Germany with him. If he were going to track down Cramer, then he would need all the help he could get. Hunt might be able to ferret out news better than he could. He was an enterprising young man.

'Do you remember a prisoner by the name of Cramer?' he asked.

'Cramer? Cramer?' Hunt shook his head. 'Not offhand. Give me a clue.'

'He was about as tall as me, fair hair, lodged with the Sawyers after the war until he was repatriated.'

'Ah, played the piano like a dream. Came from Dresden.'

'That's the one. The Sawyers have asked me to try to find him when we get to Germany.' Bob had grave doubts of success. Europe was awash with displaced persons.

'That won't be easy; he could be anywhere by now. God knows if he had any chance of finding his family, if they'd been there during the raids.'

'Yes, poor devil.' Bob could remember the prisoners' reactions as the war came to a close. There had been anger at the destruction, shame as the cruelty of the concentration camps had been uncovered, and desperation to know if their families were all right. 'Anyway, I'm going to need your help.'

'Only too glad to be of use, sir.'

That was the response he had expected from Hunt, so Bob sat back and relaxed. He might as well forget it for a while because he couldn't do anything until he arrived in Berlin.

Long after the car had disappeared, Angie was still standing by the window, and her heart rate had slowed at last. That kiss had been like nothing she had ever experienced before. She'd had a few boyfriends, but now she could see that they had been just that – boys. Bob Strachan was a man. His kiss had urged and coaxed her to enjoy the embrace. And she had. Alan's kisses had been selfish and only took, not giving anything in return.

Turning away from the window, she pulled a face. Judging by the speed with which Bob had left, he'd regretted kissing her. And what had he meant when he'd said he would be back when he could? It had sounded rather vague and made her wonder if she would ever see him again . . .

'Auntie!' Danny burst into the front room. 'Em's mum said we could have tea with them.'

Was it that late already? Angie glanced at the clock

on the mantelpiece. Nearly four – where had the time gone?

'Please, can we?' Danny jumped up and down impatiently.

'Of course. What time did she say?'

'Now!'

'Okay, go and wash your hands.' They were filthy as usual. 'Give them a good scrub.'

Danny thumped up the stairs and was soon back, holding his hands out for inspection. When she nodded, he turned and headed for the back door.

'Danny!' she called. 'We'll go to the front.'

He appeared again, looking puzzled. 'But I always go this way.'

She grinned. 'I'm not crawling through the hedge. The hole isn't big enough for me, and you'll get all dirty again and I'll tear my frock.'

This took a bit of thought, and Angie could almost see his mind working behind his clear grey eyes. They really were beautiful.

'Em don't care. And I could wash my hands again, I suppose.' It didn't appear to be a very enticing prospect.

He seemed to relish a bit of dirt ever since he'd lived here. When they visited the farm, she always had to take a change of clothes with her.

She couldn't hide her smile as she pictured the little girl's total disregard for her pretty frocks. If she were Sally, she'd put Emma in dungarees. 'Can you see me on my hands and knees trying to get through the hedge?'

Danny giggled then, holding his arms out wide. 'We'd have to make the hole this big.'

'Well, not quite that big,' she said, holding out her hand to him. 'Let's arrive like proper guests, shall we?'

They didn't have a chance to knock on the door before it was thrown open by Emma.

'We've got tinned fruit and my daddy's home,' she declared, dragging Danny inside.

'Hello, you must be Angie.' A man of around five foot eight, with light brown hair and an appealing smile, held out his hand. 'I'm Joe, Sally's husband.'

'I'm pleased to meet you.' She took an instant liking to him. He was very slim and wearing a pair of horn-rimmed glasses.

'Come in. I'm sorry I wasn't here when you moved in, but I've been working as a long-distance lorry driver and was away.'

'That was the last trip, though.' Sally beamed and hugged her when they reached the kitchen. 'After Joe was demobbed two years ago, he had to take whatever work he could get, but now he's going to teach in the local school.'

He looked more like an academic than like a lorry driver. 'What branch of the service were you in?'

'RAF ground staff; my poor eyesight stopped me doing anything exciting.'

'You'll have enough excitement round here.' Sally raised her eyebrows. 'You'll have Emma to deal with everyday from now on.'

They were all grinning at the thought when the children scrambled on to chairs, ready for their tea.

Later that evening, as Angie tucked up Danny in bed, he gazed up at her, eyes troubled.

'Why haven't I got a daddy like Em?'

Her heart skipped a beat. She had known the question would come one day, and seeing Emma with her father must have made him wonder. She sent up a silent prayer for help to deal with this wisely. She wasn't going to tell him any lies.

'You have got a daddy, darling, but we don't know where he is.'

'Have you lost him?'

'Your mummy said he had to go away before you were born.'

Danny's bottom lip trembled. 'Why didn't he come back? Didn't he love me?'

'He would love you so much if he saw you.' Angie was alarmed. Danny had made wonderful progress since they'd been here and she didn't want to see him unhappy again. But how did you explain to a three-year-old? 'He doesn't know you've been born.'

'Can you find him and tell him, Auntie?' A single tear trickled down his cheek. 'I want a daddy like Em.'

'I'll try to find him for you, darling.' John and Hetty knew something, and it was about time she insisted on answers. She had been reluctant to do anything about tracing his father, quite happy to have Danny to herself, but she was being selfish. Whatever her feelings, this lovely little boy must come first. And if she ever did find him, he was going to be in real trouble for not coming back to see if Jane was all right after seducing her. All right, Jane hadn't told him about the baby, but he shouldn't have disappeared like that. He should at least have left her some way of contacting him if she needed to.

How could his daddy be lost? Danny pretended to be asleep until he heard Auntie leave the room, then he got up, trotted over to the chair in the corner and picked up his teddy bear. Then he clambered back into bed, slid under the covers and hugged the soft animal to him ever so tightly.

He wanted a daddy. Perhaps Em would share hers with him. He'd give her an extra long go on the swing.

10

Finding the teddy bear in Danny's bed the next morning drove Angie into action. This was to be his first day at the Mothers' Relief session, and, with Emma there, Angie was sure she would be able to leave him for an hour or so. She chatted away as she got him ready, explaining what fun the morning was going to be, and by the time they left the cottage she had coaxed a smile out of him.

It was bedlam when they walked into the church hall. There were eight children of varying ages from toddlers to about four. Sally and another young woman were doing their best to control the mayhem. Danny took one look and, spotting Emma, rushed straight into the fray, his sombre mood disappearing.

Sally was sitting on the floor with a tiny girl on her lap and mopping up her tears. She grinned at Angie. 'Danny's fitted in right away.'

'So I see.' She shook her head as she saw him happily daubing paint on paper, himself and Emma.

'Don't worry, Angie, it's only coloured water.' With the little girl's tears now stemmed, Sally stood up. 'Are you going to stay?'

'I need to see Hetty first, but I'll be back in about an hour. Will that be all right?'

'That's fine. You'll be able to help with lunch,' Sally said with a perfectly straight face, but her eyes were alive with laughter.

Angie raised her eyebrows. 'Oh, good, I'd hate to have missed that treat.'

'I'll introduce you to the Rector when you get back,' Sally called as Angie headed for the door. 'When I told him you can type, he said you were the answer to his prayers.'

With a final wave Angie hurried out of the church hall. If she walked very briskly, she should reach the farm in fifteen minutes, another fifteen back, leaving half an hour to talk to Hetty and John, if he was around. They knew more about Danny's father than they were saying. She felt guilty that she hadn't pushed harder for the truth, but fear had stopped her, and in a way she'd been relieved they hadn't given her a name. But the problem couldn't be ignored any longer, because Danny was at an age when he noticed things and asked questions. She quickened her pace as worry gnawed at her. All the time Danny had seemed unaware that he didn't have a father, she had been happy to leave it, but it wasn't going to be something she could easily push aside now. She had to find out for Danny's sake.

'Angie!' Hetty greeted her with real pleasure. 'Where's Danny?'

'At the church hall with other children.'

'My goodness you have been hurrying, you're out of breath. Come and have a cup of tea.'

'Thanks. I've only got half an hour. I must get back in time to help with the lunches. Is John around?'

'He's at the market this morning.' Hetty filled the kettle and put it on the stove. 'You look worried. What's happened?'

'Last night Danny asked me why he hasn't got a daddy like Emma.' Angie watched Hetty's face pale. 'I believe you know who he is.'

'Yes, we do.' Hetty sat down heavily.

'Then I think it's time you told me.'

Hetty's eyes clouded for a moment, then she nodded. 'He worked here for a while just after the war ended. He was such a nice young man and we were very fond of him . . .'

'What did he look like?' Angie urged when Hetty stopped speaking.

'Tall, fair hair and grey eyes, just like Danny. He used to sit at our piano in the evenings and play for us. He was a wonderful pianist.'

'So Danny has inherited his musical talent along with his looks?'

'Yes.' Hetty ran a hand over her eyes. 'But we didn't have any idea Jane had fallen for him. They were very discreet. And, to be truthful, we still considered her a child, which was very short-sighted of us.'

'We need to find him because Danny's asking questions.' The kettle boiled and Angie made the tea, seeing Hetty needed time to compose herself. When she'd done that, she sat down again and the questions tumbled out. 'Where did he come from? How old was he? Why was he working here? Where did he go when he left here?'

'We don't know, Angie.' Hetty was getting agitated now. 'I can't tell you more than I have.'

Angie narrowed her eyes in suspicion. 'Can't or won't?'

'We won't.' John strode into the kitchen. 'We don't want you prejudiced against him before you've met him.'

Angie shot to her feet, furious. 'This nonsense has gone on long enough, and I'm getting very tired of you evading my questions. And how the hell am I going to meet him, if you won't tell me where he is?'

'Sit down, please.' Hetty caught her arm. 'Don't be angry with us.'

John took hold of her shoulders and eased her back in her chair, then began to speak earnestly. 'We do have a vague idea where he might be, but finding him will be difficult, especially if he's moved around a lot.' He stirred two spoonfuls of sugar into his tea, his expression grim. 'We know he must be found and a friend of ours is looking for him now, but it could be an impossible task.'

'But he must have had a home address. You saw his identity card, surely? Where did he live before he came here?'

'Angie,' John said, shaking his head, 'we don't have an address for him; if we did, we'd have contacted him already. If our friend can find him, we'll explain everything.'

'If he does come across him, he isn't going to tell him about Danny, is he?' Angie was exasperated. They shouldn't have done this without asking her first. Danny was her responsibility, not theirs.

'No, no, Angie.' John leant towards her. 'Don't be upset. You must trust us; we would never do anything to hurt you or Danny. If he turns up here, we'll send him round to you. It will be your decision how much you tell him. We don't want you forming an opinion about him until you meet him face to face.'

'What the hell is wrong with him?' She exploded; this was too much for her quick temper. 'I'm completely bewildered by this secrecy about his identity.'

'We know you are. There is nothing wrong with him, but we feel it best if you form your own opinion when you meet him.' Hetty reached across the table and took hold of her hand. 'We are doing what we feel is right for all concerned. Please trust us, Angie. Any decisions you come to about him will be up to you. We won't interfere in any way.'

Angie's anger faded as quickly as it erupted. John and Hetty were taking steps to trace him. She would have to be satisfied with that for the moment. 'At least tell me his name. Is it Cramer?'

'Yes, it is.' Hetty gave a sad smile.

So that confirmed it. Jane had put the father's name on his birth certificate. 'What's his first name – is it Daniel?'

'No,' John said firmly, 'and we won't tell you his Christian name, but it's something like Daniel.'

'Jane obviously chose her son's name carefully.' Hetty's gaze was appealing. 'I know this is confusing and frustrating, but one day, God willing, you'll understand our reasons.'

Angie's mind was in turmoil. This whole business was impossible to understand. First Jane's refusal to identify him, and now John and Hetty were keeping things from her. Her sigh was full of frustration. She wasn't going to get any further with this. Once John and Hetty made up their mind about something, nothing would shift them. She had soon found that out when she came to live here. 'But you liked him?'

'Yes.' John drained his cup and put it back on the table. 'I must admit to being furious when I found out he had taken advantage of our Jane, but, when we look at Danny, it's impossible to feel anything but pleasure. Giving birth to him may well have shortened Jane's life, but you said she loved him dearly and never regretted it.'

'No, she didn't.' Angie swallowed the emotion as she remembered her cousin. 'He was the light of her life, and he is mine as well. How could we regret the birth of such a lovely child?'

'Then we must learn to forgive.' Hetty smiled at last. 'Everything will turn out well in the end, I'm certain of it.'

'Ever the optimist,' John chided his wife. 'But this time I pray you're right. As I've said, if he is found, you'll make the decision as to whether he meets his son and has access to him. But the boy is yours, legally and morally, that was Jane's wish, and we won't let anyone interfere with that. We'll be right beside you to support you in whatever decision you make.'

The tension eased. Angie couldn't ask for more than that, and knowing that they would provide help, should she need it, was a great comfort. They looked very relieved now the questions had stopped. She glanced at her watch and jumped to her feet. 'I've got to see the Rector about his typing. You'll let me know if you have any news, won't you?'

'Of course, but we must warn you that our friend believes the chances of finding him are very slim.' Hetty hugged her for a moment. 'When are you bringing Danny to see us? I swear the chickens are pining for him.'

'Oh, dear, we can't have that,' she joked, though it was the last thing she felt like doing. The mystery of Danny's father was frustrating, but she couldn't be angry with John and Hetty. They had their reasons for acting like this, just as Jane had, but she was really worried now. Turning her mouth up in a smile, she said, 'How about tomorrow afternoon? He's having his first piano lesson today and he can show you what he's learnt.'

Hetty's smile was wistful. 'He'll soon be playing for us. His father told us that he could play almost before he could walk.'

She caught the warmth and affection in Hetty's voice and felt her spirits rise. 'If Danny's the image of his father, I can't fail to like him, can I?'

John squeezed her arm. 'If he is found, just give him a chance.'

'I will, for Danny's sake.' Glancing at the time, she stood up, knowing there was little point in continuing to question them. They had said all they were going to say on the subject of this mystery man. They had asked her to trust them, and she would. 'Now I must dash. We'll see you tomorrow.'

All the way back Angie kept running names through her head, trying to find something that sounded like Danny, without success. In the end she gave up. At least she had gleaned a bit of information and would have something to tell Danny if he brought up the subject again. She wouldn't mention it if he didn't, though. The thought of a strange man turning up with a claim on Danny was worrying, but John and Hetty had made no secret of their affection for him. They were keeping secrets, just as Jane had. It was all very puzzling, and she'd found it hard to hold on to her temper, but what good would it have done to demand they tell her who he was? None at all, she suspected.

There wasn't any point in getting into a lather. She strode out, head high, enjoying the warmth of the sun, the smell of freshly cut hay and the sound of birds chattering in the hedgerow. He might never be found, and, as Danny got older, the boy would accept the situation. And she might be able to find him a daddy of her choosing; someone he would love and respect. He already cared for Bob, and she wondered how long it would be before he came home on leave.

*

As soon as she walked through the church hall door, Danny charged towards her, holding out a plasticine model of a horse. 'Look, Auntie Angel, see what I've made.'

She made a point of inspecting it carefully, looking suitably impressed. 'That's really good, Danny.'

'Yeah.' He beamed at the praise, then tore back to join in the fun again.

Angie watched his animated face as he talked to the other children. This was so good for him. She didn't know of any group like this where they had lived in London.

Looking up, she found an elderly man watching her, hands in his pockets, and with a slight stoop. The dog collar told her that this was the Rector. He looked docile enough.

He smiled. 'You must be Angie.'

'Pleased to meet you, Rector.' He had a firm grip when they shook hands.

'Call me Geoff. We don't stand on ceremony around here.' His dark eyes crinkled at the corners. 'I heard your boy call you Angel, and that's just what you'll be if you can help me with my typing.'

'I'd be pleased to.' She liked him instantly. There was a sense of humour lurking behind his eyes.

'That's a relief.' He put his hands together and looked up at the ceiling. 'Thank you, Lord.' Then he winked at Angie. 'Our prayers are answered when the need is great.'

'Well, you should know, Geoff.' Sally joined them,

giving him a teasing grin. 'Are you going to stay and help us feed the children?'

A look of horror crossed his face. 'I'm urgently wanted elsewhere.'

'I thought you might be.' Sally shook her head at Angie. 'It's strange, he's quite happy to come and play with the children, but mention feeding time and he's off.'

Geoff chuckled. 'I'm too old to deal with that mayhem. Now, Angie, would you be free to help me the day after tomorrow, in the afternoon? I have something urgent needs doing.'

'That would be fine. Can I bring Danny with me?'

'I'll look after Danny for you.' Sally glanced at the children. 'Our two are practically inseparable now anyway.'

'Good, good.' Geoff headed for the door, muttering to himself. 'That's all settled, then.'

'Come on,' Sally urged. 'Let's get this lot fed; afterwards they can go home and sleep.' She rolled her eyes. 'Bliss!'

'What time do you pack up?' She followed Sally to a small kitchen in the back, which was firmly in the control of a rotund middle-aged woman.

'Usually around twelve, but every Thursday we keep going until two. We feed the little ones and it gives the mums a longer break.'

'Except for the helpers,' Angie pointed out.

'We've got a rota system going and this task comes around only once in four weeks.' Sally gave her a cheeky grin. 'I've put you on the list with me.'

'Oh, thanks, I think.'

'Are you two going to help or stand there all day gassing?'

'Sorry, Mavis.' Sally held up her hand in an apology. 'This is my new next-door neighbour, Angie.'

'Nice to meet you, Angie. I'm the cook.' A fork was held out. 'You can mash the spuds. Don't want no lumps or the little ones will spit it out.'

That danger was enough to make Angie concentrate on the job until the potatoes were fluffy, with not a lump in sight.

When the children had their dinner in front of them, Sally and Angie stood back, alert for any need to rush in and avert a disaster.

'Good heavens!' Sally knocked Angie's arm. 'Did you see that?'

'No, what happened?'

'Emma just gave Danny a spoonful of her mashed potatoes. She loves mash.' Sally gaped in disbelief. 'I think she's in love with him.'

Angie stifled a giggle. 'And Danny, being the perfect gentleman, refused it, did he?'

'No, he ate it.'

They howled with laughter, unheard above the noise of the children shouting at each other. All Angie's earlier worries dissolved at that moment. Hetty was right: everything was going to turn out well. There wasn't anything to get in a stew about. She was letting her stupid imagination get the better of her.

After they'd washed up the dishes and all the children had been collected, Angie and Sally had a quiet cup of tea. Danny and Emma were playing with the plasticine again and concentrating hard on their creations. Probably trying to outdo each other.

'Do you think we can persuade Danny to play Joseph in the Nativity Play? Emma's going to be in it.'

Angie nearly choked on her tea. 'What as?'

'Haven't decided yet.' Sally grinned. 'But if Danny's going to be Joseph, then she'll want to be Mary!'

'Oh, dear.' Angie was crying with laughter. 'I don't think they'll be much of an advert for domestic bliss. If we put them together, there's liable to be a fight.'

'I know.' Sally's face was glowing with amusement and anticipation. 'Should be fun.'

Angie shook her head in disbelief. 'Are you looking for trouble? I'm beginning to think Emma takes after you.'

'She does.' Sally chuckled. 'But I grew out of it – almost.'

'How does Joe cope with the two of you?'

'Oh, he loves it. There's never a dull moment in our house.' She winked at Angie.

'I can imagine.' Angie glanced out of the window and saw the clear blue sky. 'Isn't it a bit early to start planning the Nativity Play? It's only early September.'

'If we don't start soon, we'll never get it sorted out.' She gave Angie a hopeful look. 'Can we drag you in to help?'

'Why not? I can see that living here will be anything but boring.'

Sally rinsed the cups and left them on the draining board. 'Great. I knew you were a sport as soon as I saw you.'

What a day! Angie collapsed on the settee and swung up her legs. Even Danny was tired out, and that took some doing. He'd been asleep as soon as she had covered him over. After leaving the church hall, they'd gone to Mrs Poulton for his first piano lesson, which he had enjoyed enormously. Then they'd had Emma round for tea and played a game of football with Sally and Joe.

She laid her head back, closing her eyes, a happy smile on her face. Moving here had certainly been the right thing to do. Life was going to be busy, what with the children's mornings, typing for the Rector and piano lessons.

They had been welcomed into the village activities and were already making friends.

And then there was the Nativity Play to arrange! Angie shook with silent laughter as she thought about it. With Danny and Emma together, it could turn into a farce.

11

After four weeks in Berlin all efforts to find Cramer had come to nothing. Corporal Hunt had even managed to find some people who came from Dresden but had drawn a blank there as well. Bob stared at the paper in front of him, trying to think what to tell John and Hetty. They were going to be disappointed, but Europe was full of displaced persons. Finding anyone was an almost impossible task.

Dammit! He stood up and prowled over to the window. It was October now and soon winter would be upon them. He'd hoped to have found out something by now, anything, but he was loath to admit defeat. 'Where the hell are you?' he cursed out loud.

'Sir.' Hunt came into the room and saluted when Bob turned round. 'Cramer: I might have something. There's a man by that name playing piano in the lounge bar of the Bayern Hotel.'

'Where is this place?' A glimmer of hope at last!

'Not too far. It's in the Tiergarten area. I'll show you.'

'Are you telling me we've been scouring Germany and he's on our doorstep?'

'Never thought to look here, sir. As his home's in Dresden, we assumed he would be there, not in West Berlin.'

'That was stupid of us, Corporal.'

Hunt pulled a face. 'If you say so, sir.'

'I do. Now what time does this man start playing?'

'Should catch him around nine, sir. But don't get your hopes up too much. It might not be him. I didn't go in to check because the place is mainly used by British officers.'

Bob looked at his watch. It was eight thirty. 'It could be him. Cramer was a damned good pianist, so come on, let's go now.'

The hotel was only fifteen minutes away by car, the way Hunt drove, and Bob strode in, taking the Corporal with him. Hunt was stared at, but, as he was with an officer, nothing was said. The sound of a piano drew them to the lounge bar and, finding a table where they could see the man clearly, they sat down and Bob ordered drinks for them.

Corporal Hunt was staring intently, a deep frown creasing his brow. 'Is it him, sir?'

'Oh, yes.' Bob sat back and let the music flow over him, remembering the evenings at the Sawyers when they had listened to Cramer playing. 'I'd know that touch anywhere.'

'He's good. Was he a professional musician before the war?'

'I think he said he'd been studying to be an engineer.' Bob sighed and watched the pianist. 'Looks as if he's had a rough time.'

'Yeah, but at least he's got a talent he can use to earn some money. I know Germany started the war, but this

136

country's in a mess and its people are suffering something terrible. I can't help feeling sorry for the poor buggers.'

Bob nodded in agreement, ordered two more drinks for them and one for the pianist. Cramer ignored it when it was put before him and continued to play without even looking up after the waiter spoke to him.

'Well, that didn't grab his attention.' Hunt downed his beer. 'Looks like he could do with a good meal instead.'

'Yes, he's a shadow of the man he was.' Bob sipped his beer, wondering about the best way to approach him. He saw people asking him to play certain pieces for them and decided to do the same. There was one tune Jane had always wanted.

Pushing his chair back, he stood up and went over to the piano. He stood slightly behind, watching the skill of the man's fingers as they caressed the keys. When he stopped, Bob used Jane's words, 'Play "Stardust" for me, Dieter.'

The start was noticeable and Bob found himself staring into grey eyes: he was shocked by the naked pain showing on the German's face. From side view it hadn't been so evident, but full view it was enough to take his breath away. Dieter Cramer was thin and drawn, with dark shadows under his eyes. He recognized Bob immediately.

'Ah, Major, you are in Berlin at last.' He went straight back to playing, but not the tune Bob had asked for.

'We need to talk. What time do you pack up?'

'I can't think what we have to talk about, Major.'

'The Sawyers are worried about you.' He saw Cramer tense at the mention of their name.

'Are they well?'

'Yes. I have a message for you from them.'

Cramer's hands swept over the keys, his head bent in concentration. 'I finish at twelve.'

'I'll wait for you.' Bob walked back to his table. He had no sooner sat down before the haunting strains of 'Stardust' filled the room. Bob nodded in acknowledgement when Cramer glanced up at him briefly.

'Ah, that's smashing.' Hunt studied his empty glass with a forlorn expression. 'Is he going to talk to you, or did he tell you to sod off?'

'He's agreed to see me when he finishes at twelve.' Bob decided to put Hunt out of his misery and ordered him another beer. 'Somehow I've got to persuade him to return to Somerset.'

Hunt perked up when another drink was placed in front of him. 'I thought the Sawyers just wanted to know he was all right.'

'I'm afraid there's more to it than that.'

'Really?' Hunt drank from the glass, his eyes fixed on Cramer, and then he gasped, putting the glass back on the table with a thud. 'Hell, Major, he's the boy's father, isn't he? I never noticed it before.'

'And that's something you'll keep to yourself,' Bob said sharply. 'Cramer doesn't know and it's not our job to tell him.'

'I won't say a word. You know you can trust me, sir.'

'I wouldn't have brought you here if I couldn't.'

'If you can get him back to England, who's going to tell him?'

'Angie Westwood, and that isn't going to be easy for her. She has no idea Danny's father is German. Angie's and Jane's parents were killed one night when they'd gone to the local pub.'

'Oh, God!' Hunt had forgotten his beer. 'She's not going to take kindly to news like this. She loves that little boy.'

'I believe she's also a reasonable girl, and will do whatever is right for the child.'

'Yeah, nice girl that.' Hunt studied his major. 'Awkward situation, what with you liking her yourself an' all.'

Bob narrowed his eyes. 'What are you trying to say?'

'Well, sir.' He turned the glass round and round in his fingers. 'Once Cramer sees his son, he ain't never gonna leave him. Awkward, as I said.'

'I understand what you're saying, but I've already told you I'm not looking for a wife!'

'So you said, sir.'

'But you don't believe me?'

Hunt sat back and smirked. 'I don't think you believe that either.'

'Ah, reading minds now, are you? You're insubordinate, Corporal.'

'I know, sir. That's why I'm with you. No one else will put up with me.'

'That I can believe.' Bob controlled a chuckle. Hunt

was a rogue, but the man was loyal and useful. They tolerated each other's ways with good humour. 'Finish your beer and disappear for a couple of hours. Come back for me at midnight.'

'Right, sir.' Hunt drained his glass and was on his feet immediately and heading for the door.

At ten o'clock Dieter went into the kitchen. Bob hoped they gave him a decent meal; he was clearly undernourished. When he returned and began playing again, Bob sat back to enjoy the music.

Two officers he knew joined him and the time passed quickly. When Dieter finished playing and closed the lid of the piano, Bob went over to him. 'I've got a car outside. Where are you staying?'

'Not far.' Dieter pocketed the tips left for him and they walked out of the hotel.

The ever reliable Hunt was by the entrance. 'Where to, sir?'

Bob glanced at Dieter as they got into the car. 'Tell my driver where you live.'

As soon as Hunt was given instruction, they were tearing away from the hotel. In no time at all they were pulling up at a building that was little more than a ruin. Windows had been boarded up, and there was rubble all around. Very little attempt had yet been made to clear up this part of town.

'You're living here?' Bob was appalled. He knew living accommodation was at a premium, but this looked like a bombsite.

'Don't look so shocked, Major. I'm lucky to have a

room here.' Dieter got out of the car. 'If you don't want to come in, then I'll meet you somewhere tomorrow.'

That was the last thing Bob wanted. After the trouble they'd had finding Dieter, he didn't want to risk losing sight of him again. 'Lead on.'

Though the outside of the building was a mess, an attempt had been made to make the inside habitable. Dieter's was a decent-sized room with a sink in the corner, a bed and two chairs. The furnishing was sparse but clean.

Sitting down in one of the chairs, Bob waited for Dieter to settle. His movements were slow, as if everything was an effort. 'Are you all right?'

'I am.' Dieter eyed Bob with a hint of derision in his grey eyes. 'Don't pretend you care, Major. You said you needed to talk?'

'When the Sawyers knew I was being posted to Germany, they asked if I would try to find you.'

'Why?'

Bob could feel exasperation rising and fought to control it. Dieter Cramer was distant, defensive, and he longed to be able to tell him that he had a son who needed him. He took a deep breath, making himself relax. Dieter's attitude was only to be expected with the man who had been his gaoler. 'Because they liked you and are worried not to have heard from you. Couldn't you at least have written to let them know you arrived home safely?'

'Home!' The word came out in a snarl. 'Have you seen my city, Major?'

'No,' he admitted. 'Tell me what has happened to you since you were repatriated.'

For the next half an hour Bob listened with mounting horror as the story unfolded about Dieter's frantic search for any trace of his family, and he told of his utter despair at the destruction.

Dieter looked up, his eyes bleak. 'There was just a great hole in the ground where my home had been. There are no graves, Major. Nothing to say my family ever existed. There wasn't even a headstone I could stand by and grieve.'

The words 'I'm sorry' were on Bob's lips, but how could he say that. It was totally inadequate in the face of this man's torment.

'Go back to England. John and Hetty would welcome you, give you a home and a chance to start a new life.' Bob paused. After hearing Dieter's story he wanted, even more, to be able to tell him that there was one member of his family alive – a three-year-old son. Once again he cursed the promise he had made to the Sawyers. 'There's more for you there than here.'

Dieter ran a hand through his hair and shook his head. 'I could not. This dark shadow will always be with me, and I'm not sure I can forgive the nations who did this.'

Sitting forward, Bob spoke earnestly. 'Many things have been done on both sides. Things we are ashamed of, but don't forget that you were part of a bomber crew unleashing death and destruction on London and other cities. Many might find it hard to forgive you for the loss of their loved ones, but we have got to learn somehow to forgive each other. If we can't do that, then we'll live with this shadow for ever and not be able to move forward. Cities need rebuilding, and lives as well, and that's the hardest part. Without forgiveness there is little hope for humanity.'

Dieter's head was bowed while Bob spoke; now he looked up. 'That was quite a speech, Major.'

'I mean every word of it.'

'I believe you do. And you are right, but it's a damned hard thing you are asking.'

Dieter's attitude seemed to have changed, and Bob pushed the point. 'The Sawyers have given me enough money for your passage back to England, and other expenses. I will also vouch for you as a DP – displaced person. You have somewhere to go and a job waiting for you, so there shouldn't be any problems.'

'Let me sleep on it, Major.' Dieter rubbed his eyes in a weary gesture. 'I'll give you my decision within a few days.'

'Right.' Bob stood up, disappointed not to have an immediate decision, but he mustn't push too hard. This would take a lot of thought. He placed a hand on Dieter's shoulder for a moment, feeling his bones through the jacket, then turned and walked out of the squalid building.

Dieter was exhausted. He undressed and slumped on the bed, too tired even to crawl under the blanket. The Major had talked a lot of sense. He'd always known him as a fair man, but he'd had no idea of the depth of his feelings. He was tough when he needed to be, like tonight, when he'd pointed out that as part of the Luftwaffe bomber crew he had played his part in killing innocent civilians. After his capture he'd seen London in flames. That guilt still lingered, even after all this time.

Turning on to his back, he stared up at the ceiling. In the gloom he could see the huge crack weaving its crazy way from one end of the room to the other. His mind went back to just after the war, when they had been allowed out to work and mix with people. Many English families had invited them into their homes, treating them with kindness. They had known how to forgive! And Jane, sweet Jane, she had loved him, even though their two countries had fought a bitter battle between them.

He sighed and rubbed his temple. Perhaps he should go back and find her again. When they had met, he had been worried to distraction about his family, and he had simply taken advantage of the comfort she had offered. Had he loved her? Had he been capable of love at that point?

It had given him a terrible jolt hearing the Major ask for her favourite tune. He could picture her now, legs curled under her in the armchair, and her bright smile as she'd asked every evening for 'Stardust'. How they had all laughed. She never tired of hearing the song, and he hadn't played it again until tonight.

How long had it been since he'd laughed like that?

Sadness welled up inside him – not just for himself but for everyone who was still finding it hard to come to terms with their losses, whatever side they had been fighting on.

Dieter turned and buried his head in the pillow and, for the first time, allowed the cleansing tears to flow.

The letter to John and Hetty was done and Bob sealed it. It was just to tell them that he had found Dieter and was trying to persuade him to return to England. He didn't hold out much hope, but assured them that he'd kept his promise and not mentioned Danny, or that Jane was dead.

Bob regretted he'd agreed to that now, but he wouldn't break his word, and if Dieter refused to go back, it would probably be for the best that he didn't know. One thing was for sure, though: if Dieter was going to stay in Germany, Bob would see that he was looked after and given every chance to pull his life together. Of all the prisoners, Dieter Cramer had been the one who had impressed him the most.

'Here we are, sir.' Hunt appeared, arms full of clothing. 'The things you requisitioned.'

Bob checked through them: socks, underclothes, jumpers, shirts, all army issue, but, from what he'd seen, Dieter had only the clothes he stood up in, so he wouldn't be fussy. And they had been given to him on repatriation. Bob could recognize the old demob suit anywhere.

'What size shoes does he take, sir?'

'No idea.'

'Hmm.' Hunt eyed Bob up and down. 'He's about your height, so why don't we take several sizes with us? If you'll sign the chitty, I'll get them now.'

After putting his name to the necessary form, Bob opened his wardrobe door. He hadn't brought many civilian clothes with him, but he might find something to fit Dieter. Hunt was right: he was about the same height as him but much thinner. He pulled out a dark blue suit. This might fit if he used braces to hold up the trousers. He rummaged in a drawer and found a pair. The weather was getting colder now, so a topcoat would be essential; he doubted Dieter had such a thing. He was still pondering the problem when Hunt returned.

'Three pairs of shoes, various sizes, sir.'

'Thanks.' Bob frowned. 'What's that you've got over your arm?'

'An army greatcoat, sir.' Hunt looked a picture of innocence. 'It was just hanging around; no one seemed to want it.'

'Hanging around where?' Bob pulled a face and held up his hand. 'No, don't tell me. I'd rather not know.'

Hunt put the coat on the pile of clothes. 'Pardon me for asking, sir, but are you going to get away with this?'

'I've had a word with the Colonel and explained the situation. I told him Cramer is one of my ex-prisoners so I'm naturally concerned for his welfare.'

'Really, sir?' Hunt didn't look as if he believed this.

Bob nodded as a smile twitched at the corners of

his mouth. The Corporal was no fool and knew him too well. 'He was very understanding after six whiskies at two o'clock this morning.'

'Ah, well, he would have been, sir.'

They both grinned. The Colonel's fondness for the drink was legendary.

'We going to give these things to Cramer tonight, sir?'

'No, we'll do it now. There's always a chance he'll have made up his mind already.'

When the door opened to Bob's insistent knocking, he couldn't believe his eyes. 'My God, man, you look terrible. What the hell have you been doing?'

Dieter stepped aside to let them in, watching in disbelief as Hunt dumped a huge pile of clothing on his unmade bed. He hadn't bothered to answer Bob's question.

The Corporal held up the suit jacket. 'The clothes should fit, sir, but what size shoe do you take?'

'Ten, English size.'

'Ah, we've got those, I think.' After sorting through the packets, he held up a pair of black shoes for Dieter. 'See if they fit you, sir.'

'What the hell is this all about? And don't keep calling me "sir"!'

Bob thought it was time to intervene. Dieter obviously wasn't pleased about their interfering. 'He calls everyone "sir". He's a cheeky sod and thinks that if he tacks "sir" on to the end of every sentence he'll be safe.

You need the clothes, and just about everything else, by the look of you.'

The shoes were hanging from Dieter's long fingers, his eyes wary. 'Is this an inducement to make me go back to England?'

'There are no conditions. As incredible as it may seem, we only want to help.' Bob's irritation grew. Did the man believe he would resort to bribery? 'Whatever decision you come to, I'll accept. It will be up to you. Now, stop arguing and see if the things fit!'

'Stop ordering me around! You are not my gaoler now, Major!' Dieter's glare was hostile. 'I don't have to take bloody orders from you any more.'

Never having been the most patient of men, Bob's temper snapped. It was impossible to help some people. But this one was going to be helped, even if he had to knock some sense into him. 'No, but you still need a kick up the backside, Cramer. Look at the way you're living, and with your intelligence you shouldn't be playing piano in a bar. Stop drifting and pull your life together. You're not the only one to have suffered in this bloody war!'

'What right have you got to be so judgemental?' In his fury the usually excellent English slipped and he reverted to German, snarling a string of abuse. 'This is a palace compared to some hovels people are living in. Or haven't you noticed, Herr Commandant?'

'I've noticed.' Bob stepped up to him, barely resisting the temptation to shake the man until his teeth rattled. 'And I'm bloody well sick to my stomach that

I can't help everyone. That's going to take time. Total war is a damned messy business, but I can help you. So stop being so pig-headed and accept a hand held out in friendship.'

Corporal Hunt had pushed his way between the two men. 'Now, now, sirs, you'll have the Redcaps here if you keep shouting like this, and we don't want that, do we?' He gently elbowed Bob out of the way and turned to face Dieter. 'Don't you take no notice of the Major, sir. He gets a bit uppity at times, but his heart's in the right place. Why don't you try the shoes on, sir? Real good they are. Chose them myself.'

Bob saw the funny side of the situation and started to laugh at the antics of Hunt. 'All right, Corporal, you've made your point. There's no need to bang our heads together.' He lifted his hands in surrender to Dieter. 'I apologize. Take the clothes if you need them, or tell me to sod off and I won't bother you again.'

'Oh, I need them, Major.' Dieter gave a wry smile and held his hand out. 'Thank you, I am grateful.'

Bob shook his hand and smiled in relief. He'd nearly ruined any chance of getting Dieter back to England by losing his temper. He should have realized that the man still had his pride and made allowances for that, not tried to order him around as if he were still a prisoner. Those days were over. It was only natural that Dieter would take offence. He studied his former prisoner as he tried on the shoes, remembering him as a quiet, thoughtful man – no, boy – he'd been little more than a boy when he had been captured, and only around twenty-four when Bob had met him. He couldn't be more than twenty-nine now but looked much older. Hardly surprising when you considered that he had been a prisoner since 1941 and that it had been six years before he'd been repatriated. He could only guess at the grief and hardship he had faced since returning to his own country – a country torn apart as the Allied troops had fought their way through it.

'These fit perfectly.' Dieter stood and walked up and down, smiling at Hunt. 'You chose well, Corporal.'

'Thank you, sir. Try the suit on now. The one you've been wearing is on its last legs.'

Dieter raised an eyebrow. 'What do these sayings mean – "last legs" and "uppity"?'

'It means the suit's worn out, and' – Hunt lowered his voice and bent towards Dieter – 'uppity means the Major gets a bit above himself sometimes. Got a short fuse, but you don't want to take no notice of that, sir. It shows he's got a heart, but he does his best to hide it, of course.'

Bob leant against the wall with his arms folded, watching Hunt placate Dieter, content to let him do what he was good at as he urged him into the suit. He'd deal with him later! The jacket was on the big side, but looked even larger because the man was so thin – it looked as if he hadn't had a good meal in months. Bob had tossed in one of his best ties and a white shirt. The effect was a huge improvement on the clothes Dieter had been wearing.

'There.' Hunt stood back and nodded in admiration.

'Real smart you looks now. Some regular food and you'll soon fill out to fit the suit.' He glanced at Bob. 'Did you say you was taking the gentleman to lunch, sir?'

He hadn't, but that was a good idea. It would give him more chance to talk Dieter round to returning to England. 'I did, and as soon as he's had a shave you can drive us back to HQ.'

'Yes, sir.' He grinned at Dieter. 'The grub ain't bad in the officers' mess.'

Bob pushed himself away from the wall. 'We'll wait outside for you.'

When Dieter nodded, they returned to the car.

'You should have been a diplomat, Corporal.'

'Had to do something, sir. I thought you was coming to blows. That man wasn't in no mood to have you throwing your weight around – if you'll pardon me saying so, sir. He didn't take kindly to you ordering him around again. You ain't gonna get him back to England like that.'

'I have a nasty feeling we won't be able to persuade him whatever we do.' Bob sighed, his brow furrowed with concern, remembering the little boy, and the lovely girl who had taken on the responsibility of bringing him up on her own.

'He ain't got nothing here.' Hunt held open the car door so Bob could get in the back. 'Couldn't you tell him about his son?'

'I'm afraid not. I promised the Sawyers, and deep down I think they may be right. If he knew, he would probably storm back, upsetting Angie and Danny.'

'Ah, I see what you mean, sir. Introduce him slowly, giving him time to adjust.' Hunt nodded. 'Might be best all round.'

'Angie will need time to adjust as well.'

'Indeed, sir, mustn't forget the nice young girl. If he does turn up in Somerset, it won't be easy for her.' Hunt sprang out of the car as Dieter came towards them, holding the door open so he could get in the back with the Major.

They didn't speak much. Dieter seemed withdrawn and troubled, so Bob left him to his thoughts, not wanting to say or do anything that would antagonize him. Cramer was in a mess, mentally and physically, and one wrong move by Bob would send him into the undergrowth. Hunt had stumbled across him by an incredible stroke of luck. If he disappeared again, they might never find him.

After seeing that Dieter had a decent meal inside him, Bob lit a cigarette and held out the packet, surveying him through the smoke. 'Have you given any thought to going back to England?'

Dieter took the cigarette he was offered but didn't light it. 'I have given it a great deal of thought, but I can't leave Germany until I definitely know if my parents and sister are dead.'

'Surely you would have heard from them if they had been alive?' It was gently put, as Bob could see that he was having trouble accepting this.

'But what if they did try, and in the chaos after the bombing, their letters never reached me?' Dieter leant forward, his face etched with pain. 'I know you think me foolish to hope, and I am inclined to agree with you, but there is nothing to show me they perished in the raids. No one appears to know exactly how many died. The figures being banded about are thirty thousand to over one hundred thousand. I must know for sure. Until then I cannot let this nightmare go.'

'Have you tried the Red Cross?'

'Of course I have.' Irritation crossed Dieter's face. 'There are thousands looking for their relatives. It will take years to deal with this terrible situation.'

Bob pulled a small notebook out of his pocket. 'Let me see if I can help. Give me your family details.'

When Dieter had done this, he paused. 'I have little hope that my parents are alive, but I pray that if anyone has survived it is my sister. Her name is Gerda and she would now be eighteen. She was only nine years old when I was taken prisoner.'

'Leave it with me and I'll see if there's any news. In the meantime I want you to consider going back to the Sawyers.'

'Thank you for your help, Major, but I will not leave until all hope has vanished.' Dieter shook his head sadly. 'I cannot get on with my life until I know.'

'You want proof.' Bob nodded understandingly.

'Yes.' Dieter whispered the word.

For the next few days, the problem of whether to stay or to return to England was constantly on Dieter's mind. He had told the Major he couldn't leave until he knew what had happened to his parents and sister, but deep in his heart he already knew. They must be dead or they would have contacted him somehow; but he couldn't seem to accept that. And until he did, he wouldn't be able to decide what to do with his life. Not knowing what had happened to them was the hardest part. It was like an open wound that would not heal until he had some kind of proof.

The Major obviously wasn't having any more luck than he'd had, or he would have been in touch before now. He hadn't seen a sign of him since he had arrived with the clothes. No, if the Major with all his connections had not been able to find them, they were gone. It was time he accepted that fact.

His fingers swept over the keys with practised ease. He had always been passionate about his music, and even at his most troubled it could calm him, lifting his mood. It was a lifesaver for him.

The bar was extra busy tonight, but he was oblivious to the activity around him, oblivious to the laughter and hum of people talking.

He bowed his head and lost himself in the music.

13

Ten days and still nothing. Bob prowled round his office. He'd pulled every string possible to get priority in tracing Dieter's family, but all the organizations that dealt with this had a mammoth task on their hands. It seemed as if almost everyone in Europe was looking for someone. People had been dragged from their homes, and even countries, into forced labour and the horror of the concentration camps. Then there was the destruction caused in the fight to defeat Hitler. Some poor souls had lost their identity, not even knowing or caring who they were.

Bob stared moodily out of the window, with unseeing eyes, when Hunt came in. He turned his head. 'Has the mail arrived yet?'

'Don't know, sir. Shall I check?'

He nodded, turned back to the window and waited. He had been aware that it would take years to rebuild and for life to return to something like normal, but it wasn't until he had arrived in Germany that he'd realized the full extent of the task facing them. It was huge, but progress was being made in some areas. There was still so much to do, though.

'It had just arrived, sir.' Hunt soon returned with a pile of envelopes in his hand. 'A letter from the Red Cross there.'

'Let's hope they've found something.' He slit open the letter and read it quickly, frowning as he did so. Then he stuffed it in his pocket and grabbed his hat, already striding out. 'Get the car.'

Hunt caught him up and fell into step beside him. 'Is there news, sir?'

'It might be a glimmer of hope.'

Once in the car Bob reread the letter. A Gerda Kramer had been traced. The spelling was different, but that could merely be a clerical error. The age was right, but where she was now was the most interesting detail.

'You come in with me,' Bob said as he got out of the car. 'You can pull us apart again if we look like resorting to blows.'

Hunt grinned. 'Pleasure, sir.'

Dieter opened the door and wordlessly stepped aside to let them in. Once in his room, he turned and faced them, his expression taut. 'You have some news?'

'The Red Cross have traced a Gerda Kramer, spelt with a "K". The age is right, but would she have used that spelling for your family name?'

'I don't see why, but it might just be a mistake on the records. It would easily be done. Where is she?'

There was hope gleaming in his eyes and Bob couldn't help feeling uneasy. If it wasn't his sister, could this man take another crushing disappointment? 'She's in York, England.'

Dieter's eyes opened wide in surprise, and after no more than a split second he lunged for a bag on the top of his wardrobe. Throwing it on the bed, he began to stuff clothes into it, not bothering to fold them. 'She's looking for me. I was in a camp up there for a while. She might have remembered that.'

'Hold it!' Bob caught Dieter's arm to stop him packing. 'The rest of the letter says that if you haven't heard from your family in all this time, then they almost certainly perished.'

'Almost!' Dieter shook off Bob's hand. 'There is doubt. I must find out. Did they give you an address for her?'

Sighing, Bob handed him the letter. 'They say where she can be found, but stop and think for a minute. The chances are that this isn't your sister. Write to her first, or let us look into it further before you rush off.'

'No, I must go to her.'

Bob knew he didn't have any right to stop him, so he would help him all he could. It was obvious from Dieter's attitude that he wasn't going to listen to any advice. 'Have you got any money?'

'Very little, but I shall hitch lifts.' Dieter put the letter in his pocket and continued stuffing things into his bag.

'If you'll just wait for a day or two, I'll see if I can get you on a flight. It will be much quicker. It could take you weeks to make your way across Europe.' Bob took the Sawyers' money out of his wallet. 'I'll pay your airfare, but take this as well. The Sawyers would want you to have it.'

'No.' Dieter shook his head. 'It wouldn't be right to take their money when it is most unlikely I shall go to them as they wish.'

'They would understand.' Bob pushed the money

into Dieter's hand. 'Pay them back one day when you are in a position to do so. Now, will you wait and let me see what I can arrange?'

Dieter's long fingers closed around the English money and he gave a sharp nod, looking calmer now. 'If you can get me on a plane, I shall be most grateful, and I shall also repay you when I can.'

'I'll do my best.'

'You will let me know quickly. I shall not wait long. Twenty-four hours at the most.'

'Go to the hotel as usual and I'll be there sometime during the evening.'

'Thank you, Major.'

When they were outside again, Hunt asked, 'Where to now, sir?'

'Templehoff Airport.'

It was eleven in the evening before Bob arrived at the hotel. He had spent the day giving orders, making people hustle to get the necessary paperwork ready, and even pulling rank when the occasion demanded. If Dieter was going to England, then he didn't want him running into any trouble and perhaps being delayed by bureaucratic procedures. Hunt had followed him around with a gleeful expression on his face and every so often muttered, 'That told 'em, sir.'

'It's been one hell of a day.' Bob slid out of the car. 'Come on, Corporal, I'll buy you a drink.'

'Thank you, sir.' Hunt followed him into the bar lounge.

Dieter looked up when they walked in, a question in his eyes.

Smiling, Bob patted his pocket to indicate that he had the ticket, then sat down, ordered drinks and waited for the time when Dieter stopped playing.

As soon as midnight struck, he closed the lid of the piano and walked over to them. 'Did you manage it, Major?'

'The flight is leaving at ten tomorrow morning.' Bob handed him the papers. 'It's going to Croydon and you'll need to catch a train to York from King's Cross. It's only a one-way ticket, so I've given you enough money to get back here if you want to.'

Dieter's hand shook slightly as he held the papers. 'You have been over generous. One day I shall try to repay you for your kindness.'

'I'm glad to help.' Bob waved away his thanks. 'I hope it is your sister, but, if not, what will you do?'

'I have not thought that far ahead, but I shall return here, I suppose.'

Bob sighed inwardly, feeling the man's hope and pain. 'Before you do that, I hope you will visit the Sawyers.'

'I will think about it.'

He couldn't ask for more than that, Bob thought, as he stood up to leave. It wasn't right to push the man when he couldn't tell him why it was important. The poor devil had enough to deal with at the moment. But he would have to make sure he didn't lose sight of him. Perhaps he would be able to arrange for him to meet Angie and Danny one day, even if he had to bring them over here, for he had no great hopes that this girl was Dieter's sister. But the man wouldn't give up and was grasping at any hope, and he could understand that. If he lost track of any of his family, he would be just the same. 'Come on, we'll give you a lift home, and I'll see you're collected tomorrow and taken to the airport.'

The next day Bob was already at the airport when Hunt arrived with Dieter. This had been arranged in a rush and he wanted to be on hand should any snags arise.

Everything went smoothly, and when Dieter was ready to board he held out his hand. 'Thank you again, Major.'

'I want you to write and let me know how you get on. Will you do that?'

'Of course. That is the least I can do to repay you for your kindness.' Then Dieter walked towards the plane and disappeared inside.

The plane taxied and turned, its engines revving at full power, then headed along the runway. As it left the ground, Bob watched until it was out of sight.

'Done all you can now, sir.' Hunt pulled a face. 'Poor bugger's going to be pulverized if it isn't his sister.'

Hunt was right, Bob realized; he'd done all he could, and now he would have to write to John and Hetty to tell them that, although Dieter was heading for England to search for his sister, it was unlikely they would see him. If the girl in York was not his sister, he would probably return to Germany, but Bob promised that he would keep track of him and try to engineer a meeting between Dieter, Danny and Angie sometime in the future. The Sawyers would be disappointed, he knew.

As the plane left the ground, Dieter remembered the many times he had taken off on a bombing raid. How sure of themselves they'd been. All young boys fighting for the Fatherland, constantly being told that the cause was just and they were invincible.

He gazed out at Berlin below him, looking nothing like the city he had known as a boy. In victory the allies had carved it up between them. Efforts were being made to clear and rebuild, but it was taking time. And the Russians hadn't helped with their blockade, but that had ended last month, thank heavens. It had only been by the airlift and determined effort of the Allies that West Berlin had survived. He closed his eyes, suddenly drained of all energy. Soon he would be back in England. Please be my Gerda, he silently prayed. Give me someone of my own. Some hope for the future.

It was only when they landed that Dieter understood just how much trouble the Major had gone to for him. He had vouched for him, and an official document stated that he had a job and accommodation waiting for him in Somerset. Again he had cause to be grateful to his former commandant, though he couldn't understand why he was helping him so much. The Major had often come to the farm for dinner while he had been working there. The man had always been polite but not overly friendly. That had been understandable, of course, for Dieter had still technically been a prisoner.

Once the formalities had been dealt with, he headed for the station without delay, determined to get a train to York that day. When he reached King's Cross, there was a forty-minute wait before his train arrived, so after buying his ticket he went into the snack bar. He paid for a cup of tea and a sandwich, found a table and sat down.

Munching on the sandwich and not caring what was in it, he gazed around the busy room. The thing that struck most forcibly was the contrast with Berlin, a city cut in half by the victors. It was a grim time for the German people, with everything in short supply and their future uncertain. This country had had a tough war and made many sacrifices. The world had thought them beaten, but he doubted if they had ever considered it a possibility. They had laughed then, and were laughing still. But he knew that underneath all the joking was a stubborn race determined to hold on to its freedom, whatever the cost. And yet at the end of the war, when the prisoners were allowed out, he had found them friendly towards their former enemy. Jane had known that he had been in the Luftwaffe and had bombed London and other parts of the country, but it hadn't bothered her at all. She had seen him as a person, and one she came to love.

Finishing his tea, he sat back and let the lively chatter sweep over him, trying not to think too much about what he might find in York. After a while he looked at the station clock and saw that the train was due in five minutes. Leaving the refreshment bar, he made his way to the platform.

The train was on time and he was lucky enough to find himself a seat by the window. It was a shame that the light was fading already. He would have liked to watch the countryside on the journey. It was still a green, pleasant land. The first thing he would do when he arrived in York was get cheap lodgings for the night, try to get some rest, and in the morning see if this girl was his sister. He hoped she was still at the address he'd been given, because he had a strong feeling that it would be her.

He had done a lot of thinking while he had been on the plane. The drone of the engines had been strangely soothing, especially knowing that they were not going to find a Spitfire on their tail. In between dozing he had taken a brutal look at his life. After his capture he had spent years sharing huts with lots of other men. Then he had lived at the farm, met Jane and been included as one of the family. The villagers had also accepted him and he had played the organ in the church for many a service. He had loved doing that.

From the time he had returned to Germany he had been alone. The only desire driving him had been to find out what had happened to his family. People had been understanding and had done their best, but the organizations dealing with displaced and missing persons were swamped with work. He hadn't sought out friendships, or wanted them, but the Major had shaken him out of his apathy. Now he wanted – needed – someone of his own. If this wasn't his sister – something he was loath to consider – then he must turn his back on the past and try to rebuild his life.

It wasn't going to be easy.

14

Giving a little wriggle, Danny settled himself on the cushions piled on to the piano stool, then leant forward to put a sheet of paper on the stand. Mrs Poulton was teaching him to read music right from the beginning and writing his lessons out for him. How a young child who couldn't yet read or write knew what the dots meant was a source of wonder to Angie, but much to her amazement he seemed to know. They had made a mark on the key of middle C, and he worked it out from there. He was only playing simple exercises, of course, and the sounds meant nothing to her.

She listened. In her opinion he was little more than a baby, but his concentration was phenomenal. A feeling of wonder ran through her. Had Jane given birth to a musical genius? There wasn't any such talent in their family, so it could only have come from his father. Who the hell was he? The next time she saw Hetty she must ask if they had heard from their friend who was looking for him. The thought of finding the father made her uneasy, but of course it was obvious why. She was selfish! She had been with Danny from the moment he'd been born, helped to look after him, and now he was hers. Her life had changed with the desire to do what was best for the little boy. And she didn't mind whatever sacrifice she had to make as long as he was happy. He hadn't mentioned his father again, and she fervently hoped that it had been a passing thought and not something he had dwelt on. Sally's Joe was a kind man and always included Danny in his games with Emma. Perhaps he had forgotten about having a daddy of his own? She hoped so, because he was far too young to understand what had happened between Jane and the man she had fallen in love with.

She sat on a chair beside the piano and Danny didn't even look up, completely absorbed in practising his lesson.

When he stopped she smiled. 'That was lovely, darling. I don't know how you understand those dots Mrs Poulton writes down for you.'

'Each dot means a note,' he told her, 'but I have to think hard to remember where they are.'

'Well, you do it very well. Your teacher told me you have real talent.'

The dimples flashed in shy pleasure. 'It's fun. Em doesn't like music, though. Her mummy said she could have lessons as well, but she didn't want to.' He looked puzzled, as if he couldn't understand someone not liking music.

'Everyone's different, Danny. We don't all like the same things. Now I think it's time you got ready for bed. Do you want milk or cocoa?'

This had to be thought over for a few moments, then he jumped down and followed her into the kitchen. 'Cocoa, please, Auntie.'

There was a thoughtful expression on his face as he sat at the table. 'Auntie?'

Angie was waiting for the milk to boil and turned her head. 'Yes?'

'Do you think Mummy knows you're looking after me now?'

A lump lodged in her throat, and she turned the gas down under the milk so she could crouch down beside his chair. 'I'm sure she does.'

He nodded, very serious. 'She always said you were my second mummy, and I was so lucky to have two mummies.'

'And we are so lucky to have you.' Angie had to go back to making the cocoa as emotion welled up inside her. He had such wisdom at times, but that didn't make him any the less a normal mischievous child. Jane had always said that he was special, but Angie had just put that down to motherly pride. Now that she was with him all the time, she knew Jane had been right. Even at this young age he was sorting things out in his mind, making his own adjustments.

She made the drink for both of them and watched him enjoy it, giving him a biscuit as a treat.

After putting him to bed and reading him a story, she stayed until his eyes closed. Her heart sang. Perhaps one day he would drop the Auntie and call her Mummy.

Dieter was lucky: he'd found a reasonably priced bed and breakfast just outside the old city walls at Micklegate Bar. The landlady had given him a map so he could find the address he wanted. It was within walking distance and that was a help. He was grateful for the money the Major and the Sawyers had given him, but it wasn't going to last long. If he stayed here for more than a few days, he would have to find a job.

As he walked along, through the Shambles and on up to the beautiful Minster, his heart beat in anticipation. He had told himself repeatedly that he mustn't hope too much, as the chances of this being his sister were slim, but he couldn't help it. It must be her! If it were, he would stay here with her. His musical talents could surely be put to use in this lovely place. He strode out, head up, and for the first time in years a tiny spark of hope began to burn in his heart.

On reaching the Minster, he stood gazing up at the magnificent structure; he couldn't help but wonder what the organ sounded like. His fingers itched. He would go in there tomorrow and have a look round, but for today he could only concentrate on one thing.

He was taking deep breaths to calm his racing heartbeat. Consulting the map, he saw that he was near High Petergate, so he crossed the road into Duncombe Place. Nearly there.

He found the house without any trouble after walking for about ten minutes. It was a rather splendid-looking place, with three floors and a front door with a brass knocker gleaming in the autumn sunlight. As he hesitated, a woman came from round the side of the house and he stopped her. 'Excuse me, I am looking for Gerda Kramer. Can you tell me if she lives here?'

'Gerda? Sure, go and knock on the side door. You'll find her there.' Then she bustled away.

She was here! Dieter almost ran to the door and couldn't keep still as he waited for his knock to be answered.

A boy of no more than fifteen opened the door. 'Yes?'

'I wish to see Gerda Kramer.'

'Oh, right, you'd better come in, then.' He led Dieter along a narrow passage and into a large kitchen, full of warmth and tempting smells. 'Gent to see Gerda.'

A large woman who was obviously the cook eyed him suspiciously, taking in his shabby appearance. 'What you want with her?'

'I need to see if she is my sister.'

The woman's expression immediately softened. 'Ah, you're German, like her.'

He nodded, his throat too tight with anxiety to speak again.

At that moment a door opened and a young girl came in carrying a large tray; she turned her back to him to put it on the draining board.

'Gerda, there's someone here to see you.'

He was so tense that it felt as if all the air had been sucked from the room as Dieter stared at her. The hair colour was right . . .

Then she turned, a smile on her face, and his world disintegrated around him. The disappointment was so cruel he moaned out loud. It wasn't her. It wasn't her. Everything went fuzzy around him, and he shook his head trying to clear it. All he could hear was a voice in his head shouting *You fool! How could you have believed it was her?*

'Oh, my, Jimmy help me with him. He's been taken real bad. Gerda, put the kettle on.'

Although he could hear what was being said, the voices seemed to come from a long way off. He was helped into a chair and he bowed his head.

'There now, you sit there quiet for a while and we'll make you a nice cup of tea. That'll soon put you right.'

The English cure for all troubles, Dieter thought, as he fought for composure. This was his own fault. He should not have set his hopes so high. But he hadn't been able to help himself.

'You drink that.' The cook placed a cup in his hands.

The tea was hot, strong and sweet. He drank it gratefully and gazed at the young girl he had come to see. She was the right age, but there the resemblance to his sister ended. At first glance she was pretty, but a scar down her left cheek and neck marred her looks.

Finishing his tea, he put the cup on the table and gave the cook a tight smile. 'I apologize for reacting so badly.'

'No need. Gerda isn't your sister, then?'

He shook his head, feeling more in command of himself again and looked at the girl. 'I hope I did not frighten you, Fräulein?'

She spoke for the first time. 'I understand. What made you believe I might be your sister?'

'Your name, age, and the fact that your home was

Dresden.' He grimaced. 'Not much to go on, but I had to see you. Were you there during the raids?'

She touched the scar. 'My mother died, but my father was away in the Panzers. When the war ended we came here. There was nothing left for us in Germany.'

'Did you by any chance know the Cramers, spelt with a "C"?'

'*Nein*. I am sorry, but it was a large city.' She stood when Dieter did. 'I do not wish to be cruel, Herr Cramer, but it was very bad. If you have not heard from your family in all this time, they must have perished.'

'I have been reluctant to admit that, but I shall have to now.' He bowed slightly to the cook, wanting to get away. 'Thank you for your kindness.' Then he dredged up a smile for Gerda. 'I am happy your father is alive and you are not alone.'

'*Ja*, I am fortunate.' She studied him with compassion in her eyes. 'What will you do now?'

'Go back to Berlin, I suppose.'

'My father would be pleased to meet you. I live here, but he has two rooms in a house near by, and I'm sure we could fix up a bed for you if you wished to stay. You would be most welcome.'

Dieter couldn't bear the thought of meeting anyone at the moment. 'I'm afraid I cannot stay, but thank you very much.'

'Why do you not see if you can remain here?' Gerda seemed reluctant to let him go.

'I was a prisoner in this country for most of the war,

and do have the offer of a job, but I do not know if that is what I want.'

'Whatever you decide, I hope all goes well for you.' She reached up and kissed him on the cheek. 'Come to us if you need help.'

'*Danke.*'

He left the house and walked blindly as sadness rolled through him. They were all dead. In his heart he had known that even before he had been repatriated, and he should have accepted it then. But he had stubbornly refused to do so. Now he must face the truth.

Feeling utterly drained, he stopped. York Minster was in front of him, standing proud and solid. Dieter's mother had brought them up to believe in God as a loving creator. It had been hard to hold on to that belief through the brutality of the war and its aftermath. All the time he had been a prisoner he had attended church services, mostly because it gave him something to do, and he loved the music. After the war, while he was waiting to be sent home, one of his great pleasures had been to play the organ in the village church. The Rector had been a kind man.

A gust of cold wind ruffled his hair and he pulled the army greatcoat around him. On impulse he stepped through the door of the Minster. It would be warmer in there and he needed time to sort out his jumbled thoughts. There were quite a few people inside, but a wonderful sense of peace pervaded the atmosphere.

He walked slowly along, gazing up at the magnificent ceiling, and pausing to admire the huge stained-glass windows. A feeling of inner quietness seeped into him. On reaching the choir area he sat, head tipped back as he imagined the sound of singing filling the place.

Closing his eyes, calm now as the hurt receded, he prayed silently. 'What shall I do now? For the last two years I have wandered aimlessly, wasting my life, refusing to face the truth. Today I have come face to face with the knowledge that my family are all gone. Nothing can change that, however much I have longed for it to be different. I must get on with my life, but do I return to Germany or go somewhere else? I cannot go back to the kind of life I had in Berlin. What shall I do?'

At that moment the organ burst into life, making Dieter gasp with pleasure. It was wonderful! Whoever was practising was a fine musician.

He shut his eyes again, feeling the sounds flow over and around him, and, as he sat there, his mind cleared. There was a job waiting for him with the Sawyers. Working on the farm would give him a chance to rebuild, to grow strong again and, most important of all, to decide what he was going to do with his life. If Jane hadn't married, he would try to see her again. What they had shared had been special. He had often wondered if he had really loved her, or just taken the comfort and love she offered after years behind barbed wire. He still didn't know, but if they could meet he might find out.

He stood up, renewed in spirit, and strode out of the Minster. He would leave for Somerset at once.

15

It was a bright early November afternoon, with a nip in the air to warn of approaching winter, and the sky so blue it seemed to sparkle. As Dieter walked into the yard, he caught the smell of animals wafting on the breeze, and the memories came tumbling back. He dropped his bag and stood facing the huge barn, expecting Jane to come out, stomping through the puddles in her rubber boots, laughing as always and waving at him.

Taking a deep breath, he closed his eyes for a moment. Oh, why hadn't he come back sooner? So much wasted time. This was such a lovely, peaceful place. How could he have forgotten?

The scrape of the barn door made him open his eyes as John came out with a young child holding his hand. He looked at Dieter, his steps faltering for a moment, then he came forward.

'Dieter.' John shook his hand. 'It's good to see you. Bob told us you were here and we hoped you'd come to us.'

'I am pleased to be here and would like to stay for a while, if I may.'

'Of course, there's nothing we would like more.'

Satisfied with the warm welcome, Dieter looked at the child, who was watching him curiously. 'And who are you?' he asked, crouching down in front of him.

'I'm Danny.' He gave a shy smile.

'That is a nice name.' Dieter smoothed a strand of fair hair away from the child's eyes.

Danny nodded, making the hair fall back again. 'This is my grandpa.'

Standing up, Dieter was puzzled. 'I thought you did not have children, Mr Sawyer.'

'We haven't, but we loved Jane as a daughter and so took on Danny as our grandson.'

'My mummy's gone to live with the angels.' Hearing his mother's name, Danny blinked rapidly, but the tears didn't spill over. 'I wish she hadn't gone.' His voice wobbled a little but then brightened. 'She liked it here, and now I live here with my auntie. Don't I, Grandpa?'

'That's right, Danny.' John smiled and ruffled his hair, then gave him a little push. 'You run along and do your practice while I talk to Dieter.'

'Okay.' The smile was back and he ran towards the farmhouse.

Dieter spun round to watch the child and saw Mrs Sawyer and a girl standing by the door. A girl with the same colouring as Jane – only she wasn't Jane. The news hurt so much he had trouble grasping it.

'Danny is Jane's child?' His voice sounded strained. 'How old is he?'

'He was three last May.' John touched his arm. 'Come inside, Dieter.'

There was a roaring in his head. Oh, dear God, it couldn't be. But, now that he thought about it, the family likeness was unmistakable. Fair hair, grey eyes, dimpled smile . . . With a great effort he managed to rasp out, 'Who is his father?'

'You are, Dieter, but I think you've already seen that.'

The shock was so severe it made him stumble back, robbed of all speech.

Angie heard Hetty give an alarmed gasp.

'Oh, no, don't be angry, please. Don't tell him yet, John!' Hetty ran over to them.

Feeling this really wasn't any of her business, Angie stayed where she was, watching the scene. Hetty was holding on to the stranger's arm and talking rapidly. Pleading? The man shook his head, turned sharply and walked out of the yard, leaving his bag where he had dropped it.

John picked it up, putting his arm around his wife as they walked towards her. Hetty was crying, and they were both clearly upset.

'Now, now,' John urged. 'It was a shock. He'll be back.'

'Oh, John,' she moaned, 'what rotten luck. I didn't want them to meet like this. I hoped we would have a chance to explain first.'

'Can't be helped, my dear. At least he's come, and you know Bob said it was doubtful that he would. Let's go inside and Angie will make us a nice cup of tea.'

Angie followed them into the kitchen and put the kettle on. 'Sit down, Hetty.'

Danny was in the other room happily practising the

piano, and she knew he would be all right for a while. He never seemed to tire of the discipline needed to learn the piano and knew each lesson off by heart by the time he went for his next one. Mrs Poulton was thrilled with her new student.

When the tea was made, she poured one for each of them and sat down, bursting with curiosity. 'Who was that man? And why did he upset you so much?'

The tears began to flow again. 'I'm so sorry, Angie, we thought we were doing the right thing . . .'

'We have done right, Hetty.' John spoke firmly. 'I've told you he'll be back when he's walked off the anger. He's left his bag behind.'

'You shouldn't have told him yet, John.'

John shrugged. 'What was I to do? Danny told him about his mother, and it didn't take Dieter long to put two and two together.'

Hetty blew her nose. 'What's happened to him, John? He's so thin and haggard.'

'They've been having a tough time over there. If we'd known where he was, we could have sent food parcels like some of the other villagers have been doing for those they befriended.'

Hetty nodded. 'Yes, he should have told us where he was. Poor, dear man.'

Angie was confused now. What was all this talk about food parcels? 'Who is he?'

'He's Danny's father.' Hetty whispered, her eyes still swimming with tears. 'Bob found him for us.'

As the shock hit her, Angie stood up so quickly the

chair nearly went flying. 'Where's he gone? Why did he run off like that? And how could Bob find him, when he's in Germany?'

John was also on his feet, straightening the chair and making her sit down again. 'It's no good you chasing after him. He didn't know about Jane and the boy, but he knew that the fair hair and large grey eyes were a trait of his family's. He'd made love to Jane and the boy smiling up at him with identical dimples was the right age. It didn't take much working out, Angie. He demanded to know who the child was. We've got to give him time to come to terms with this.'

She was shaking. The thing she had been half dreading had happened. Danny's father had arrived, and the coward had run away at the first sight of his son. That didn't make her very hopeful about the future.

'Will you stay here tonight, Angie?' Hetty's expression was pleading. 'You'll be able to talk to him when he comes back.'

'No.' She shook her head firmly and stood up. 'I'm not sure if I want anything to do with him. If he wants to see us, he'll have to come to me. If he doesn't, he can just go back where he came from. He doesn't deserve to have a lovely son like Danny. He couldn't even stay to talk to him. The bloody coward!' She was distraught now. 'He left Jane pregnant. What kind of a man does that?'

'All right, Angie.' John sighed. 'You're not going to like this either, but before you go there's something you should know. Danny's father is German. He was a prisoner at Goathurst Camp.'

The breath left Angie's lungs in a rush and the room swam before her eyes. They'd known. Bob had known. They'd known he was German! No wonder they had refused to tell her about him. She was so angry, and frightened. Very frightened. Now she knew why Jane had kept his identity a secret. How could she have fallen in love with a man whose country was responsible for their parents' death? That dreadful time came back to her as if it were yesterday, along with the pain and loss.

Her hands clenched into tight fists as she tried to gain control of her emotions. She had to keep a clear head. 'He can't take Danny away! He's my son, legally.'

'I'm sure he won't do that.' Hetty spoke gently, trying to calm her. 'He's a nice man. He didn't know. Dieter is the one who has been wronged, Angie. Jane shouldn't have kept news of his son from him. I know she believed she had her reasons, but she wasn't right.'

It was a rare censure of the young girl they had loved so much. The shock was fading, but she was still having difficulty grasping the news. A picture of the man walking away came to her, the sun glinting on his fair hair, head bowed. Even in her dismay, she could understand what he must have been going through. She sat down again. 'You'd better tell me all about him.'

John took up the story. 'Dieter was taken prisoner in early 1941. He baled out when his plane was shot down during a raid on London.'

Angie's head shot up, anger blazing in her eyes again. The news just got worse and worse. 'He was in the Luftwaffe?'

'Yes, a navigator,' John continued, ignoring her fury. 'He was the sole survivor out of his whole crew. He was only twenty, Angie, just doing what he'd been ordered to do, like all the young men on both sides. He was sent from camp to camp, until he ended up here. When the war was over, they were allowed out and Dieter came to lodge with us and work on the farm.'

'And that's when Jane met him.' Angie couldn't believe this. She had spent hours wondering who Danny's father was, but never in her wildest dreams – no nightmares – had she considered this. He might have been up there in the sky when their parents had been killed.

Hetty gave a wan smile. 'We didn't know there was anything between them. You must believe us.'

'I do.' Angie looked at John. 'Even if Jane wouldn't tell him where she lived, why did he go away without giving her an address where she could contact him?'

'I think he knew he didn't have a home address any more.'

'I don't understand.'

'He comes from Dresden, Angie.' John gave a ragged sigh. 'After the terrible bombing there, he didn't hear from his family, and he was frantic to get back. Repatriation took such a long time, and it was late in 1947 before they shipped him back to Germany. He was out of his mind with worry by then, and we never heard from him again.'

'When we knew Bob was going to Germany, we asked him to try to find Dieter and persuade him to come back here,' Hetty said, her hands trembling. 'We asked Bob not to tell him about Jane or Danny, hoping we would be able to break the news to him gently. It was rotten luck that Danny was here when he arrived. He was furious the news had been kept from him.' She was still clearly distressed. 'He looks so ill . . .'

'Don't upset yourself again.' John placed an arm around her as her tears welled up. 'When he comes back we'll be able to look after him.'

Danny rushed into the kitchen. 'Did you hear me?'

'Yes, darling, that was wonderful. Mrs Poulton will be very pleased with you.' Angie pushed aside her worry and smiled approvingly at the little boy. This news hadn't touched him yet, and she was going to make damned sure he got to know his father before being told who he was. That's if the man stayed around long enough. From what she had seen in the yard, he would probably run straight back to Germany. And if he did, she would shout good riddance. There was a niggling feeling that she was being harsh and judgemental, but she didn't care. Her darling boy's happiness was at stake here.

She stood up, not wanting to be around when he did return for his things. 'We'll be going now. Say goodbye to Granny and Grandpa.'

There were hugs all round, and, as Hetty held Angie tightly, she whispered in her ear. 'Give him a chance, Angie. Please.'

'I'll see.' She would find it difficult to like this man who had seduced Jane and then left her, never bothering to try to find her again. Heartless, that's what he was. But her cousin had loved him. She had said in her letter that he had great problems. He might have lost his family in that terrible bombing. Although Angie had always been the stronger of the two girls, she did have a compassionate side, but it was going to be a struggle to be polite to him. She sighed as the disjointed thoughts tumbled through her head. What a mess!

'I'll take you both home.' John held out his hand to Danny, and they disappeared into the yard, where the old truck was parked.

She had to get away from here now, because she was so angry and would be tempted to punch the man on the nose if he came back.

He was dazed, unable to think straight. Dieter leant on a gate and gazed across the field with unseeing eyes, his mind unable to believe what he had just seen and been told by John Sawyer. Slowly the peace of the countryside began to work its magic, and the turmoil he'd experienced when he'd seen the boy began to wear off. Then his mind started to race. It had been like looking at himself at that age: same hair, eyes and even the dimples flashing as he'd smiled. And adorable Jane had died a few months ago. Dear God, that was unbelievable. What had happened? He had been too stunned to ask.

He bowed his head in deep sorrow. She should have told him. He had still been in this country when the child had been born. It was true he had been moved to another camp just before he'd been repatriated, but Major Strachan could have found him.

The Major! Dieter ground his teeth. Now he understood why the swine had gone out of his way to make him come back. He knew, and should have told him. At least he would have been prepared for the meeting. The shame that ripped through him at that moment made him double over as if in pain. Jane had needed him, and he hadn't even bothered to find out if she was all right. All he had thought about was returning to Germany and finding his family. But there hadn't been anyone left to find. He should have come back then, but he hadn't. He had just drifted around in a state of shock. What wasted time when he could have been with Jane and his son.

He heard a slight huffing sound and felt warm breath on the side of his face, along with a strong animal smell. He looked up and found himself eye to eye with a donkey, which was surveying him with interest. He reached out and stroked the velvet face.

'Sorry, I haven't any carrots.'

As if it understood, the animal turned and ambled off to join a horse on the other side of the field.

Dieter stood up straight and watched as they greeted each other with playful affection. A feeling of awe swept over him as the reality of the situation dawned on him. He had believed that he was alone, all his family lost, but that wasn't true. He had a son.

He continued walking – through the village, past the pub and finally stopping in front of the church. It didn't look as if anything had changed over the last couple of years. He gazed at the church for a few moments, then retraced his steps. After the bitter disappointment in York, he had come here in an effort to sort out his life, but what he'd found had thrown his life into even greater confusion. His mind grappled with the news.

He had a son!

He ran back to the farm and John opened the door as soon as he reached the yard.

'Where is he? I must talk with him.' Dieter bent over, out of breath.

'Come in and have something to eat.' Hetty held his arm and urged him inside.

'Is he here? What is his name?' Dieter allowed himself to be pushed into a chair at the kitchen table.

'His name's Danny, and he lives in the village with Jane's cousin, Angie Westwood.' Hetty placed a plate of hot food in front of him. 'Eat that before you do anything else.'

'You will stay with us.' John studied him carefully. 'We've put your bag in the room you had before.'

'Thank you.' Dieter began to eat; he had no interest in the food, but it was clear they were determined that he had a meal. As soon as the plate was cleared, he stood up. 'Tell me the address, please.'

'Leave it until tomorrow,' John said. 'Let us explain first.'

'No.' Dieter shook his head. 'We shall talk later. Now I must see the child.'

'I'll come with you.' John stood up and reached for his coat.

'I wish to go alone.' He paused at their concern. 'I shall not cause trouble for Danny or his aunt. You can trust me.'

John gave a grim smile. 'We know we can. They're in the first cottage in the village. No. 2.'

Dieter bowed slightly and left the house, heading for the village once again.

It was impossible to settle. Angie tossed aside the book she had been attempting to read. Her insides felt as if they were tied in knots. Danny was fast asleep in bed, oblivious to the drama about to unfold around him, and that was how she was determined to keep it. He couldn't suddenly be presented with a father he didn't know. That would frighten and confuse him. They would have to be introduced to one another slowly. What had Hetty called him? Dieter? Yes, that was the name. No wonder they wouldn't tell her his first name: she would immediately have known that he wasn't English. It was a nice name, though.

She wandered into the kitchen to make a cup of cocoa. Perhaps that would help settle her insides. There was a knock on the door just as she was about to put the milk into the saucepan. A glance at the clock showed that it was nine o'clock and she hoped it wasn't the Rector with more urgent typing for her. She didn't think she would be able to concentrate at the moment.

When she opened the door, her heart missed several

beats. She was looking into Danny's lovely grey eyes, only these were worldly-wise, not innocent and trusting like her darling boy's.

'I wish to see my son.'

'He's asleep.' She was surprised to see that he was on his own. Hetty and John must have told him where she lived, and she would have expected one of them to come with him. But if they hadn't thought that necessary, it showed they trusted him. She was going to have to do the same, but she really didn't want him in her home.

'I will not awaken him.'

'Come back tomorrow.' She noticed how he planted his feet slightly apart and saw he wasn't going to move.

'No, I will see him now.' He held his hands out, palms up. 'I will not disturb him.'

She didn't miss the steely determination in his eyes, but he had asked politely, with no sign of anger or aggression, so she stepped aside. As much as she wanted to, she couldn't deny him this right. Giving a slight bow, he walked in and waited for her to shut the front door.

'This way, but you must be quiet.' She made her way upstairs to Danny's room. The bedside light was still on, casting a warm glow around the room and lighting up the small figure in the bed. He was on his back with arms thrown above his head and, much to her relief, fast asleep. She didn't want him to wake up and find a strange man in his room.

Dieter stood beside the bed, staring at the child. He didn't try to touch him; he just stood there for ages, unmoving. 'He's beautiful,' he whispered after what had seemed a lifetime.

'Yes, he is, and I love him very much.' Angie felt it was wise to let his father know this right away.

Dieter nodded and reached out to pick up the toy truck from the bedside table. 'Ah, the wheel is loose. I shall fix it.'

She pointed to the photograph they had found in Jane's tin. Danny always kept it by his bed. 'Is that you with Jane?'

'Ah, yes.' He reached out to gently touch the image of Jane. 'Another prisoner from the camp found an old camera, but it did not work well. I did not know Jane had kept it.'

'She treasured it.'

He spoke huskily. 'She was a very special girl.'

They had been talking in whispers, and Angie touched his arm, afraid if they stayed much longer they would wake Danny. 'We must go downstairs now.'

'Of course.' With a last lingering look, Dieter followed her out of the room.

In the bright light of the kitchen Angie could see tears in the German's eyes as he gazed at the wooden toy in his hands. She could only guess at the torment he was going through. She had been determined not to like him, but her heart softened. 'I was about to make cocoa when you arrived. Would you like some?'

When he looked up, two dimples flashed for a moment. 'Thank you, I would like that.'

'Please sit down.' Angie turned to the stove, her heart

pounding. If he weren't so gaunt-looking, he would be exactly like his son. Had he laughed and run through the fields with Jane? Had they helped with the harvest and fed the animals together? Had their time together been happy? Yes, she was sure that for Jane it had been, but it didn't look as if he had been really happy for some time. A glimpse of what he had been like was still there. No wonder Jane had fallen in love with him.

The milk nearly boiled over while she had been lost in thought. She turned off the gas just in time.

Dieter was bent over the truck, his long fingers wielding a small penknife as he fixed the wheel. She put the drink in front of him, and, without speaking he left the toy and wrapped his fingers around the mug.

'I'm so sorry . . . so sorry.' His words were hardly audible. 'Jane should have told me. I would never have left her alone. I had to go back to Germany, but I would have returned. I am so sorry.'

When Angie had found out that Danny's father was a German ex-prisoner of war, she had been dismayed, but this man was racked with guilt. She would never have believed she could feel pity for a man who had not only seduced her cousin but had also taken part in the bombing of this country – but she did. It made her realize that the past had to be forgiven, if not forgotten. The only thing that mattered now was Danny's future. Her own personal feelings must be put aside. She owed it to Jane and Danny to give this man a chance.

'There is much to be sad about,' she said firmly, 'but

you must never be sorry about what happened between you and Jane. She loved Danny and never for a moment regretted having him. I believe she did what she felt was right by not telling you, but I think there is something you should see.'

She stood up, went into the front room and returned with Jane's letter, handing it to Dieter. 'Jane left me this. I think you have a right to know how she felt about you.'

His hands shook as he read the letter, then he folded it carefully and handed it back to her. 'Thank you for allowing me to see that. Will you tell me exactly what happened to Jane?'

Angie went back to the time Danny was born, explaining what joy the little boy had brought to them both. She left nothing out about Jane's death and the bad time Danny had had since then. 'I brought him here in desperation, hoping that a change would help. It did, and we decided to live here. He's happy now with friends of his own age, and looks upon John and Hetty as his grandparents.'

'You have done all the right things. I'm sorry there won't be any grandparents from my side. My entire family was killed in the bombing.'

'So were ours, mine and Jane's.' It was hard to keep the sharpness out of her voice.

Dieter's head shot up, and what little colour there was drained from his face. 'Jane never told me.'

'She wouldn't. My cousin was very loving and wouldn't do or say anything to upset anyone. To forgive came easily to her.'

'And what about you?' He spoke gruffly. 'Could you find it in your heart to forgive the man who might have dropped the bombs that killed your family?'

Angie shrugged helplessly. This was still an open wound for her. 'We are both going to have to try to do that, for Danny's sake.'

He sighed wearily. 'There are so many shadows between us.'

'There is only one way to dispel shadows.' She sat up straight, her lips set in a determined line. 'And that is to let in the light. I will not deny you the right to get to know your son, but he is mine now. I have legally adopted him, as Jane wanted. You must not tell him who you are until I decide the time is right.'

'I would like to tell him now, but you are right. I would not wish to do anything to upset him. I shall try to be patient.'

'Good.' Angie breathed a silent sigh of relief. Although she didn't know him, he seemed a reasonable man, and she hoped he would keep his word.

Danny woke up hearing voices downstairs, and then noticed that the truck wasn't on the table. Scrambling out of bed, he crawled around the floor. It was gone! He had to find it. He mustn't lose it!

Holding tightly to the banister, he walked down the stairs and into the kitchen, where someone was talking. Auntie Angel was sitting at the table with a man. She saw him at once.

'Hello, darling, what are you doing up?'

'My truck's gone,' he whispered, very worried.

'It is here.' The man spoke. 'I have mended the wheel for you.'

He took it from the man and smiled in relief, running it along the table to see if it worked properly. It did. 'Thank you. Em broke it, so I won't let her touch it again.'

'Very wise. Who is Em?'

Auntie hadn't told him to go back to bed, so he clambered on to a chair between her and the man. 'She's my friend, but she breaks things easy.'

'Ah, well, you mustn't let her do that.'

'I don't. She's bossy, but I like her.'

'Good.'

Danny looked at the man intently. 'You talk funny.'

The man laughed. 'That's because English is not my native tongue.'

He didn't know what that meant but didn't ask, too interested in what Auntie had in her mug. 'Is that cocoa?'

'Yes, would you like some?'

'Please.' He'd be able to stay up a bit longer if he had a drink. He watched while his auntie poured some of hers into his own little mug. Before picking up the drink, he pushed the truck towards her, just to be on the safe side. He didn't want the man to go off with it. He guzzled his cocoa, looking from one to the other with a big grin between gulps. The man was staring at him, but he must be nice because he'd mended his truck.

When he finished his cocoa, Auntie helped him off the chair and took his hand.

'I think you ought to go back to bed now, Danny.'

Giving a big yawn, he picked up his truck.

'Say goodnight to . . . Dieter.'

'Night, night.'

'*Gute Nacht, mein Sohn.*'

Danny glanced at his auntie and giggled. What funny words.

16

There was a bright moon shining as Dieter walked back to the farm. The air was clear, and a slight frost was forming on the grass verges. It was all so clean and fresh after the noise and dust of Berlin. He felt as if he had been transported into another existence. He should have come back sooner and married Jane. They may not have had much time together, but they would have been happy. She had been easy to love, with her wide-eyed innocence and ready smile. Her cousin was like her in colouring, but he sensed she was a different person. There was something about the way she stood, the directness of her gaze, that told him she had a determined nature. But she also had a clear sense of what was right, for she had allowed him to see his son, even though he was sure she didn't want him anywhere near the boy.

He stopped and gazed up at the moon, overcome with the wonder of seeing Jane's child – his child. Lifting his arms high, he tipped his head back and shouted at the bright orb, spinning round and round on the spot. 'I have a son! I've talked to him and he smiled at me. I believed the war had robbed me of my youth and family, but I have a son!'

Lowering his arms, he glanced around, embarrassed

at his outburst, but the lane was empty. The only ones around to hear were some sheep in a field, and they didn't appear to be interested in him. He gave a wry smile, feeling like a child again.

When he walked into the farmhouse kitchen, John and Hetty were still up, which was unusual, as they started work at dawn every morning. He could tell from their faces that they had been waiting anxiously for him to return.

'Hello, Dieter.' Hetty smiled. 'Would you like a hot drink?'

'No, thank you, I had one with Angie and Danny.' He didn't miss their look of relief. They had wanted to come with him, but he'd felt it would be better if he had his first meeting with Jane's cousin and Danny alone. And he'd been right. It had all gone much better than he could have hoped. The girl had been cautious and possessive, but that was only to be expected. He was a stranger to her, and he had obviously come as quite a shock – not the Englishman she had assumed was the boy's father.

'Well, sit down for a moment and you can tell us how you got on.' John pulled out a chair from the table. 'You saw Danny, then.'

Dieter sat down and nodded. 'He was asleep in bed when I arrived, but I was allowed upstairs. After that we sat in the kitchen talking and Danny came down. He was upset because his truck was missing. I had noticed a wheel was loose, so I brought it down with me and mended it.' He gave a sad smile. 'He thanked me politely and then pushed it towards his auntie in case I kept it. I wanted to tell him that I had made the toy and given it to his mother, but I couldn't. His aunt guards him well and has made it clear that I must not tell him anything.'

'Your turning up will cause her much heart searching. I believe that deep down she hoped you would never be found, but she will do whatever is right for Danny.' Hetty leant towards Dieter and touched his hand lightly. 'You see, from the moment Jane arrived home pregnant, Angie supported her and the child. Not only financially but emotionally as well. She has now given up her life and home in London because Danny was unhappy, and has done this without any thought for herself, as she loves him so very much. He has asked why he hasn't got a father like all the other children, and for that reason she wanted you found. It's right he should know who his father is.'

'I do not think that she likes me, but she was kind.' Dieter glanced at John. 'She is not like Jane. Tell me about her, please.'

John rested his elbows on the table. 'You're right; the two girls were very different in nature. They both came to us after their parents were killed in a raid.'

Dieter clenched his jaw. 'I did not know about that until she told me tonight. Explain please.'

John told him how both sets of parents had been killed, and then continued with the story. 'Angie was older than Jane and couldn't settle here. After only six months she returned to London and went to work in a factory until the end of the war. Angie was always the stronger and more determined of the two, but Jane was happy with us and stayed.'

'Did you not know about Jane's heart?'

'No.' Hetty shook her head. 'Sometimes we would find her curled up asleep in an armchair. When we expressed concern, she would smile brightly and jump up, declaring that she was fine. She was such a happy girl and we assumed she had tired herself out by running around the farm. Even Angie didn't know until after Jane died, and we have a suspicion that Jane didn't know how bad it was until she became pregnant.'

Dieter thought about the words in the letter she had left for Angie, and remembered her with admiration. 'She had been gentle, but she must have had much courage.'

'She also had Angie.' John spoke again. 'As Hetty has already told you, when Jane returned to London, Angie looked after her, and when Danny was born she insisted that Jane stay at home while she went out to work. She provided for all three of them. They brought up Danny together, and she loves him as if he were her own son.'

'I am sure of that.' Dieter ran a hand over his eyes. 'The news of his birth should not have been kept from me. I was not repatriated until late 1947. I was still in this country when he was born.'

'That was wrong.' Hetty looked alarmed at his tone. 'I know how you must feel, Dieter, but please don't upset things. Danny was a very troubled little boy when she brought him to us. He is just beginning to settle down.'

'I shall be careful, but I am here now and nothing will make me leave. Before I left Germany, Major Strachan told me that we all have things to forgive, and without forgiveness there is no future. That is true. It won't be easy, though.'

'Difficult but not impossible,' John said.

'We shall do it, no?' Dieter's smile was tight as he stood up. 'What time do you wish me to start work in the morning?'

'Six o'clock as usual.'

'I will see you then.' He bowed slightly and made his way to the room at the top of the house. It was the same one he'd had when he had worked here just after the war. There was a welcoming feel to the old farmhouse, and it almost felt like coming home, except this time there would not be a laughing, loving girl to brighten his days. The fact that she had died so young was a great sadness to him, but their loving had produced a beautiful child. Jane had not regretted that, and neither could he.

Much to Angie's amazement, she had slept soundly, and so had Danny. But, as she woke and remembered what had happened the day before, she knew that things would never be the same again. However, she was not going to allow Danny's father to come in and disrupt their lives if she could help it. He had a right to see his son, and she wouldn't – couldn't – deny him that, but she would not leave them alone together. She had a terrible fear he would disappear with Danny, and they might never be able to find him again. Her stomach heaved at the thought of such a danger. She was probably misjudging the man, but it would be criminal to take chances with a vulnerable little boy's life.

'Morning.' Danny rushed in and climbed on her bed. 'What we doing today?'

She ruffled his shining fair hair and smiled. 'First there's the church hall, then lunch and your lesson with Mrs Poulton, then tea with Granny and Grandpa. How does that sound?'

'Smashing.' He was already on the floor again, ready to spring into action for the exciting day ahead. 'I'll clean my teeth. Can I have boiled eggy for my breakfast? One I collected from the chicks myself?'

'Of course, and some of Grandma's home-made bread and jam?'

He nodded and shot towards the door, only to stop and look round before disappearing. 'Get up, Auntie. We mustn't be late. I'll tell Em that a nice man mended my truck.' Then he was gone with the sound of little feet tearing towards the bathroom.

Since they had been here, he never seemed to do anything at a normal pace. It was no wonder Emma got on so well with him: she was just the same.

After breakfast Angie dressed Danny in a pair of long trousers that she had made for him. They weren't as good as the ones Jane had made, but it was cold outside and they would keep his knees warm. He always beamed with pride when he wore long trousers, and she would try to make a better pair for his next birthday.

It troubled her when she thought about his birthday – the day his mother had died. How on earth was she going to make it special with that sad memory hanging over them? Ah, well, she had plenty of time to think about it. May was a long way off yet.

After breakfast they made their way down the street to the church hall.

When they walked in, it was bedlam, as usual, and Danny couldn't wait to join the other children.

'Thank heavens you're here.' Sally's hair was in a tangled mess, her skirt smeared with paint. 'We're shorthanded. Can you stay?'

Angie glanced around and grimaced. 'Good job I put my old clothes on.'

'With Emma around all I've got are old clothes.' Sally's chuckle was infectious. 'Danny's the only one who can keep her in order. Can I adopt him?'

'Not a chance!'

'Thought you'd say that.' Sally wiggled her eyebrows. 'I'll have to have one of my own. Wonder what Joe will think of that idea?'

Angie roared with laughter. 'He'll be absolutely thrilled.'

'Yeah.' Sally looked smug.

Angie removed her coat and sat on the floor to prise apart two toddlers who were fighting over a toy rabbit. 'Now stop it, you two. There's a whole box of animals here.'

The time flew by, and Angie was crawling around the floor pretending to be a dog, when the Rector came in.

'Feeling brave today, Geoff?' Sally called. 'We've got to feed them soon.'

He visibly blanched and shook his head. 'Another appointment.'

'Yeah, yeah, we've heard that before,' Sally teased.

The Rector's next words had Angie sitting back on her heels and staring at the door.

'Dieter, my dear boy, it is you, isn't it?'

'Hello, Rector.' They shook hands.

Geoff beamed. 'It's good to see you again. Are you visiting the Sawyers?'

'Yes, but I'm going to stay and make my home here.'

'Splendid, splendid.' The Rector's eyes were fairly gleaming with delight. 'Erm . . . I don't want to make a nuisance of myself as soon as you've arrived, but, if you're staying, may I pressure you into playing the organ for us now and again?'

'I would be pleased to.'

'Good, good. What a treat that will be.' He patted Dieter on the shoulder. 'Lovely to have you back. You are most welcome. Come and see me when you have time.'

'I will.'

'Good, good.' The Rector leant towards him. 'Must fly now. They're going to feed the children and I can't cope with that. Too much for an old man like me.'

As soon as the Rector disappeared, Danny ran over to Dieter, dragging Emma with him. 'I saw you last night. You mended my truck.'

Angie watched anxiously as Dieter crouched down in front of the children.

'I did. Is it all right now?'

'Works lovely.' Danny pushed Emma forward. 'This is Em. She broke my truck.'

'Hello, Em.'

The little girl eyed him carefully for a while, as if sizing him up to see if she could play a trick on him, then she pulled a face. 'I didn't break his rotten truck.'

'It isn't a rotten truck. It was in my mummy's special tin.' Danny looked scandalized. 'And you did break it. You sat on it.'

'Didn't.'

'Did.'

'Uh-oh, I can see a fight coming on.' Sally moved towards the children, with Angie close behind. It was best to stop this before it got out of hand or the whole group would join in.

'There was no great harm done.' Dieter seemed quite unperturbed by the bickering. 'It was easily mended.'

Emma was about to say something else to Danny, but stopped and stared at Dieter with her mouth still open and eyes wide with surprise.

Danny giggled. 'He talks funny. Say what you did last night. Go on, please, let Em hear.'

'Gute Nacht, mein Sohn.'

'Of course, that's who Danny reminds me of, but I hadn't made the connection.' Sally whispered, bubbling with delight. 'Dieter.'

He stood up and frowned at Sally.

'I'm Sally. Don't you remember?' She held out her hand. 'You had tea with us now and again.'

The frown disappeared and he stepped forward. 'Of course. I did not recognize you at first.'

'I'm not surprised. There's a lot more of me than there used to be.'

Angie could only watch, speechless. Did everyone in this village know him?

'You remember that squalling baby I had? Well, she's grown a bit. This bundle of mischief is Emma.'

A genuine smile crossed his face. 'She takes after you, perhaps?'

'How did you guess?'

A wail cut through the air as one little boy cried that he was hungry.

'Oops, feeding time. Will you come and see us sometime, Dieter? We live next door to Angie now.'

'I would enjoy that.' Dieter inclined his head as Sally hurried into the kitchen; then he turned to Angie. 'Good morning. I hope you slept well?'

'I did, thank you.' Was he always the polite gentleman?

He stooped to say goodbye to the children, then stood up, gave a slight bow to Angie and left without another word.

Angie found Sally waiting for her in the kitchen, in a high state of excitement. 'Does Danny know?'

'Know what?' Angie pretended ignorance.

'That Dieter is his father. Come on, Angie, the likeness is unmistakable. When you told me Danny was Jane's child, I knew she must have met someone while she was here, but I never guessed it was one of the prisoners.'

'Danny doesn't know, and I don't want him told.' This was becoming more difficult by the moment. 'The man has only just turned up, and I don't want Danny upset. He's settling in so well. Don't say anything, Sally, please!' Angie rubbed between her eyes as a headache began to pound. 'Tell me why you all know him.'

'We knew quite a lot of them. After the war ended, they were allowed out; some were billeted on farms and worked while waiting to be sent home. Local families adopted one or two and invited them in for meals, Christmas and things like that. We received such heart-rending letters from some when they returned home. There have been terrible food shortages, and we've all been sending clothing and food parcels. Dieter was much liked and respected, but he never gave John and Hetty an address where they could contact him.'

'I see.' Angie chewed her lip.

'I don't think you do, Angie.' Sally took her hand and made her sit down. 'I know your parents were killed in a raid, and you probably have no love for the men who did that. They were all young men carrying out their orders, just like our own. Dieter was twenty when his plane was shot down. He spent four years behind barbed wire and another two waiting to be repatriated. God knows what he found when he finally arrived home, but, by the look of him, I would say he's had a bad time. I didn't recognize him at first. He's a good man, Angie, and I expect Jane found it easy to love him.'

'I'm sure you're right.' Angie covered her face with

her hands as her head pounded with tension. 'When Danny asked why he didn't have a daddy like Emma, I knew we had to try to find him. But I never expected anything like this. I'm frightened, Sally.'

'I'm sure there's no need to be.'

Angie shook her head, worried sick. 'I love Danny so much and would do anything for him, but this is all such a shock. How is he going to take it when he finds out?'

'He's a child.' Sally smiled at her. 'He isn't yet lumbered with our prejudices, likes and dislikes. If Dieter is kind to him, and I'm sure he will be, then Danny will accept him. He won't give a damn that his father is German.'

'Of course he won't.' Angie hadn't noticed that she'd shed a few tears, and dried her face with her handkerchief. 'I'll try to remember that and be sensible. Is it all right if I'm still a little frightened?'

'Quite all right. You wouldn't be human if you weren't.'

17

That afternoon Danny was in with Emma, playing with her train. Angie's head was pounding so badly she could hardly see. She hadn't expected Dieter to turn up at the church hall like that, and to discover that he was well known in the village came as quite a shock. If Sally had noticed his resemblance to Danny, how long would it be before others did the same? She had foolishly believed that there would be plenty of time before they needed to tell Danny, but if people started to talk, the other children would pick up on the gossip and chatter away in all innocence. Danny mustn't find out about his father in that way. It would be cruel.

The worry was making her feel ill. She stretched out on the settee and closed her eyes, at a complete loss about what to do for the best. Should he be told now, or would it be better to wait until he was older and knew Dieter better? This is what she wanted to do, but was she right? It was such a responsibility, and she dreaded the thought of making a mistake. Rubbing her head, she gave a ragged sigh. She must rest.

A piercing scream had her sitting up, startled, and fully awake. Danny was standing in front of her, eyes closed, fists clenched and screaming at the top of his voice.

'Danny!' She lunged forward and swept him up, falling back on the settee with him in her arms. 'What is it? What's the matter?'

His little fists beat on her chest as he struggled to get down, his cries of terror ripping the heart out of her. 'You was leaving me.'

'No, darling. No, I wasn't. Please tell me what's the matter.'

He stopped struggling and locked his arms around her neck, the screams turning to tortured moans. 'Mustn't leave me,' he sobbed.

'I'm not going to leave you, darling.' Oh, God, what had happened?

The back door burst open, and Sally rushed in with Emma at her heels. 'What's the matter?' She was out of breath.

Angie looked over the top of Danny's head. He was still sobbing out of control and shaking so badly that his teeth chattered. 'I don't know.'

'Mustn't leave me.' Danny was gulping in terror. 'Angels took Mummy. Mustn't have you.'

'Oh, dear Lord.' It suddenly dawned on her what this was all about. Danny must have come in and found her in the front room, sound asleep. He believed she was dead, just as his mother had been. That dreadful day was still very clear in his mind.

She lifted his head from her shoulder so he could see her face. 'I'm fine, and I'm never going to leave you. I was asleep, that's all.'

He buried his head in her shoulder again. 'Sleep in

bed, not here. Don't wake up again in here.'

'That isn't going to happen to me, sweetheart. Your mummy was sick. I'm not.' Angie was furious with herself. How stupid of her. She should have rested on the bed. It never worried him to find her asleep there. In his mind that was where you slept. It must have been terrible for him when he'd seen her in the front room, unmoving. The memory of finding his mother like that had terrified him. It was only six months since she had died, and far too soon for him to have forgotten. If he ever would.

'Is there anything we can do?' Sally sat beside her, and for once Emma was silent.

'We were supposed to go to the farm for tea, but we can't now. Could you somehow let John and Hetty know?'

'I'll go at once.' Sally hurried out, taking Emma with her.

Danny was still crying, and she held him tightly, whispering gentle words of comfort. Just when he seemed to be settling down into the normal, happy boy he had been before, this had to happen. She should have realized how fragile his peace was. She was a blasted idiot!

How long they sat there she didn't know. Danny maintained a fierce grip on her. His sobs had ceased, but quivers rippled through his body.

Suddenly the room was full of people. Sally had returned with Hetty, John and Dieter.

Dieter loomed in front of her. 'What has happened?'

'I had a headache and fell asleep on the settee.'

Angie's voice broke. 'Danny found me and thought I'd died.' She was back in the nightmare of when they had found Jane. And, because of her thoughtlessness, so was her darling little boy. Quiet tears of remorse filled her eyes and dimmed her vision.

'You will make us all a cup of tea, yes?' Dieter touched Hetty's arm, and, when she stood up, he took her place next to Angie. He ran his hand gently over Danny's tousled hair. 'Danny, everything is good. See, we are here with you.'

The only response from the frightened child was to tuck his head more firmly into Angie's neck.

Dieter sighed, a deep frown on his face. 'His love for you is great.'

'It was Jane and me from the moment he was born, and after she died there was only me. He must think that if I go away he will be left alone.'

'That might have been true a few months ago, but he will never be alone now. He must be told that. It is clear he does not feel secure.' Dieter spoke firmly. 'You have had to deal with this on your own, but now you have many people to help.'

Angie lifted her head and gazed around the room, seeing Sally, Emma, looking worried for her friend, John and Dieter. Hetty was coming back with a tray of tea and a glass of milk for Danny. People who loved her and Danny surrounded them. She wasn't alone. Dieter obviously wanted to tell Danny that he was his father, but this was not the time. She was not going to let him force her into doing something about it until she was certain it was right. Her lips thinned into a determined line as she stared at Dieter. Right or wrong, she would have her way in this. 'You will say nothing until I agree.'

He didn't have a chance to answer as Hetty put the tray on the small table by the window and said, 'Dieter, why don't you play something for us? Danny loves music.'

Without a word he went over to the piano, removed the cushions Danny used to reach the keys and sat down, his long fingers sweeping over the keyboard.

As the beautiful strains of 'Stardust' filled the room, Angie felt Danny move and lift his head. The sound he made was something between a sigh and a gulp. Gradually the tremors ceased, and by the time Dieter was on another tune he was kneeling on Angie so that he could see over to the piano. When Dieter swept into a lovely classical piece Angie had never heard before, it was too much for the little boy. He slid off the settee and went to stand beside Dieter, listening intently and leaning against his leg. Then he ducked down to watch his feet on the pedals, his tear-stained face a picture of concentration. When the pedals under the piano had been fully examined, Danny stood up again. He was about eye level with Dieter's hands, his own fingers twitching in anticipation.

Dieter stopped playing and smiled down at him.

'What you doing with your feet?' Danny's voice was husky after his distress.

Sally had poured the tea and Angie took a cup from her, never taking her eyes off Danny as Dieter demonstrated the difference in sound the pedals made. It never ceased to amaze Angie that a boy of only three and a half should have such an ear for music. But perhaps it wasn't so surprising, now that she had heard his father play. The man was brilliant.

'I can't reach them.' The signs of Danny's upset had started to fade as he thought only of the music.

'You will be able to when you are taller. It doesn't matter for the moment, but when you can play they will add light and shade to your music.' Dieter played a sweeping chord loud and then soft. 'See what I mean?'

Danny nodded again, his tongue caught between his front teeth.

'Let's try something else.' Dieter reached down and swept Danny up until he was sitting on his knees. 'Put your hands on top of mine, by my fingers. Now try to keep them there.'

Dieter began to play a lullaby, making the breath catch in Angie's throat as she watched the two heads bent over the piano. They were so alike. She knew the tune well, because it had been the one she had sung with Jane when Danny had been fretful and teething. Neither of them could sing, but he had watched them from his cot, eyes swimming with tears, and eventually fallen asleep. The memory tugged at her heart. They had been such happy days. How she missed Jane.

When it was over, Danny looked up at Dieter and gave a little smile, his grey eyes beginning to sparkle again. 'What was that first tune you played?'

'It is called "Stardust".'

'I liked that. Play it again.'

'It was your mummy's favourite tune.'

Angie almost dropped her cup in alarm, making to get up. He was going to ignore her demand that Danny not be told yet. He was going to tell him!

'He knows what he's doing, Angie.' John gave her a warning look.

She sat back again, hoping that John was right.

'Did you know my mummy?'

'Yes,' Dieter said, smiling, 'she was lovely and I liked her very much.'

'The angels are looking after her now.' Danny's bottom lip trembled. 'I wish she hadn't gone away.'

'They'll take good care of her.'

'That's what Auntie said. But I wish she'd stayed with us.'

'So does everyone, Danny, but she was ill. We can be happy that she is being looked after now, can't we?'

Danny nodded and the threatened tears didn't appear as he turned his attention back to the piano. 'Can we play that tune together?'

'Of course. Put your hands on mine.'

Relief swept over Angie. Dieter had dropped the subject of Jane, and with it the danger that he was going to tell Danny that he was his father. But she was not daft; she had seen the look in his eyes. He had talked about Jane so naturally, and by bringing up the subject he was forming a link between himself and his son. She studied him with fresh eyes. He was talented, and no fool. He had calmed Danny and endeared himself to the child. It should have made her happy, but she knew nothing about this man. She must never underestimate him, however charming he may appear. And he was – there was no other way to describe him – charming and attractive.

It felt like he was playing. Danny concentrated hard on keeping his hands on top of Dieter's. It wasn't easy and they came off sometimes, but he soon put them back again.

When the tune was finished, he clapped his hands together in wonder. He was going to play like that one day.

'Shall we have tea now?'

Danny nodded, a bit disappointed that the music had stopped, but as soon as he was put back on the floor he ran over to Auntie. When she smiled at him, he clambered on to the settee and shuffled across until he was on her lap. He was still frightened, but he felt safe there.

'Do you want a piece of cake?' she asked.

He didn't want to eat. His tummy felt funny, so he shook his head.

'Have some milk, then.' Grandma held out a glass and he took it. He liked milk. He took a mouthful and looked up. 'Did you see, Auntie? It was like I was playing.'

'I did.' She smiled and he snuggled up closer.

'I'm going to do that soon.'

'I'm sure you are, darling.'

He finished his milk and watched the man as he sat beside them. 'You're better than Mrs Poulton.'

'My goodness, that is high praise.' Dieter opened his eyes in mock surprise, making Danny nod firmly.

Everyone else was laughing. It made him feel all warm with these nice people here. He didn't want to be frightened any more. It was nasty.

Em's mummy took the glass from him and he yawned. His auntie hadn't gone away. Laying his head on her shoulder, he closed his eyes. He'd stay near her, though. He was very tired now.

Angie felt Danny relax and knew he was fast asleep. 'Thank you,' she said to everyone, including the man sitting beside her.

He inclined his head in acknowledgement, and she was struck by his quiet dignity.

'We'll leave you now.' Sally stood up. 'If you need anything, Angie, just let us know.'

She held out her hand in gratitude. Sally was turning out to be a good friend, and she couldn't ask for better neighbours.

Emma hung back, her eyes fixed on Danny. She had been unusually quiet. 'Is he all right?'

'He will be in the morning.' Angie was touched by the little girl's concern. 'He's had a bad fright.'

'Must have been a whopper.'

'I'm afraid it was.'

'Come on, Emma,' Sally said to her daughter. 'Say goodbye to everyone.'

She didn't attempt to leave but turned large, thoughtful eyes on Dieter. 'You don't half play good. Just like on the wireless.'

'Why thank you, Princess.' Dieter smiled.

She shuffled and gave a titter. 'Why'd you call me that?'

'Because you look like a fairy princess.'

This took a bit of thinking about. 'Mummy, can I be a princess in the Christmas play?'

'There aren't any princesses, but you can be a king if you want to.'

'Nah, I'll be the one with the dolly.' She pursed her lips. 'That's good, isn't it?'

'Perfect.' Dieter smiled at her again.

Peering at him, she lifted her hand and pointed at his face. 'You got dimples, just like Danny.'

Sally took hold of her daughter's hand. 'We must go now. If you don't stop chattering, you'll wake up Danny.'

With a last glance at her sleeping friend, she left with her mother.

'Would you like me to stay the night, Angie?' Hetty still looked worried.

'That would be lovely, thank you.' Angie was pleased with the offer, because, to be truthful, she was badly shaken and didn't fancy being alone in the house tonight. 'You can have Danny's bed and he can come in with me. I don't think he's going to let me out of his sight for a while.'

'That's a good idea.' John got to his feet. 'I must get back to the farm. Stay longer if you want to, Dieter.'

'Another hour, if that is all right? I can walk back.'

'Fine. We'll knock ourselves up a meal when you arrive.' John kissed his wife, Angie and Danny, careful not to wake him, and then he left.

'We'll have something later as well.' Hetty gathered up the tea things and went to do the washing-up.

'Are you all right?' Dieter spoke softly when they were alone.

'I'm shattered.'

'Pardon, what does that mean?'

'It means I'm completely exhausted.' Dieter's English was excellent, but he still found some of the phrases strange. 'You play beautifully. Were you training to be a musician when the war came?'

'That is what I wanted to do. I had dreams of becoming a concert pianist, but my father thought it not a suitable ambition for his only son. I gave up the idea and began studying to become an engineer.'

'That's a shame. I will never try to dictate what Danny must do with his life. He loves music, and if that's what he wants to do, then that's fine. If he wants to be a road sweeper, then that will be fine as well. All I'll ever want is for him to be happy.'

Dieter nodded. 'He must be free to make his own way in life. I had no such choices. As young boys we were all expected to belong to the Hitler Youth. I joined quite willingly with all my friends, and it was fun. We went camping, on marches and did all sorts of things young boys find exciting. Little did we guess what it was all leading up to.'

He fell silent with an expression of utter sadness on his face.

'You weren't to know.'

'No, and it is all history now. But even as a young boy some things that were happening made me uneasy; I pushed the doubts aside. I was part of a Germany that was going to be great again. Hitler promised it and we believed him. Who was I to doubt such a powerful man? Two friends I'd grown up with became Nazis. They strutted around as if they owned the world and believed themselves to be above the law. I did not recognize them any more.'

Angie was intrigued and wanted to know more about him. 'You didn't follow their lead?'

'No.' He looked straight at her, holding her gaze. 'I was never a Nazi, Angie. When I was captured, the British Intelligence questioned me. They had a system of grading prisoners, white, grey and black. Black were the hardened Nazis. I was classed as a white German.'

'I see.' Angie moved Danny to a more comfortable position, as her arms were becoming numb with his weight. He remained asleep, clearly exhausted.

Dieter gave her an assessing look. 'Does that put your mind at rest?'

'It helps.' And it did. But she needed to find out more about what this man was really like.

'I tell you these things because I want to acknowledge my son. We are not going to be able to keep this a secret for long. The likeness between us is strong. Even a young child has noticed it.'

'She's very observant.' Angie's insides rebelled. He was pushing to have his way in this, but she couldn't let him – not yet. 'Danny has enough problems at the moment. We must wait until he knows you better and is able to accept the news.'

'Christmas.' Dieter reached out and pushed a strand of fair hair from Danny's eyes. 'I will wait no longer than that.'

As Dieter walked back to the farm, his mind ran over what he had found out today. His son was obviously still a troubled child, but Angie was looking after him well and cared deeply for him. Danny also had a love of music, and that filled him with joy. It had always been so important to him as well. He had taken a chance mentioning Jane, but it had seemed the right thing to do. Danny's reply, that his mother was with the angels, had given Dieter much to think about.

He slowed his pace and absorbed the quiet of the countryside. His mother, father and sister were with the angels and being looked after. It was a comforting way to think of them. His deep breath was ragged with relief. The good memories would always be with him, but a small child had shown him the way to let his family go.

18

'What do you want for breakfast?' Hetty called up the stairs to Danny, who was on the landing. 'Grandpa's brought fresh eggs and some lovely bacon – would you like some?'

'Yes, please, Grandma.' Danny trotted back to Angie in the bedroom. 'Grandpa's here with Dieter.'

'I expect they want Grandma to cook their breakfast as well.'

He nodded, watching her every move as she made the bed. He was still pale, but had slept well, waking only a few times. Once he'd seen she was close by, he'd gone straight back to sleep again. Angie had hardly slept at all, afraid to drift off in case he had a nightmare. Much to her relief he hadn't, and she had high hopes that the fright would soon be forgotten.

Angie laced up his shoes and ruffled his hair. 'Let's go down for breakfast. I'm starving, aren't you?'

He stood up and reached for her hand as they made their way downstairs. 'I like bacon.'

'So do I.' Fortunately he hadn't yet associated fried bacon with the pigs he was so fond of.

'Good morning, everyone.' Angie stopped in the doorway, watching Danny greet them all in his usual affectionate way. 'My goodness, we'll never all be able to eat in here.'

'That's okay.' John was already holding a plate piled high with breakfast. 'Me and Dieter will go in the other room.'

While Danny enjoyed his food a little colour began to seep back into his face.

Dieter and John came back with their empty plates just as there was a thump on the backdoor. It shot open and Emma skidded in, a piece of hedge sticking out of her hair.

'Morning.' She gave them all a brilliant smile. 'Mummy said I've got to tell you that I've had my breakfast.'

Hetty's shoulders were shaking in silent laughter. 'Oh, that's a shame. I've got a slice of bacon left over.'

Emma pursed her lips. ''Spect I could eat that. Can't waste it. Er . . . have you got an egg left over as well?'

'I have.' Hetty broke the egg in the frying pan. 'How about a bit of fried bread?'

'Cor, thanks.' Emma scrambled on to the chair just vacated by Angie.

'Emma!' Sally came in. 'You're not cadging food, are you?'

'I told them like you said,' she protested. 'Mrs Sawyer's got it left over. You're always saying we mustn't waste food 'cos of the rationing.'

'Sit down, Sally.' John was chuckling. 'Would you like some as well?'

'No, thanks.' She pulled a face at her daughter. 'That girl's a bottomless pit where food is concerned.'

Emma smirked as the plate was put in front of her, then she held out one of her precious trains to Dieter. 'Can you fix this? A bit's come off the back.'

Sally gazed up at the ceiling as if praying for divine help. 'Not only does she cadge another breakfast, but now she's bringing her toys here to be mended.'

'It needs fixing.' Emma concentrated on cutting the bacon. It was a tricky job for a three-and-a-half-year-old.

'I can do this.' Dieter sat down and took out his penknife, which had all sorts of attachments on it, and bent to the task. Danny had finished his breakfast and sidled over to watch what he was doing.

'I give up.' Sally threw her hands into the air. 'Why didn't you ask Daddy to mend it instead of bothering Dieter?'

Emma stopped chewing as a look of utter disbelief crossed her face. 'Daddy can't fix anything. You said he couldn't . . . 'nize a booze –'

'Emma!'

'. . . mutter . . . in a brewery.' She popped the last bit of egg in her mouth, looking a picture of innocence. 'Don't know what it means anyway.'

'She's got ears like radar.' Sally was trying to look stern. 'Sorry about that.'

They were all laughing except Dieter. 'I do not know what it means either.'

'I'll tell you later,' John promised.

Having scraped her plate clean, the little girl was now off her chair and leaning on the table the other side of Dieter. After another couple of minutes he handed the train back to her.

'There you are. Good as new.'

'Thanks.' Emma shoved it across to show Danny. 'Look, Deeder's so clever.'

'That's not his name,' Danny snorted in disgust.

''Tis.'

''Tain't.'

Sally groaned.

'Deeder is your name, isn't it?' Emma scowled, offended.

'That's close enough, Princess.'

'There.' She pulled a face at Danny. 'You say it, then.'

'It's Dieter.' He emphasized the 'T'.

'That's what I said.' Obviously satisfied that she was right as always, she said to Angie, 'Is Danny all right now? Can he come and play?'

'If he wants to.'

'I was frightened, that's all.' Danny gave Angie a loving look. 'But it's okay now.'

'Yeah.' Emma smirked. 'I can scream louder than you.'

'Bet you can't.'

Emma took a deep breath and opened her mouth.

Sally clapped her hand over her daughter's mouth. 'Don't you try it! Breathe out slowly.'

The girl was red in the face as she held her breath but did as ordered, very disappointed that she hadn't been able to let out a piercing scream.

Danny was giggling in delight at his friend's antics. 'Let's go and play with your trains.'

Both children ran out the backdoor, completely

ignoring Sally's yell as she tried to make them go in the front way.

Angie was laughing in sheer relief. It had been wonderful to hear Danny bickering with Emma, and then see him tearing off to play.

'Looks like he's over it now.' John was nodding with satisfaction.

'Yes, thank heavens, but I must be more careful in the future.' Angie glanced at everyone in the room. 'Thank you all so much for your help.'

'Think nothing of it, Angie.' Sally was watching the children wriggling through the hedge. 'We're going to have to make that hole larger. I've asked Joe several times, but it takes him ages to do anything. You can't rush into these things, he always says.'

As a rumble of laughter went around the room, Dieter joined Sally at the window. 'I could cut an archway and put a small gate there. That's if your husband would not mind.'

'He'd be delighted.'

'Good. I will do it tomorrow.'

The sheep trotted towards Dieter as he drove the tractor into their field with feed for them. Nearly all of them were starting to show signs of being with lambs. It was going to be a busy time next year. He watched them munching away and shivered as a gust of cold wind ruffled his hair. Nearly December and he could almost smell snow in the air. Perhaps they would have a white Christmas? They would have to get the sheep in if the weather turned really nasty.

A smile touched his lips as he wondered what Danny thought about snow. Did he laugh and tumble and throw snowballs? Had Jane played with him and helped to build a snowman? That thought felt like a physical pain. It was so hard to accept that she was no longer with them, or to forgive himself for the wasted years when he could have been with her and his son.

'Oh, Jane,' he murmured, suddenly sad. 'You should have told me. I would have married you and we could have been a family, even if only for a short time.'

He climbed back on the tractor, started the engine and headed for the gate, his mind still lingering on Danny. What was he going to do now? He wanted so desperately to be a part of his son's life, to tell him that he was his father; but Angie was resisting that – resisting him. It was understandable, of course. She was suspicious of him, and there was no mistaking how much the child loved her. Did she fear that if Danny knew he had a father who loved and wanted him, the boy might be drawn away from her and she would lose him?

That would not happen. After what he had seen yesterday, with Danny clinging to her as if his life depended upon her, he could never take him away from her, but he would not be shut out of Danny's life. He thought she was wrong to insist that they do not tell him yet. It might help to make the boy feel more secure. In his opinion it would have been more sensible to explain who he was as soon as he had arrived from

Germany, but Angie was adamant that it was to be done her way. He was under no illusions about her character. She was strong, determined, and he suspected that her only vulnerability was the child.

Dieter jumped down and closed the gate behind him, standing for a moment drinking in the tranquil scene of sheep grazing, but it did nothing to ease his turmoil. What would happen when they did tell him? Danny would expect him to live with them, as all fathers should. That could not happen, of course. As far as he was concerned, he did not mind what the villagers thought, but Angie would. One thing was certain, though: he was determined to have a hand in bringing up his own son, and if that meant a fight with Angie to exert his rights as a father, then so be it. He had been overjoyed to find that Danny had inherited his love of music. The talent came from his mother's side of the family. How his mother would have loved her grandson, and his darling sister would have spoilt him at every opportunity. It was devastating to know he was never going to see them again. He remembered Danny's words again, and when he thought of Jane and his family with the angels it did ease the pain a little. Angie had shown wisdom when she had told the distressed child that.

Getting back on the tractor, he drove into the yard, parking the vehicle and jumping down. He wandered over to the pigs. Cleaning them out was not his favourite job, but it had to be done.

The next time he managed to see Angie on her own

he must tell her that he intended to support them. He had only his wages from the farm work, but he would try to find another way to make some money. If he was in London or somewhere like that, he would have little trouble earning money playing piano, but nothing was going to make him leave this village.

He clenched his jaw. Danny was going to have a better life than he'd had. If he wanted to play piano for a living, he would make sure the child had the best training available. His talent was not going to be stifled, as his had been. And he prayed the world had learnt its lesson so that the youngsters of today would not be called upon to kill, or to spend years as prisoners.

John looked over the fence. 'I've collected Hetty from Angie's and she's cooking lunch. Ready in half an hour.'

'Right. I've finished here so that will give me time to wash and change.' He wrinkled his nose. 'Not the kind of smell to bring to the meal table.'

With a wave of his hand, John walked away, grinning.

Dieter was ready for lunch within the half an hour. He was already beginning to put on some weight, and feel so much better since he'd been eating regular meals.

'Ah, there you are.' Hetty smiled as he walked into the large farmhouse kitchen. 'Hope you don't mind a simple lunch today. I haven't had time for much, but I've got a nice apple pie for afters.'

Dieter watched as she ladled a rich vegetable stew and dumplings into a bowl and put two large chunks of home-made bread on his plate. He spoke softly, remembering the shortages in Germany. 'Please do not apologize, Mrs Sawyer. This would be several days' rations in Germany.'

Hetty shook her head. 'It's terrible. And that awful blockade of Berlin by the Russians must have been dreadful. Thank heavens that's over now. After you left us we were so worried about you. We could have helped if we'd known where you were.'

Dieter gave a wry grin. 'The Major soon sorted me out with clothes and food. I also received a sharp lecture on how I should stop drifting and come back here. Pull myself together, I think you say in English? I objected to his attitude and we had a big argument. But he was right.'

John helped himself to more stew. 'He wanted to tell you about Danny and Jane, but we swore him to secrecy. We thought it would be better if you came back because you wanted to, and then we would break the news to you gently.'

'We never got the chance, though, because the first person you saw when you arrived was Danny.' Hetty refilled Dieter's plate and gave him more bread. 'That wasn't how we planned it. We were disappointed when Bob wrote and said you were coming to this country to look for your sister, but that it was unlikely you would come to see us. This is where you belong, Dieter.'

'That is true, and I shall now make this country my home. When I discovered that the girl in York was not my sister, I did not know what to do, but I couldn't go

227

back to the life I was leading in Berlin. Then I remembered your kindness and how lovely it was here.'

'It must have been a terrible disappointment to find that she wasn't your sister, but now you have found your lovely son.' Hetty smiled fondly at him.

'Danny will soon grow to love you. You've made good progress with him already, and little Emma also likes you. Did you say you were going to fix the hedge for the children?' John's grin spread. 'Emma's always got a bit of it on her somewhere.'

'I'll do it tomorrow during my lunch break.'

'There's no need for that, Dieter.' Hetty was shaking her head. 'I won't hear of your missing a meal.'

'Go to Angie's after lunch today. There's some spare wood in the barn you can use for a gate.' John nodded to Hetty as she put a slice of apple pie in front of him. 'I'm sure you're anxious to see if Danny has fully recovered.'

Dieter was touched by their kindness and understanding. 'Has Angie ever told you what she had to deal with after Jane died?'

'A little, but I suspect she's held a lot back.' Hetty put the kettle on to make tea. 'But seeing the state Danny was in yesterday made me realize she's had a very difficult time.'

Dieter nodded. 'I thought that also. She is very protective, but she is going to have to let me into his life.'

'She will, just give it time.' John stood up. 'I'm off to mend a couple of broken fences this afternoon.'

'Can I help?' Dieter followed John out to the yard.

'No, I can manage. Make the gate and get it fixed up. You can take the truck.'

'Thank you, Mr Sawyer.'

It didn't take Dieter long, and it was only two o'clock when he loaded the gate and his tools into the truck and headed for the village.

Angie opened the front door as he walked towards it. 'I saw you arrive. Danny's next door with Emma.'

'I've come to fix the hedge. Mr Sawyer has given me time off to do it today. Is the side gate open?'

'Yes.'

'Good. I will take my tools round to the garden that way.' He returned to the truck, unloaded it and carried everything round the back.

Angie met him in the garden and examined the gate admiringly. 'The children will be thrilled with that.'

He smiled at her praise. He had taken a great deal of trouble building it, even carving both their names on the top, Danny's on one side and Emma's on the other. As they were alone, he decided that this would be a good time to talk about Danny's upkeep. He propped the gate up against the hedge and turned to face her.

'I wish to support you and Danny. Please tell me how much to give you each week.'

'That won't be necessary.' Angie gaped in surprise. 'We're managing.'

'That is hardly the point.' He could tell from her face

229

that this was not something she wanted to do, but he would not give in. 'Danny is my son and it is right that I should do this.'

'I don't want to take your money. I know you arrived here with nothing.'

'The only thing I need is to be a part of my son's life.' He gave a dismissive wave of his hand. 'Nothing else is important to me.'

Angie held his gaze with determination. 'I can understand how you feel, but I will not leave you with nothing. Perhaps when you are more settled, we can talk about this again.'

'No. We will settle this now, Angie. I insist on helping to support Danny.' He placed his feet apart and stood firmly, determined not to give way on this point. She said she didn't want to take what little money he had, but he believed it was more than that. Angie Westwood was trying to keep him at a distance, and she would not be able to do that if she took money from him. But he was here and he was Danny's father, and that was something she would have to accept.

'I see.' She chewed her lip, holding his gaze. 'Danny would like two piano lessons a week instead of one, and he is growing so fast clothes need replacing often. I would appreciate your helping with those things, but I cannot allow you to support me as well.'

Dieter nodded. It was a small concession, but it was a start. 'As you wish. I shall pay Mrs Poulton for the lessons and when Danny needs clothes we shall buy them together.'

He could see that she was not happy about this suggestion, but he would not give too much ground. 'Does he urgently need anything now?'

'Well, yes, shoes. The ones he's wearing are a little too small now.'

'Then he must definitely have new. We shall all go to Bridgewater on Saturday to buy them. I shall collect you at ten o'clock. Now I must fix the hedge.' He picked up the gate and walked away, not giving her a chance to object. She was going to find that he could also be determined and stubborn.

For the next hour Dieter worked steadily until he had cut an elegant archway in the hedge, and the gate opened and closed smoothly. He was just packing up the tools when the children erupted out of Sally's back door.

'Deeder,' Emma shouted. 'What a smashing gate.'

Danny beat her to him, his face glowing with pleasure. 'Yippee! We won't have to crawl through the mud any more.'

'Oh, no.' Emma was clearly disappointed at that thought, but she was soon bouncing again. 'Can you give us a push on the swing?'

'Of course. Who is to be first?'

'Me, me,' they both cried.

Dieter winked at Danny. 'Ladies first, I think, don't you?'

Danny giggled. 'Her mum says Em doesn't know how to be a lady.'

'We will pretend she is, shall we?' Dieter spoke softly as they enjoyed the joke, and when he looked down at the little face gazing up at him, he almost wept with joy. Oh, Jane, his heart whispered, you have given me a wonderful son. How sad you will not see him grow to be a man, but I shall, and I thank you for that with all my heart.

He pulled his thoughts back to the children as they enjoyed themselves. 'What a lovely swing,' he said, as Danny clambered on for his turn.

'Uncle Bob did it for us,' Danny shouted, as he was swung high into the air.

'Who is Uncle Bob?' Dieter was puzzled.

'The Major.'

Major Strachan? Now what had he been doing building Danny a swing? Dieter had been under the impression that he had merely been the Sawyers' messenger, but *Uncle Bob* sounded personal. How involved was he with Angie? Oh, Lord, it would be damned difficult if he married Angie. She was young and attractive and was bound to fall in love and marry.

A chill rippled through him. This was something he had not before considered. He did not want another man bringing up his son. The prospect filled him with alarm.

19

'Congratulations, Lieutenant-Colonel, this is a well-deserved promotion.'

Bob saluted the General. 'Thank you, sir.'

'Shame your father can't be here to see this day. Enjoying his retirement, I suppose?'

'Yes, sir. He manages to keep busy, though.'

'I'm sure he does. Never was one for wasting time.' The General gave a wry smile. 'Now, I believe there is to be a celebration this evening.' He raised an eyebrow. 'You're not supposed to know about it, but make sure you're in the bar by eight thirty.'

'I'll look surprised, sir.'

'Good. The first round will be on you.'

'No doubt.' Bob's mouth twitched as he marched away.

Corporal Hunt was waiting for him when he arrived back at his office. He didn't miss the worried frown creasing his driver's forehead. 'I brought your mail along for you, Colonel.'

'Thanks.' Bob flicked through the letters and saw two from Somerset.

'Sir?'

Bob looked up.

'Now you've got your promotion, will they be assigning you another driver?'

He was tempted to have a little fun at Hunt's expense, but he would put him out of his misery. 'You're stuck with me. I wouldn't inflict you on anyone else.'

The frown disappeared in a flash. 'Very wise, sir.'

Bob kept his head down to hide his grin as he slit open the first envelope. The letter was from John and Hetty, giving him all the news about Dieter's arrival. He wasn't surprised to learn that the girl in York hadn't been Dieter's sister. It had been a long shot, but at least it had got Dieter back to England, and he had gone straight to the Sawyers from York. The poor sod must be devastated, though.

'The gentleman's okay, then, sir.'

'You still here?' Bob laid the letter on the desk. 'It seems so. The girl wasn't related to him, and he went to Somerset, as we'd hoped. Would you like to read the letter?'

'That won't be necessary.' Hunt smirked. 'I'm good at reading upside down.'

'Another of your doubtful talents?'

'Quite useful at times.' Hunt pointed to the other unopened letter. 'I'd say that's from the gentleman himself. Got more than a letter inside.'

'Have you steamed it open?'

'No, sir.' The Corporal looked suitably offended. 'From the feel of it, I would say it has money in it.'

Did nothing get past this man's sharp eyes? When Bob opened the letter, he found that it contained a brief note and the money he'd given Dieter for his return fare. The note thanked him, and said that he wouldn't be returning to Germany.

'Ah, an honest man, sir.'

'I must be careful not to read anything of importance while you're around.' Bob felt the urge to laugh but managed to control it.

Hunt was going to hate this next order. 'Go and pack your gear: we're leaving at oh-six hundred hours.'

'Where to, sir?'

'Manoeuvres.'

'Man —' The word died on his lips as a look of panic flitted across his face.

'Yes, you know, where we get to play at being soldiers, digging holes to sleep in, hiding in bushes, crawling through the mud. Things like that.'

'But . . . but, sir, you can't do that. Not with your poor leg. And it might rain . . . or even snow.' The last word came out in a horrified gasp.

Bob was enjoying this. He'd really poked the wind up him. 'I'm touched by your concern, but I shall be in a tank.'

This took Hunt a few seconds to absorb, and then the jaunty expression was back. 'Ah, well, that's different, sir. I can drive a tank.'

'Can you? I didn't know that.'

'If it's got pedals and gears I can drive it.' The Corporal looked smug. 'And you can't drive it, sir . . . Not with your poor leg.'

'Will you stop acting like a mother hen? I'm perfectly fit, as you well know. And leave my leg out of this.'

'Can't do that, sir.' Hunt shook his head, a crafty glint in his eyes. 'It's my job to look after you. You was limping real bad after putting up the kids' swing. Hope the little chap is happy. Nice boy that, and his auntie too, of course.'

'Don't change the subject. We're going on manoeuvres for the next ten days, whether you think I'm up to it or not. Where I go, you go. Now get your kit together. We're leaving at dawn for West Germany. The destination is secret, but why the hell we bother is a mystery to me. The Russians know every move we make.'

Hunt was crestfallen again, not the slightest bit interested in the location of the manoeuvres. 'Ten days?'

Bob nodded and watched his dejected driver start to walk out of the office. 'And don't forget to pack your marching boots, Sergeant.'

Hunt stopped, turned his head and looked over his shoulder. 'What did you say, sir?'

'Don't forget to pack your marching boots.'

'No, sir, after that.'

'Oh, you mean Sergeant.' Bob chuckled. 'You've been promoted as well.'

Hunt spun back to face him. 'That's very good of you. Not that I don't deserve it, of course.'

'I thought you would be less of an embarrassment to me with extra stripes on your sleeve. You would blend in better with a more elevated rank.'

'Very wise, sir.' Hunt was beaming from ear to ear now. 'Perhaps these games won't be so bad, and ten days ain't long.'

'Keep that in mind. The other good news is that we are going on fourteen days' leave over Christmas.'

'That is good news.' The new sergeant's eyes took on a calculating shine. 'Would there be any chance of a flight home, sir?'

'I'll arrange it for both of us. I want to go back as well.'

'If you could summon up a car in England, I could drive you to Somerset. You will be going to Somerset, sir?'

'You won't be on duty. I'll catch the train.' He knew just what Hunt was after.

'It wouldn't be no trouble, sir. I'd like to visit there myself.'

'Would you?' Now there was a surprise. 'In that case I'm sure the landlord's daughter will be pleased to see you. You can book us rooms at the pub for a couple of nights.'

'I'll send a telegram as soon as these *manoeuvres* are over.' He grimaced at the thought of playing soldiers.

'You'd better get off and pack now.' Bob glanced at his watch. 'I've been ordered to attend a surprise party.'

'I'll wake you at oh-five hundred hours, sir. If I can.' The Sergeant was laughing as he left.

'Get your stripes stitched on and you can join us,' Bob called to his retreating back.

'Thank you, but one of us must be in a fit state to get up in the morning.'

'Cheeky sod.'

What a lot of people. Danny trotted along, holding tightly on to Auntie's hand. He was going to get new

237

shoes. Dieter had come along too. He gazed up at the tall man walking on the other side of him. Perhaps he was having new shoes as well?

He was nice. He could play piano smashing, and Em's mum had said he could play the organ in the church. He'd like to hear that. Danny reached up and slipped his hand into Dieter's and was given a nice smile.

They went into a shop, and he sat on a chair while a lady looked at his feet, then brought him a shiny pair of black shoes. She slipped them on him and sat back, smiling. He had a good look at them and wriggled his toes about. He couldn't do that in his others.

'How do they feel?' Auntie asked.

Dieter lifted him off the chair. 'Walk up and down, Danny. See that they are not too tight.'

He walked slowly, head down, never taking his eyes off the shoes. They felt funny, all stiff, but they were nice.

'Are they all right?'

'Yes, Auntie.'

Dieter knelt in front of him and pushed on the toes. 'There's plenty of room for his feet to grow.'

'Good. We'll take those, then.' Auntie made him sit down again and took the shoes off.

'Are you having new shoes as well? Danny asked as Dieter was taking some money out of his pocket.

'Not today, but I'm taking you and Auntie out to lunch when we've done our shopping.'

'Can we have fish and chips?' Danny beamed in

excitement. That was his favourite. 'With lots of salt and vinegar on them?'

'Of course.'

'Oh, good.' What a lovely day they were having.

Angie wasn't happy about Dieter paying for Danny's shoes. Children's clothes were so expensive. Her mothering instincts were telling her to keep him at a distance and not to let him into their lives any more than she could help. But how could she be so cruel? Anyone could see how much he adored his son, and how anxious he was to take on the role of father. She couldn't blame him for that. When she had seen him walking away from John and found out who he was, she had believed it would be hard to like him. But that wasn't true: it was proving all too easy.

She watched him at the cash desk. He was a tall man with a haunted look in his eyes, wearing clothes that had obviously been given to him, along with an army greatcoat. Nothing fitted properly, and yet there was an unmistakable air of dignity about him. He had arrived in this country with only a small bag and the things he was wearing. He had lost his family, home and country. It was impossible to imagine what pain that must have caused him. John would be paying him a farm labourer's wage, and, although she didn't know what that was, it couldn't be much. He couldn't afford to be doing this, but he looked so proud to be buying shoes for his lovely son.

Her eyes clouded. His son. How had he felt when

he'd found out? It must have torn him apart to discover that Jane was dead and she'd had his child. Angie had no idea if he had loved her cousin, or if it had only been a passing attraction for him, but she was certain of one thing: Jane had loved him.

Dieter came back and handed the parcel to Angie, and then he swept Danny up in his arms. 'I think it is time for our fish and chips now, don't you?'

Danny slipped his arm around Dieter's neck and grinned. 'I'm hungry now.'

It always gave Angie a jolt to see them together like this. Danny was a little duplicate of his father. As they walked out of the shop, she said quietly, 'You must let me pay for lunch.'

'I would not dream of allowing you to do such a thing.' He hoisted Danny higher and smiled at her. 'Do not be concerned. I have enough money to pay for this.'

The smile made her heart flutter. His intense grey eyes and flashing dimples were almost identical to Danny's. There were deep shadows in this man's life, as there were in hers, but he had suffered far more, and it showed. Each time she saw him she liked him more.

She nodded agreement to his paying and couldn't help wondering what the future held for the three of them. She was under no illusions that it was going to be easy. There were tough times ahead, and adjustments and compromises to be made by each of them.

They found a fish and chip shop with a few tables in the back of the shop, ordered and sat down.

Once Danny was settled on his chair, he swivelled

round to Dieter, who was sitting next to him. 'Em's mum said you can play the organ.' His expression was animated. 'Can I hear you?'

'I'll ask the Rector if we can go in the church, shall I?'

'Oh, please!'

'I shall also arrange for you to have two piano lessons a week with Mrs Poulton. Would you like that?'

Danny's eyes opened wide as he reached across the table to grab Angie's hand. 'Can I do that? You said we couldn't afford it.'

'Dieter is going to pay for your lessons, darling. He's very impressed with you.'

'Are you?' He shunted back again to face Dieter. 'Do you think I'll be good like you?'

'I am sure you will be better if you try hard and keep it up.'

'I will, I will.' Danny wriggled with pleasure and gazed up at Dieter in admiration.

'Thank Dieter for the lessons, Danny.' She couldn't help wondering if Dieter had been this enthusiastic about music at such a young age. But then she remembered that he'd said he could play almost before he could walk. This was a talent Danny had inherited from him.

'Yeah, thank you.' He knelt on the chair and leant over to kiss Dieter on the cheek, blushing shyly.

Angie was sure she saw tears cloud Dieter's eyes at this show of affection. Her heart ached for him and she wanted to tell Danny at that moment, but there were practical details to be worked out first. Danny obviously liked him and would probably accept him as his father, but what was Dieter going to do? Was he going to stay in this country for the foreseeable future, or did he intend to return to Germany soon? If they told Danny and then he disappeared again, the little boy would be dreadfully upset. Or, even worse, he might try to take Danny back to Germany. That possibility made her feel ill. He had no legal right to do that, of course, as she had adopted him. In a way she wished there was some doubt about his being the father, because fear of what he might do was casting a shadow over her. If only she could be hard-hearted and keep him out of their lives as much as possible, but when she saw them together, she just couldn't do it. He was such a likeable man and she didn't want to doubt him.

She gazed down at her hands and silently prayed for the strength and wisdom to deal with this in the right way. And the only way was what was best for Danny. She was trying so hard to put him first, but her own feelings for Danny kept getting in the way. She loved him so much. But she must not forget one important thing. Jane had trusted her with her son; trusted her to do what was right for him. Her own selfish fears must not get in the way. But, oh, how hard that was proving to be.

'Angie.' Dieter touched her arm. 'Do not let your meal get cold.'

She hadn't even noticed the plate being put in front of her. 'Sorry, I was miles away.'

Dieter was carefully cutting Danny's fish to make sure there weren't any bones, and when he'd finished he looked up and spoke softly. 'Do not be so worried. We shall work it out.'

He'd read her mind. She nodded, picking up her knife and fork to eat a meal she no longer wanted. It was no use ignoring the situation any longer. Dieter was here, he loved his son, and it was time they sat down and discussed what was to be done. 'We must talk.'

Relief showed in his eyes. 'Tonight. We shall talk tonight.'

By seven that evening Danny was so tired he could hardly keep his eyes open and prepared for bed quite willingly. It was often a tussle to get him to bed, for he seemed to have boundless energy, but not tonight.

When he was washed and dressed in his pyjamas, he trotted up to Dieter. 'Night, night. I've had a nice day.'

'And I also. Practise your scales and do as Mrs Poulton tells you. At the end of each week you shall show me what you have learnt.'

'I will.' Danny gave an impish smile. 'You won't forget about the organ, will you?'

'I promise.' Dieter stooped down and received a kiss from Danny.

Two in one day, Angie noticed. It was definitely time to sort out what they were going to do.

As Danny was too tired for a story, she was soon back in the front room. There was a good fire burning, and the room was warm and cosy. So much better than London, she thought as she sat down, sighing deeply. Dieter was watching her every move, his lovely eyes quiet, waiting for her to speak first.

She pitched straight in. 'The thing worrying me most is whether you are going to stay in this country. And I don't mean for a few months, I mean for years. I don't want Danny to find out who you are if you intend to go back to Germany soon.'

'I'm staying here until my son is a grown man.' He waited for her to speak again.

'Will you find that hard to do?'

'I do not believe so. There is nothing for me in Germany. Everything I want is right here.'

That eased her mind a little, but there were still gnawing worries. Was her darling boy too young to understand? 'How often do you want to see Danny?' She immediately regretted the question when she saw his expression change.

'Every day!' He spoke sharply. 'I was denied the first three years of my son's life; I shall not be kept from him a moment more.' He stood up and faced her. 'If you are trying to limit my visits, then I shall not allow it. I do not want to fight you, but I will if I have to.'

'I didn't mean it like that.' Angie was alarmed at his warning; his eyes had turned a stormy grey. 'I only meant that we will need to set aside time for you to be with him. He goes to the church hall twice a week. Two piano lessons a week, and then there are days with John and Hetty. He plays with Emma . . .' She was babbling.

'And I have my work at the farm.' He glared down

at her. 'I shall come every spare moment I have. It does not matter if he is doing something. I will watch.'

Oh, good gracious, she was making a terrible mess of this.

'Would you have been this obstructive if I had been English?'

The question jolted her. 'It wouldn't have made any difference. I'm only concerned about Danny.'

'You lie, Angie.' He sat down again. 'Let us be honest with each other, yes?'

'All right!' He was far too perceptive. 'I'll be honest. In the beginning it knocked me for six when I found out you were German and had been in the Luftwaffe, but that doesn't matter now that I know you better. Jane was only seventeen when she met you. You shouldn't have made her pregnant. That was wrong. Your home is in another country, and you'll want to go back there. I just know it.'

Dieter waited until she ground to a halt, and then said gently, 'I have promised that I will stay in this country. I do not lie about that. I could not leave my son now I have found him. If neither of us can see through these shadows, then we are going to make a lovely boy very unhappy.'

'I know you're right, but it's so hard.' She took a deep breath, trying to still her agitation and fears.

'For me also. Do you not think that I feel shame about Jane? I should never have left her, whatever she said. And when I finally arrived home, do you not think I raged with despair when I saw my home razed to the ground? I was consumed with grief when I could find no trace of my family.' He was leaning forward now, elbows on knees. 'I am not proud of my country's part in the terrible war, or my own, but it is over now and we must put the past behind us.'

'You are right, and you have as much right to be angry as me. The war blighted many lives.'

'The only important one to be considered is a small child who is not responsible for this tragedy. Now, I will see him as often as I wish, and when he is more used to me being around, we shall tell him who I am. That decision I will, reluctantly, leave to you, but it must be soon.'

'Christmas is only three weeks away. We'll all be at John and Hetty's, and that will be the time to tell him. If that's all right with you?'

'I agree.' Dieter stood up. 'Now you must rest.'

As soon as she heard the front door close, Angie curled into a tight ball in the armchair, exhausted. She hadn't meant to say all those things, but they had just poured out. He was right. If they couldn't put aside the past, there wasn't much hope for the future.

20

The large barn was leaking badly, and Dieter was on the roof, where he could see that it needed extensive repairs. He sat astride the ridge and looked down at John as he appeared at the top of the ladder.

'You stay there, Mr Sawyer. Slide the planks of wood up to me and I will fix them in place.'

'Be careful.' John frowned. 'Doesn't look any too safe up there.'

Dieter tested a section with his foot, but it held firm. 'It is not too bad where I am. The trouble is right in front of me. That is where the rain is getting in. The roof is rotten just there.'

John swore fiercely. 'I should have checked it before winter set in.'

'Well, if it stays dry for a few hours we should be able to make it watertight.' Dieter peered up at the grey sky, threatening heavy rain. 'We will have to work quickly, though.'

With another muttered curse, John disappeared, and Dieter shoved his hands in his pockets to keep them warm while he waited. There was a biting wind whistling around him in this exposed position. He gazed across the fields and let his mind wander. Christmas would soon be here, and he was looking forward to spending more time with his son. He wanted to give Danny and Emma a present, but he didn't have much money left after yesterday, so he would make them something. Quite a few of the prisoners in the camp had made wooden toys for the local children, and he was sure he could still do it. The last one he'd made had been the little truck, and as Jane had loved the toy he had let her keep it. He sighed deeply. Little had he known she was going to have a son who would also love the toy. It had brought back many memories when he had seen it on Danny's bedside table, but also pleasure to know how much he treasured it. He would make Danny a car this time, and perhaps a dolls' house for Emma. Oh, dear me, no. He chuckled. She was a pretty girl, but she didn't seem to have any interest in girls' toys. He had better make her a station house, or a control box for her train set. Yes, that would please her more.

John cut off his musing by appearing at the top of the ladder again, hauling up a stack of planks on a rope. 'I've told Hetty to keep lunch for us later. We'll never finish before the light fades if we stop to eat.'

Blowing on his hands first to bring some life back into them, Dieter reached out to catch the rope John had thrown to him. Tied in a bag on the stack of wood was a hammer and nails. It was a shame they had to do this today, when Danny and Angie were here for their Sunday visit, but it couldn't be helped. There had been quite a gale blowing last night, and that had ripped away some of the rotten roof. With more bad weather threatened, it had to be done immediately.

Holding nails in his mouth, he edged forward and began to hammer. It was a long job and by the time the last plank was in place the light was fading fast. The days were so short at this time of year. He was looking forward to the spring. He would take Danny out to many places. Perhaps they would get bicycles and ride around the country lanes. They would have fun together.

'Come down now,' John called.

'Just a moment more.' Dieter stretched out until he was almost flat, checking to see if the roof was secure.

'You can't see what you're doing now.' John held on to the ladder they had laid across the roof to enable Dieter to climb to the top.

'I'm coming.' He rested both feet on the top rung and edged his way down to John.

'Good lad.' John caught his ankles and guided him to the same ladder he was on. 'You can leave that one on the roof. It's tied securely. We'll take it down some other time.'

Once on the ground they went into the barn and shone torches up to inspect the repairs.

'Looks good.' John patted Dieter on the back. 'That's enough for today. You've done a grand job, and you've hardly seen Danny.'

'That is true, but you did let me have time off yesterday so we could go to buy him new shoes.'

'And he's real proud of them.' John became serious. 'If you're short of money —'

Dieter shook his head. 'I shall manage on what you

pay me, Mr Sawyer. I am going to see if I can get work playing piano in the evenings. I wish to pay back the money you gave me.'

'We don't want it back.' John waved away the suggestion. 'Now, let's go in, I'm starving.'

Dieter followed. They might not want to be repaid, but he owed them a debt. They would get their money in full, along with his gratitude for their kindness to him. It was the least he could do. The Rector had asked him to play the organ at the Carol Concert three days before Christmas, but he would not take payment for that. He would make inquiries in Bridgewater; there should be something there.

'Ah, there you are at last.' Hetty came into the kitchen just as they arrived. 'Sit yourselves down. You must be famished. Just wash your hands. Don't bother changing.'

'We're filthy,' her husband protested.

She eyed them up and down. 'When is that a novelty working on a farm?'

John winked at Dieter and spun a chair out from the table so he could sit down. 'Looks like we've been let off a wash and brush up tonight.'

Dieter sat down just as Danny came in.

'I saw you on top of the barn.' He scrambled on to a chair beside Dieter. 'It's very high. Was you scared?'

'No, I used to go higher than that in an aeroplane.' Dieter began to eat the meal Hetty had placed in front of him. He was famished.

'Did you drive it?'

'I was a navigator. I used to tell the pilot where to go.'

'Would he have got lost without you?'

'Definitely.' Dieter's smile died when he saw Angie glaring at him from the doorway. He sighed inwardly. She still did not trust him. All he was trying to do was feed Danny bits of information so he would know something about his father.

Dieter held her gaze, daring her to protest, but she remained silent.

'Do you want a cup of tea, Angie?' Hetty said, putting out the cups.

She nodded and sat next to John.

Danny was now kneeling on his chair and leaning towards Dieter. 'Is it good in an aeroplane?'

'Sometimes, but it is not so good when someone is trying to shoot you down.'

'Boom, boom, like that?' Danny's eyes were wide. 'Who was shooting at you?'

'Spitfires.' He heard Angie draw in a deep breath, but he didn't look up. Danny had to know he was German. It would give him time to get used to the idea. Dieter knew he was taking a chance, but this was the perfect opportunity, while the people who loved Danny surrounded him.

'Why would they do that?' He looked puzzled.

'Because I was in a German bomber. War makes ordinary people do terrible things, whatever nationality they are. I am German, Danny.'

This seemed to take a bit of working out, and Danny

chewed his lip in concentration. 'Is that why you talk funny?'

Dieter nodded. There hadn't been any adverse reaction to the news, and he was pleased.

'Did you drop bombs?'

'Yes, just as the RAF and Americans dropped bombs on my home.' Dieter laid his knife and fork down. 'War is a terrible thing, Danny, but it's all over now, and we are friends once again.'

'Yeah.' Danny nodded vigorously, then tipped his head to one side. 'Did they shoot you?'

'They did and I came down on a parachute. I was put in a prisoner-of-war camp near here.'

His little face became serious. 'Did you meet my mummy here?'

'I did, and she was lovely.'

'I loved her.' Danny's eyes filled with tears for a moment, and just as quickly disappeared. He peered at Dieter's plate. 'Are you gonna leave that tato?'

Dieter pierced it with his fork and popped it into the little boy's mouth.

Danny chewed, swallowed and grinned. 'Will you play the piano now?'

'Of course.' He helped Danny off the chair and they went into the front room.

As soon as they left the kitchen, Angie sagged in relief. All her worrying, and Danny had accepted it just like that. No questions, no upset, nothing, only curiosity. But then why would he react any differently? He was a child born after the war, and innocent. He was part of a new generation who were not tainted with the memories or prejudices of their elders. Pray God they stayed that way.

'Are you all right?' Hetty touched her hand.

She looked up with a smile. 'Oh for the uncomplicated mind of a three-year-old.'

'It was far better for Danny to find out from Dieter than to run the risk of someone else telling him.' John lifted his head as the sound of music echoed through the house. 'When are you going to tell Danny that Dieter is his father?'

'Christmas.' Angie worried her bottom lip. 'I'm dreading it. How is Danny going to take the news?'

'Much like he did today, I expect. Only with more joy.' Hetty was clearing the table and stopped what she was doing for a moment. 'He already likes Dieter.'

'I know he does, and that's a relief.' Angie clasped her hands together tightly. 'But once he's been told, it could cause more difficulties. Is he going to understand why Dieter doesn't live with us, like Emma's father lives with her?'

Hetty's glance was compassionate. 'This is only a problem because Jane decided not to tell Dieter about the baby. That is the legacy we have to deal with, and it can't all be smoothed out in an instant. But Dieter is a fine man; he will respond to Danny's concerns calmly and kindly. It isn't going to be easy on any of you, but it can be done. It must be done.'

'I know. I just wish I had your confidence.'

*

Later that night Angie tossed and turned, unable to sleep. She was glad she wasn't dealing with this on her own in London. Here she had friends around her who were more than willing to help all they could. She was very grateful for that, because Dieter was a most unsettling man.

Swinging her legs out of bed, she stood up, put on her dressing gown and made her way quietly downstairs. She would make herself a cup of tea.

Angie sipped her tea, deep in thought. She wanted to know more about Dieter. How had he dealt with those years as a prisoner of war? It must have been terrible for a young man of just twenty to have found himself behind barbed wire for an indefinite time, all normal life cut off. Then, as the war ended, he had heard about the destruction of his country, and particularly of his home. What anguish that must have caused him. She was beginning to understand why Jane hadn't told him she was pregnant. Dieter had had to go home; there was no question about it, and she might have done the same thing if she'd been in her cousin's position. He would have been frantic about his family, and Jane knew she might die and the baby never be born. What a dilemma her young cousin had faced; and, although her decision did not seem right now, Jane had done what she felt she had to at the time. No one could fault her for that.

She covered her face with her hands. Oh, dear Lord, what an awful situation they had both faced. And with such courage. She straightened up and lifted her head.

She must stop thinking about herself – what she might lose. Her fears were selfish shadows, and if she didn't learn to overcome them, she was going to cause all of them more pain. Whatever the rights and wrongs of things, it was essential to put the past aside and concentrate on the future. The war had happened, and nothing could change that. Young men had been torn from their families and put in a situation where it was kill or be killed. She prayed that their sacrifices had made the world a safer place for the generation to come. Children like Danny and Emma must never have to face the grief and heartache caused by total war.

She stood up and climbed the stairs. Once back in bed she stared up at the ceiling. She really would try to be more understanding. From now on she would treat Dieter with respect, and encourage Danny to get to know his father. Christmas was only three weeks away, and that would be the time to tell him. She had nothing to lose and everything to gain by seeing her darling boy happy.

21

It was chaos in the church hall, with all the children shouting at the tops of their voices, trying to outdo each other. Danny was rolling on the floor, yelping as Emma tried to get a brightly coloured ball from him. The little girl wasn't having much luck, because, although there were only about three months between them, Danny was beginning to shoot up. He was going to be tall, Angie thought with pride, smiling as she watched their antics.

Suddenly Danny let the ball go, clambered to his feet and rushed towards the door. Angie turned and saw Dieter catch him, swinging him high in the air. Here was someone else who was changing before her eyes, she noted. He was bigger, stronger and in much better health since he had been working at the farm and eating Hetty's cooking.

Danny whispered in Dieter's ear and he nodded, walking over to the Rector. After exchanging a few words, Dieter put Danny down and came over to her.

'I promised Danny that he could hear the organ. The Rector has given me permission to go to the church now.'

'Oh, I can't get away at the moment.' As soon as the words were out of her mouth she knew she'd made a big mistake.

Dieter's mouth tightened as he studied her face intently. 'There is no need for you to come if you are busy. My son will be quite safe with me,' he added softly so that only she could hear.

'Of course.' She smiled down at Danny. 'Enjoy yourself, darling. I'll try to come along later.'

As they walked out the door, Angie cursed vehemently under her breath. Damn, damn! What had she decided last night? Wasn't she going to stop being fearful and selfish? She was pathetic.

'Where's Danny gone?' Emma was pulling at her skirt. 'Why didn't Deeder take me too?'

Angie stooped in front of the very hurt-looking little girl. 'They've only gone next door to the church. Dieter is going to show Danny the organ.'

'Oh.' She didn't look quite so cross now. 'He likes music.'

'Yes, he does, and everyone says he's going to be very good when he grows up.'

''Spect he will.' A gleam of something like pride shone in her eyes. 'I'm gonna marry him when I've growed.'

'My goodness.' Angie just managed to stop herself from laughing out loud. 'Does Danny know about that?'

She nodded and smirked. 'I told him.'

'And what did he say?'

'He said to stop being daft.' Her grin was confident. 'But he'll see.'

'And once she makes up her mind she always gets what she wants.' Sally had been standing behind

Angie, and they both began to shake with helpless laughter.

Just then there was a lull in the noise and the sound of the organ could be heard. The Rector tipped his head to one side. 'Oh, my, just listen to that sound. That dear boy makes our organ sound magnificent. Oh, my, beautiful, beautiful.' Turning on his heel, he hurried out.

'Mummy, Deeder's playing, so can we go and listen?' Emma was jumping up and down.

'But you've always said you don't like music.'

'Danny likes it, so I like it now.'

'Ah, well.' Sally grinned at Angie. 'That's true love for you.'

'Can we go, Mummy?' Emma was getting impatient.

'Give us ten minutes and we'll all go.'

'He might stop by then. I'll go now.'

Sally just managed to grab her daughter as she charged towards the door. 'Oh, no you don't. You'll wait for me, Emma. If you go, you'll have to be very quiet, no running around and making a noise.'

'Why?'

Sally sighed. 'Because Danny will want to listen. You know how still he sits when there's music on the wireless.'

Emma drew a circle on the floor with the toe of her shoe, and then looked up, a picture of innocence. 'I can be quiet.'

Sally muttered under her breath, 'That's news to me.'

*

Fifteen minutes later they stepped into the church and Angie stopped in utter amazement. The Rector was in one of the choir pews, eyes closed and an expression of complete bliss on his face. Danny was next to him, absolutely still, with his gaze fixed on Dieter. Nor was the rest of the church empty. There were men in working clothes, women with shopping baskets, even one or two teenagers. It looked as if the glorious music had enticed in quite a few people.

Sally held her finger to her lips as Emma started to fidget. They slid into the back pew and settled down to listen.

Dieter was lost in playing, and Angie was sure he wasn't even aware that he had an audience. He was playing classical music, and she was sorry she didn't know anything about it, as it was so lovely. As she watched, all the lingering doubts melted away, and her heart went out to the talented man. How sad that he had never been allowed to pursue a musical career. Then the war had come and robbed him of his youthful years. It could have blighted his life, but she could see now that he had inner strength.

The organ roared, filling the small church with breathtaking sound. A smile touched Dieter's mouth at that moment, and she understood what solace he gained from making music.

Sally wiped away a tear, and even Emma was quiet – only she was watching Danny, not the organist.

The next twenty minutes were the most relaxing, healing moments Angie had had since Jane's death. She seemed to ride on the sound, feeling the tension and worry melt away.

When the music stopped, Dieter bowed his head as if willing himself to come back to the real world again, and there was a stillness in the church you could almost taste. When applause rippled from those present, Dieter lifted his head, startled at the sound. He acknowledged it with a slight bow of his head and stood up.

Danny was the first to reach him, with the Rector right behind.

'That was wonderful.' Sally smiled at her daughter. 'You were a very good girl. Now you can go to see Dieter.'

Emma was off before her mother had stopped speaking, running full pelt down the aisle.

Everyone wanted to thank Dieter, so Angie and Sally waited until they had all left, then made their way down to the organ.

'Ah.' The Rector beamed when they approached. 'I hope you're all coming to the Carol Concert. We're in for a real treat, with this dear boy playing for us. Such talent, such sensitivity. Ah, yes, a real feast.' He wandered off, still muttering under his breath with a huge smile on his face.

'Wasn't that good, Auntie?' Danny's eyes were glowing as he gazed at Dieter in wonder. 'The organ's got three lots of keys and knobs to pull out. An' there's all things on the floor. Not just two pedals but lots.'

Angie smiled down at his excited face. 'It was really lovely, darling.'

Emma had nipped across to have a look at the organ,

and came back with a puzzled expression on her face. She tugged at Dieter's sleeve. 'Deeder, how did you make all that noise come out of that?'

'It wasn't noise, Emma.' Sally corrected her daughter firmly. 'You make noise. Dieter makes music. There's a big difference.'

The little girl screwed up her face and tipped her head back to look up at Dieter. 'I can sing music.'

Danny giggled and received an offended glare from his friend.

'You must sing for me sometime.' Dieter's shoulders were shaking in silent mirth.

Sally looked appalled. 'Oh, I don't think you'll want to hear that, Dieter.'

He schooled his expression. 'I'm sure Emma's very good. I shall look forward to it, and I shall accompany her on the piano.'

Now Emma looked smug and she gave Danny a shove. 'There. Bet you can't sing.'

'Bet I can.'

Gurgling with laughter, the two children began to chase each other round the pews with Sally in hot pursuit, growling that this was a house of God and not a playground.

When they disappeared out of the door, Angie turned to Dieter. 'I really enjoyed that, but I'm afraid I don't know anything about classical music.'

'I shall be pleased to teach you, if you wish.'

'Thank you.' Angie suddenly felt shy, which was surprising, because it was something she had never been prone to. They were alone in the church, and he was standing rather close. 'Erm . . . would you like to have lunch with us?'

'Thank you, I would like that very much.'

He gave his usual slight bow that she found so appealing. He was always so polite.

'Let us go and find the children, shall we?' He placed a hand under her arm, and they walked out together.

Sally appeared from behind a bush, panting and holding each child firmly. She was still grinning. 'Heaven help us. By the time we've finished rehearsals for the Nativity Play this afternoon, we'll be exhausted.'

'Do I *have* to cuddle that dolly, Mummy?' Emma scowled. 'Can't we have a teddy bear instead?'

'No, you can't. If you don't want to play Mary, say so now and we'll find someone else.'

Emma kicked a stone and sighed.

Bending down, Angie tried to help Sally with her disgruntled daughter. 'Jesus was a little baby boy, so you must have the dolly. It wouldn't be right with the teddy bear.'

'S'pose.'

'Danny's going to be Joseph. That's Mary's husband.' Angie wanted to laugh when she saw Emma's expression change at that piece of news.

'I'll be Mary, then.' She looked hesitantly at her mother. 'Can I just rock the dolly in the cot?'

'No, this is the Rector's play and he wants you to hold it, but only for a little while when the Three Wise Men give their gifts. Then you can put it back.'

Another stone went tumbling along the path. 'S'pose that'll be all right. Long as they don't take too long.'

'A small concession,' Sally muttered under her breath. 'Though I really don't know what she's got against dolls. Now we'd better all get moving if we're going to be back at the hall by two.'

It didn't take long to cook sausages and mash for their lunch. Angie had made an apple pie the night before, and she popped that into the oven to warm through.

Dieter was in the front room with Danny, playing the Moonlight Sonata. She knew that one. Pausing for a moment, she listened, picturing Dieter's head bowed over the keys and Danny sitting entranced. He never seemed to tire of hearing Dieter play, and the poor man was continually being dragged towards the piano. She waited until he had finished playing another piece, then called them for lunch.

They both appeared immediately.

'Oh, good.' Danny sat down. 'Sausages and mash. I like that, don't you, Dieter?'

'My favourite.'

'What was that last piece you played?' Angie put the meal in front of them and sat down herself.

'*Liebesträume* by Liszt.' Dieter picked up his knife and fork. 'Did you like it?'

She nodded. 'It was beautiful.'

'Yeah.' Danny beamed at them both. 'Mrs Poulton's gonna start learning me a tune next week.'

'Teach,' Angie corrected gently. 'Mrs Poulton's going to teach you.'

He nodded and chewed on a piece of sausage. 'She teaches, and I learn. Is that right?'

'Yes, darling, that's the right way round.' It was amazing: he never seemed to mind being corrected. If you tried that with Emma, you would end up in a fierce argument.

'What's it like in Germany?' Danny made a lightning change of subject.

'It is in chaos at the moment, but in a few years it will be beautiful again. One day I will take you to see the rivers, forests, and we will visit grand concert halls and listen to the finest artists.' A brief look of sadness crossed his face, but it was soon gone and he smiled at Danny. 'You will see how lovely it is.'

'Smashing. We'll take Auntie Angel with us as well, won't we?'

'Of course, we would not go without her.'

He nodded and cleared the last bit of mash from his plate. 'Is it a long way? Could we go in an aeroplane?'

'I expect so, but we shall have to see when the time comes.'

'Okay.' Danny looked at his empty plate and then at Angie. 'Have we got afters, Auntie?'

'Yes, there's an apple pie.' She stood up, cleared the empty plates away and took the pie out of the oven. It looked really appetizing. Her pastry had improved since she had been living here and doing more cooking. John had set aside a small field for fruit trees and the apples were lovely.

Danny watched as she cut three slices, put them on plates and handed them round. He had his spoon ready. 'This is a lovely day.'

'It is,' Dieter agreed, giving his son a gentle smile. 'And it is not over yet. You have the rehearsals this afternoon for the Nativity Play.'

'Can you come and watch?'

'No, I'm sorry, Danny. I have to go back to the farm as soon as I have eaten this wonderful pie. But I shall look forward to seeing it later.'

Danny gazed at his plate, and reluctantly decided he couldn't manage another mouthful. 'I'm full, Auntie. Can we keep that for my tea?'

'Of course. I'll put it in the larder for you.'

'Thanks.' He swivelled round to look at Dieter. 'You really gonna let Emma sing?'

'I promised.' Dieter glanced at Angie and winked. 'Have you heard her?'

'Yeah.' He scrunched up his face.

'Is she any good?'

'She's loud.'

Angie had to concentrate on her pie in an effort to remain quiet, when she was really bursting to giggle. Such a girlish thing to do, but she felt unusually light-hearted all of a sudden. Danny was discussing this so seriously with Dieter. It was good he had a man to talk to. For the first time since he had arrived, she was glad he was here. It hadn't taken long for his quiet patience to drive out her shock. But though he gave the impression of being a gentle man, it would be a mistake to take that for weakness. Under that gentlemanly exterior was a strong and forceful personality.

'In that case she should be able to make herself heard in the church. Perhaps we should ask her to sing at the Carol Concert?'

Danny's mouth dropped open.

'I think that's a lovely idea.' Angie smiled broadly. 'Sally and Joe would be so proud.'

Dieter stood up. 'I shall ask her. Now, if you will excuse me, I have to return to my work. Thank you for an excellent meal.' He ruffled Danny's hair, bowed to Angie and walked out.

'Do you think he'll get Em to sing?' Danny looked very doubtful about that idea.

'I really don't know. What do you think?'

'Nah, she won't do it.' Danny shook his head.

'Oh, what a shame.'

They both collapsed in a fit of the giggles.

22

A week before Christmas and Angie was nervous. The Nativity Play was at six tonight, and the last two weeks had been a mixture of hilarity, frustration and a certain belief that this was not going to work. But whether the children were ready or not – and Angie believed it was *not* – the play was being performed this evening.

Sally and the Rector seemed unconcerned, but Angie had never been involved in anything like this before and really didn't know what to expect. All the children were very young.

There was a rap on the back door and Sally peered in. 'Hi, Angie, can I scrounge a cup of tea?'

'Of course.' Angie put the kettle on. They had become good friends since moving here, and she loved Sally's bubbly nature. You were always sure of a laugh when she was around.

'Lovely, thanks, I'm gasping.' She plonked herself in a chair. 'I've come to ask if you'll give a hand with the chairs this afternoon.'

'Sure.' Angie poured them both a cup of strong tea and joined her friend at the table. 'It will give me something to do and take my mind off worrying about tonight.'

'You don't have to worry.' Sally ladled two spoons

of sugar into her tea. 'All the parents are so proud to see their kids on stage that the odd disaster or two doesn't matter. In fact it adds to the fun.'

'Hope Emma and Danny don't start arguing.' Angie pulled a face. Rehearsals had been difficult, with Emma trying to tell Danny what to do – as well as anyone else she thought needed putting right. When Sally pointed out that the Rector was in charge and they all had to do as he said, Emma declared that she was only trying to help.

'Once she has an audience in front of her, she'll be as good as gold.' Sally tipped her head to one side, listening. 'Danny's practising, I hear.'

'He does his lessons faithfully and doesn't seem to mind the discipline or time it takes to learn something. It never ceases to amaze me that a child so young can be that dedicated.'

'Hmm, Dieter must have been like that.' Sally spoke softly. 'Are you going to tell him soon? They get on well together.'

'Yes, they do. We've decided to tell Danny on Christmas Day, when we're all at John and Hetty's.'

'Good, then we can talk about it openly. Everyone has guessed, Angie.'

'That isn't difficult when you see them together. They're like two peas in a pod.' Angie gave her friend a smile. 'Where's Emma? You haven't left her alone, have you?'

'No fear. She's gone with Joe to do her Christmas shopping.'

'Has Dieter managed to persuade her to sing at the Carol Concert?'

'No, she's flatly refused. I think he was quite disappointed, and so was Joe, but no amount of coaxing will make her change her mind.'

'Ah, never mind. It's going to be a good get-together tonight, isn't it?' she said wistfully. Angie gave a deep sigh as sadness crept into her thoughts. 'We're going to miss Jane dreadfully, but it will be a blessing to have so many friends around us. And Danny is being kept too busy to think about it at the moment. He's bound to miss his mum, though, and so will I. Do you know, Sally, this will be the first Christmas we haven't been together since Jane was born?'

Sally gave Angie's hand a sympathetic squeeze. 'It's hard, I know, but on Christmas Day Danny will find out that he has a father. That will be a great joy to him.'

'I'm sure you're right, but I can't help being apprehensive.'

'That's only natural, so don't upset yourself over it. I'm sure everything will be all right.'

Angie brushed away the worry, sat up straight and smiled. 'Of course it will.'

Checking that everything was ready, Angie stepped back from the table. She had cheese sandwiches, bread, butter and a sponge cake with some of Hetty's home-made plum jam as a filling. The sponge had risen nicely, and she was quite proud of it.

She glanced at the clock and saw that it was nearly

three, so she called upstairs, where Danny was happily drawing in his bedroom. He seemed to like having short times on his own. John, Hetty and Dieter would be here in half an hour. She was helping Sally and the Rector get the children ready for the play, which meant that she would have to be at the hall by five. It would be a hectic hour before the curtain went up, and then they would see if all the hard work had paid off. No one appeared to believe it would be anything but a resounding success. A smile hovered on her lips when she remembered the chaos some of the rehearsals had been. But what did it matter? She had never had so much fun.

There was a sound behind her, and she turned to find Danny had wandered into the kitchen. 'Oh, there you are. I was just coming to get you.'

He stood on tiptoe to look on the table. 'What a lot of tea.'

'Your granny, grandpa and Dieter are coming to tea, then they're all coming to the play.'

He nodded and yawned, making her laugh. There wasn't any sign of nervousness about tonight. 'Come on, let's get you changed, ready for tonight.'

They made it with only five minutes to spare. Danny had just gone into the front room to watch for them out of the window when he yelled, 'They're here!'

Everyone enjoyed the tea Angie had prepared, and it didn't seem any time at all before they had to go to the church hall. When Sally, Joe and Emma arrived, Angie considered the pile of washing-up and was waved away from the sink by Hetty.

'I'll see to this. You get off.'

John pushed back his chair and stood up. 'And us men will just have time for a beer to steady our nerves. You'll join us, Joe?'

'Good idea, thanks.' He held his hands out, pretending to shake with fright.

'Just a minute,' Hetty called as they tried to disappear into the front room. 'You'll only have one each. I don't want you turning up reeking of drink.'

'Don't worry.' John winked at Angie. 'We've only got time for one. The rest we'll save for later.'

'Come on, Mummy.' Emma tugged at Sally impatiently. 'We'll be late. We've got to get dressed up an' everything.'

A quarter of an hour before the play would start. Angie and Sally joined the others in the main hall and collapsed on their seats. The place was already full, and there was an excited buzz of conversation and laughter. It was a nice dry, clear evening, and it looked as if everyone in the village had come.

'Is everything ready?' Dieter asked Angie.

She mopped her brow. 'As ready as it will ever be. The Rector's in charge now.'

The curtain opened, cutting off all further conversation, except for the ahs of the audience as they saw the little children in their costumes. Some were so fascinated by the audience that they forgot what they were supposed to do, and had to be prompted by the Rector until they took their right places. The audience loved

271

it, and Angie was aware of Dieter shaking with quiet amusement beside her. The Rector was narrating the story, so fortunately there wasn't a lot of dialogue. All went reasonably well until one of the Wise Men refused to part with his gift. Emma, clearly fed up with holding the doll, snapped, 'Put it down!'

He threw it at her feet and stormed off in a huff, only to be led back by the Rector. The little boy was clutching another parcel, with an expression on his face that said he was jolly well going to keep this one.

The curtain came down to thunderous applause, and the children poured off the stage, making for their families to receive the expected praise.

Emma and Danny went tearing past them towards someone at the back of the hall, their long robes flowing behind them.

'Uncle Bob!'

Both children threw themselves into the arms of Robert Strachan.

'My word, what a welcome.' He crouched down and scooped them up.

'Did you see us?' Emma had her arms around his neck.

'I did, and you were both excellent.'

Danny beamed at his praise. 'Are you back for good now?'

'No, I'm only here for a couple of days.' He put the children down again.

'Ow.' Emma was disappointed. 'We was gonna ask you to build us a see-saw.'

'I'll do that next time I'm on leave.' Bob shook hands with John and Hetty, then bent his head and kissed Angie on the cheek. 'You and Danny are looking well.'

'So are you.' Angie studied his uniform. 'Promotion?'

'Yes.' He grinned as Danny gave him a smart salute, which he returned.

'Are you a general now?'

'I'm a lieutenant-colonel, and that's one up on a major.'

'I bet you're gonna be a general one day.' Danny gazed at his smart uniform in admiration, swinging on his hand and beaming with pleasure at seeing him. 'Did you come in your big car?'

'Of course.'

As everyone crowded round Bob, Dieter watched with narrowed eyes. Danny appeared to be much too fond of Strachan, and the kiss Angie had been given troubled him. It looked as if there was more than friendship between them. If that was so, then it could be a problem. He didn't begrudge Angie happiness, but army wives followed their husbands around the world, and that meant Danny would go as well. He couldn't bear for that to happen. This obvious affection between Angie and the Colonel was deeply worrying. He had to find out just how serious their relationship was.

'Dieter.' Bob came over to him. 'I'm sorry you didn't find your sister, but I'm glad you came here after all.'

They shook hands. 'Congratulations on your promotion, Colonel.'

Bob gave a brief nod in acknowledgement. 'I must say you look a lot better than you did the last time I saw you.'

'Good food and finding Danny has made all the difference.' Dieter placed a possessive hand on his son's shoulder.

'Uncle Bob.' Danny tipped his head back to look up. 'Dieter can really play the piano, and the organ.'

'Yes, I know. I've heard him. How are you getting on with your own lessons?'

'Mrs Poulton says I'm doing good, but it's gonna take a long time before I can play properly. I don't mind, though, 'cos it's fun.'

'Children!' Sally clapped her hands. 'Let's get you out of those costumes; then we can go home and have a party.'

John rubbed his hands in anticipation. 'You'll join us, Bob?'

'I'd love to.'

Sally and Angie took the children backstage to get changed, which didn't take more than five minutes. Then they all went back to Angie's cottage.

Miraculously, food appeared from the back of the truck, along with beer and even a bottle of whisky.

'My goodness, Hetty, when did you do all this?' Angie got out plates and glasses.

'This morning. It didn't take long, and I thought we'd all have a nice time after the play.'

The small front room was packed, but no one appeared to mind. The men stood, the women sat and the children ran around from person to person.

As soon as the opportunity presented itself, Dieter cornered the Colonel. He needed to talk to him.

'I gather you haven't told Danny yet.' He handed Dieter a glass of beer.

'No, we are going to do that at Christmas.' Dieter couldn't waste time. 'Forgive me for being rude, Colonel, but I wish to know if there is something serious between you and Angie?'

Bob's eyebrows lifted. 'I consider that an impertinent question.'

Dieter bowed his head in apologetic agreement. 'It is something I must know. I have just found a son I didn't know I had and will not allow anyone to take him away from me.'

'And you think I'd do that?' Bob was clearly annoyed. 'Damn it, man, I was the one who tried to make you come here. I wouldn't separate a man from his child.'

'You could not help it. If Angie became your wife, she would go everywhere with you. If that were to happen, I would lose my son. Do you know what that would do to me?'

'Yes, it would be more than you could stand. But Angie will marry some day. If not me, then someone else.'

'I know that well, but I want to be a part of my son's life, to watch him grow into a man. I cannot do that if he is taken away.'

Bob's mouth straightened into a firm line at Dieter's vehemence. 'Perhaps you want her for yourself?'

'She would never consider me as a husband. Oh, she is polite and outwardly friendly, but I see the shadows in her eyes when she looks at me. I am a German, and, although she denies that it matters, she does not easily forget that her parents were killed in the bombing.'

'You misjudge her!' Bob snapped. 'She would act the same with anyone who was Danny's father. Her reticence is merely her concern for the child. It has nothing to do with your nationality.'

'I wish I could be that sure, but I can't. So, I need to know, Colonel.'

'Call me Bob, for heavens sake! I can't answer your question. I had vowed never to marry again, but, if I do change my mind, it will be to someone like Angie. If it weren't for you and Danny, I think I would consider marrying Angie now, but I'm not a fool. I know the situation is hellishly complicated.' Bob gazed at Angie, who was on the other side of the room, then back at Dieter. 'I can't tell you what I'm going to do because I don't know myself.'

Dieter nodded. 'Thank you for your candour, but it does not make me feel any easier.'

'Dieter!' Hetty called. 'Play us some Glenn Miller tunes.'

'Of course.' He put his untouched beer down and sat at the piano. He could do no more at the moment. The Colonel obviously didn't have any immediate plans, but the worry niggled at Dieter. It wasn't just the thought of another man bringing up his son, though that was bad enough; it was the realization that he was jealous of the affection between Angie and the Colonel – he couldn't call him Bob. He didn't know why he was so jealous every time he saw them together. He kept telling himself it was because he was afraid of losing his son. He admired her, but he wasn't in love with her. The idea was ridiculous.

'"In the Mood", Dieter,' Sally called, pushing Joe into the middle of the room so they could jive.

His hands swept over the keys, and he began to play the request, pushing his troubled thoughts away as the lively tune filled the room.

There really wasn't enough room to jive, so they paired off in couples and just shuffled round the floor. Angie danced with Bob, Joe and John as they all changed partners continually. There was a great deal of laughter as Dieter swung from one lively tune to another. He could play anything, and he blessed the talent. It had helped him through many troubled years.

The party broke up about nine, as it was well past the children's bedtime and they were getting tired and ratty.

Dieter was relieved to see the Colonel leave when they all did, but he hadn't missed the earnest conversation between him and Angie – or the brief kiss. Oh, hell!

Dieter didn't sleep well that night.

23

'Good morning, sir.'

Bob, in his civilian clothes, glanced up from his newspaper to see that Hunt was wearing them as well. 'Sergeant, join me for breakfast.'

'Thank you, sir.' Hunt spun a chair out from the table, sat down and ordered a cooked breakfast from the landlord's daughter. The cheeky wink made her laugh as she walked away. 'Any plans for today, sir?'

'I'm taking Angie and Danny to do some Christmas shopping in Bridgewater. I'll use the car.'

'Do you need me to drive, sir?'

'Good Lord, no. I'm quite capable of driving that distance.' Bob gave his sergeant a quizzical look. 'My *poor* leg will stand it for a few miles.'

'Right, sir.' Hunt smirked and tackled his breakfast as soon as it was put in front of him. 'Good job you didn't have to crawl through ditches in the mock battles. Being a Colonel kept you out of that.'

A deep rumble of laughter echoed through Bob. 'And being a sergeant didn't do you any harm either, did it?'

'No, wasn't as bad as I thought it was going to be.' Hunt pursed his lips. 'You forgot to mention that I would be your batman and driver during the war games. But then you will have your little joke, sir.'

When they'd reached West Germany and Hunt had discovered that he wouldn't be forced on long marches or freezing in open trenches, his relief had been so great he had almost wept. The expression on his face was something Bob would remember for a long time. Hunt was a damned good driver but a reluctant soldier. Only compulsory National Service had dragged him into the forces. 'I thought you needed to be reminded of what it was like to be a proper soldier.'

Hunt's shudder was visible. 'Basic training was enough for me. Now, sir, have you decided how long we'll be staying here?'

'I'll have to leave tomorrow afternoon about fifteen hundred hours. My parents are expecting me. You can drop me off in Wiltshire and keep the car for the duration of our leave. I'll have my own car at home.'

'Thanks, sir, I'll go straight on to London, then. I'll be able to take my sister's nippers out for a ride, if that's all right with you.'

'Just bring the car back in one piece when you collect me on the second of January.' Bob stood up. 'You have plans for today?'

'Yes, sir.' Hunt glanced over at the landlord's daughter and gave her another sly wink.

'I'll see you in the morning, then.' Bob shrugged into his topcoat and left the pub. It was only a short drive up the road to Angie's. They had arranged this trip last night, and, as he pulled up outside her cottage, Danny burst out to meet him.

'Where's your uniform?' Danny's salute froze halfway in disappointment.

'I decided not to wear it today.' He came to attention and saluted, making Danny giggle and bring his hand up sharply.

Angie joined them, smiling at their antics. 'Good morning. You can't salute out of uniform.'

'Yes, he can,' Danny said. 'He's a big officer now and can do what he likes.'

'Don't I wish.' That made Bob chuckle as he held the passenger door open for Angie. He couldn't resist kissing her on the cheek. She really was quite lovely, with the pale winter sun making her beautiful chestnut hair come alive with a multitude of hues. He was drawn to her and had to find out if he could feel more than affection for this charming girl. And, if he did, would he want to marry again? There were rather too many obstacles facing them. The age gap, for one. Then there was his army career, which would mean they wouldn't have a permanent home for some years. And not forgetting Danny and Dieter – now there was a complication! He really should walk away from all of them, but he couldn't seem to do it.

He slid into the driver's seat and started the car. This was not the time to mull over the possibilities. They were going to have a relaxing day out.

'Uncle Bob.' Danny was wriggling about on the back seat, unable to keep still with excitement. 'I've got money to buy presents. Granny and Grandpa give it to me.'

'I'm sure we'll find some lovely things for you to buy.'

Danny chatted all the way to Bridgewater, giving Angie and Bob little time to talk to each other. He was a lively and obviously talented little boy, but Bob suspected that he was quite demanding. Angie had certainly taken on a big responsibility when her cousin had died so tragically, but he had never heard her complain or seem anything but delighted at the prospect of bringing up the child. He suspected that she loved him unreservedly, and would make any sacrifice to see him happy. She really was a rather special girl.

Bridgewater was busy, but Bob managed to park near the shops. It was Saturday morning, and the place was crowded. There remained an air of austerity about, even four years after the end of the war. Food was still rationed, but clothes rationing was lifted last February. Petrol remained in short supply, but Bob's car was an official army vehicle, so they were all right, and his father seemed to manage on his ration by using the car only occasion-ally. Shops had been decorated, though, and some of the colourful displays had Danny beaming in delight.

Bob couldn't stop his thoughts returning to Berlin, and the whole of Europe. Rebuilding was a huge task, and he wondered how long it would be before many of the towns and cities looked like this again. Poor devils like Cramer had lost everything, and there were countless thousands like him . . . Danny's voice broke through his thoughts.

'Look!' He was pointing. 'There's a picture of Father Christmas. What does it say?'

Bob swept Danny up. 'It says, "Come in and see Father Christmas." Do you want to meet him?'

Danny nodded, beaming in excitement.

There was a queue of children, so Bob paid the sixpence required to see Father Christmas and wandered off to buy a couple of presents of his own. He found what he wanted and was back in half an hour.

Danny was just coming out of the hut, his face gleaming, clutching a brightly wrapped present. He was talking to Angie and jumping up and down. Bob watched them for a couple of minutes, feeling more than a pang of regret that he'd never had children. Perhaps he ought to consider marrying again before he was too old. Affection and liking would be enough for him; he'd had the wild passion, and that had ended in bitterness. He would look for a very different marriage second time around. His step faltered when he realized he was actually considering it.

Danny spotted him and waved a package. 'I've got a present!'

Bob strode over and stooped down to Danny's level. 'Do you know what it is?'

The boy shook his head. 'I'm gonna keep it for Christmas. Grandma's having a huge Christmas tree to put all the presents round.'

'You don't have to keep it, darling,' Angie told him. 'You can open it now if you want to.'

'I'll keep it.' He gave it to Angie to put in her shopping bag, and then fished in his pocket for his money. 'I want to buy Em and Dieter a present. Have I got enough money, Auntie?'

'Plenty. You've got three shillings and sixpence.'

'Come on, my boy.' Bob picked up Danny so they could make their way through the crowds.

'Am I your boy?' Danny stared at him, puzzled.

'Of course you are.' Bob weaved his way through the crowds. 'What did you think of Father Christmas?'

'He had a funny beard and something stuffed up his coat to make him look fat. I know 'cos I saw it sticking out.' He whispered in Bob's ear, 'I want to buy Auntie a present too.'

'What do you think she'd like?'

'Dunno.'

'Well, let's have a cup of tea while we think about it.'

The day went quickly. Bob found presents for his parents, younger brother and other members of his family. Angie had a bag full of purchases, and Danny had a scarf for Dieter, a colouring book and pencils for Emma, and a pair of bright red woollen gloves for Angie. These had cost more than Danny had, but Bob had slipped some of his own money in without the boy's noticing.

By the time they arrived back at the cottage, Danny was fast asleep. Bob picked him up from the back seat and kicked the car door shut as he straightened up, hitching the child into a more comfortable position.

Angie was rummaging through her bag, searching for her door key. He looked over her shoulder, resting his chin on the top of her head. 'Lost it?'

'I know it's here somewhere. Ah, here it is.' She held it up triumphant.

A feeling of being watched made Bob look up as Angie opened the door. His eyes locked with Dieter's. He was standing a few yards away, absolutely still, his gaze on Danny's sleeping figure in Bob's arms.

'Dieter!' Angie had also seen him. 'Come in and have a cup of tea with us.'

There was only a slight shake of his head before he turned on his heel and walked away.

'Why didn't he come in?' Angie frowned. 'He didn't look well.'

'I have a feeling he was upset to see me with you and Danny.' The front door was open now, and they made their way into the kitchen, where it was warmer. The old black leaded grate was always alight and kept the small room very cosy.

Angie immediately put the kettle on to make tea. 'But he must understand that I will have friends, and Danny will know them as well.'

'I expect he finds it hard to accept.' Bob spoke softly so as not to awaken Danny.

'I know, and I don't want to do anything to upset him, but I do have a right to a life of my own, don't I?' She chewed her lip and looked at him with pleading eyes. 'Must I always be on my own because he can't bear to see another man with Danny?'

'I'm sure he wouldn't expect that of you, however much he may wish it. He's a reasonable man, Angie. Talk this over with him.'

She sighed. 'I'll have to do that. Now we must get Danny to bed. He's tired out after such a lovely day.'

Bob carried him upstairs and watched as Angie put the sleeping child into his pyjamas, tucked him in and kissed his head gently. All this had been accomplished with only an occasional mutter of irritation from Danny, but he hadn't woken. Bob could see by her tenderness that although she hadn't given birth to the child, he was her son. There was no mistaking that. As she bent over the bed, with the soft light from the small lamp on her face, it became very clear what he was missing by not having a family of his own. His wife, Sylvia, had never wanted children. That had been a mistake, because she might have stayed with him if they'd had a family. No point thinking about it now. That part of his life was over, and, standing here watching Angie with the child, he could hardly remember what she had looked like. Their love had been passionate and explosive, but they hadn't been right for each other. It would have come to an end when the passion died.

Angie patted the bed covers, straightened up and smiled at Bob standing quietly just inside the door. She put her fingers to her lips. 'He's still fast asleep.'

They went back to the kitchen, and she took a milk saucepan out of the cupboard. 'Would you like a hot drink?'

He walked over to her, placed his hands on her shoulders and rested his forehead against hers. 'What am I going to do about you, Auntie Angel?'

She lifted her head until their lips were almost touching. 'I really don't know. Only you can answer that.'

Lowering his head the last couple of inches, he brushed his lips gently over hers. Then he eased back, a question in his eyes. 'What I'd like to do is take you back upstairs and make love to you.'

Her head moved slowly from side to side. 'You're a very attractive man, Bob Strachan, but all that's on offer here is cocoa.'

'I thought that's what you'd say.' He gave a dramatic sigh, lifted his hands in acceptance and stepped away from her, his lips quirked in a rueful smile. 'Cocoa it is, then. Though I must warn you that I'm finding it very hard to walk away from you.'

'And that's a problem?' She poured milk into the saucepan and put it on the stove, not looking at him. Their friendship was changing to something more affectionate, and she hadn't missed the thoughtful expression in his eyes when he'd looked at her and Danny.

'It could be.'

He said no more and she didn't ask. She knew his background, and also knew how difficult it would be for him to form another deep relationship after the failure of his marriage. As for her own feelings? Well, like him, she wasn't sure. They would both have to wait and see how things worked out.

*

Dieter walked slowly back towards the farm, head down, as a feeling of hopelessness swept through him.

If he'd ever had any doubt about the Colonel's intentions towards Angie, they had been swept aside by the intimate scene he had just witnessed. The picture of them outside the cottage, loaded with parcels and standing so close together, was burnt into his memory. And *his* son's little arms around Strachan's neck, fast asleep.

He'd had to fight the need to rush up and take Danny away from him. He is my son, he had wanted to shout. I should be holding him, not you! You have so much. Must you take Angie and my son away from me as well?

But he hadn't. Strachan was an affluent man, able to give them such a lot, whereas he had only the things he stood up in, and most of them had come from the Colonel. He shouldn't begrudge his child and Angie the security that man could give them – but he did!

Dieter straightened up. He had no money, no home, and little prospect for the immediate future. He was grateful to the Sawyers for giving him a job and a place in their home, but he had nothing that he could give his son – except his great love. He hadn't even known this little member of his family existed until a few weeks ago, and he could still feel the joy he had experienced on finding him. But was he now going to be expected to stand aside and let him go to another man?

Everything in Dieter rebelled at that idea. He couldn't do it, nor should anyone expect such a sacrifice from him. He had already lost three years. He had never seen his first smile, first step, or heard his first words.

Spinning round, he began to walk back the way he had come. A strong drink was what he needed to calm the tumult inside him. Slipping his hand in his pocket, he stopped and swore fluently in his own language, angry now. After paying for Danny's piano lessons this week, he didn't have enough money left for even a pint of beer.

He had to do something!

Without knowing how he had reached there, he was in front of the farmhouse again. The first thing he did when he walked into the kitchen was look for the latest local newspaper.

'Hello, Dieter.' Hetty came in. 'You're back early. I thought you were going to see Danny.'

'They are with the Colonel. Mrs Sawyer, do you have a recent local newspaper?'

'It's in the front room, I expect.' She studied him thoughtfully. 'Why would Bob's being there stop you from seeing Danny?'

'I would have been in the way.' Without waiting for her reply, he swept into the other room and picked up the newspaper. 'May I borrow this, Mr Sawyer?'

'Of course. You don't need to ask, Dieter.'

'What do you want it for in such a hurry?' Hetty had followed him into the front room.

'I need work as a pianist. In the evenings, of course, when I've finished my duties here.' Dieter saw their concerned expressions and threw his hands up in a gesture of hopelessness. 'I have to earn some more money in case I need it in the future.'

Hetty looked alarmed. 'What's happened, Dieter? You know we'd help in any way we can.'

'You are both very kind, but I have to rebuild my life – make it more secure. I can't waste any more time.'

'I see.' Hetty glanced at her silent husband, who was shaking his head sadly.

'I do not think you do, Mrs Sawyer.'

As he strode out of the room he heard Hetty say, 'There's trouble, John.'

It took Dieter only two days to find a job. It was in a rather smart club on the outskirts of Bridgewater. The pay wasn't huge, but it would be a big help. John had insisted that he take the truck, as he didn't finish until midnight and there wouldn't have been any public transport. He was grateful for their understanding and support, and he made sure he worked hard for them during the day, no matter how tired he was feeling.

After another long day and evening, he crept up the stairs, not wanting to wake them. He wasn't needed at the club until Christmas Eve now, which was just as well because there was the Carol Concert tomorrow evening and he wouldn't like to let the Rector or the village down. Everyone was so looking forward to it.

24

The Carol Concert last night had been wonderful, and Angie smiled to herself as she unpacked their things in the bedroom they were using over Christmas. Danny and Emma had been allowed to stay up late, and the candles and the singing had entranced them. There had been cups of tea afterwards and much laughter as the villagers got into the Christmas spirit. Everyone had appreciated Dieter's playing.

'Come on, Auntie.' Danny dragged her downstairs to put the presents round the tree. It was a splendid sight, covered in sparkling decorations, making Danny crow with delight.

'When do we open the presents?' he asked.

'Before lunch tomorrow – Christmas Day.' She handed him another parcel to put in place.

When the presents were arranged to Danny's satisfaction, he went out with John to see the pigs, both of them wrapped up against the biting wind.

Angie wandered into the kitchen to see if she could help with the evening meal.

'All settled in?' Hetty glanced up from peeling potatoes.

'Yes. Danny's disappeared with John. Can I help?'

'You can do the sprouts, if you like.'

Angie put on the spare apron and set to work. 'Where's Dieter?'

'He won't be back until late. He's found a job as pianist in a club just outside Bridgewater.'

'Oh, I didn't know that.' Angie was surprised he hadn't said anything to her. 'Doesn't he work for you any more?'

'During the day he still works for us, and in the evenings he plays piano till all hours.' Hetty gave her a disapproving glance. 'The dear boy's working himself much too hard.'

'But why?'

'Because he needs the money, of course.'

Angie didn't miss the sharpness in Hetty's voice. She put the knife down and turned to face her. 'What's going on? We've only seen him a couple of times since the play, and he didn't tell me he'd taken another job. He wanted to support Danny and me, but I wouldn't let him do more than pay for Danny's piano lessons and a pair of shoes he insisted on buying. I know he hasn't got anything, and I would never take money from him, however much he wants to help. But he's a proud man and hard to refuse.'

Hetty sighed. 'You know we think the world of him, and have done ever since he came to us from the POW camp. We were so happy when he turned up and met his son. It was lovely to see him smile again, but ever since Bob came on leave, he's changed. I think he's worried you're going to marry Bob and take Danny away from him.'

'But I'd never stop him from seeing Danny. He

knows that, and we've agreed to tell Danny who he is.'

'But what if you travel the world with Bob – how would he see him then?'

'Hetty, this is ridiculous! Bob hasn't asked me to marry him. I really believe he doesn't want any permanent commitments.'

'And how do you feel about that?'

How could she answer that? The attraction between them was strong, and, to be honest, she would like to be closer to him. In that way they could find out if there was any hope of a future for them together. But how could they do that when he was here one minute and gone the next? Bob had said he would never marry again, but he hadn't tried to hide the fact that he found her attractive, and she felt the same about him. But there was Dieter . . .

'Angie, you haven't answered my question.' Hetty touched her arm.

'We're attracted to each other, but a man wouldn't want to take on another man's child. My last boyfriend said that no one would marry me while I had a young child to care for. And nothing in this world would make me give up Danny.'

'That boyfriend of yours was a selfish bastard.' Hetty smiled sheepishly. 'Pardon my language, but he didn't know what he was talking about.'

'Maybe.' Angie picked up the knife and continued to prepare the sprouts, swallowing hard to control the emotion. 'I'm a young woman and would naturally hope to marry one day, but, if that doesn't happen, I'll be content with Danny. Bob likes me, but after one failed marriage I'm pretty sure he wouldn't risk it again.'

'That isn't what Dieter believes. I think he's so worried that he wants money in case he has to try to stop you taking Danny out of the country.'

'You're all jumping to conclusions! A man pays me some attention and you've got me walking up the aisle. It's nothing.'

'Then tell Dieter that, Angie. He has a right to know if anything will affect his son.'

'I will.' Angie felt guilty. She should have spoken to him after he had seen them all together after the shopping day out. But he'd come round the next day, listened to Danny playing through what he'd learnt and never mentioned anything, or voiced his fears. Like a heartless fool she had just left it at that. She shouldn't have done that. Her sigh was ragged. She had no right to cause him more pain.

It was one o'clock in the morning when Angie heard Dieter creeping up the stairs. Slipping out of bed, she put on her dressing gown and opened the bedroom door just as he was walking past.

'Dieter,' she whispered. 'I need to talk to you. Let's go down to the kitchen.'

He nodded and followed her, surprised.

She made them both a cup of cocoa, and then sat opposite him at the large kitchen table, wondering how to start. He looked strained. 'How's your new job?'

'It is all right. The pay is reasonable.'

Angie sipped her drink. There was only one way to do this, and that was to go straight to the point. 'I want you to know that I would never do anything to separate you from Danny. I've given you my word. There is no need for you to work day and night.'

'Is there not?' The stunning grey eyes focused on her. 'What if you want to take Danny out of the country? How would I see him if I do not even have the money to travel? I have seen how he loves you. I could not take him away from the person he has known from birth and adores. I have considered it, very seriously, but it is not possible.'

'This is our home now. I'm not going to take him anywhere.'

'Oh, you say that with such conviction, but what if Strachan wants to marry you? He is a career soldier, moving about all the time.'

'Bob hasn't asked me to marry him!' She was getting cross now.

'Not yet, but I have eyes.' He sighed wearily.

'Dieter,' she said, leaning towards him, 'whatever happens in the future, I would never, *never* take Danny away from his real father.'

Dieter sat back, his gaze searching. 'You would sacrifice your own life and happiness for Danny?'

'What a daft question to ask! Of course I would. He is the most important person in my life. And looking after him is no sacrifice! If there are ever to be any changes, we will discuss it together. Believe me, Dieter. The last thing I want to do is hurt anyone.'

He let out a long breath. 'I believe you.'

'Good.' How dare he doubt her. 'Now, let's forget all this nonsense. Are you still set on Danny being told that you are his father?'

'Yes, tomorrow, before lunch.'

Angie chewed her lip in concern. 'Okay, I'll tell him when he's relaxed and opening his presents.'

'I will tell him, Angie. It is my right.'

'He might accept it better if it came from me.' She gave him a pleading look. 'He isn't four until May, and this will be so hard for him to understand. If I told him . . .'

Dieter shook his head. 'I will explain carefully. I love him as well.'

Angie stood up, seeing little point is discussing this any longer. His mind was made up. 'Very well, Dieter, we'll do it your way.'

She left him sitting at the table, and, on reaching her bedroom, she stood by Danny's bed, looking down at her precious child, praying they were doing the right thing. He'd had such a terrible time after finding his mother dead, but he was much better now and enjoying his new life here. It frightened her to think they might be doing him more harm than good by suddenly presenting him with a father. If only he were older and could understand . . .

Slipping back into her bed she stared up at the ceiling, eyes wide open. She was probably worrying too much. Danny liked Dieter and would most likely throw himself into his arms in delight.

She turned over and thumped her pillow into shape. There was something niggling away at her, and she couldn't shake it off. Danny had asked only that one time about his father, and he'd never mentioned it again. It was strange, and the nearer they came to telling him, the more uneasy she became. Why had he dropped the subject so completely? It was as if he didn't want, or didn't need, to know any more.

With a sigh she buried her head in the pillow and tried to sleep. Her imagination was running riot. Why was it that in the middle of the night fears magnified, and small problems grew out of all proportion?

Christmas Day and the kitchen was full of the most wonderful smells. Although food was still rationed, living on a farm did have its advantages. There was a goose in the oven and lots of lovely fresh vegetables. Danny was out with John and Dieter, helping to feed the animals. It was a task that had to be done whatever the occasion.

'This is going to be a wonderful meal, Hetty. My mouth is watering already.' Angie grinned; her fears of last night had vanished with the dawn. She could hear Danny laughing and chatting outside in the yard, probably getting in the way as he tried to help.

Hetty glanced at the clock. 'Nearly ten – the men will be in soon. I'll make the tea and then we can open the presents. I can't wait to see Danny's face.'

'Nor me.' Angie wiped her hands and pushed her hair away from her eyes. It was hot working in the kitchen. 'As this is our first Christmas without Jane, I thought it might be difficult, but Danny seems so happy and excited. Here, let me take that.'

'Thanks.' Hetty gave her the loaded tray to take into the front room.

There was a lovely log fire burning in the grate, casting flickering lights on to the Christmas tree, making its decorations sparkle. Angie put the tray on a small table by the window, a warm feeling of pleasure surging through her. The presents were stacked around the base of the tree. Her darling boy had lovely gifts, and he was going to be so excited.

The door burst open and Danny rushed in, followed by John and Dieter. Their faces were glowing from the keen north wind. This was such an exposed spot, and when the wind was blowing it fairly howled across the fields.

'We've fed the animals.' Danny stood in front of the tree, grinning. 'Is it time for presents?'

'I don't think you can wait any longer.' Angie laughed and knelt down by the packages, handing him each one and telling him who to give it to, watching with a smile as he trotted from person to person.

When they all had their presents, Danny sat on the floor and began to rip open each of his. He gurgled with delight over an army tank sent by Bob, showing it to everyone. Then he went back to opening the rest of his presents. As soon as the wooden car was in his hands, Dieter sat with him.

'Cor, it looks like my truck.'

'That is because I made them both.'

Danny ran his fingers over the bright paint. 'I 'member, you gave it to my mummy.'

'That is right.' Dieter paused for a second, then continued. 'I knew your mummy very well, but after the war she went back to London and I returned to Germany. She did not tell me you had been born.'

Danny was watching him, not saying a word, and Angie was finding it hard to breathe. Please don't let this talk of Jane upset him again, she prayed silently.

'It was a great joy and surprise when I saw you for the first time.' He ran his hand gently over his son's bright hair. 'I am your father, Danny.'

The atmosphere in the room was tense. John and Hetty were sitting by the fire, watching intently. For a minute, though it seemed longer, nothing happened; then Danny's reaction shocked all of them. He dropped the toy and scuttled away from Dieter, heading for Angie. He grabbed her legs and pulled himself up on to her lap.

Once he was safely with her, he whispered rather loudly, 'He's telling fibs, Auntie. Mummy said it's wrong to tell fibs.'

Dieter was on his feet, his expression stricken. 'What is this "fibs"?'

'Lies.' Angie held the agitated child close. 'He thinks you're lying.'

'It is the truth, Danny. I would not lie to you about such an important thing.' Dieter tried to take hold of his son's hand, but Danny pulled away. 'You're not my daddy! You're not! Mummy told me . . .' He was in a panic now.

'Shush.' Angie smoothed her hand over his silky fair hair. She was completely bewildered by this reaction.

'What does he mean?' Dieter's voice was husky. 'What did Jane tell him about me?'

'I don't know, I swear I don't.' Angie lifted Danny's head so she could look at him. 'Darling, Dieter isn't telling fibs. He really is your father. What did your mummy tell you?'

His mouth set in a stubborn line. 'He's not my daddy. Uncle Bob's my daddy.'

Angie felt as if she had been hit by a prizefighter, and she saw Dieter reel back in shock. Where the devil had he got that idea from?

'That's not true.' Dieter raised his voice. 'He doesn't look anything like Strachan. He is the image of me!'

'Don't shout at my auntie.' Danny had wriggled round to face Dieter, his little fists clenched in fury. 'Naughty to tell fibs. Uncle Bob is my daddy. I know. You go away.'

With a feeling of utter helplessness, Angie watched Dieter leave the room. This was terrible, and unbelievable. She had been concerned about telling Danny when he was so young, but never for an instant had she imagined that this would happen. Her worry had been that he wouldn't understand and become confused – not that he would reject Dieter so firmly. He liked Dieter, so what on earth was going on in his mind?

Danny slid off his auntie's lap. He still had presents to open, but he felt nasty inside. He'd get his mummy's truck; that always made him feel better. Running as fast as he could, he went upstairs and found the truck. He wished his mummy was here. She wouldn't tell fibs.

Clutching the precious reminder of his mother to him, he started back down again. Auntie was at the bottom waiting for him, so he walked very carefully, not wanting to fall. Was she cross with him? He watched her face as he came down one step at a time, and when she bent and kissed his cheek, he gave a smile of relief and ran past her into the front room.

He put the truck next to the pretty car. They were nice. Mummy would have put the car in her special box as well. Dieter was clever, but he was naughty. He shouldn't have said those things. It had upset him, and he didn't want to be upset on this lovely day. Granny and Grandpa had made it all nice for them, and so many presents!

There was a great big parcel he hadn't opened yet. His fingers worked feverishly until the box was open.

'Ooh!' He held up a train. 'This is better than Em's. Wait till she sees it.'

'I'll show you how it works, shall I?' John sat beside him on the floor.

He nodded eagerly. He liked Dieter and was disappointed he told fibs; he shouldn't have done that. He knew who his daddy was. He wouldn't think about nasty things any more.

Angie watched in consternation. Apart from the loss of colour in his face, Danny appeared to be all right and not overly distressed, now that Dieter wasn't here. Seeing that he was fully occupied, she slipped out of the room, looking for Dieter.

She could see from the kitchen window that he was in the yard, leaning on the old tractor, head down and not wearing a coat in the bitter wind. Slipping on her coat, she took his greatcoat off the hook and stepped outside. He'd catch his death of cold out there.

'Dieter,' she said when she reached him. 'Put your coat on.'

He seemed oblivious to her, so she draped the coat across his shoulders. 'Come inside. It's freezing out here.'

When he turned, she gasped and her heart ached for him. His face was wet with tears. 'Oh, Dieter.' She stepped forward and slid her arms around him. 'It'll be all right. I'll find out what this is all about.'

'I should have listened to you.' He wrapped his arms around her and buried his face in her hair. 'But I wanted so much for him to know that I am his father.'

'I know, but I don't think it would have made any difference who told him. He's obviously got this idea that Bob is his father, but I don't understand why.'

Dieter held her away from him, searching her face. 'You do not believe that?'

'Of course not. Any fool can see he's your son, and Jane put your surname on his birth certificate. Danny's full name is Daniel Cramer Harris.'

'I did not know that.' He wiped a hand across his wet face.

It tore Angie apart to see him so upset. In the few

301

weeks she'd known him, her respect had grown steadily. She had found him to be a kind, talented man, with a strong sense of honour. She was certain that if her cousin had told him she was expecting his child, he would never have left her, no matter how worried he'd been about his family. He would have had to return to Germany for a while, but he would have come straight back.

'I don't understand where he's got the idea that Bob is his father.'

'From Strachan!'

Angie looked up, surprised by the vehemence in his voice. 'Oh, I can't believe that. Why would he do such a thing?'

'Because he wants you, and what better way is there to accomplish that than to convince Danny he is his father?'

'He wouldn't do such a thing, surely?' Angie chewed her lip as doubt began to surface. Had she been taken in by his smiles and kisses? She was sure he wasn't the marrying kind . . . but was he trying to cause trouble? She shook her head from side to side. No, she couldn't believe that of him.

'The man is a born soldier, Angie, and will use any strategy to win what he wants.' Dieter put on his coat, his expression grim. 'If he has done this, I shall never forgive him.'

'There must be another explanation.' Angie was very reluctant to believe Bob would act in such an under-hand way.

'What else is there? Why would Danny believe this

unless the Colonel had told him?' Dieter turned and began to walk out of the yard.

Angie caught his sleeve. 'Where are you going?'

He shrugged. 'I do not know, but my son has rejected me.'

'So you're going to run away and leave me to deal with this disaster?' Sympathy evaporated and her anger bubbled over. 'This was your idea, Dieter, and now that it's all gone wrong you're going to disappear. I thought you had more backbone than that!'

'If I come back, he will be upset again.'

'I expect he will.' Angie almost stamped her foot in exasperation. 'But this has to be sorted out, so let's face this together. My God, you are both alike, aren't you? Stubborn as hell when you get an idea lodged in your heads.'

A glean of amusement flickered in his eyes as he watched her fuming. 'I shall take that as a compliment, shall I?'

'Men!' The corners of her mouth turned up and she held out her hand. 'For some bizarre reason this boy of ours has got the wrong end of the stick. Let's all have lunch together and see if we can find out where he got this daft idea from.'

Dieter's long fingers curled around her hand. 'What is this – wrong end of the stick?'

'It means believing something that isn't true. Come on.'

They walked back to the farmhouse, hand in hand.

25

Dieter's heart was pounding badly, not only for the disaster he had caused by insisting that Danny be told, but with despair. They had been getting along so well, and now he had alienated his son from him. He was going to have to start all over again to win his love and confidence. What a terrible mistake he had made. Angie had been right; he should have listened to her! In his eagerness to become a part of his son's life, he had ruined everything.

However, there was one gleam of hope. By her impassioned outburst, Angie had shown that she accepted him. Her words – 'this boy of ours' – had echoed through him like the strains of a beautiful concerto. Her calm, controlled exterior held a fiery centre, just like her hair when the sun shone on it. She was very different from her cousin. Jane had been gentle through and through, and had come as a balm to him at that anxious time. As much as he had been capable of then, he had loved her, and he wished he'd had the sense to stay with her. He would always regret that. This was another shadow in his life, and he wondered when he would see enough sunshine to sweep them away.

John was waiting for them in the kitchen with two

glasses in his hands. 'Here, drink this. The two of you look as if you could do with a stiff brandy.'

'Thank you.' Dieter downed his in one gulp, shuddering slightly as it burnt its way into his stomach. It reminded him of the brandy he had been given after his plane had been shot down. He would never forget that bizarre moment in someone's garden. Hostility had been expected, but instead he'd found tolerance and even kindness.

'How's Danny?' Angie only sipped her drink.

'He's all right, so stop worrying.'

'Have you any idea what he was talking about, John?' Angie took another sip and grimaced. 'Hell, this is awful.'

'Give it to Dieter.' John laughed at her expression of distaste. 'He doesn't think it's too terrible. And no, I haven't any idea what the lad was on about, but, if I were you, I wouldn't mention it again today. Hetty tried while you were outside, but he clammed up tight.'

'I might be able to get him to talk when I put him to bed.' She glanced hesitantly at Dieter. 'Do you agree we leave it until then?'

He nodded. 'I am not about to go against your advice again.'

Hetty came into the kitchen. 'He's playing again. Give me a hand with the lunch, Angie.'

'Let's get out of their way.' John smiled. 'Come into the front room, Dieter, and I'll refill your glass.'

He followed John and stood in the doorway, gazing at the child playing with his toys, and it felt as if someone had squeezed his heart. Then he saw the old truck next to the new car he had made and his worry lifted a little. Perhaps there was hope; Danny hadn't abandoned his gift.

At that moment he made a decision. He would leave Angie to talk to Danny, but he would see Strachan, if he could, and have this out with him.

'Dieter?' John held up a bottle.

'No, thanks, Mr Sawyer.' He walked up to him and spoke softly. 'Do you know if Colonel Strachan is still in this country?'

'Yes, he's here until the New Year. Staying with his parents in Wiltshire, I believe.'

'Do you have his address? I would like to see him before he returns to Germany.'

John took a sheet of paper out of the sideboard, scribbled the address and gave it to Dieter. 'I know what you're thinking, but there's no way Bob would have told Danny that he was his father. The little lad has got this in a real muddle in his mind.'

'That may be so, but I must find out. You understand?'

'I do, but wait until after tomorrow. You can't barge in on his family during the festivities.'

'I want this settled now, and if there is a misunderstanding, I am sure Strachan would want to know.' He dredged up a smile, though in truth he felt like weeping.

John nodded. 'You'd better take the truck.'

'Thank you. I appreciate your kindness.'

'You haven't opened your presents.' Danny voice was accusing and put a stop to their conversation.

'That is so.' Dieter's hand shook slightly as he picked up a parcel. At least his son was talking to him. There was a shirt from the Sawyers, a jumper from Angie and a woollen scarf from Danny. He held it up admiringly. 'What a lovely scarf, and just what I wanted. Thank you, Danny.'

'S'all right. Uncle Bob said you'd like it.' He turned his back on Dieter, still obviously upset.

The pleasure drained out of Dieter. Damn the man! He turned and faced John. 'I shall definitely go tomorrow, Mr Sawyer.'

'There's enough petrol in the tank to get you there and back. And I think it's time you called us John and Hetty.'

'That is kind of you.' Dieter bowed slightly. 'I shall pay for the petrol I use, of course. Would you not mention to Hetty and Angie what I am going to do, please?'

John squeezed his shoulder. 'This will be just between us.'

'Come and get it.' Angie looked into the front room and smiled at Danny. 'Come on, darling. We've got goose, Christmas pudding and mince pies.'

Danny got to his feet and ran into the kitchen, where the huge wooden table had been transformed with candles and crackers to pull.

'Oh, pretty. Where am I sitting, Grandma?'

'Over here, next to me.'

Dieter sat at the other end of the table, keeping his distance from Danny in case he upset him again. The meal passed off well, and though Danny never spoke directly to Dieter, he didn't seem too troubled by his presence. Angie watched with mounting disbelief, wishing she could see into the child's mind. But she didn't need to be a mind reader to know what Dieter was thinking. He was devastated.

After lunch they went back to the front room to drink coffee in front of the fire and to relax after the enormous meal.

'I'm sure you don't feel like it, Dieter, but would you play for us?' Hetty asked.

'Of course.' Without hesitation, he stood up and walked over to the piano.

Angie couldn't help being struck, once again, by his dignity. No matter how much he was hurting, he was the perfect gentleman. Danny often showed the same qualities, as if politeness were ingrained into him – until today. She had never known him to be rude or hurtful to anyone. It was so out of character.

As soon as Dieter began to play, Danny stopped what he was doing, his head on one side as he listened. As upset as he had been, he could never resist the music. He didn't edge towards Dieter, as he normally would have done, but stayed where he was.

Angie closed her eyes and let the music flow over her. She felt exhausted. He was playing lovely tunes from the war years and she allowed herself to drift, half asleep, half awake. Was this what Jane had done? Had she fallen in love as she'd listened to him?

She dragged her eyes open. Dieter's head was bent

over in the now familiar attitude, as his expert fingers caressed the keys. Oh, yes, he would be so easy to love. Danny was lucky to have such a wonderful father . . .

Danny's voice snapped her awake. The light outside was fading and the log fire sending flickering lights around the room. She must have fallen asleep for a while.

'I learnt a tune last week.'

'You had better play it for me.' Dieter stood up and stepped away from the piano.

Danny trotted over, put two cushions on the stool and sat down. He started to play 'Silent Night', giving it his whole concentration.

Dieter leant against the wall, his eyes closed as he listened. When Danny had finished, he pushed himself upright. 'Good, Danny, but you rushed the middle part. Here, let me show you.' He reached across and played the tune again. 'Did you hear the difference?'

Danny nodded.

'Play it again and we shall sing.'

They joined in, but Angie stopped when she heard Dieter's deep baritone voice singing in German. It was beautiful. Danny could only pick out the tune, so Dieter was playing the left hand for him.

When the tune came to an end, they all applauded, making Danny blush with pride. He glanced hesitantly at Dieter, obviously wanting his approval.

'You are making good progress, and in about two years I shall teach you the organ.'

Danny's eyes opened wide. 'Mrs Poulton said I would have to be about ten before I could do that.'

'You will not be able to reach with your feet, but there are many things to learn about the organ. I shall show you, and when you are tall enough, you will play.'

The dimples flashed, but didn't quite develop into a smile, as Danny slid off the stool and went back to his toys.

Angie smiled at Dieter and nodded in approval. He had handled that very well and had gone a long way towards getting things back to normal between them.

By the time Danny was ready for bed, he was so tired it wasn't possible to talk to him, as she had planned. As much as she wanted to question him, it would have to wait until the morning. And perhaps it was for the best: he'd had quite enough excitement for one day.

The next morning, when Danny was dressed, Angie sat him on the bed and knelt in front of him to lace his shoes. Then, staying where she was, she placed a hand on his knees to keep him sitting on the bed.

'Danny, I want you to tell me why you think Uncle Bob is your father.'

'He told me.' He wriggled, eager to go downstairs for his breakfast.

'What did he say?'

'He said I was his boy. I'm hungry, Auntie.'

'Just a minute, darling.' She held him firmly in place. 'When did he tell you this?'

'When we saw Father Christmas. Em said that's what daddies do. They build you swings and take you to see Father Christmas; and her daddy calls her "my girl".'

Angie sat back on her heels in astonishment. The children had obviously been discussing this, but it didn't make sense. Bob would not do such a thing. She just knew he wouldn't! 'Uncle Bob isn't your father, whatever he may have said. Dieter is your daddy.'

She could see that he was confused, so she took a deep breath. Somehow she had to make him understand. 'Dieter plays the piano, doesn't he?'

Danny nodded.

'And you want to do the same. Your teacher says you are talented, doesn't she?'

He nodded again, watching her with large beautiful eyes.

'Darling, you have that gift from your father. Your mummy couldn't even play a penny whistle,' she joked. 'You have the same colour hair and eyes as Dieter, and you even have the same dimples when you smile. You are going to look just like him when you grow up.'

Danny pursed his lips and huffed as his young mind tried to work this out. Then his expression lightened. 'Have I got two daddies, like I had two mummies?'

'No, you've only got one. What did your mummy tell you?'

He swung his legs and looked into space, concentrating hard. 'She said daddy had a uniform and gone a long way away.'

Angie waited, and when he didn't say anything else she was disappointed. 'Is that all she told you?'

'Can't 'member.' He tipped his head to one side. 'Uncle Bob lives a long way away and he's got a uniform.'

Oh, Lord, she wasn't getting anywhere. His mind had accepted one thing, and it seemed as if nothing would shift it. He'd remembered a couple of things Jane had said, and Bob fitted, as far as his mind was concerned. There was little point in pursuing this any longer. She would have to leave it for the moment. He was only going to get in more of a muddle.

Standing up, she held out her hand. 'Let's go down to breakfast, but I want you to do something for me. You hurt Dieter very much by telling him to go away. He didn't deserve to be treated like that, Danny, it was very rude, so I want you to tell him you're sorry and didn't mean it.'

'All right, Auntie.' Then he was off, clattering down the stairs.

When she reached the kitchen, he was already sitting at the table, waiting for his boiled egg and soldiers.

'Where's Dieter?' she asked, seeing he wasn't there.

'He's gone out for the day.' John continued to eat his eggs and bacon, not meeting her eyes.

'Do you know where, John?'

He did look up then. 'Said he had to see someone.'

'Oh, he didn't say anything about it yesterday.' Angie glanced at Hetty, who shrugged.

'I expect it's something to do with his music.' Hetty put a plate of cooked breakfast in front of Angie. 'I made sure he had a good meal inside him before he left. He's taken the truck so I don't suppose he'll be long.'

John pushed his empty plate away. 'He said he'd be back later this afternoon.'

Picking up her knife and fork, Angie gave a mental shrug. She knew he was trying to earn extra money, but she was surprised that he hadn't mentioned it. Still, he didn't have to tell her everything he was doing, did he?

Danny looked up, egg around his mouth. 'Can't say I'm sorry if he's not here, can I, Auntie?'

'No, but you must as soon as he comes back.'

He nodded obediently and then grinned at his grandparents. 'I've got two daddies.'

'No, you haven't, darling. You've only got one, and that's Dieter.'

'Mummy said you were my second mummy, and you're my auntie.' His mouth set in a stubborn line. 'So Uncle Bob is my daddy.'

Angie groaned inwardly and threw her hands up in defeat. Their little talk had done no good at all. In fact, the situation was even more confusing. How on earth was she going to make him understand?

'Don't worry about it, Angie,' Hetty laughed. 'It's his artistic temperament. If it isn't to do with music, he gets it in a muddle.'

'What do you mean, Grandma?' Danny swivelled round to face Angie. 'What's it mean, Auntie?'

Angie reached over, pulled a face and dug him in the ribs. 'It means you're potty!'

He giggled and stood up. 'Is it time to milk the cows, Grandpa?'

'That's already been done, but you can help me with the pigs. Come on.'

Alone with Hetty, Angie rested her elbows on the

table and cupped her chin in her hands. 'I'll bet this confusion is Emma's doing. That little girl has very firm opinions on just about everything, and, from what I can gather, she's been talking to Danny about daddies.'

Hetty sat next to her. 'They're still only babies.'

'I know, and I wish I had been firmer with Dieter and made him wait until Danny was at least five, but he wants his son so very much.'

'He knows he made a mistake.' Hetty patted her hand. 'But it's done now; he'll listen to you in future.'

26

Pulling over to the side of the road, Dieter stopped and spread the map over the steering wheel. Strachan lived in a place called Chilmark, and John had said that it was about fifty miles away, as the crow flies. He must be almost there.

He traced the road with his finger. There it was. If he turned right at the next crossroads, it would bring him straight into the village. He started the truck again and set off. Within fifteen minutes he was making his way up a long driveway towards an impressive old gabled house. To Dieter it looked like a mansion surrounded by large gardens.

After getting out of the truck, he stood gazing at the building. There were three floors and a fine oak front door in the centre of the house. He felt that it must be more than a hundred years old and only a family with money could own such a lovely place. The Colonel had much to offer Angie and Danny. He himself had no material security that he could give his son, but he had something far more valuable: the love of a real father. He could nurture and guide his talented son as no one else could, for he understood his passion for music.

While he was still standing there lost in thought, the front door swung open and Bob Strachan strode out.

'Dieter, what the hell are you doing here? Has something happened to Angie or Danny?'

'They are all right, but it is necessary that I talk to you.' That piece of information didn't look as if it were going down too well, but he hadn't driven here just to be turned away. He had come for answers, and he was going to get them.

After only a slight hesitation, Bob said, 'You'd better come in.'

Dieter followed him into a room on the ground floor. The walls were lined with bookshelves, and dark brown leather chairs were placed around a blazing log fire. It looked as if the Colonel had been reading, because there was a book open on a small table beside one chair and a cigarette smouldering in an ashtray. Through an archway Dieter caught sight of a beautiful grand piano.

'Do you play?' he asked, hesitating before stating the reason for his visit. He did not want to pitch straight in and argue with the man. It would do no good to accuse him of something he might not have done. Dieter knew from his time as a POW that the Colonel exploded very easily, and he did not wish to cause a scene in this man's own house, but they were going to get to the bottom of this. He would not leave until they had.

'No, but my mother does.' Bob frowned. 'Now, what was so urgent that you had to come all this way on Boxing Day?'

Before Dieter could answer, a tall, elegant woman with silver hair came into the room.

'Robert, Cook said lunch will be served in thirty minutes.'

'All right, Mother.' He smiled at her. 'This is Dieter Cramer.'

'Ah, Herr Cramer, my son has mentioned you.' She shook hands with him. 'Will you join us for lunch? I'm sure your business can wait for an hour.'

'That is very gracious of you.' Dieter bowed. 'But I did not intend to put you to any trouble. My business with Colonel Strachan will only take a few minutes, then I shall leave.'

She waved away his hesitation. 'You have come quite a distance?'

'About fifty miles, madam.'

'Then you cannot return without a meal.' She looked at her son. 'I insist, Robert. You must persuade Herr Cramer to join us. Your father will be most interested to meet him.'

'I'm sure Dieter would appreciate something to eat after a cold journey.' He watched his mother leave the room and smiled fondly. 'You'll have to accept. My mother is an immovable force once her mind is set on something.'

'I shall of course do so. I would not wish to offend your mother.' Dieter sighed inwardly. This was not at all what he had expected or planned. He wanted to find out what Strachan was up to and then be on his way as quickly as possible.

'You would be wise not to.' Bob walked over to a table of drinks, chuckling to himself. 'Would you like a sherry or whisky before lunch?'

'Whisky, thank you.' There was no way out of this. He was going to have to curb his impatience. Dieter took the glass from him. 'I had no intention of intruding upon you and your family for any longer than was necessary.'

'Think nothing of it.' Bob sipped his whisky and studied Dieter. 'I must say I'm damned curious to know what this is all about, but I'm afraid it will have to wait until after lunch. There goes the bell, so you'd better bring your drink with you.'

Feeling rather bemused by the unexpected welcome, Dieter followed the Colonel into the dining room, where a man who must have looked just like his son when he was young greeted him with a smile.

'Good of you to join us.'

'It is my pleasure, sir.' Dieter inclined his head and returned the smile, not wanting to be impolite to the charming couple.

'Sit here next to me.' The father pulled out a chair for Dieter. 'I have questions to ask you.'

Dieter did as ordered and wondered what sort of questions.

They had hardly finished a delicious tomato soup before he found out.

'Now Dieter – I may call you that?' On receiving a nod, Bob's father continued. 'My son has told me a little about conditions in Europe, but I would like to hear how things are in Germany at the moment.'

While they enjoyed a meal of roast beef, Dieter told them of the destruction he had found on his return home, and of the shortages of all basic needs. By the time he had finished, they had reached the coffee stage, and the elderly man was shaking his head.

'Dear God, I knew things were bad, but what you have just told us is appalling.' He glared at his son. 'I hope the army is doing all it can for these poor civilians.'

'Things are beginning to improve, but rebuilding is a massive undertaking, Father.'

'Robert tells us that you have not been able to find your family.' Mrs Strachan refilled Dieter's cup.

'I am afraid not. It has taken me a long time, but I have finally accepted that they are dead. If I could have found out where they had been buried, it would have helped me to come to terms with the loss sooner.'

'I shall find out for you.'

Dieter glanced at the elderly man in surprise. 'That is kind of you, sir, but I fear there is little you can do after all this time.'

'I still have connections. Europe is full of displaced persons and a dedicated group of us are doing what we can to help. We are often asked by the larger agencies, the Red Cross amongst them, if we can help them.' He stood up and retrieved a camera from the sideboard. 'Let me take a couple of photographs of you in case they are needed.' Once this was done, he put the camera away again. 'Now I believe you have business with my son. Come, my dear, let us leave them to it.'

The parents left, and Bob and Dieter remained at the table drinking coffee.

Bob lit a cigarette and offered Dieter one. When that was refused, he sat back. 'My father enjoyed talking to you. He is greatly concerned about conditions in Europe.'

'How does he think he can find out anything about my family, when we have already exhausted all avenues in our search for information?'

'I doubt very much that he can, but that won't stop him trying. As a retired general, he has many connections, and both my parents are involved in trying to unite people with their families. It is a difficult task, but they've had a few successes.'

'That is good of them.'

'They are good people.' Bob stubbed out his cigarette. 'I think it's time you explained why you are here.'

'Yesterday I told Danny I was his father.' Dieter watched the Colonel's expression carefully. 'He rejected me. He is convinced that you are his father. I believe you have designs on Angie, and winning over Danny will aid you in that plan. I will not allow you to take my child away from me. I wish an explanation, please.'

There was silence for a moment, and then Bob surged to his feet. 'My God, you have a very low opinion of me if you believe I would mislead a small child in that way.'

Dieter was also on his feet, too heartbroken to stop his voice rising. 'Danny told me to go away. You were his father, not me. Tell me, Colonel, why would he believe that if you had not told him?'

'I don't know, but I'm bloody well going to find out.'

Dieter caught his arm as he stormed into the hall-way. 'Just a minute, Colonel – are you denying you told him this?'

Bob spun round to face him, furious. 'Of course I am. What kind of a swine do you think I am? If my intentions towards Angie were serious, and I'm not saying they are, then I wouldn't need to act in such an unprincipled way.'

Dieter realized that was true. Colonel Robert Strachan was an impressive man, with wealth and posi-tion. He would be a good catch for any girl. He stepped back. 'I apologize if I have insulted you, but this does not solve the mystery of why my son believes you are his father.'

'No, it doesn't.' The fury left Bob's face and he grimaced. 'This must have caused you a lot of anguish. We must get to the bottom of it at once. I'll follow you back to the farm in my car.'

By this time they were back in the library, and his parents had obviously heard the argument.

'I have to go back with Dieter. There's something we need to sort out.'

His mother nodded and looked at the clock. 'You know we have guests at eight o'clock, Robert – will you be back in time?'

'Should be. I'll take my car.'

His father got to his feet. 'How far is this place?'

Bob shrugged. 'Fifty miles, give or take.'

'That's a hundred-mile round trip. I'll drive you.'

'There's no need, Father. I can manage.'

'I insist.' His father was already on his way. 'I'll get the car.'

Mrs Strachan smiled at Dieter. 'I hope you solve your problem. My son has told me that you're a wonderful pianist. I'm sorry you won't have time to play for us.'

Dieter bowed at the compliment. 'You also play, madam.'

She laughed. 'My talent is mediocre, but it gives me pleasure.'

'I am sure you are too modest. I should have enjoyed hearing you play.' Dieter doubted that anything this charming woman did was mediocre.

She held out her hand. 'You must come again, and we shall entertain each other.'

'That would be most enjoyable.' He shook her hand, bowing slightly. 'Thank you for your hospitality, madam.'

'We must be going, Dieter.' Bob kissed his mother's cheek. 'Don't worry, we'll be back in time.'

'I don't doubt it, the way your father drives.' His mother raised her eyebrows. 'Do try to make him go at a reasonable speed.'

'I'll try.' Bob was laughing as they left the room and headed outside.

'We'll follow you,' Bob said as they reached the car. His father was already behind the wheel.

Dieter eyed the gleaming Rolls-Royce, then looked at the battered old truck he was driving. 'Um, you will be able to travel faster, so go ahead, but I must ask you not to say anything to Danny until I arrive.'

'I'll make sure you're there.' He joined his father in the car, and they headed down the drive with a deep purr coming from the Rolls.

They were out of sight by the time Dieter had rattled his way out into the road.

'Are you going to tell me what this is all about?' Bob's father gave him an inquiring look as they sped along. 'Couldn't help hearing your raised voices. That young man was angry with you, so what have you done?'

'For some odd reason his son believes I'm his father, and Dieter is convinced that I told him that.' Bob settled back in the comfortable leather seat and told his father the whole story.

'Hmm, I'm not surprised you ended up in a shouting match. That little child will be very precious to him.' His father cast him a withering glance. 'You must have done something. I was hoping you had matured with age, but it looks very much as if you are still causing trouble.'

'I had nothing to do with this muddle.'

'Are you sure?'

Bob held on to the door as his father took a corner much too fast, his anger beginning to surface. 'For God's sake, slow down. We don't want to arrive too far ahead of Dieter. And what do you mean? Of course I'm sure!'

'If you've been showing this girl a lot of interest, the boy may well have assumed you were his father.'

'That's ridiculous.'

'The child is only three, Robert, and from what you've just told me, has had a traumatic time after losing his mother. He will be vulnerable and quite liable to flights of fancy. He knows his father went away and is probably looking at each man and wondering if he's come back at last. May I give you some advice?'

Bob snorted. 'No, but I don't suppose I can stop you.'

His father chose to ignore that remark. 'If I were your commanding officer, I would order you to retreat. You loved your wife to distraction, and I don't believe you'll ever feel like that again. Don't complicate Angie's, Danny's and Dieter's lives. God knows they have enough problems without you stirring things up. If you're beginning to hanker after another wife, then find someone like your mother.'

'That's impossible.' Bob laughed, his anger disappearing as quickly as it erupted. 'You know she is the only one of her kind.'

'I agree with you.' The General nodded. 'Will you take my advice?'

'I'll think about it, but this mess must be sorted out before I make a decision.'

His father began to chuckle. 'I keep forgetting you're a grown man. I haven't talked to you like this since you were in your teens.'

'If I remember rightly, you had to lecture me quite often.'

His father's grin spread. 'As I've said, you were, and still are, volatile. The army was the only place for you, and, apart from nearly getting yourself killed, you've made a success of being an officer.'

'A compliment, Father?'

The only answer was a deep rumble of laughter as they took another corner much too fast.

The rest of the journey was accomplished in companionable silence, and Bob closed his eyes. He had the greatest love and respect for his father, always listening to his advice, even if he didn't agree with him. He would make up his own mind, but was he being fair to Angie? Was he being fair to any of them?

His thoughts drifted back to the day they'd taken Danny out shopping. He was a delightful child, and one he would have been proud to call his son. The picture of Angie putting Danny to bed that night had tugged at him and made him realize what he was missing by not having a family of his own. But there was so much against marrying Angie. He began to tick off the things in his mind. He was so much older than her. She was a London girl – would she be able to cope with army life and the other officers' wives? And the little boy she had taken on would always come first in her life and affections. Could *he* accept that? He had demanded so much from his wife – too much, and she had finally left him. He wasn't good husband material. He would expect everything and everyone to fit in with his army career. The child was artistic and obviously talented; he needed someone who had the time and understanding to help him reach full potential. And Dieter was the one to do that.

Oh, hell.

'Nearly there.' His father's voice broke through his thoughts. 'You'll have to direct me to the farm from here.'

Bob sat up straight and gave directions. They were soon pulling into the yard.

Somehow, Dieter had managed to stay with them, and he arrived no more than two minutes later.

They all got out and made for the kitchen door of the farmhouse.

27

Laughter filled the room as everyone played 'I Spy'. Sally, Joe and Emma had joined them for tea, making for a lively afternoon, but Angie couldn't relax. Where was Dieter? What was taking him so long? Why hadn't he told her he wouldn't be here today? She missed him, liked him being around; liked seeing him with Danny. But he had been shattered by his son's reaction; she had seen it in his eyes, and felt his anguish. He had lost so much, and she had no idea how he would take this blow. She was so worried about him.

With a heavy heart she stood up and wandered over to the window for the umpteenth time, gasping in surprise when she saw the truck, a Rolls-Royce and three tall men striding towards the kitchen door.

All she had time to say was 'Hetty!' and they were in the front room.

Pandemonium broke out as Danny and Emma threw themselves at Bob.

Emma quickly turned her attention to Dieter. 'Deeder, my station house is lovely.'

He swung her into the air. 'I am pleased you like it, Princess.' After receiving a kiss he put her down again.

'We apologize for descending upon you unannounced.' Bob's father shook hands with everyone. 'But

I believe the matter is urgent. I'm Robert's father, by the way.'

'Would you like some tea?' Hetty looked flustered.

'Thank you. That would be most welcome.' The elderly man fixed his gaze on Danny. 'Ah, you must be the young man who is causing all the trouble.'

Danny stood in front of him, eyes wide and unblinking. Emma was doing the same, as was everyone else in the room. Angie wasn't surprised by the reaction. The three men filled the room with their presence, and the other two, she noticed, did not diminish Dieter. In fact he emanated just as much power and strength, but his was tempered with an unassuming dignity.

'Auntie?' Danny edged towards her, his gaze still riveted to the man. 'What have I done?'

'Nothing bad, Danny.' Bob stepped in before she could answer. 'You must meet my father, General Strachan.'

'General!' Danny forgot his nervousness and edged back towards Bob's father. 'Where's your uniform?'

'I'm retired now, but I still have it at home. You must come to visit and then I'll show it to you.'

'Can I come too?' Emma piped up. 'I'm Danny's bestest friend.'

'Of course, I shall expect you to come as well.' The General's smile encompassed everyone in the room. 'You must all come in the New Year.'

'Angie.' Bob stood beside her. 'Bring Danny into the kitchen. Dieter told me what happened and we must put this right.'

She nodded, and, as Hetty returned with the tea, she took Danny's hand and followed Bob and Dieter into the other room, her heart thumping. So Dieter had been to confront Bob. She wished he had told her what he was planning.

Once Danny was seated on a chair, Bob crouched down in front of him. Dieter stayed in the background, watching with narrowed eyes.

'Danny, I want you to tell me why you believe I'm your father.'

When Danny shot her an alarmed look, Angie sat beside him. 'It's all right, darling. There's nothing to worry about. Just tell Uncle Bob what you told me this morning.'

He swung his legs and studied his feet, and, without looking up, said, 'You built me a swing, and took me to see Father Christmas.'

'Uncles do that kind of thing.' Bob uncurled himself and sat on the edge of the table.

Danny pursed his lips and glanced up. 'Em said daddies do that. And you said I was your boy.'

'When?' A deep frown furrowed Bob's brow.

'After I'd seen Father Christmas.'

It took a few seconds for Bob to remember. As realization dawned, he lifted his hands. 'Oh, hell, I picked you up and said, "Come on, my boy."'

Danny nodded, still appearing troubled by this strange talk.

Bob squatted down to his level again. 'That's just the way I talk. I wasn't saying that you are my son. Dieter is your real father, and he's come a long way to find you.'

The child took a deep breath and huffed it out again, looking completely confused. 'Was you telling fibs?'

'No.' Bob shook his head. 'I'll try to explain in a way you can understand. When I was young, my parents sent me to a private school. When I did something wrong, the Master used to say, "Come on, my boy, one more prank like that and I'll put you on a charge."' He had changed his tone of voice to imitate that of the Master, making Danny giggle.

'Was you naughty?'

'I'm afraid I was.' Bob stood up again, rubbing his left leg. 'So you see, the Master wasn't saying I was his son, it was just a way of talking. Do you understand?'

Danny pursed his lips, looking thoroughly confused. 'You'll still be my uncle, though?'

'Of course. I'll be proud to be your uncle.'

Angie breathed a quiet sigh of relief and intervened for the first time. 'Didn't you have something to say to Dieter, darling?'

He nodded and snuck a shy glance at Dieter, who was standing at the end of the table. 'I'm sorry I told you to go away. I didn't mean it,' he added hastily. 'Grandma said I get 'fused.'

'I accept your apology.' Dieter stepped forward then. 'Do you now believe that I am your father?'

'S'pose.' Grey eyes met grey eyes. 'Mummy said you had a uniform.'

'I did. A German Luftwaffe uniform.'

Danny gave a puzzled huff. 'Why did you go away? Didn't you love us?'

Angie saw the pain on Dieter's face as he knelt in front of his son.

'I loved your mummy very much, but she didn't tell me about you. If I had known, I would *never* have left you.' He took hold of Danny's hands. 'You are too young to understand, but I promise that when you are older I shall tell you the whole story.'

'You won't go away again?'

'I shall never leave you again.'

Danny nodded. 'Auntie said I look like you.'

'You do.' Dieter swept him from the chair and into his arms. Walking over to a mirror on the wall, he tipped his head until it was touching Danny's. 'See, we have hair the same colour, and almost identical grey eyes. Your fingers are long like mine – pianist's hands, and I believe you will be tall like me as well when you are older.'

Danny peered at their reflections while Dieter juggled to take a wallet out of his back pocket. He flipped it open and showed Danny a photograph, much dog-eared by years of use.

'I was older than you in this photograph, but you can see that I looked just like you when young.'

The child stared at the picture. 'Who's the baby?'

'My little sister.'

'Hmm. Where is she?'

'I do not know.' Dieter's hand shook slightly.

Danny gazed up at him. 'Have you lost her?'

'Yes, I have.' He slipped the wallet back into his pocket. 'Do you see how like me you are?'

Danny nodded. 'Em looks like her mummy. Why don't I look like my mummy?' He swung round and held his hand out to Angie. 'Why isn't my hair red like yours and Mummy's?'

Seeing that he was about to become upset, Angie joined them at the mirror. 'Our hair colour is called chestnut, darling, and only girls in the family seem to have it.' She ruffled his hair playfully and grinned. 'It looks nice on girls, but I don't think you would like it. Everyone would call you copper knob.'

He wriggled back and studied Dieter's hair. 'Hmm, this is nice for boys. Have you got more pictures?'

'My family photographs have been lost in the war. That is the only one I have of me as a young boy.' Dieter put him down when he struggled, then stooped to his level. 'I am your father, and we shall have fun together. I shall help you with your music and teach you lots of things. Would you like that?'

Danny nodded and shuffled uncomfortably. 'Do I have to call you Daddy now?'

'I would like that, but not if you don't want to. You can call me Dieter, as you have always done.'

'Is that okay, Auntie?' Danny took hold of her hand, gazing up at her, his little face puckered with worry and confusion.

'If your daddy said it's all right, then you can call him by his name.' Angie saw the look of gratitude flash through Dieter's eyes when she referred to him in that way. But they had done all they could for today. Danny was a bright child, but he couldn't take in anything else at the moment. He had believed one thing and now he was being told something different. It would be best if they let him take his time in trying to understand what was going on. 'Now we had better go back to the other room. Grandma made tea and it will be getting cold.'

When they walked back into the front room, Emma was leaning on the General's knees, explaining the finer points of her train set.

He looked up, his gaze sweeping over all four of them and settling on Danny. 'All sorted out, young man?'

He nodded and let go of Angie's hand so that he could go to stand next to Emma.

'Good lad.' The General smiled in approval. 'And all done without tears. That's a brave soldier.'

The dimples flashed at the praise. 'I got muddled. I've never had a daddy.'

'Well, you have now.' The General hauled himself to his feet. 'We must be moving, Robert. Your mother will be furious if we're late for our guests.'

They all trooped outside to see them off, but they were further delayed as the children had to thoroughly examine the Rolls-Royce. It was only after Bob's father had driven them round the yard a few times that they were allowed to leave.

Angie hung back when they returned to the house, wanting to talk to Dieter alone. They remained in the porch by the kitchen.

'I wish you'd told me you were going to see Bob.'

'You think I did wrong?'

'No, no.' She caught the defensive tone in his voice. 'You did the right thing, but I was worried not knowing where you were.'

'Why?' He frowned.

'I was afraid you wouldn't come back.'

Dieter ran a hand over his eyes. 'Perhaps it would be for the best if I went away. Danny says he understands, but he does not. How can he? How can I explain to him about being in prison for all of those years, what was between his mother and myself, and why I left and never came back? How do you tell a young child such things? You told him I am his real father, and so has the Colonel, but still he does not believe it.'

'Oh, I'm sure you're wrong.' Angie put her hand on his arm, touched by his sadness.

'No, I am not.' Dieter dipped his head and closed his eyes. 'He likes me because of the music, but he does not want me as his father. He would accept Strachan without a moment's hesitation. Did you not see how he laughs and hangs on his every word? That is the father he wants.'

'If you are right, then he will have to change his mind.'

Dieter's head lifted slowly and he opened his eyes, studying Angie intently. 'Why should he? Strachan can give you much in life. If you marry him, my son will have security and love in his life.'

Her temper snapped. Was this the same man who

had insisted that his son be told about him? The one who wanted to support him and be part of his life? Was he trying to back away now? 'How the hell do you think I can marry him or anyone with this mess Jane has left behind? And what's happened to all your fine talk about watching your son grow into a man? Is it all getting too much for you, Herr Cramer?'

As she turned away, he caught her arm and spun her round to face him, pulling her into his arms and kissing her long and hard. After releasing her, he growled, 'What is it like to kiss a German, Fräulein Westwood? Does it repulse you? And does it surprise you that my only concern is for what will be best for my son? It will tear me apart to see him go to another man, but what am I to do? Tell me! You will no doubt one day marry. Must I then break Danny's heart by attempting to take him away from you? Separate him from the person he loves so much? Is that what I am going to have to do in order to keep my son? Tell me, for you appear to have all the answers. I do not know what to do any more.'

Angie wasn't sure who was the more shocked by what she did next. She burst into tears. It was just as well she didn't understand the stream of words coming from Dieter. It didn't take knowledge of the language to know he was swearing with ferocity in his native tongue.

'I'm sorry,' she sobbed. 'I didn't mean to insult you. I lost my temper, and when that happens I can't control what I say. I wouldn't give a damn if you came from

Timbuktu. Jane's dead, you're Danny's father. I love my darling boy so much and I just want this whole blasted thing sorted out so we can live a normal life. And don't threaten me, Dieter. It frightens me.'

Dieter cradled her head on his shoulder. 'I am at blame here. You have had much to cope with, and I have been an added burden with my impatience. I am the one who should be begging forgiveness. Jane was so young and I should never have walked away after taking advantage of her love for me. I am, and always shall be, greatly ashamed of that. I do not mean to frighten you, but I am at a loss to know what to do.'

She lifted her head, fished a handkerchief out of her pocket and blew her nose, then gave him a watery smile. 'Let us accept that we both acted in the heat of the moment, shall we? I'm proud that Danny has such a fine father. One I'm sure he will grow to love and respect.'

Dieter ran his fingers down her tear-stained cheek. 'Thank you, Angie, that is gracious of you. Now you need to splash your face with cold water to remove the tears. The others must not see that I have made you cry or I shall never be forgiven.'

She washed her face and dried it. 'Is that better?'

'Yes, much better.'

'Dieter,' she said before they went into the front room, 'be patient. Don't do anything in haste, and, above all, please don't leave us. Danny needs you.' And so do I, she added silently to herself. The kiss had been given in anger, but it had stirred up something inside

336

her. 'I promise that I will never, knowingly, do anything to jeopardize your relationship with your son. I will put him first, whatever my personal needs and feelings are. I am sure that in the future we are all going to have to compromise, but we will face this together. No matter how difficult things become, you must never walk away from us.'

'I shall not go away again, that I promise.'

It was eight o'clock before Sally and Joe decided to leave. Emma was standing in the middle of the room, coat on, her arms overflowing with presents and a huge grin on her face.

'She won't sleep for ages yet.' Sally pulled a face. 'Just look at her, she isn't a bit tired.'

There were kisses all round, and the little girl made sure Danny received one from her as well. As her parents made their way towards the door, Emma stopped and trotted back to Dieter.

'Deeder, would you make me a truck like Danny's?'

'Emma!' Sally came back for her daughter. 'How many times must I tell you not to ask for things?'

She glanced quickly at her mother, and then back to Dieter, who was shaking with amusement. 'Deeder don't mind. He's nice. Can I have a bright red one?'

'Of course.' He bowed. 'It will be my pleasure to make you a truck, Princess.'

Emma shot her mother a look of 'See, I told you so' triumph, then scuttled out to catch up her father.

Sally lifted her hands in defeat. 'She should have been

a boy, she really should. You don't have to do this, Dieter.'

'I shall keep my word.'

When he smiled the worry and upset of the last two days disappeared. The transformation was so marked that it literally took Angie's breath away. He was such a good man, but, more than that, he was a gentleman through and through, sensitive and kind. Of course, he also had his faults, like everyone. He had a dogged determination and would not be swayed once he made his mind up. Qualities like that must have been a great help to him while he'd been a prisoner of war in this country. Dieter was a complicated man, one who felt deeply. Oh, Jane, she thought with sadness, why did you ever let him go?

It was at that moment her stomach lurched. Was she beginning to find him attractive? Oh, Lord, she mustn't do that. Dieter had loved Jane. She mustn't let herself become too fond of him. She had enough problems without that. Friendship between them was all she could hope for. But one thing had to be admitted: she was in an emotional mess.

Watching Sally and her family drive out of the yard, she turned and held her hand out to Danny. 'Time for bed, young man.'

He pulled a face. 'Must I bathe, Auntie?'

Angie made a pretence of sniffing him. 'Hmm, you haven't been near the pigs today, so I'll let you off tonight. You can have one in the morning before we go home.'

He smiled as he kissed his granny and grandpa good-night. Then he glanced at Dieter. 'Are you gonna live in our house now?'

'That is not possible.'

'Why? Em's daddy lives with her.'

Dieter bent to his level. 'Emma's parents are married. They can live together.'

'You're not a proper daddy, then?'

'I am your father, but I can't live with you.' He gave Angie an anguished look. 'How can I explain?'

'You can't.' Angie touched Dieter's shoulder in sympathy. 'He's too young to understand, and he's already confused. He sees Emma with her family and wonders why it isn't the same for him.'

'You are right. I have done much damage by insisting he be told now.'

'It's as much my fault as yours. I felt this wasn't the right time and should have tried harder to make you see that.' Danny was looking worried, so Angie stroked his hair. 'It's all right, darling. There's nothing to worry about.'

'You did try, but I did not want to listen.' Dieter unwound himself and stood up, still holding Danny's gaze with his own. 'I will be a proper daddy to you, I promise.'

Seeming satisfied with that, and his auntie's comforting smile, he said 'Night, night' to everyone. Then he let Angie take his hand and lead him upstairs.

Dieter watched the small figure of his son until he disappeared at the top of the stairs. Danny's words,

'You're not a proper daddy, then', had felt like a knife slipping into his ribs.

Wandering over to the piano, he sat down and began to play softly, the beauty of the music seeping into the dark shadows of his life and lighting a tiny flame. He bowed his head as if in prayer, and allowed his fingers to sweep over the keys.

Upstairs, Danny snuggled under the covers and tipped his head to one side, listening to the music. 'Playing,' he said, and closed his eyes, instantly asleep.

28

There was great excitement as they gathered in Angie's small front room at ten o'clock on New Year's Day. Sally, Joe, Emma, Dieter, Danny and herself were going to visit Bob's parents today. The General had sent a message insisting that they come for the day. Hetty and John had also been invited but had declined, unable to leave the animals all day, but they had insisted that Dieter have the day off for the visit.

The children had their noses pressed against the window so that they could see the car as soon as it arrived.

Angie watched them with a smile on her face. Since the upset at Christmas, Danny was almost back to his normal self with Dieter. He hadn't once called him Daddy, but he watched him shyly and appeared happy when he was around. Angie was sure acceptance wasn't far away. Children had such a talent for adapting quickly to changing situations, and she wished she had the same ability. In the beginning she had fought against Dieter becoming a part of their lives; that had been wrong and cruel of her.

'He's here!' both children yelled at the top of their voices and began to tear around the room.

Angie managed to catch hold of them as they tried

to rush towards the door. 'Whoa! You'll tire yourself out before the day has even started.'

'It's the great big car.' Danny jiggled impatiently.

Sally patted her hair. 'I'll feel quite posh riding in a Rolls-Royce. I wonder what the house is like.'

'Very large.' Dieter helped Angie on with her coat. 'And most elegant.'

'Oh, dear.' Sally gave her daughter a doubtful glance. 'I'll have to tie her down.'

Joe opened the door to the General. 'We're all ready.'

'Good.' He strode in. 'Now where is everyone going to sit?'

They went outside and stood beside the car, and after some discussion it was decided that Danny should sit in the front on Dieter's lap, and the rest of them in the back with Emma sitting on Joe. Arranged in that way, they could all fit in comfortably. If Hetty and John had come, they would have needed to use the farm truck as well.

It was a lively journey, with the children chattering and asking questions all the way. They were at the age when they wanted to know everything.

When they turned in through some large gates and drove up to the house, Angie gaped in amazement. She had known Bob was well educated and used to having money, but she had never imagined anything like this. The house was huge.

Bob's mother was waiting for them in the hall, which was so big it had a fireplace and a log fire burning in the grate. The entire ground floor of her house would have fitted into this entrance hall, Angie thought, as she gazed around in wonder. She had never seen anything so grand.

'I'm very pleased you could come.' Mrs Strachan greeted them with a smile. 'Come into the library. There are refreshments waiting for you.'

Angie noticed a slight Scottish brogue, but of course Strachan was a Scottish name. The accent had probably been educated out of Bob and his father.

Their coats were hung in a small cloakroom off the hall and they followed Bob's mother.

'Don't touch anything,' Sally hissed to her daughter, but she was talking to her back. She was already running after Mrs Strachan.

A deep rumble of amusement came from the General. 'Don't worry about the children, my dears. We have two grandchildren and are quite used to their tearing around the place.'

'I didn't know Bob had children.' Joe placed an arm around his wife's shoulder.

'He hasn't, much to his mother's disappointment. We have a younger son. They are his children.'

If Angie had been impressed with the entrance hall, she fell in love with the library. It was warm, inviting and very homely. A room where you could relax and be comfortable.

'Please do sit down.' Mrs Strachan went over to a table laden with tea and lovely things to eat. 'I'm sorry Robert isn't here to greet you. He's had to go out, but will be back in time for lunch. I thought we would be more comfortable in here. It's our favourite room in the house.'

Emma was standing by the table on tiptoe to get a better view of the food, while Danny had spied the piano and was edging his way towards it.

'Ah, I see your boy is interested in music.' Mrs Strachan handed Angie a cup of tea.

'Yes, he's learning to play and read music.'

'Inherited that gift from his father, no doubt.' She smiled at Dieter. 'When you've had your tea, I'm hoping to be able to persuade you to play for me.'

'Of course, madam.' Dieter drained his cup and stood up. 'What would you like to hear?'

'I would love Beethoven's Piano Sonata No. 8, if that is possible. It's one of my favourites but is too much for me, I'm afraid.' She gave Dieter an appealing look. 'And then perhaps the Warsaw Concerto?'

'It would be my pleasure.' Dieter made his way through the archway to the piano.

Danny was already gazing at it in wonder.

'The music is in the stool.' Mrs Strachan had followed Dieter. 'I shall turn the pages for you.'

'Thank you. It is some time since I have played this piece.'

'He's gonna play that great big piano.' Danny tore back to Angie, his face alight with pleasure.

'Won't that be lovely?' Angie spun Danny round again as he reached her, giving him a little push. 'Go and sit near him. He won't mind.'

Needing no further encouragement, he crept back and sat on a chair where he could see clearly.

With the music on the stand and Mrs Strachan

standing by to turn the pages, Dieter began to play.

As the music filled the room no one moved, not even Emma, as Sally had a tight hold on her. Angie had never heard this before and watched in amazement as Dieter's hands flew over the keys in some sections. And the second piece had such power she could see Bob's mother was moved by it.

'My God,' the General murmured, 'the boy is wonderful.'

When the piece ended, there was utter silence. It was as if everyone was afraid to break the spell by speaking.

It was Danny who spoke first. He got off the chair and stood beside Dieter. 'What was that? And how did you make your fingers move so fast?'

'Years and years of practice.'

'My dear chap.' The General strode towards the piano. 'You should be earning your living by teaching and playing, not labouring on a farm.'

'Perhaps one day I shall be able to do that, but for the moment I must stay where I am.'

'Understand.' He patted Dieter's shoulder and smiled at his wife. 'We must see what we can do for this talented young man, my dear.'

His wife nodded. 'I've already set things moving.'

'Good, good. Now, Danny, you've heard how excellent your father is. You'll have to practise very hard to be as good as he is one day.'

'I do practise – every day.' He glanced up at Dieter. 'Don't I?'

'You do, and if you keep it up you will be better than me.'

Danny didn't look as if he quite believed that, but he flushed at the praise. 'You said I could see your uniform, General.'

'So I did. Bring Emma and we'll go upstairs right now.'

When the three of them left the room, Dieter said to Mrs Strachan, 'Will you now play for us, madam?'

'After listening to such artistry I do hesitate, for I cannot match your skill or touch. However, I did promise, so I shall play something a little easier. What do you suggest?'

'Moonlight Sonata? That is one of Danny's favourites.'

'Ah, yes.' She sat on the seat vacated by Dieter. 'I believe I can manage that.'

In fact she more than managed it. Angie knew the piece by now, for it was the one Mrs Poulton had played when she had first taken Danny for lessons. It was so beautiful.

'You are an excellent pianist,' Dieter said when she had finished.

'Ah, that is kind of you, but I play only for my own enjoyment.'

At that moment the children came tearing back into the room, faces glowing with excitement.

'The General's got loads of medals.' Danny held out a small badge for Angie to see. 'Look, I can keep this. Em's got one too. Ain't it smashing!'

'It's lovely, darling. You must take good care of it.'

'Oh, I will.' Danny rushed over to Dieter and showed him as well. 'Did you have things like this on your uniform?'

Angie's eyes misted over as she watched Dieter admiring the badge. She had been right. Danny had accepted him very quickly and was now going to him quite naturally. It was an encouraging step forward. He wasn't calling him Daddy yet, but she was sure that would soon come.

'I did, but all I have left are the fabric Luftwaffe badges.'

'Will you show me?' Danny was swinging on his leg.

'Of course, I shall find them and bring them to you tomorrow.'

'What's luft . . . ?' Emma, who had joined them, couldn't get her tongue around the word.

'It means the German Air Force.'

'What a funny word.' Nevertheless, she appeared impressed as she showed him her badge. 'You got pictures in your uniform?'

'A couple, yes.'

'Show us!' Both children spoke at the same time.

Dieter took the wallet out of his pocket and produced the photos, as everyone crowded round to have a look. One was of him standing beside a Dornier bomber with the rest of his crew; the other had been taken in the POW camp at Goathurst, with Bob talking to him and leaning on a walking stick.

'That's Uncle Bob.' Emma pointed, as sharp-eyed as usual.

'He was in charge of the prisoner-of-war camp. I expect he was telling us off for doing something we shouldn't have been.'

'Did they lock you up?' Danny knew what prisoner meant.

'Yes, for a very long time.'

Emma was more interested in the aeroplane. 'That's very big.'

'Pass them round, Dieter.' Joe took one of them from his daughter, who looked as if she was going to keep it.

When they reached Angie, she studied the one of him with his crew and saw a group of young men, relaxed and laughing. Her heart ached for them. They had only been boys, and now they were all dead, all except Dieter. Once they had been the enemy; now they would have been friends – if they had lived. What a terrible waste of life the war had been.

'Did you have to do what Uncle Bob told you?' Danny wasn't finished with the interesting subject.

'We did; he was very stern.' Dieter smiled easily. 'But we got up to all sorts of things he never knew about.'

The General laughed. 'I can imagine, but it must have been hard for you to spend so many years as a prisoner.'

Dieter sobered at the memory. 'My greatest deprivation was not having a piano. I used to spend long times just going through the music, listening to it in my head and imagining my fingers on the keys. It was the only way I had to keep up with the practice. When I went to work at the farm, they had an old piano. It needed tuning and I did this in my spare time, until it was in a good-enough condition to play. That was a great joy for me.'

At that moment Bob arrived wearing his uniform. The children stood up straight and saluted, receiving one of Bob's best in smart military style, making everyone laugh.

'I apologize for not being here when you arrived, but I had to go up to London unexpectedly.'

'Dieter was telling us how you tried to keep them in order at the camp.' His father chuckled. 'I felt sorry for the poor devils when they gave you that posting, for you were in a foul mood after being refused permission to return to the fight.'

'Ah, yes.' Bob gave Dieter a wry smile. 'It took some doing. They were an enterprising bunch, but I don't believe for one moment that they were frightened of me.'

'You're just in time, Robert.' His mother kissed his cheek. 'Lunch will be ready in fifteen minutes.'

The phone rang and Mrs Strachan waved her husband down again as he began to get up. 'I'll take that in the other room. It's probably the call I've been waiting for.'

It was almost half an hour before she returned, full of apologies. 'I am so sorry to have kept you waiting. We had better go in to lunch, or Cook will be cross with me.'

Both children were well behaved at the table. Emma knew this was the one place her mother insisted on good manners.

The meal of soup, succulent lamb and trifle with fresh cream was thoroughly enjoyed by everyone. There was cheese to finish, but Angie couldn't manage another mouthful. There was a good deal of lively talk and laughter round the table. Bob's mother seemed rather pleased after her long phone call.

Coffee was taken in the library, and, as Angie watched the maid busy with the cups, she wondered what it would be like to have staff to cook your meals and wait on you all the time. Her family had been considered well off, as they had owned their houses, and she'd had a decent education, but her background didn't compare with this sort of wealth and luxury.

Her gaze turned to Bob, who was talking with Joe and laughing about something. The soldier she had met on the train had become a friend – and more than a friend. They were attracted to each other, he got on well with Danny, and she hadn't looked further than that.

'Children!' The General clapped his hands to gain their attention. 'Why don't you look behind the chair in the corner? There might be something there for you.'

Danny and Emma couldn't move fast enough and, after scrambling on their hands and knees, emerged triumphant with a parcel each. The paper was torn away with cries of delight. A colouring book and a box of coloured pencils were inside.

They thanked Bob's parents nicely, without any prompting, then sprawled on the carpet and began to fill in the pictures. Silence reigned as they concentrated.

'That was very astute of you,' Joe laughed.

'We didn't want them becoming bored.' Mrs Strachan gazed fondly at the children.

Bob stood up, walked over to Angie and said something to her.

She nodded and they left the room together.

Dieter noticed the gentle squeeze of Angie's shoulder as Bob spoke to her. He knew Bob was returning to Berlin the next day, so was he going to take this opportunity to propose?

They made a fine couple, and he couldn't blame Angie if she took this chance for a secure future, but how he wished she hadn't fallen for a career soldier. If it had been someone who lived in this country, they could have worked something out. He watched his golden son with a heavy heart. Wherever Angie decided to go, he would have to follow her. He couldn't give up Danny.

It was half an hour before they returned, but Dieter could deduce nothing from their expressions. He waited anxiously for an announcement to say they were engaged, but nothing happened. So they were keeping to themselves whatever had been discussed.

Mrs Strachan claimed his attention by asking how Danny was enjoying his piano lessons. Dieter pushed his concerns aside. He liked this charming, aristocratic-looking woman very much. She reminded him of his own mother.

'Dieter, I realize that you want to stay near your son, but would you allow me to see if I can find you more suitable employment?'

'Doing what, madam?'

'I was thinking of a music master in a school somewhere.'

He started in surprise. 'But that would not be possible.'

'Why not? You've had a good education, have you not?'

'It was cut short by the war, but, yes, I have been well educated.'

She nodded. 'That is evident, and you are obviously qualified to teach music. You have a slight accent, but your English is excellent.' She studied him thoroughly. 'What is your objection?'

'I do not object. It is something I would love to do, but I am German.'

Her eyes opened wide in surprise. 'What difference does that make?'

'Parents may not like to have a German teaching their children.'

'You are quite wrong about that, Dieter.' She reached out and touched his arm. 'The war is over, and many prisoners of war opted to remain in this country. There are Germans and people of other nationalities making new lives for themselves here, and they are welcome. You can do the same. Let me make inquiries for you.'

'Thank you.' Dieter was touched by her sincerity. 'I should be most grateful for your help.'

'Leave it with me. Now, we must have tea before you all return home. It has been such a pleasant day.'

The refreshments were brought in, but Dieter couldn't eat a thing. He wouldn't allow his hopes to rise too much, but if he could have a teaching position it would solve a few problems. He would earn more money, and with decent holidays he could travel to wherever Danny was and spend time with him. It wasn't ideal, of course, because he wanted to be with him all the time. But if he could establish himself in a good job and find a house for himself, perhaps Danny would come to stay with him in the holidays.

He put a stop to his planning. Mrs Strachan meant well, but this might come to nothing. Nevertheless, it had made him think. He must not sit around worrying what Angie intended to do. He must build a future for himself in this country.

It was time to put the past behind him.

29

As the Rolls-Royce drove away with everyone waving, Bob felt his mother slip her hand through his arm.

'Come inside. I wouldn't be surprised if it snowed soon.'

Back in the library, Bob warmed his hands by the fire. 'Hope the bad weather holds off until I get back to Berlin.'

'I want you to take this with you.' She handed him the photograph of Dieter. 'You may need it if we can trace his family.'

Bob took the picture and pursed his lips. 'You're wasting your time, Mother. If they had been alive, we would have found them by now.'

'I know.' She sighed sadly. 'But you know our little group has had some success, and we shall see what we can do for him. It must be terrible not knowing for sure what happened to them. I believe that if he could, at least, know where they are buried, he would be able to get on with his life.'

'I agree, but it might only be a communal grave.'

'Even that would help, if we can find it. Perhaps he would be able to grieve properly at last, for I doubt that he has done that.'

He slipped the photograph into his wallet and smiled

at his mother. She cared so much about the plight of displaced persons. 'Of course it will.'

'The phone call I received before lunch was to tell me that two of our team have arrived in Germany. I have taken the liberty of giving them your address and phone number, should they need your help.' She tipped her head on one side and held his gaze. 'I hope you don't mind, but you may be able to cut through the bureaucracy.'

'I'll be pleased to help.' Bob still wasn't very happy about this enterprise. 'I hope you haven't raised Dieter's hopes.'

'I'm not a fool, Robert.' She spoke sharply. 'All we have said is that we will see if we can find out anything. No more than that.'

Bob held up his hand. 'I didn't intend to criticize you. I'm concerned for Dieter, that is all. He was in a state when we found him, and he looks so much better now.'

'We will be cautious. He is a fine young man. In fact they are all lovely people.' She had a speculative gleam in her eyes. 'Is there something between you and Angie?'

'Mind your own business, Mother.' He hid his amusement, knowing that he was about to receive a grilling.

'Never. So, do I take it that you are more than fond of her?'

He knew he would tell her in the end, but for the moment he would make her wait. 'I've talked things over with Angie and we have come to an agreement.'

'What kind of an agreement?'

Bob grinned. 'As I've already said, mind your own business, Mother. This is between Angie and me.'

'That is where you are wrong!' She was becoming exasperated with him. 'There is the child and his father; you cannot ignore them.'

'I am well aware of that.' Bob studied his mother through narrowed eyes. 'I can almost see your mind working. I know I can be a selfish bastard at times, but I wouldn't hurt them. Don't you trust me to do what is best for all concerned, regardless of my own personal wishes?'

'You are a tough, determined man, and I do not believe you would knowingly hurt them, but I believe you like the girl, and if you marry her you will be causing a lot of anguish. You find her attractive, and the idea of a ready-made family appealing.'

'You know me so well.' He had teased her enough, so he leant forward and squeezed her hand. 'Don't worry – Angie is a sensible girl, and' – his mouth twisted in a sad smile – 'I don't think she loves me.'

'Ah.' His mother smiled then. 'Then she is a sensible girl. That must have been a shock for you.'

Bob tipped his head back and roared with laughter. 'You have a very low opinion of your elder son.'

'I know his faults and love him still. Marry for love, Robert.'

'I did that the first time,' he said, shaking his head. 'I won't fall into that trap again. If I do marry again, it will be for comfort and companionship.'

'And Angie would fit the bill, would she?'

'She would.' Bob prowled the room. 'If it were only the two of us, I would try to persuade her to marry me, but Dieter and the boy complicate things.'

'So you have decided to walk away?'

'Oh, no.' Bob smiled at his mother. 'I am going to be Danny's uncle, and Angie's friend.'

'And how does Angie feel about that?'

'She agrees it's for the best.' Bob sat down and stretched out his legs. There was no way he was going to tell her what else he had proposed to Angie. 'The main passion in her life is Danny, and you know that half-measures would never suit me.'

Mrs Strachan poured herself a cup of tea from the fresh tray that had just been brought in, and then measured out a small whisky. She gave the whisky to her son. 'This couldn't have been an easy decision for you, but you have done the right thing.'

Bob drained the drink in one go and grimaced. 'You're right it wasn't easy; I was sorely tempted. She's a fine young woman, but I could have ended up hurting everyone, including myself. I'm not good husband material.'

'Sadly that's true, but you're a good man none the less.'

'I thank you for those few kind words.' He held out his glass for a refill, a gleam in his eyes. 'Of course, I could change my mind, tell everyone to go to hell, and take what I want.'

His mother gave him a withering look. 'Robert, I do despair of you at times.'

*

The children were tired after their lovely day and had fallen asleep still clutching their presents.

Dieter was talking quietly to the General, Sally and Joe silent in case they woke their daughter. Angie settled back in the comfortable seat and closed her eyes, listening to the hum of the tyres on the road. It was a soothing sound.

She felt more content than she had done for a long time. The talk she'd had with Bob had cleared the air, and her mind. He had been perfectly straight and blunt. He had asked if she would be willing to marry him and bring Danny out to Germany to live with him. When she had vehemently refused, he'd nodded, saying in that case marriage between them wouldn't work. He would expect a wife to follow him wherever in the world he was posted. She had told him that wouldn't be possible. She would never take Danny away from Dieter.

They had talked everything over in a rational way, without emotion clouding the issue, and they had both recognized how wrong it would be for them, not to mention the heartache it would cause Dieter. She adored Danny and there was no way she would disturb his life now that he was settling down. She had told Bob that as much as she would like to marry one day, Danny would always come first. If that meant she would have to stay single, then so be it.

He had then made an outrageous suggestion that she had turned down very firmly. She found him very attractive and would certainly have given marriage to him serious consideration, but there was no way she would agree to become his mistress whenever he was in this country.

She smiled to herself as she remembered his reaction. He had shrugged with a glint of devilment in his eyes, saying that he hadn't expected her to agree, but he'd had to try, hadn't he? And to let him know if she ever changed her mind!

When she couldn't stop a rumble of amusement coming from her, Sally turned her head.

'What's amused you?'

'Just something Bob said.' She changed the subject. 'It's been a lovely day, hasn't it?'

'Yes, it has.' Sally closed her eyes again.

Angie did the same and returned to her thoughts. In the end they had agreed that they should remain friends. Though the kiss he had given her then had not been the sort given between *friends*. He had grinned and said that was something for him to remember when he was in his lonely bed.

She doubted he had trouble coaxing women to spend the night with him. Life with Robert Strachan would not have been dull, but it couldn't be, and she was relieved they'd had a frank talk. While they had been talking she had also realized just how concerned she was for Dieter's happiness as well as Danny's. He was now an important part of their lives and she wanted it to stay that way.

'Here we are.' The General stopped outside Angie's cottage.

They all got out and, after thanking the General, Sally and Joe took their still sleeping daughter indoors.

'I'll wait for you,' Bob's father said to Dieter, who was carrying Danny, also fast asleep.

'That is kind of you, sir, but I shall walk back to the farm after Danny is in bed.'

'Right, then I'll be off.' He opened the car door. 'It's been a real pleasure to have you join us today. You must do it again soon.'

'Would you like a cup of tea before you go?' Angie didn't like to think of him just turning around and driving straight home again.

He beamed at her. 'No, thank you, my dear.' After getting back in the car, he waved and sped up the road.

'It won't take him long to get home,' Angie said drily, as she opened the front door. 'Better take Danny straight upstairs, Dieter.'

The little boy was soon in his pyjamas and tucked up in bed.

'He never even woke up.' Dieter gazed down at his son.

'No, he's worn out. It's been a long day for him.' She turned on the dim night-light and they crept out, leaving the bedroom door open in case he woke suddenly and called for her. He didn't do it so often now, but she was still alert in case he did. It always calmed him at once when he saw her there with him.

'Would you like cocoa?' she asked, when they reached the kitchen.

'I would prefer coffee, if you have some.'

'Of course.' She chatted about the day as she made the drinks. 'Are you hungry?'

'No, thanks.' Dieter laughed. 'I have eaten far too much today.'

Angie put the cups on the table and sat down. 'And me. I don't think I'll be able to eat anything for a week.'

The kitchen was warm and cosy, and in the relaxed atmosphere Dieter told her about Mrs Strachan's suggestion that he try for a job as a music teacher.

'That's a wonderful idea!' Angie was enthusiastic. 'It would be perfect for you, and I'm sure you'd enjoy it.'

'I would.' Dieter nodded in agreement. 'But I would not wish to let John and Hetty down. They have been very kind to me.'

'They would understand.' She smiled encouragingly. 'I know they would be happy to see you settled in work you love and are suited for. With your talent it's a terrible waste to be working as a farm labourer.'

'I will talk to them, but this might come to nothing. With my background it might not be easy to find a school willing to employ me.'

'You mustn't think like that.' She reached out and took hold of one of his hands, marvelling at the elegance of his long fingers. 'Parents would be pleased to know that someone with your talent was teaching their children. Go for it, Dieter!'

He smiled into her animated face, cradling her hand in both of his. 'Very well, I shall *go for it,* as you say. Mrs Strachan is going to make inquiries on my behalf, but I shall begin searching as well. If I can find something, it must be near here, for I would not wish to be far from Danny.'

She nodded. 'You must stay close and see him often. He likes you, and I feel it won't be long before he accepts you as his father.'

Dieter held her gaze. 'You will not take him away from here, will you, Angie?'

'I have already given you my word on that. And now Danny has been told who you are, you must not disappear from his life. It would cause him much distress now.'

'I promise I shall never leave him.'

Angie wasn't going to marry Bob. He was sure of it. Dieter shoved his hands into the pockets of the greatcoat to keep them warm as he walked back to the farm. She would never have said those things if she had such plans.

He kicked a stone along the track, feeling more hopeful about the future than he had done for many years. Now he had something to aim for – a new and secure life to make for himself and Danny.

John and Hetty were sitting by a huge log fire when he arrived.

'Did you have a good day?' Hetty asked.

'It was very pleasant. The Strachans are nice people.'

'They are.' John indicated a tray on the sideboard. 'Do you want anything? The tea's still hot.'

'No, thank you.' Dieter sat down. 'I wish to talk to you.'

He spent the next ten minutes explaining about Mrs Strachan's suggestion, and how much he would like to become a music teacher, if at all possible.

'That's a wonderful idea.' Hetty nodded, beaming in agreement. 'We've been hoping you would try for something like that.'

'We certainly have,' John said. 'As much as I appreciate your help around the farm, this is not what you should be doing.'

'You are both very kind.' Dieter was touched by their obvious pleasure. 'I shall start looking in this area at once. If I am successful, would you like me to move out?'

'Certainly not!' They both spoke together, looking horrified at the suggestion.

'We love having you here,' Hetty said with a gentle smile. 'This is your home for as long as you want to stay.'

'In that case if I do have another job, I shall pay you rent.'

John gave a dismissive wave of his hand. 'We'll talk about that when the time comes.'

Sleep did not come easily that night; Dieter's mind was working overtime. He had spent another hour talking with John and Hetty. They had given him a list of schools in the area whose students were ten years old and upwards. There was one just outside Bridgewater, near Durleigh. He would try them at the start of the next term. If he couldn't find anything, perhaps Mrs Strachan would be more successful.

Placing his hands behind his head, he stared up at the ceiling, wide awake. How fortunate he was to have the support of so many kind people. When he had returned here after York, sad and dispirited, he hadn't known what he was going to do. Now he did. He would consider this country his home. One day, when Europe had recovered from the war, he would take his son to see Germany, for it would be beautiful again once the scars had healed.

30

Three weeks into the New Year and the threatened snow had arrived. At least four inches had fallen during the night and it was still coming down. Angie and Sally stood at the kitchen window watching the antics in the garden. The children were bombarding Joe and Dieter with snowballs and chasing them. Joe slipped, caught hold of Dieter for support and they both ended up on the ground. With squeals of delight, Emma and Danny jumped on them. All four were rolling in the snow in a mass of arms and legs.

Sally smirked. 'I thought we had only two kids between us, but it looks as if we've got four.'

Angie's shoulders shook with laughter. These Sunday lunches together were becoming a regular thing. The two girls took turns to cook, and this week it was Angie's job. The children loved it, Joe and Dieter had become good friends, and it gave Angie and Sally a chance to have a gossip.

When Angie looked back now, it was hard to remember what life had been like in London. This was so much better. They had been accepted into village life and were surrounded by friends.

She returned to the cooking, opening the oven door to check on the joint of beef John had given her. 'Fifteen minutes and we can dish up.'

'Right.' Sally opened the back door and yelled that lunch was almost ready.

Four bedraggled figures erupted into the kitchen, faces pink, noses red, and sopping wet. Pools of water began to form where each one stood.

Sally whipped a mop out of a cupboard, brandishing it at them. 'Get those wellingtons off and put your wet coats upstairs in the bath. We'll dry them by the fire when they've stopped dripping. Quickly. Look at the mess you're making.'

There was a scramble to remove the offending footwear, then the four of them thundered up the stairs, seeking rapid escape from Sally and her mop.

They came down again just as the meal was being put on the table, hungry as wolves after their games in the snow.

After lunch the dishes were stacked on the draining board to be dealt with later, and they took the tea into the front room. The warmth of the fire after a good meal inside them was too much for Emma and Danny. The friends squeezed into one armchair and promptly fell asleep.

'Just look at them,' Sally whispered to Angie. 'They look like a couple of kittens.'

'How are you getting on with your search for a teaching job?' Joe asked Dieter.

'I have finally had a reply from the school near Durleigh. They've asked me to see them tomorrow morning at ten o'clock.'

'Oh, that's wonderful news!' Angie was thrilled. Dieter had applied for quite a few positions without success, and even Mrs Strachan with her connections hadn't been able to find anything in this area. To have had a reply from the one she knew Dieter really wanted was encouraging.

'We must not get too excited. They have asked to see me. That is all.'

Sally grinned. 'They'll love you, Dieter, and when they hear you play you'll get the job.'

Joe glanced out of the window. 'You might not get there if this weather doesn't let up.'

'I shall keep my appointment even if I have to slide all the way there.'

From the determined set of his mouth, Angie had no doubt that a bit of snow would not make him miss this appointment. She sent up a silent prayer that he would be taken on. If anyone deserved a slice of good luck, it was Dieter.

Emma woke up, fighting her way off the chair and disturbing Danny. She ran over to the window. 'It's stopped snowing! Can we build a snowman before it all goes?'

Danny was also wide awake now. 'Can you give us a carrot for his nose, Auntie?'

'I've got some in the kitchen.' She stood up. 'Then I'd better get on with the washing-up.'

It didn't take Sally and Angie long, and as soon as the dishes were stacked away they went into the garden to join in the fun.

*

The next morning Dieter was up early. He was relieved to see that a lot of the snow had melted, so he shouldn't have much difficulty with the short journey. This interview meant a lot to him and he was nervous as he sorted out what he was going to wear. Not that there was any choice. The suit and tie Strachan had given him were smart enough still, and the suit fitted him better now that he had put on some weight. He'd bought a new shirt and pair of shoes.

He had just finished dressing when John knocked on his bedroom door and came in with a coat over his arm.

'It's still cold out there, and you can't wear that army greatcoat.' He held out the coat. 'Here, take this. I never wear it.'

The black wool coat was soft, warm and fitted Dieter perfectly. 'That is very kind of you, John. I shall be grateful to borrow it, for I did not know what I could wear. I was going to slip the army coat off and fold it up when I arrived at the school.'

'I don't want it back. You keep it. The moths will only get at it otherwise.'

Before he could protest, Hetty bustled in. 'Let me look at you, Dieter.'

He turned in a circle and she nodded in approval. 'You look every inch the perfect music teacher.'

Doubt assailed Dieter. Everyone was so sure he would get the job, but he didn't dare hope too much. 'I do not have proof of my qualifications. All papers were lost . . .'

'They will understand that.' Hetty was brimming with confidence. 'You'll impress them without pieces of paper.'

'I shall do my best.'

'Take the truck.' John's smile was amused. 'Only leave it out of sight of the school and walk the last bit. Don't want them to see you arrive in a heap of junk.'

With a laugh, Dieter was on his way. The roads weren't too bad, but he still had to drive with care. Even so, he was twenty minutes early when he walked through the school doors. He stood in the corridor wondering where he should go.

'Can I help you?' A middle-aged woman stopped beside him.

'I have an appointment to see the Headmaster, Mr Hargrove, at ten o'clock. I am a little early.'

'He'll like that. He's a real stickler for punctuality.' She gave him an assessing look. 'Go to the end of this corridor and you'll see his office right in front of you.'

Dieter bowed slightly. 'Thank you, madam.'

She began to move away but stopped again. 'Are you the new music master?'

'I hope so, madam.'

She smiled then and made for a classroom further along the passage.

He followed her directions and, before knocking on the door, took a deep, steadying breath. He liked the feel of the place and wanted the position very much. It would be a big disappointment if he was turned down, but he knew that that was a distinct possibility.

He knocked, and waited.

'Come in,' a voice called.

Dieter turned the handle and stepped into a room littered with books, files and papers. The man behind the desk was nearer fifty than forty, hair greying, but with shrewd brown eyes that took in the appearance of the man standing in front of him.

He hauled himself stiffly out of the chair, smiled and held out his hand. 'You're Mr Cramer, I take it?'

'Yes, sir.' Dieter shook hands with him.

'Glad you made it. Wretched weather. Please sit down.'

He tried to relax as he watched Mr Hargrove read the letter he had sent in. That was put aside and another one scrutinized for some moments, then he looked up and smiled. 'Mrs Strachan speaks highly of you. Her letter arrived the day after we received yours.'

'I wasn't aware she had approached you.' Dieter was surprised, but he shouldn't have been because he had kept her in touch with what he was doing. A good word from her might give him more chance. His hope increased.

'Ah, yes, I've met her a few times. I served with her husband for a while until I had an accident on a motorbike. Now tell me about yourself.' Mr Hargrove settled back in his chair.

Dieter ran through his childhood education and the war years. He kept it brief and to the point.

When he finished, the Headmaster nodded. 'I take it you don't have any proof of your musical education?'

'All was destroyed.' Dieter's heart beat erratically. Was

this going to be the thing to hold him back with English schools? 'If you would allow me to play for you, sir?'

'Best thing to do.' He stood up, grabbed a stick from the corner of the room and, leaning heavily on it, walked towards the door. 'We'll go to the music room. It will disrupt Class Eleven's lesson, but I don't suppose the little devils will mind.'

Dieter was reminded of his old school when he reached the room. There were around a dozen children scattered about, each holding a different instrument, with various excruciating sounds coming from them as they tried to tune up. In the centre was a fine grand piano.

The Headmaster rapped his stick on the wooden floor. 'Quiet!'

All eyes turned towards them and silence fell.

'What are you doing taking this class, Baker?'

A young man of no more than twenty-one flushed. 'There isn't anyone else available at the moment, Mr Hargrove.'

'Well, they won't learn much from you.' The Headmaster snorted in disgust. 'You're tone deaf.'

Dieter hid a smile as the group of ten-year-olds sniggered. He was becoming more hopeful by the minute. This school was in desperate need of a music teacher.

'Right, Mr Cramer, play us Beethoven's Piano Sonata No. 5, first movement. The music is all filed in order over there.' He pointed to an alcove full of shelves.

'I do not need the music, sir.' He removed his coat, sat at the piano and played the piece as ordered.

'Hmm.' The Headmaster pursed his lips when the

music stopped. 'Impressive. You can read music, I take it?'

'You choose and I'll play it.'

Mr Hargrove leant on his stick and surveyed the shelves stacked with sheet music. 'Need something you don't know . . .'

'Sir.' A boy stepped forward. 'What about the piece I wrote for last year's summer concert? He won't have seen that before, and I'd love to hear him play it.'

'Splendid, Philip, get it for us.' The Headmaster raised his eyebrows at Dieter. 'That will test your sight-reading skills.'

'I am sure it will.' Dieter bowed to the boy as he put the sheets on the stand. 'You will turn for me?'

Philip nodded.

It's a simple-enough piece, Dieter thought, as he scanned the first sheet, hearing the music in his head. Without hesitation he began to play. Some of it was unstructured and could use some further work, but there was a decent passage near the end, as if the composer had suddenly decided where he was going. The boy had promise.

After the last note he took his hands off the keys and waited.

'Gee, sir, I've never heard it played like that before.' Philip's face was flushed with pleasure. He dragged a chair up to sit beside Dieter, took the music off the stand and shuffled through the sheets until he found what he was looking for. 'This section isn't right, but I just can't see how to change it.'

'A pencil, please.'

The boy fished one out of his jacket pocket and handed it to Dieter.

'I believe something like this is needed.' He began to write on the music. 'This can easily be rubbed out if you don't care for it.'

Philip was oblivious to anything else and watched the changes with fascination. 'Play it, please, sir.'

Dieter ran through the section again, and by now all the children were clustered around the piano. Time passed unnoticed as they discussed and made changes. Dieter was so absorbed in what he was doing that he had forgotten he was only there for an interview.

'Now you play it for me.' He stood up and made Philip take his place at the piano. He listened with eyes closed. It really was rather good, and the changes he had suggested were only slight.

There was much applause when Philip finished.

Dieter smiled. 'You show a great deal of promise.'

'Thank you, sir, I can see where I was wrong now.'

'You've got an accent.' Another boy was staring at him in a curious way. 'Are you Polish?'

'No, I am German.'

'Your English is good.' A girl spoke this time.

'That is because I was taught it at school, and I spent many years here as a prisoner of war.' Dieter wasn't going to hide anything from these curious children. If he did get the job, he wanted everything out in the open.

'Did you go back home after the war?'

The questions were coming from all directions now.

'Yes, but there was nothing for me there. My home and family were gone, so I came back to this country. This is my home now, and I am happy here.'

'Right, boys and girls, that's enough questions. Back to your music.' The Headmaster broke up the group. 'Come with me, Mr Cramer, we have things to discuss.'

As they left the room, Philip whispered, 'Hope you get the job, sir.'

'Thank you. Keep on with your composing.'

'I will.' He waved and so did every child in the room.

'Well, you appear to have made quite an impression.' Mr Hargrove sat behind his desk again.

Dieter waited . . . hardly daring to breathe. The next few minutes would be vital to his future.

The truck came to a sudden halt outside Angie's cottage and she rushed to open the front door. She had been on tenterhooks all morning, wondering how Dieter was getting on. He walked in, turned to face her, his expression serious.

He hadn't got the job! She was bitterly disappointed for him. 'What happened?'

He shrugged, then lunged forward, lifting her off the floor, spinning her round and round, his laughter filling the front room. 'I have been given the job.'

'Oh, you tease.' She wrapped her arms around his neck. 'I thought you hadn't got it. This is wonderful. I'm so happy for you. When do you start?'

'After the Easter break. The other teacher is leaving

then. He wasn't there today because he was sick, but I met some of the children.' He put Angie down after giving her a crushing hug. 'Where's Danny? I must tell him.'

'He's next door. Joe will be home for lunch and they'll be eager to see you.'

She watched him stride across the garden, a spring in his step. He opened the small gate and ducked through the archway. Never had she seen him so happy; he seemed almost boyish, and so like Danny.

At last things were turning around for him. The future was looking better and better for all three of them.

31

The first snowdrops were in bloom, their tiny bells dancing in the sunshine, and daffodils were pushing their way through the soil. Spring was almost here.

Dieter couldn't remember when he had felt this happy and so full of hope. He was looking forward to his new job in a couple of weeks, and Danny had begun to follow him around like an adoring puppy. He still hadn't called him Daddy, but this was enough for the moment. He wasn't going to make the same mistake again and rush things. And the little boy's burgeoning talent made him so proud of his son. Angie knew nothing about classical music. The popular tunes of the day were what she liked. Some of the classical music was lovely, but a lot she just didn't understand. He was enjoying introducing her to different composers.

The post had just been delivered and he glanced idly through the letters before leaving them on the kitchen table for John and Hetty. They had taken some time off and gone shopping. He was about to toss them down when he noticed one addressed to him. Frowning, he studied the postmark. Frankfurt? Who could be writing to him from there?

He hastily tore open the envelope and inside was a

short note from General Strachan and a couple of photographs.

> Dieter, we are in Germany at the moment trying to help a woman find her daughter. She was shipped here from Poland during the war as a slave labourer and has never returned to her home. The Red Cross haven't had any success, so they have asked us to see what we can do.
>
> During our inquiries we have come across a few people who lived in Dresden, and have enclosed some photographs in case you recognize any of them. A long shot, I agree, but we have learnt to follow up every lead, however tenuous.
>
> You can contact us at the above address in Frankfurt should you need to.

Dieter sat down and gazed at the people in the pictures, shaking his head. He had never seen them before, but it had been a big city, so that wasn't surprising. They would have to be personal family friends or near neighbours for him to recognize them.

After shuffling through them again, he was about to slip them back into the envelope when something caught his attention. There were four people in one photograph: a mother, father and two grown-up children, one boy and one girl.

What he saw had him surging to his feet and tearing upstairs for the small magnifying glass he kept in his bag. His hand was shaking as he held it over the girl. Gerda! No, it couldn't be. The name on the back said she was Helga Manstein.

Slithering down the stairs, his feet hardly touching them, he rushed into the kitchen and picked up the General's note again. His heart was beating uncomfortably as he read it right through, but it gave no information about the family in the photograph.

He sat down, taking deep breaths to try to calm his racing heart. Then he gazed at the photograph again. He didn't care what she was calling herself, or why she had changed her name: this was his sister. He was certain. She had grown into a young woman, but he would recognize her at any age.

He had to get out there!

A quick glance at the clock told him there would be a bus to the station in ten minutes. Thank heavens he had money saved from playing piano in the evenings.

It took him only five minutes to shove things into his bag, scribble a note for John and run for the bus. He made it just in time.

'Auntie.' Danny came through the gate in the hedge and stood beside Angie as she did some weeding. 'I'm gonna practise my lesson before Dieter comes to hear me.'

'All right, darling.' She followed him into the front room. This was a regular Friday-afternoon visit and one Danny looked forward to – and, to be honest, so did she. She no longer denied that her affection for Dieter was growing all the time.

As Danny arranged his cushions on the stool, Angie

picked up the letter she had left on top of the piano and tucked it behind the clock on the mantelpiece. She was receiving regular letters from Bob. They were chatty and often funny, but he never mentioned their discussion or his improper proposal. A bubble of amusement rose in her. He was quite outrageous. His mother had hinted that as a child her son had been a handful to control, and, now that she knew him better, Angie didn't doubt that for one moment.

While Danny was practising, she went into the kitchen and began to lay the table for tea. There was bread, butter, home-made jam and a fruitcake she had baked last night. Emma often joined them for tea but not on a Friday. This was just for the three of them.

She tipped her head to one side and listened. It just sounded like a jumble of notes hesitantly played, and she wondered how long it would be before he could play something she would recognize. Danny didn't seem to mind the slow progress, though. Of course he was far too young at the moment, and she couldn't help wondering what Dieter had been like at that age. Had he shown the same fascination with the sounds a piano could make? Yes, she was sure he had.

The piano stopped and she wandered back into the front room. Had Dieter arrived and she hadn't heard him? He had his own front-door key.

Danny was standing on tiptoe, his eyes fixed on the clock. 'What does it say, Auntie?'

'Half past five.'

He ran over to the window, craned his head to look

up the road and came back to her, looking puzzled. 'He's late. It is Friday, isn't it?'

'Yes, darling, I expect he's been delayed.'

'He's never late on Friday. It's my special practice.'

'Perhaps one of the animals isn't well and he's had to stay to help your grandpa.'

'S'pose.' His disappointment was great and showed.

She tried to cheer him up. 'Tell you what, let's have our tea and I'll make fresh when he comes. I've made a lovely cake, and you can stay up if he comes later.'

After another look out of the window he followed her into the kitchen.

By eight o'clock there was still no sign of him, and even Angie was becoming concerned. This wasn't like Dieter. Danny was so disconsolate that he made no protest about going to bed.

'We'll go to the farm in the morning,' she told him as she tucked him up. 'There'll be a good reason why he couldn't come today.'

Downstairs again, Angie couldn't settle to anything. There was a nasty feeling in the pit of her stomach that something unexpected had happened – though she couldn't imagine what it could be or why they hadn't even been sent a message. She would have liked to run to the farm to see what was going on, but she couldn't drag Danny out into the cold at this time of night.

She poked the fire, hoping a cheerful blaze would dispel the feeling of disaster creeping through her. This was ridiculous! Annoyed with herself for allowing her imagination to run riot, she threw herself into an armchair and picked up a book she had been reading.

It was immediately tossed aside when she heard the truck stop outside. He was here. Thank goodness.

But it wasn't Dieter. John and Hetty were standing on the step, and from their expressions it wasn't good news.

'What's happened?' She stood aside to let them in, feeling faint with panic. 'Where's Dieter?'

Hetty gulped, unable to speak, and John fidgeted uncomfortably.

'For God's sake, tell me!'

John cleared his throat. 'I took Hetty to Bridgewater to do some shopping and see a film as a treat. When we got back, there was a note on the kitchen table from Dieter.' He held a piece of paper in his hands, turning it round and round.

She couldn't take her eyes off the note. 'What does it say?'

'Well, it's hard to read because it has obviously been written in a great hurry . . .' John looked sad. 'He's gone back to Germany, Angie.'

'No!' She shook her head fiercely. 'No, he promised he wouldn't do that.'

'He has.' Hetty was stricken.

Angie was furious, and more hurt than she could ever remember. Losing her parents and Jane had been devastating, but this was a different kind of pain. She had trusted him, believed in him, and even come to love him. 'Why now? Everything is going well for him. He has Danny, a new job, and he's been so happy. I don't understand. Has he taken all his things with him?'

'Only his working clothes are in his room, but he didn't have much.' Hetty sat down and bowed her head in exhaustion.

'What do you mean he didn't have much?' Angie was incandescent with fury now. 'He had Danny, he had me, he had the love and respect of everyone here. What more did the swine want?'

'He says he'll be in touch.' John gave a helpless gesture.

'What the hell does that mean?' She grabbed the paper from John's hand, reading it through several times. 'He might have had the decency to say why he was leaving in such an all-fired hurry.'

It was at that moment Angie realized it wasn't just the three of them in the room. Danny was just inside the door, his face ashen, body rigid and fists clenched.

Angie fought to control herself. 'Oh, I'm sorry, darling, did we wake you?'

'He's gone away.' His bottom lip trembled. 'He promised he wouldn't, Auntie. He promised.'

She knelt in front of him, smoothing a lock of hair away from his eyes. 'We don't know why he had to go so suddenly, but he'll be coming back.'

Danny shook his head so wildly he nearly toppled over. 'He won't! He told fibs. He doesn't love us.'

As a tear trickled down his cheek, she gathered him into her arms and sat down, cradling the devastated child. If she could have got hold of Dieter at that moment, she would have killed him. How could he do this to Danny? How could he leave without an explanation? He had betrayed both of them. She would not have believed he could do such a hurtful thing. To leave like this, without an explanation, without facing them, was cruel. It was also out of character; but, nevertheless, he had gone.

'I'll make some tea.' Hetty disappeared into the kitchen.

John sat opposite Angie, looking helpless and somewhat bewildered. 'I can't believe he's left for good, Angie. That note was scribbled in such a hurry it's almost illegible. Something bad must have happened to make him leave like this.'

Angie was beginning to calm down a little. She knew her quick temper erupted suddenly, but it usually subsided just as quickly. Now the fury had been replaced with utter sadness. Danny had stopped crying and was sitting up listening to John.

'Is he hurt, Grandpa? Is that why he left?'

'We don't know.' John managed a smile. 'But I do know he loves you very much, and he's got the new job to start soon. You know how excited he is about that.'

Danny pursed his lips. 'P'raps he don't want it now.'

'I don't believe that, sweetheart.' Hetty returned with a tray of tea and a glass of milk for Danny. 'We'll hear from him soon and then he'll tell us when he's coming back.'

'He went too quick.' Danny slid off Angie's lap and

took the glass Hetty was holding out to him. He guzzled, looking over the rim, eyes wide and wet with the tears he'd shed. 'It was naughty, wasn't it, Auntie?'

'Yes, darling.' She sipped her tea, hands still shaking from the shock. 'When he gets back, we'll tell him off for upsetting us.'

Danny finished his milk and nodded, looking much happier now everyone was saying Dieter was coming back.

'And he'd better have a damned good explanation,' John muttered under his breath.

'You find him, Auntie, and tell him he's naughty.'

'He'll get the biggest telling-off of his life!'

He leant on Angie's knees, his grey eyes imploring. 'Make him come back soon.'

'I will. Now it's time you went back to bed. Say good-night to Granny and Grandpa.'

'Night.' He gave them a wan smile and went obediently upstairs with Angie. Once he was tucked up, she waited until he had fallen asleep. Gazing down at his tear-stained face, she felt numb with disbelief. Dieter must have known how this would upset his son, so why had he done it? Why disappear without an explanation? What was so urgent that he couldn't take half an hour to see Danny first? And was he going to come back? All he'd said in the note was that he would be in touch – not a word about returning. That was her biggest worry because they had told Danny that he was definitely coming back to them, and her darling boy had accepted that. But suppose he never did?

She wandered downstairs to John and Hetty. They were staring silently into the fire.

'Danny's asleep.' Angie sat down, bowed her head wearily and then looked up. 'Okay, what the hell do you think this is all about? Has Dieter done or said anything lately to make you suspect he was going back to Germany?'

'Nothing at all.' John sighed. 'He's been very happy, what with Danny and the new job.'

'That's what I thought.' Angie cast her mind back over the last couple of weeks, trying to remember if he'd said or done anything to give a hint that he might leave. But she couldn't think of a thing.

'I don't know what would have had him tearing off in such a hurry that he couldn't even leave a proper note.' Hetty put her hand on the teapot and, finding it still warm, poured herself another cup of tea.

John also held his cup out. 'I think I'll drive over to Bob's parents tomorrow. They might know something.'

'I'll come with you, John. I can leave Danny with Sally for a few hours.' Angie rubbed between her eyes as her head began to pound with tension. 'I'll also write to Bob and tell him what's happened. He found him once, so perhaps he can do it again.'

John stood up. 'Come on, Hetty, let's leave Angie to get some rest. I'll pick you up around ten in the morning.'

'Okay, John, and thanks for coming over.'

She saw them to the door and watched them drive away. The cups were left in the sink and she dragged herself upstairs. There wasn't anything else she could do tonight. It felt as if all the energy had been drained from her. Danny's worried little face, when he had begged her to find Dieter, was imprinted on her memory. Just when things seemed to be going so well, this had to happen.

After cleaning her teeth, she leant on the sink and bowed her head. The shock of Dieter leaving for Germany without an explanation was bringing feelings to the surface that she had denied. She wanted him to be here not just for Danny's sake but because she had grown fond of him.

She stood up straight and sighed deeply. No, it was more than that. Time to admit the truth. She loved him.

'Oh, Dieter,' she whispered as she crawled into bed. 'Please be in touch soon. And please, *please*, have a very good reason for leaving in such a hurry.'

John arrived just before ten. Angie was ready and they were soon on their way.

'Is Danny okay?' John glanced at her worriedly.

'Very subdued this morning, but I think he's happy to spend the day with Emma and Sally. They won't give him a chance to brood. I'm sure he wanted to believe it when we told him Dieter would come back, but nevertheless, with all that's happened to him this last few months, he must have doubts.'

'Poor little devil. He's had a lot to deal with in his young life.'

'Yes, and just when I thought we were coming out into the light, this happens.'

Angie battled with a mixture of sadness and fear. For all her anger with Dieter, she was worried sick about him. She could have sworn he was not the type to just take off, leaving his son and the new life he was building so successfully for himself here. She had become used to having him around and couldn't imagine life without him. And it would be worse for Danny. He had just found his father and to lose him now would be devastating. She knew children were resilient, but another blow for such a young child would be too awful to contemplate.

'Let's hope we can find out something today.'

Angie nodded, and sent up a silent prayer that they would.

When they arrived at the house, it looked deserted. No one answered their insistent knocking.

'Doesn't look as if anyone's at home.' John wandered along, peering in the windows. 'Not a sign of life.'

'Can I help you?' A man appeared from the side of the house, a shovel in his hands.

'We've come to see the General and Mrs Strachan.'

'Ah, well, miss, you're out of luck, I'm afraid. Gone away, they have.'

Angie's spirits plummeted. 'Do you know where? It's most important we speak to them.'

'They've gone overseas somewhere. Often do that. Don't know where, but they left a week ago.'

'Do you know when they're due back?' John asked.

''Fraid not. You never can tell with them. I'm only

the gardener. I come in twice a week, do my job and leave. The rest of the staff have all taken time off, so there isn't no one who can help you.' The gardener shrugged apologetically. 'If you come back in a week's time, the housekeeper will be here.'

'That's too late, but thanks anyway.' John led Angie back to the truck. 'They left a week ago, so it can't be anything to do with Dieter. All we can do now is wait and hope he gets in touch like he said in his note.'

'Ow, a wheel's come off my best train.' Emma held it out for Danny to see. 'Deeder'll fix it for me.'

'No, he won't. He's gone away.'

Emma looked crestfallen. 'I'll have to wait till he gets back, then.'

'He isn't coming back.' Danny pressed his lips together hard, determined not to cry. Auntie said he would, but he wouldn't.

''Course he is.' Emma peered at her friend's unhappy face. 'My daddy used to go away, but he always came back.'

'He's gone a long way. Over the sea. My mummy said he did that before and he didn't come back to see us.'

'He will this time.' Emma, ever the optimist, sounded confident.

'Won't.'

'Will. He's got to mend my toys when they get broke.'

'He don't care about your toys. He don't care about any of us.'

'He does! Deeder's nice.' Emma looked outraged. "Spect he's just had to go off and do things daddies do.'

'Like what?'

'I don't know!'

It turned into a full-scale bickering match, and it made Danny feel better to let all the hurt out.

'Will you two stop it?' Em's mummy stuck her head through the doorway and shook a duster at them.

There was a moment of silence as they waited until she had disappeared again, then the friends began to roll on the floor, shrieking with laughter.

32

The curses coming from Bob as he read Angie's letter could be heard by anyone within thirty yards of his office.

'Your father's here to see you, sir.' Hunt barely managed to hide his smirk as he entered the office of his furious colonel.

Bob hauled himself out of the chair just as his father swept in. 'What the blazes are you doing here?'

'Come to see for myself what's going on in this poor benighted city.' The General glanced at Hunt. 'Sent him to the best schools money could buy and they still couldn't drill good manners into him. I could do with a stiff drink, Sergeant.'

'Coming right up, sir.' Hunt opened a filing cabinet, took out a bottle of whisky and two glasses. After pouring generous measures, he handed them to father and son. 'Anything else I can do for you, sir?'

'No, I'll call you if I need you.' Bob took a good swig of the drink. This was turning out to be a hell of a day, and his father turning up was the last thing he'd expected. Though the General was very unpredictable, just like his elder son, Bob thought. There wasn't much doubt about which parent he took after. His younger brother was normal, much to his mother's relief.

As Hunt left the office, Bob held his glass up in greeting. 'You know I'm pleased to see you, but what are you really doing here?'

'Exactly what I said. I've left your mother in Frankfurt while I have a look around.'

Bob nearly choked on a mouthful of whisky. 'Mother's here as well?'

'Of course. We're trying to find what happened to a girl who was shipped to a labour camp and hasn't returned home.'

He shot his father a furious look. 'I've just had a frantic letter from Angie, saying that Dieter has returned to Germany and they don't know why. Is this anything to do with you?'

'Has he now. Shouldn't think so.' The General drained his glass. 'We sent him some photographs, that's all. Unless . . .'

Bob narrowed his eyes. 'Unless what?'

'There're a few people we met who came from Dresden, and we wondered if he might know them. We did promise we'd help him if we could.' His father helped himself to another drink. 'Dieter knows we're in Frankfurt, so he might turn up there.'

'He better bloody well had.' Bob glared at his father. 'And if he does, you make sure he gets back to England.'

It had taken Dieter three days to reach Frankfurt by boat and train. He didn't have an address for the Mansteins, but he hoped the General was still at the same hotel, or this wild dash would have been for nothing. Now the first rush of panic was over, he knew that he should have waited and asked the General to find out more about the girl. But he hadn't been able to wait. He was so sure! After giving up all hope of finding her, the shock had been overwhelming, wiping everything else from his mind.

He walked into the hotel, tired and dishevelled, and asked at reception for the General, sighing with relief when they picked up the phone and announced that he was here.

'Room 42, Herr Cramer. Up the stairs and turn left at the top.'

'*Danke*.'

Mrs Strachan answered his knock. 'Dieter, what a surprise. Come in and tell me why you're here.'

He stepped into the room, put down his bag and gazed around. 'Your husband sent me photographs. Is he here?'

'He's gone to visit Robert in Berlin. Do sit down. Can I get you something to eat and drink?'

'Tea and sandwiches would be very welcome.' He grimaced. 'I have not stopped for anything. I was so afraid you may have left here.'

She picked up the phone and ordered the food. When this was done, she studied him intently. 'Tell me why you've come in such a hurry.'

'There is a girl in one of the photographs. The name on the back is Helga Manstein, but she is my sister.'

She sat up straight in disbelief. 'You must be mistaken. She is their daughter.'

'I don't care who they say she is, or what she is calling herself. She *is* my sister.' He pushed hair out of his eyes. 'I would know her anywhere. I must see her.'

'Of course, if you are that sure, then we must get to the bottom of the mystery.' She reached for the phone again. 'But first we must settle you in a room here.'

'I cannot afford to stay here, madam. I shall find somewhere else.'

She dismissed his protest with a wave of her hand. 'You are here because of us. We shall pay for your room and food.' Her understanding smile softened the firmness of her words.

The food arrived while she was booking him a room, and she signalled for him to eat. He did so without further urging. He was famished.

'That is arranged, Dieter. You have the room next to ours. They are bringing the key to us now. When you have eaten, you must unpack and then we shall go and see the girl.'

He ran a hand over his chin, feeling the bristles. 'I will have to shave and freshen up first.'

'While you're doing that, I'll try to contact my husband and let him know you're here.'

By the time Dieter had demolished the plate of sandwiches and drunk all the tea in the pot, his key had arrived. He stood up. 'It will not take me more than half an hour to get ready. Will that be suitable for you?'

393

'Take your time, Dieter. I know you are anxious to see if this girl is your sister, but she isn't going anywhere.'

That was a comfort, but he still washed, shaved and changed his clothes as quickly as he could.

Bob was about to take his father to the mess for lunch when the phone rang. He answered it, listened for a while, and then said, 'Hold on Mother, he's here with me now.' He held the phone out to his father, and then sat back, arms folded. Thank God! Dieter had turned up at their hotel.

Fifteen minutes later his father put the phone down. 'You can stop glowering like that. Dieter's with your mother. I told you he would probably go there, didn't I?'

His father's unconcerned expression was too much for Bob's fragile temper. He exploded. 'Do you know how much trouble we had getting him to leave Germany in the first place? Now you've brought him back on the off chance you might have found someone who knows him.' He surged out of his chair and began to pace the room, knowing just how worried everyone would be back in Somerset. 'The man was settling down, happy to be with his son, and with the prospect of a new career. He had finally accepted that his family was dead, and by your meddling you've dragged up the whole thing again.'

'Don't blow your top.' The General was completely unfazed by his son's fury. 'We have to explore every possibility, however unlikely.'

'Don't . . . ?' Bob spun round to face him. 'Hell, Dad, are you going senile in your old age? Angie's worried sick and Danny is upset. They've no idea what's going on. All Dieter left behind was a hastily scribbled note saying he was returning to Germany. They don't even know if he's going back to them.'

'Of course he will. I'll see he has a return ticket. We're going back at the end of the week and we'll take him with us.'

'You make sure you do.' Bob rotated his shoulders, easing the tension. 'Did Mother say why he's come here?'

'She did. Dieter believes that a girl in one of the photos I sent him is his sister.'

'What?'

For the first time the General looked uncertain. 'It can't be, though. Her name is Helga.'

The groan was audible as Bob ran his hand over his eyes. 'Then the poor sod's in for another disappointment. Father, you should be shot!'

The General stood up. 'Nothing we can do about it now. I'll go back to Frankfurt in the morning. Today, you can show me round the place and buy me a meal. I'm starving.'

Bob gave a resigned sigh and prepared to give him a guided tour of British HQ, Charlottenburg. It was near Spandau, so his father would undoubtedly want to see the prison as well. Then there would be a riotous evening in the mess as his father revelled in army life again.

His mouth twitched at the corners. There was never

a dull moment when his father was around. He would have to warn Hunt to wake them both early in the morning.

Mrs Strachan was ready when Dieter returned to her room.

'Good, you look more refreshed. The house is only ten minutes away from here.' She closed her door and they walked towards the stairs. 'I managed to contact my husband, and he's coming back tomorrow.'

When they were in the street, she took Dieter's arm and looked up, her face showing sympathy. 'You mustn't raise your hopes too much, for I'm sure you're mistaken.'

'I am not.'

'We shall soon see.'

They walked the rest of the way in silence, until they reached a terraced house. Dieter was too tense to take much notice of the place, but his impression was of a small family house. He stood back and let Mrs Strachan knock on the door.

It was opened by a man in his middle years, hair greying at the temples and several inches shorter than Dieter's six feet. He smiled with pleasure and spoke in quite good English.

'How lovely to see you again. Come in, come in.'

'This is Dieter Cramer.' Mrs Strachan introduced him to Herr Manstein and his wife. 'We sent him a photograph of you, do you remember?'

'Ah, yes.' Herr Manstein looked at him closely, and

then shook his head. 'I am afraid I do not know you.' He turned to his wife. 'Do you?'

Dieter could not stand politely by any longer. 'We have never met, but I believe the young girl in the photograph is my sister.'

The colour drained from their faces, and Frau Manstein, a petite woman with brown hair and dark eyes, clutched at her husband's arm.

He patted her arm and cleared his throat. 'I am –'

He was stopped in mid sentence when the door opened and the girl came in, laughing with the son from the picture.

Dieter stared hard, holding his breath in anticipation. Then the elation was so overwhelming he wanted to shout for joy. He stepped towards her eagerly, arms outstretched to gather her to him. 'Gerda!'

She stopped laughing, stepped back away from him and frowned. 'My name is Helga.'

'No, it isn't.' His arms dropped to his sides, stunned by her reaction and denial. 'I am your brother, Dieter. Do you not recognize me?'

Looking alarmed, she walked over and sat beside Frau Manstein, who placed a comforting arm around her shoulder. 'I do not know you.'

'What is it, Dieter?' Mrs Strachan had been unable to follow the conversation, as they were all now speaking in German. 'Is it your sister?'

'It is, but she says she does not know me. That cannot be, for without a doubt this is Gerda.'

The first surge of joy had quickly changed to disbelief and confusion. He wanted to hug Gerda, but she was looking at him with large frightened eyes – eyes he knew so well. It cost him all the strength he had to make him stay where he was. Fixing his gaze on the man, he demanded, 'You will explain why my sister believes she is someone else.'

'Please, Herr Cramer, do not be angry. We will explain.' Frau Manstein was close to tears. 'It was a week after the bombing. Our daughter had been struck by flying masonry. We sat with her in the hospital, but nothing could be done and she died. There was a lovely girl in the next bed who did not even remember her name . . .'

Dieter gasped.

Herr Manstein took up the story. 'She did not appear to have any living relatives, so we brought her with us and moved here. We gave her our daughter's name and made her part of our family. We love her very much. She has brought us great joy.' He lifted his hands in apology. 'We hoped her relatives would never come to claim her.'

Dieter was stunned, but also grateful to them for taking her in and giving a stranger a secure and loving home. But that didn't change the facts. 'You have been most kind, but she is Gerda Cramer, my sister. I have been searching for her.'

'Are you absolutely certain?' Frau Manstein's eyes were pleading. 'General Strachan told us that you were a prisoner in England for a long time. Your sister would have grown in that time.'

He understood how they felt. They had taken her in

place of the daughter they had lost, and loved her very much. His voice was gentle when he spoke. 'She is my sister.'

The girl was staring at him without any sign of recognition. 'I do not know you.'

He went and crouched in front of her chair, taking her hands in his. She gazed at their clasped hands. 'Long fingers; you play piano?'

'Yes.' He was sure then that the memories were just under the surface. 'What else do you know about me?'

Her eyes closed as she tried to remember, then she shook her head. 'Nothing . . . and yet I have a feeling that I should know you.'

'That is enough,' Herr Manstein said firmly. 'She has said she cannot remember you and we will not have her upset.'

Disappointed, Dieter sat in his chair again. He had expected a happy reunion when they saw each other again, not this. It hurt so much to find she did not know him, that she couldn't remember the laughter and affection of their youth.

'Dieter.' Mrs Strachan touched his arm. 'Leave it for today. Come back again tomorrow.'

Reluctantly, he stood up. 'May I return tomorrow morning and see Gerda again?'

'Of course.' Frau Manstein smiled at last.

He held his hand out to his sister. 'And may I give you a big hug, just like we always used to?'

She got to her feet and nodded shyly.

He drew her close and rested his cheek on hers, never

wanting to let her go. It was a bitter-sweet moment. The dear sister he had thought dead was alive, but she didn't know him. With a tremendous effort of self-control he managed to step away, give a slight bow to everyone in the room, then turn and walk away. It was the hardest thing he had ever done.

That evening he dined with Mrs Strachan, and she tried to distract him with stories of the people they had been able to help. Getting no response, she eventually brought the subject round to his sister.

'What are you going to do?' She folded her napkin and placed it beside her coffee cup. 'I believe that she is indeed your sister. Although her colouring is slightly darker, there is a family resemblance.'

'I am going to try to persuade her to come to England with me.'

'I doubt she would want to do that. They are the only family she knows.'

'That is true.' Dieter ran a hand distractedly through his hair. 'I shall see her again tomorrow and talk to her alone.'

'Yes, that would be best, Dieter. You look exhausted. My husband will be back sometime tomorrow, and he might be able to help.' She smiled. 'He can be very persuasive at times.'

After breakfast Dieter read the newspapers, waiting for a suitable time to call on the Mansteins. Mrs Strachan had said she wouldn't come with him today, and he had been roaming around since six o'clock, anxious to see Gerda again.

Ten o'clock finally arrived and he could wait no longer. After a sleepless night he had come to a decision. He had a good job waiting for him, and there was Danny. If Gerda returned with him, they could be a real family, and, though it would be a wrench for her, she would soon settle down. She might even regain her memory if she was with him all the time.

He hurried to the house and found the whole family waiting for him. It didn't look as if any of them had had a decent sleep. They all appeared very strained, which was understandable in the circumstances. A stranger had turned up to claim the girl they had nurtured and loved.

His sister greeted him with a shy smile. 'Would you like to sit in the garden?'

Dieter smiled and nodded. Gerda had always loved to be outside, whatever the weather. It had been nearly impossible to keep her in, even when it was pouring with rain.

The Mansteins left them alone, but the son, Heinrich, hovered, never taking his eyes off the girl he thought of as part of his family. They were clearly very fond of each other. He had said nothing yesterday, but today he looked very worried.

There was an old wooden bench against a brick wall in the small garden. It was sheltered from the breeze and a lovely suntrap. They sat down while the boy sprawled on the grass a discreet distance away.

'Gerda.' When he saw her start, he apologized. 'Forgive me, but I cannot call you anything else.'

'I understand. Will you tell me what your life is like in England?'

'Do you not want to hear about us when we were children, about our parents?'

Clasping her hands together, she stared straight ahead. 'I do not wish to know about the past.'

This saddened Dieter, but he must try to put himself in her place. Perhaps she knew, deep down, that something terrible had happened that would be too painful to remember. So he spent the next hour telling her about his son, Angie, the good friends he had made, and the new job he was about to start.

'I want you to come back with me. It is a lovely place and we could have a good life together there.'

'But I am happy here. And I am sorry, but I do not know you.'

Before Dieter could reply, the General strode into the garden with the Mansteins.

'Hello, Dieter. Got back as soon as I could. So this lovely young girl is your sister.' He looked from one to the other. 'Yes, yes, I see the family resemblance.'

'I have been trying to persuade her to come to England with me, but she does not want to.' Dieter couldn't hide the disappointment he was feeling. To have found her after he had given up all hope was beyond belief, and even if she didn't know who he was, he wanted her with him.

'Hmm.' The General frowned, deep in thought. He

had a reasonable grasp of the language, and after a few moments he spoke to Gerda. 'I understand Dieter's desire for you to be with him, and your desire to stay here, but what about a compromise? Come back to England with us. Consider it a holiday and a chance to get to know your brother again. If you want to stay, you can; if not, I will personally see that you return here.'

Dieter realized at that moment what a wise man the General was. He should have thought of that himself. He was confident that once Gerda had settled in and made friends, she would want to stay.

The family were naturally reluctant to let her go, but they agreed after a long discussion. However, Heinrich was not at all happy and argued fiercely against it.

'I shall not be gone for long,' Gerda assured him. 'Dieter is my brother. A brother I cannot remember, so it is right I should get to know him and meet his little son.'

After another long discussion it was agreed that she should visit England.

'That's settled, then.' The General appeared satisfied. 'Leave everything to me. I'll make all the arrangements.'

Dieter took a silent breath in relief. Gerda didn't really want to come, but once they were in England and she got to know him again, she was bound to want to stay. She might even get her memory back in time.

33

Over a week and still no news. Bob would have received the letter by now: it had been an airmail Forces letter. She waited anxiously every day for the postman, but it was too soon for a reply.

Danny never mentioned Dieter now, and he wasn't taking his piano lessons with the same enthusiasm. Emma's shriek made her glance out of the kitchen window and smile. They were chasing each other and yelling at the tops of their voices. The exuberant little girl was good for Danny. He was a thoughtful, sensitive boy and could easily have become too serious without her. The shock of losing his mother had changed him for a while, but Emma had pushed him back into being a lively child once again. She could remember walking into Jane's house and always finding them laughing about something or other.

If only Dieter had stayed.

The sound of the truck pulling up outside the cottage had her running to the front door.

John got out and came towards her, his expression serious. 'Get Danny, Angie; you must both come with me.'

'What's happened? Is there news? Is he back?'

He nodded. 'You'll see. Get Danny.'

She turned and ran into the garden. 'Danny,

Grandpa's here and we're going to the farm for tea.'

'You were gonna have tea with me.' Emma looked disappointed.

'I know, but we have to go out. Tell your mummy we'll come tomorrow instead.'

'Okay, I'll eat your jelly. S'pect it won't last till then.' Giving Danny a gleeful push, she ran into her own garden.

Not wanting to ask John what this was all about in front of Danny, Angie remained quiet on the short journey to the farm.

When they pulled into the yard, Hetty came out of the house with two other people. Angie felt her breath leave her body as relief flooded in.

'Daddy!' Danny was running as fast as his legs would carry him. 'Daddy.'

Angie fought to control her emotions as Dieter scooped up his son and swung him high. This was the first time he had ever called him Daddy. All thought of being angry with Dieter vanished in the joy of having him back. She gazed at John, her eyes swimming.

He squeezed her arm. 'Everything's all right, Angie.'

'Thank heavens he's back, but who is that with him?'

'Come and see.'

When they reached the group, Dieter put Danny down and gathered Angie into his arms, hugging her fiercely. 'I apologize for worrying you, but I had to leave quickly. I might not have been able to find her if she had moved on again.'

'I'm just so pleased to see you, and so is Danny. He called you Daddy.'

'I know. I thought he would never do it. My happiness is now complete.'

Angie turned her attention to the young girl who was staring at Danny as if mesmerized.

'This is my sister,' he said quietly to Angie.

The girl bent down and reached out to touch Danny's hair. 'Dieter?'

Danny shot Angie a perplexed glance, then turned back to the girl. 'My name's Danny.'

Dieter took hold of her arm and made her stand up. 'Danny is my son.'

A deep frown creased her brow. 'Of course; he is like you.'

'Yes. Do you remember me as a child?'

She began to talk rapidly in her own language, and Dieter tried to calm her.

Not wanting to intrude, Angie went and stood beside Hetty. 'This is his sister?'

'Yes, but she has lost her memory. It looks as if Danny has triggered something, though, so there's hope she will remember in time.'

There was a slight resemblance in features, Angie noted, but the girl's hair was slightly darker. If they were brother and sister, then Dieter had been given all the golden looks. But she did have a beauty of her own, only it was marred by her confused expression.

Angie's heart went out to the brother and sister. What had this poor girl gone through that had caused her to forget even her own brother?

'Speak in English.' Dieter was holding her hands still

and looking at her with love in his eyes. 'I know you can. We used to talk like that all the time, much to father's disapproval. Do you remember?'

She sighed and shook her head.

'It will come back, Gerda. In time your memory will return.' He smiled encouragingly. 'When you saw my son, you thought it was me. You were not born when I was his age, but there were many photographs of me when I was that young. Something deep inside you remembered that.'

Dieter reached out for Danny, who was now holding on to Angie's skirt and watching wide-eyed. 'Come and meet your Aunt Gerda.'

He went towards his father and gave his new auntie a dimpled smile. 'Hello.'

'I am pleased to meet you.' She spoke with a strong accent but had a reasonable grasp of the language. Then she smiled and the family dimples were in evidence.

'And this is Angie.' Dieter caught her hand and pulled her towards his sister.

'Are you the little boy's mother?'

'No, that was my cousin. She died a while ago.'

'Ah, yes. Dieter told me. That is sad.' She shook Angie's hand. 'He is a beautiful child.'

The same air of politeness and dignity she had always seen in Dieter struck Angie. These two had been well brought up.

'Now that we all know each other, shall we go inside?' Hetty hustled everyone through the door. The kitchen was warm and filled with the appetizing smell of cooking and freshly baked bread. 'You all go in the front room. It will take me only half an hour to finish off lunch.'

'Daddy, are you going away again?' Danny was trotting along, holding Dieter's hand and gazing up at him.

He stopped and bent down. 'I had to go to find my sister, but I shall not go away again.'

Danny watched as his new auntie went into the other room and whispered, 'Was she lost?'

'Yes, but she will be all right now. You will make her smile again.'

Angie watched the rapport between father and son. At last their relationship was acknowledged and secure. It was a good day.

'Don't she smile?' he whispered.

'Not very much at the moment.'

'Let Em see her. She'll make her laugh.'

Dieter chuckled. 'I am sure she will.'

'I've been doing my lessons,' Danny informed him proudly. 'I've got lots to show you.'

'You can play for me after lunch.' He looked quite overcome when Danny took his hand again.

When Dieter looked up at Angie, she gave a thumbs-up sign to let him know how pleased she was about everything.

They joined the others in the front room and Angie sat down, leaning forward, anxious to hear how Dieter had found his sister. 'Will you tell us what happened?'

'I must first apologize for upsetting you all.' Dieter ran a hand through his hair and gazed affectionately at his sister, as if he couldn't believe his eyes. 'The General and Mrs Strachan had been in Germany about a week when I received a letter saying they had found some people who came from my home. They included photographs. I did not recognize anyone, except for one girl. It was Gerda. I had not seen her for nine years, and she had grown up in that time, but I was certain it was her. All I could think about was getting to her. I was afraid that if I didn't get there quickly, she might disappear.'

He gave Angie an appealing look. 'I am afraid I panicked. You understand?'

She nodded. 'We felt you must have had a good reason for taking off like that. But it would have saved us many anxious days if you'd said you had found your sister and would be back soon.'

'I am very sorry, but I did not know what I was writing.' He lifted his hands, palms up in a gesture of apology. 'I could not waste a moment getting to Germany.'

'We know that now, Dieter.' Angie smiled gently. 'All is forgiven. Now, what happened next?'

'I had the address of the hotel where the Colonel's parents were staying, so I went there immediately.' Dieter then explained what had happened in Frankfurt. 'I knew it was her as soon as I saw her, but she did not know who I was, and at first did not believe I was her brother. With the General's help we managed to persuade her to come to England with us.'

The girl spoke for the first time. 'I do not remember anything about my past.'

'Gerda is going to stay here for a while.' Hetty came

in from the kitchen. 'I've made up the room next to Dieter's.'

'If I wish to stay, Mrs Strachan has offered me work and a home with them.' Gerda sighed. 'They are very kind people.'

'That will be wonderful.' Angie liked Bob's parents more and more. 'It's a lovely house.'

'They showed me photographs. It is very grand, and' – she glanced shyly at her brother – 'it is not too far away, no?'

'Of course it isn't.' John smiled encouragingly. 'And when you have time off you must come and stay with us.'

'You are all very kind.' She chewed her lips anxiously. 'If only I could remember, but perhaps I would not like the memories.'

'They will be painful.' Dieter spoke to her kindly. 'But we shall all be here to help you through it. This is your family now, Gerda.'

Danny, who had been sitting quietly all this time, could contain himself no longer. 'Will you play?' he whispered. 'I missed you.'

'Of course.' He stood up. 'I shall play you one of your Aunt Gerda's favourite pieces. Chopin's *Fantasie*.'

Angie had never heard it before; it was beautiful. She saw a slight smile on Gerda's face as she listened. The melody obviously tugged at her memory. Perhaps being with her brother would help her to recover.

'Lunch is ready,' Hetty called as soon as the music stopped.

It was a tense meal. Everyone was doing all they could to make Gerda feel comfortable, but she said little and only toyed with her food. A deep sense of unease was seeping through Angie. In his eagerness to have his sister with him, Dieter had taken her away from the only people she knew, and for whom she had great affection. The man who claimed to be her brother was a stranger, and this a foreign country to her. Was it any wonder that she looked confused and unhappy?

Angie helped Hetty with the washing-up. 'It's going to take time for Gerda to settle down.'

'Yes, it is, and unless she gets her memory back, I have my doubts she ever will. Evidently the General suggested that she come for a holiday to see if she likes it here.' Hetty shook her head sadly. 'But Dieter intends her to stay, and I fear he is going to be disappointed.'

'Perhaps we're worrying too much.' Angie stacked the last of the plates, and hung the teacloth by the stove to dry. 'Once she gets used to being here, I expect she'll settle down.'

'Ah,' said Hetty, 'Danny's showing Dieter what he's learnt while he's been away. Let's go and listen.'

Angie grinned. 'You sure? I don't find scales, or whatever they are, very interesting.'

'Give him a couple of years and beautiful music will fill your little cottage.' Hetty took her arm and pushed her through the door, laughing.

'I can't wait.'

*

The April term had started and Dieter was enjoying the first week of his new job. A few of the older students showed promise, though others just wanted to make a noise with any instrument to hand. He was trying to give lessons that were as much fun as possible and spending extra time with those who had a love of music.

Much to his delight he had not met with any hostility because he was German – quite the opposite in fact. The welcome he had received from everyone was friendly.

The sun was warm on his back as he watched a group of boys playing football during the lunch break.

'Come on, sir.' A boy named David kicked the ball towards him. 'Come and join us. We're one short on our side.'

Without hesitation Dieter dribbled the ball towards the goal and fired. It just skimmed the top of the bar. He was out of practice. They had spent hours playing in the POW camp, but he hadn't kicked a ball since that time.

'Good try, sir.' There was a chorus of approval as he joined them.

Half an hour later he was puffing and laughing. The game had been boisterous and a draw, which he didn't think was a bad thing. The youngsters were very competitive in everything they did.

He wandered off to make himself a cup of tea in the staff room. There was a spring in his step. Everything was good. Danny was calling him Daddy. He had found his sister and she was now with him.

Angie was showing a real liking for him, even affection. That made him very happy. She had courage, strength and could also be compassionate and understanding of other people's problems. And, as Jane had been so cruelly taken from them, that made her the right person for his artistic son. His heart was full of love for his son, and his auntie was a very special woman. He really enjoyed being with her, watching her smile and seeing the sun light up her beautiful hair. There was so much about her that was appealing.

Once his tea was made, he sat down. The staff room was empty so he could snatch a little quiet time to himself. He now had a job he loved, and a growing closeness to Danny and Angie. The only concern was Gerda, who was rather withdrawn, but that was only to be expected. They had taken her out to see the beautiful countryside, visited charming tea places and introduced her to all their friends. She hung back shyly and said little, but it was early days yet. She would eventually adjust to life in Somerset. Everyone was doing their best to make her welcome and happy. How could she not like it here? It was a beautiful place to live.

With a smile of contentment on his face, he stood up and made his way to the music room for his next class.

34

Two weeks had passed, and Gerda had made no attempt to go to Bob's parents or to join in the life of the village. Dieter was settling into his job as music teacher at the school, but Angie knew he was worried about his sister. She was listless and said very little; her smiles, when they came, were forced. It wasn't that she didn't understand what was being said. Her English was not as good as Dieter's, but it was adequate.

Angie took the rock cakes out of the oven and tipped them on to a wire rack to cool. After putting the baking tray in the sink, she stared out of the kitchen window, deep in thought. Dieter was overjoyed to have found his sister alive, but Angie caught a glimpse of something in her eyes at unguarded moments. Gerda wasn't happy. No, it was more than that. The girl was lost, utterly lost.

A knock on the front door cut off her concerns, and she wondered if that was the Rector with more typing for her. She spent one morning a week with him while Danny was in the church hall, but he often turned up with 'just another little job'. He had let her bring the typewriter home now, so she could work in the evenings when Danny was asleep, if she wanted to. The arrangement suited her perfectly.

She was smiling when she opened the front door and was surprised, but pleased, to see Gerda there. 'Hello, do come in.'

'You are on your own?' Gerda hesitated before stepping inside and looking round anxiously.

'Danny's next door with Emma. Please sit down. Would you like a cup of tea?'

'No, thank you.' Gerda sat on the edge of a chair, twisting her hands together.

'What is it?' Angie sat opposite her. 'Can I help?'

'Yes, please.' Her eyes filled with tears. 'I do not know who else to go to. Dieter has much affection for you. I ask you to talk to him for me, please.'

'Tell me what's troubling you.' The girl's pallor alarmed Angie. 'Has your memory returned?'

She shook her head. '*Nein*, and I do not wish it to. The doctor at the hospital said I had been in a horror and my mind has shut it out. It is best that way.'

'Tell me what I can do for you.' Angie spoke gently, not wishing to upset her any more than necessary.

'I am pleased I have a brother, and to know my real name, but . . .' She gulped in a shaking breath. 'I do not belong here. I wish to return to Germany and to the family I was with in Frankfurt.'

'And you can't bring yourself to tell Dieter, so you'd like me to do it for you?'

When Gerda nodded, her eyes pleading, Angie felt her stomach churn uncomfortably. How could she tell him that the sister he adored wanted to leave?

'I have tried to tell him, but I shall hurt him so much.'

The tears were running down her face now. 'But I cannot stay. I have a letter from the Mansteins, and they ask when I am returning. I am like a daughter to them. They miss me and I them.'

'I can understand how you must feel.'

'You are all most kind, but I am unhappy for my own country.'

Angie reached out to touch her arm in sympathy. 'Dieter is coming round this evening, and I'll tell him then. Would you like to be here when I do?'

'No, no.' Gerda shook her head. 'I am a coward. He will be much upset.'

'I know he will, but he is a kind man.' Angie stood up and smiled, though it was an effort. She was dreading what she had been asked to do. 'Now that's settled, let's have a cup of tea. I've just made some rock cakes.'

Gerda followed her to the kitchen, looking more composed now that she had unburdened herself.

It was nine o'clock that evening before Angie had time alone with Dieter. Danny was fast asleep upstairs, and, though the evenings weren't as chilly now, Angie put a match to the fire in the front room. She felt chilled right through after Gerda's visit.

Dieter was sitting in an armchair, looking happy and content. How she hated to do this to him, but she had promised. Better get it over with.

'Gerda came to see me this afternoon.'

He looked up and smiled. 'That is good. She has not been interested in going out.'

'There is a reason for that.' Angie paused, looking at Dieter anxiously. 'She talked frankly to me and has asked me to tell you how she feels.'

He frowned and sat forward. 'I know she is finding it difficult to adjust to life here, but why did she not tell me if something is bothering her? And I know that it is.'

'She is afraid of upsetting you.'

A shadow passed across his eyes, and his gaze held hers. 'You had better tell me what this is all about.'

Taking a deep breath, Angie pitched straight in. 'She isn't happy here, Dieter. She wants to go back to Germany and to the family she was with when you found her.'

Angie had known it was going to hurt him, but she hadn't been prepared for the naked pain on his face. She carried on talking, allowing him time to digest this piece of unwelcome news. 'Gerda told me she is happy to have found her brother, and to know her real name, but she doesn't belong here. She longs for her own country.'

'But what if her memory comes back?' Dieter had recovered and was now pacing the room. 'If she returns to Germany, I will not be there to help her.'

'It's been five years, Dieter. If she were going to remember, it is probable she would have done so by now. She doesn't want to know what happened to her, and can you blame her for that?'

'No, I cannot.' He turned to face her. 'I must go to her now, let her know I understand. Tomorrow I shall make arrangements for her journey.'

'Will you go with her?'

'I cannot ask for time off from school yet. I have only just started and I would not want to jeopardize my position there. I love the work.'

'Will she be able to travel on her own?'

'I shall try to get her a flight to Frankfurt, and telegraph her friends to let them know when she is coming. They will meet her, I am sure.' He slipped on his coat. 'Thank you for telling me, for, as much as I want to keep her with me, I would not wish my sister to be unhappy.'

She wanted to hug him, to give some comfort, and reached out to clasp his hand in hers. 'You'll be able to keep in touch now you know where she'll be.'

'Of course. Thank you, Angie.' He gathered her into his arms and held on tightly for a few moments, then he kissed her forehead gently and stepped back.

With a slight dip of his head he was off, striding up the road. Her heart went with him. This would be a terrible blow.

The light was still on when Dieter walked into the kitchen of the farmhouse. His sister was sitting at the table looking so unhappy and lost, and he knew he had made a terrible mistake in urging her to come to England with him. It had been a great joy to find her, and all he had thought about was having her with him so he could take care of her. His pleading with her had been completely selfish, but he had convinced himself that she would settle down and love it here as much as he did. But all he had done was to take her away from everything and everyone she was familiar with. He had made her unhappy, and cursed silently that he had been too stubborn and blind to recognize what he was doing. He had no right to do this to her. She was not the little sister he remembered, but a grown woman who would make her own decisions. She had problems, certainly, but she had been a level-headed child, and that wouldn't have changed.

He stood silently in the doorway, watching her toy with the cup in front of her, knowing he had to let her go. 'Gerda.'

She jumped at the sound of his voice, scrambling to her feet, searching his face anxiously. 'Angie has told you?'

'Yes.' He took hold of her shoulders and made her sit again. With an effort he managed a teasing smile. 'Am I so frightening that you could not come straight to me with your unhappiness?'

'I know how much you want me to stay with you. I was afraid you would be hurt and angry with me, so I went to Angie. She understands. I like her.'

'If you could not bring yourself to tell me, then you went to the right person.' He sat opposite her. 'But I could never be angry with you. Tell me how you feel and why you want to go back to Germany.'

'I do not belong here, Dieter.' She rested her arms on the table and leant towards him. 'Although I do not remember about our family, somewhere deep inside I know you are my brother. Many things you do are familiar. The way you smile, move, the tilt of your head when you are amused. I know the gestures, and I knew you played the piano like a master even before I heard you.'

'You always loved me to play for you.' His smile was wistful.

'Your son is just like you. He has inherited your love of music, I think. Was it from our father that the talent comes?

'Good Lord, no.' Dieter laughed at the suggestion. 'Our father had no time for music and I would never have touched a piano if it had not been for our mother. She was the talented one and made sure I went to a school where musical ability was nurtured.'

'I know I do not play.' She gazed into space. 'That is a pity, for I am sure it would have brought solace during the months I was confused.'

'It has helped me to cope with everything.'

She was talking freely now, and Dieter allowed her to take the lead and jump from one subject to another. She would tell him, in her own time, how she was feeling.

'I am sorry the girl who gave birth to your son is dead. Did you love her very much?'

'I didn't know at that time what I felt, but, looking back, I can honestly say that I did love her as much as I was capable of in those troubled times. I had spent four years in a POW camp, and suddenly I had a taste of freedom by working on the farm.' He paused for a moment, and then told her all about Jane. How ashamed he was that he had taken advantage of her love for him, and then left her.

'Ah, that is sad, but you must not blame yourself too much. Jane obviously knew the risks she was taking and she sent you away. You did not know about the child.'

'That is true, but it does not make me feel any better. I should have insisted she keep in touch with me, and should have returned here instead of drifting around Germany.'

'We are all very wise with hindsight.' Gerda smiled at him. 'But you have a beautiful boy, and Angie loves him much. She is a good mother to him.'

'Yes, she is. I could not wish for Danny to have a better person to bring him up.'

'You will marry her, yes?'

He gave her a startled look. 'She is in love with the General's son, Colonel Strachan, but she has promised she will not take my son and travel the world with him.'

'She will deny her own happiness for you and your son?'

'That is a sacrifice I believe she is prepared to make.'

'And you will allow her to do this?' Gerda studied him intently.

He lifted his hands. 'What choice do I have? I have only just found my son. I cannot be parted from him. I am selfish, Gerda. Jane risked her life to give birth to Danny, and, although she is not here to tell me so, I'm sure she would want me to help him grow into a fine man. I love him all the more for her sacrifice.'

Gerda studied him thoughtfully. 'I do understand that, but you have not said what your feelings are for Angie.'

'She is kind, determined and loves Danny very much. My gratitude and admiration for her have grown.' He stopped and gave a deep sigh.

'And that is all – admiration? Is she not beautiful and desirable as well?'

'Well, yes, of course she is . . . What is this cross examination about?'

'I am just trying to find out the truth. I believe your feelings for her are deeper than you will admit.'

His smile held amusement. 'You always were perceptive, little Gerda.'

She nodded and her smile widened. It was the same teasing expression he remembered from their youth, making him lean forward and kiss her cheek. Now he felt it was time to bring the subject back to her. 'Why do you not feel able to stay here with us?'

'You have spent many years in this country and come to know its people. You have a son, a job and friends who love you.' She clasped her hands together tightly. 'Apart from you I have nothing to keep me here; I have no memory of life before I woke up in the hospital. The Manstein family took me with them to Frankfurt when I was strong enough. They gave me love and a new life, and I was happy. After a while, it no longer bothered me that I knew nothing of my past. I heard about the bombing, and I think it best if I do not remember.'

'Perhaps that is so.' Dieter looked at his sister with sadness in his eyes. 'But I do wish you remembered me. We laughed together so much as children. I adored you then, and I still do. I had resigned myself to never seeing you again, so it was such a great joy to know you were alive, but a terrible shock to discover that you did not know who I was.'

She reached out and caught hold of his hand. 'I do know that you are my brother and that we love each other. I am also happy to know my family name. It gives me a sense of identity I did not have before. But I cannot stay, Dieter, I must return to the only place I know as home.'

'I understand that now.' He felt as if his heart were breaking but still he smiled. 'It is Saturday tomorrow and we shall visit the General to see if he can help get you back without delay. He is very influential in arranging things like that. And we must also tell Mrs Strachan that you will not be going to live with her.'

'Thank you. I shall write to you every week.'

'You be sure you do.' Standing up, he pulled her out of her chair and hugged her, burying his face in her hair, so she wouldn't see his tears.

The next day the General and Mrs Strachan listened sympathetically to Gerda's desire to return to Frankfurt.

'Forgive me for coming to you with this, but I hoped you might help my sister fly back. I cannot take time from my new job at the school to accompany her overland, and she wishes to travel as soon as possible.'

'Only too pleased to help.' The General looked at Gerda. 'I'm sorry you don't want to stay with us, my dear, but we quite understand. I promised to get you back, and that's what I shall do.'

'Of course you must return to Germany if you are unhappy here.' Mrs Strachan gave Dieter a quick glance that said she knew how this must hurt him.

'Give me a couple of days to make the arrangements, but we should have you safely back with your friends within a week.'

'Thank you, sir.' Gerda was brighter already. 'You are very kind.'

'Think nothing of it.' The General beamed at his wife. 'Tell you what, I'll take Gerda back myself, and then I can stop off and see Robert again. Never did get a proper look at the place.'

She raised her eyebrows as she looked at her husband. 'He'll love that! Two visits in a month.'

This produced a deep rumbling chuckle. 'Do him good. Keep him on his metal.'

Dieter didn't understand that saying, but the Colonel's parents found it highly amusing.

'I do wonder who is watching whom when you two are together.' Mrs Strachan gave an amused smile. 'They would deny it, but they are very alike in temperament.'

The General laughed at his wife, and then became serious again. 'I will see you home myself, Gerda.'

'That is good of you, sir.' Dieter breathed a sigh of relief to know that his sister would not be travelling alone. 'Please let me know how much the journey will cost for both of you.'

'No need for that, my boy.'

'I insist you let me pay for the tickets.' Dieter was

well aware that they were a wealthy family, but this was his responsibility.

'You may pay for your sister,' Mrs Strachan said, 'but my husband is going out there for his own pleasure and he will pay his own fare.'

'Quite right, my dear.' His face was alight with mischief. 'I'm going there to torment my son.'

'Exactly!' She turned to Dieter. 'We will let you know how much one ticket will cost. You may pay my husband when it's convenient for you.'

Dieter nodded in acknowledgement. He had only just started his teaching job and hadn't been paid yet. He'd had to buy himself some new clothes, but he still had some money put aside from the weeks he had played piano in the evenings.

'Dieter.' Gerda was looking worried again. 'I am sorry I cannot stay.'

He squeezed her hand. 'Please do not worry. I do not wish you to be unhappy. You must return to Germany; but I want you to write every week and let me know what you are doing. I shall need to know how you fill your days, how you are feeling.'

The frown disappeared from her face and she laughed. 'I promise – long, long letters.'

'That is all I ask.'

'Good.' Mrs Strachan stood up. 'Now that's all settled, you'll stay and have lunch with us.'

35

Sunday morning and Angie had just finished getting Danny ready for their day at the farm when the truck arrived.

'Daddy's come for us.' Danny was pulling open the front door.

Dieter swept him up for a hug, and Angie was relieved to see him looking relaxed and happy. She hadn't seen him since Friday evening, when she'd told him that Gerda wanted to return to Germany, and she was dying to know what had happened.

They bundled into the old truck, and as soon as they were on their way he told her about their visit to the Strachans. 'She is already much more cheerful knowing she will be going back in a few days.'

'That will be hard for you, Dieter.'

'Yes, it will, but I can see that I was wrong to insist she come to England with me. But at least I shall know she is alive and where she is. It is more important that she is happy, no?'

'Much more.' She nodded. 'And you will be able to see her during holiday times.'

'That will be something to look forward to.' He drove into the yard and helped them both out.

After a quick wave to his grandparents, Danny was

off to check on his favourite pigs and chickens. Once he'd done this, they all went into the front room. Angie was delighted to see the change in Gerda. She was smiling and more animated than she had ever seen her.

'Angie.' Gerda greeted her with warmth. 'I do thank you for your help. Has Dieter told you I am to go home soon?'

'He has, and I'm pleased to see you looking so happy.'

Gerda pulled a face and studied her brother. 'I have been a great trial to Dieter, but he is a kind man and understands.'

'Auntie Gerda?' Danny was gazing up at her. 'Daddy said you're going in a plane. Will you be scared?'

'*Nein*, I came here in one. It is very fast.' She crouched down in front of him. 'You must come and visit me one day.'

'Daddy said he'd take us when I'm older.'

'Well, that will not be long. How old are you now?'

That took a bit of working out and he chewed his lip in concentration. 'I'm gonna be four soon. Is that right?' he asked Angie.

'That's right, darling.' Angie held her breath, hoping he had forgotten what had happened on his last birthday.

But she knew he hadn't when he went very quiet and sidled up to Angie, looking near to tears. But before he could be too upset, Dieter had swept him up and plonked him on the piano stool. He began to show his son how to play a simple tune.

As she watched, Angie was numb right through. So

much had been going on just lately that she hadn't given his approaching birthday much thought, but it was only four weeks away, and the previous one was obviously still vivid in his mind. How on earth was she going to make it special and happy for him with that shadow hanging over them?

By Tuesday afternoon Angie still hadn't come up with an answer. 'What am I going to do?' she asked Sally as they enjoyed a cup of tea while the children played on the swing in the warm sunshine. 'It has come round so quickly.'

'We could have a big party and invite all the local children. If Danny's surrounded by screaming and shouting kids, he might not think about his mother too much.'

'That's an idea.' Angie gazed into space. 'We need something very special, though. Something to make it different from anything else he's had in the past.'

'Well,' Sally stirred her tea, and then grinned. 'I know. Joe can do a magic act for them.'

'Can he?' This was the first Angie had heard of Joe's magical talents.

'Oh, yes, he used to be quite good. We've even got a cloak and pointy hat in the loft somewhere.'

'Can he pull a rabbit out of a hat?' Angie giggled at the thought of Sally's serious husband in a pointy hat.

'Yep. Not a live one, of course.'

They were both chortling with amusement now.

'It will certainly be different.' Angie composed herself. 'Will you ask him?'

'I'll get him up in the loft to look for the things tonight. Whoops!' Sally was on her feet and rushing towards the door. 'Time to get the magician's dinner.'

Angie felt much happier as she set about preparing their meal. It was so good to have a friend like Sally. She was someone she could pour out her heart to and know she would receive cheerful help. It had been an eventful and traumatic year. She had known that Danny's birthday was going to be a difficult time, but it had always seemed a long way off. It had crept up on her, and now the problem had to be faced.

She put the pan of potatoes on the stove and lit the gas, giving a deep sigh. Where had the time gone? Almost a year since Jane had died. It was unbelievable. Her thoughts turned back to the birthday. She would ask Dieter if he had any ideas. The day would not be easy for any of them, so it would be best if they were all so busy they didn't have time to dwell on Jane's sudden passing.

It was ten o'clock that evening when there was a knock on the front door. Frowning, she put aside the book she had been reading. Who could that be this time of night?

When she opened the door she was surprised to see Dieter standing on the step, head bowed and hands stuffed in his pockets. 'Dieter! Why didn't you use your key?'

He looked up. 'I thought it might frighten you if I walked in this late. I saw your light still on. May I come in for a moment?'

429

'Of course.' She stepped aside, and then closed the door behind him. 'Would you like a cup of cocoa or something?'

'No, thank you.' He sat down looking bone weary.

'What's the matter?'

'Gerda's gone. The General arrived at six o'clock today and said he had managed to get an early flight for them, but that they must leave at once.' An expression of utter sadness crossed his face. 'She could not wait to leave. She was so excited about returning to Germany.'

'I'm so sorry we never had a chance to say goodbye.' Angie could feel Dieter's pain.

'She would not allow me to see her off.' He gave a helpless shrug. 'But perhaps it is better this way.'

'It doesn't make it any easier, though, does it?'

'No.' He forced a smile. 'I hope you do not mind me calling? I was feeling low.'

'You are welcome at any time, you know that, Dieter.'

'Thank you.' He bowed his head in acknowledgement of her understanding. 'Danny is sleeping well?'

'Yes, but I'm a bit worried about his next birthday.' Angie hesitated, not wanting to burden him further, but thought it only right she should discuss this problem with him. 'Sally came round this afternoon while the children were playing in the garden. We were trying to decide what we could do to make his birthday special at the end of next month. I'm afraid he's going to associate it with the day his mother died, and I would like to do something really special. Do you have any ideas?'

'That will be a difficult day.' Dieter nodded in agreement. 'Fortunately it is a Saturday, so I shall be able to spend the whole day with you.'

'That will be lovely.' So he had already been thinking about it, and worked out which day it would be. She then told him about Sally's suggestion that they give him a big party, with Joe doing magic tricks for the children.

'That I must see!' The sadness and worry cleared from his face and he laughed. 'I think this is a good idea. And perhaps we could take Danny to a concert somewhere in the evening. Make it really special by allowing him to stay up late. Just this once.'

'He'd love that. Will you see what you can do?'

'Of course. I should be able to find a show of some kind.' He stood up. 'Now I must leave you to get some rest.'

At the door he hesitated, looking down at her upturned face. He said softly, 'You are very understanding, Angie, and so lovely.' Without touching her, he lowered his head and kissed her, his lips lingering on hers, then he stepped back. 'Thank you for being someone I can come and talk to; someone who can make me laugh when I'm sad; someone who loves and cares for my son as much as any mother would.'

Then he left, closing the door quietly behind him.

She gazed at the door with unseeing eyes. The kiss had been so gentle she had wanted to wrap her arms around him, hold on tight and never let him go. It had only been his lips that had touched hers, but the warmth and tenderness had made her head swim. But he had quickly stepped away.

The joy she had felt when he'd kissed her now evaporated, and she bowed her head in sorrow. Gratitude, that's what he was saying he felt for her, but she wanted more than that from him – much more. It had been foolish to complicate her life like this, but how did you stop yourself from falling in love? She certainly didn't know the answer.

There was a bright moon shining, but Dieter was oblivious to the beauty of the night as he walked back to the farm. He hadn't been able to resist kissing Angie as she had gazed up at him with compassion and understanding. The desire to stay there with her, to hold her in his arms and make love to her, had been overwhelming, but somehow he had managed to control himself. They had a sound relationship now and he didn't want to ruin that by showing her attention she might not want.

Lifting his head, he looked up at the full moon hanging in a clear sky. She hadn't resisted, though. She could have stepped away at any time, but she hadn't moved.

Two days later Bob walked into his house, dumped his bag in the hall and headed for the library. He often wondered why they had such a large house, when they used only this one room all the time.

'Robert!' His mother put down the newspaper she

had been reading. 'What a surprise. I wasn't expecting you.'

'Managed to wangle leave at the last minute.' He bent and kissed her cheek. 'And I cadged a lift on an RAF flight.'

'But your father has taken Gerda back to Frankfurt, and said he was going to visit you.'

'He arrived and I spent a few hours with him. He's staying with General Steadman, and I've left Hunt to look after him.' Bob poured himself a small whisky and held up the decanter. 'Do you want a drink?'

His mother shook her head. 'Do you know how long he's staying?'

'Only a couple of days.' Bob sat down, chuckling. 'He's thoroughly enjoying himself.'

'I expect he is.' She gave a faint smile. 'He misses the life, you know. Never says as much, but I know him too well to be fooled. Now, how much leave have you got?'

'Seven days. I thought I'd go down to Somerset for two of them, spend two with you, then I'm meeting father in Frankfurt before returning to Berlin.' Bob changed the subject. 'How did Dieter cope with his sister leaving?'

'He was very sad, of course, but he hid it well. He knew she wasn't happy here and had to let her go. That young man has had a lot to cope with in his life, but he has great courage, I think.'

'Must have been hard for him.' Bob finished his drink and put the glass on the small table beside him. 'I'll set off early in the morning and see everyone while I'm in the country. Then I'll come back here and take you out for a slap-up meal.'

'That would be lovely, Robert. I'll look forward to it.'

He hauled himself out of the chair. 'Now I'm going to have a long soak in the bath to ease my aching bones. There were only bench seats in the plane, and it was a damned uncomfortable journey.'

'Don't make it too long. Dinner will be in an hour. I'll warn Cook you are here and see if she can rustle up some of her famous apple pie. I know how much you like it.'

'I think she's already making it. I saw her when I arrived and she muttered something about apples.'

The train was crowded, but Bob found a carriage with only four people in it. Throwing his bag on to the rack, he sat by the window. He always found the rhythm and sway of trains soothing, and his mind wandered to the time when Angie and Danny had been sitting opposite. Little had he realized then how much he was going to be drawn into their lives, or how fond of them he was going to become. He had been giving Angie a lot of thought. He was attracted to her, but it wasn't love. To be brutally honest with himself, being single suited him and the kind of life he led. For a while the cosy picture of having a family of his own had tempted him, and Danny was a good kid, but it wouldn't be right for any of them. And something had been niggling at him ever since they had all visited in the New Year. When Dieter had been playing, Angie had caught his attention. He had watched her through half-closed eyes and seen something she was trying to keep a secret. In that unguarded moment her feelings had been visible. Now that he had the time, he was going to get to the bottom of it, even if he had to force the truth out of her.

Opening the window at the top, he lit a cigarette. If he had gone ahead and tried to persuade her to marry him, he would have made four people very unhappy – Angie, Danny, Dieter and himself. If what he believed was true, then his role in this complicated set-up must be one of friendship and to act as an uncle to the boy. He liked all of them far too much to just walk out of their lives. A bond had been formed on that other train journey, and it was one he didn't want broken.

The train pulled into his station and he was surprised. He had hardly noticed the time passing.

He was lucky and managed to catch a taxi as it dropped passengers at the station. It took him to the pub in the village and he booked in for two nights. Then he walked up the street to Angie's.

The door opened before he could knock.

'Bob, what a lovely surprise. Come in. Is this a flying visit?'

'I'm staying for a couple of days.' He stood in the middle of the small front room and smiled down at her. 'I've come to spend some time with my nephew and his auntie.'

That made Angie laugh. 'Well, your nephew is in the

garden with Emma, and they'll be as pleased to see you as I am.'

'Good.' His eyes took on a devilish gleam and he reached out to take hold of her arms, drawing her slowly towards him. 'How about a proper welcome?'

She placed both hands on his chest to make him keep his distance, shaking her head in mock displeasure. 'I thought we'd settled this ages ago, Bob. We don't love each other, and I will not be a convenient mistress for you.'

'All I want to do is give a good friend a kiss.' He pretended to be offended, but couldn't hide his smile.

Her look told him she was suspicious of such an innocent request, and he thought again what a damned shame it was that they hadn't met under different circumstances.

She tapped her cheek. 'Just a peck, then.'

'You're a hard woman, Angie Westwood,' he joked as he lowered his head.

36

Closing the front door quietly, Dieter eased the key out of the lock. So, the Colonel was back.

Damn him! After the kiss they had shared, he was hoping for a chance to show Angie how much he cared for her, and to find out if she had any affection for him. Not as Danny's father but as himself. He had been sure she did, but, after what he had just seen, he knew who had her love. The Colonel.

He could hear the children in the back garden and he went to the side gate.

'Deeder.' Emma shrieked with delight, seeing him first.

Then he was nearly knocked off his feet as both children threw themselves at him.

'Give us a push, Daddy.' Danny dragged him towards the swing.

It was hard to dismiss from his thoughts the scene he had nearly walked in on. All Angie's denials that there wasn't anything between her and the Colonel could no longer be believed. He had seen their love for each other with his own eyes.

He wasn't allowed to brood, though. Not with two lively youngsters claiming his attention.

'Emma.' Sally peered over the gate. 'Come in now. We're going to see Grandma. Hello, Dieter.'

'Ow, Mum, Deeder's only just come,' Emma protested. 'He's gonna play with us.'

'Another time.' Sally held out her hand. 'We mustn't be late.'

Giving a dramatic sigh, Emma went obediently.

When they were alone, Danny said, 'You were going to show me your badges, Daddy. That was a long time ago. Have you lost them?'

'No, they are in my room. I'm sorry, Danny, there has been so much going on that I forgot all about them.'

'Can we go and see them now?'

'I do not see why not.' Dieter hesitated, wondering if he should knock and tell Angie where they were going. His mind conjured up a picture of what she might be doing, and he decided against it. If he carried Danny, they would be at the farm and back within an hour. She wouldn't even know they had left the garden.

'You'd better go to see Danny while I make some tea.'

Angie watched Bob walk out and shook her head in amusement. Colonel Robert Strachan was a real handful, but she couldn't have a better friend, which was all he could ever be to her. Singing to herself, she filled the kettle with water.

Bob came back into the kitchen. 'He isn't there.'

'Oh, he's gone into Emma's, then. I'll go and get him.'

'I'll come with you and say hello to Sally.'

They went to the front and Sally answered when they

knocked. 'Hello, Bob, nice to see you. I'm afraid we're just going out.'

'We've come for Danny.' Angie smiled at Emma, who was being swung in the air so she could hug Bob.

'Danny's with Deeder,' Emma informed them when she was on the floor again.

Although it was a warm day, Angie went cold. When she had been fooling around with Bob, she thought she'd heard the click of a door closing. Had Dieter arrived, seen them and drawn the wrong conclusion?

'Don't look so worried, Angie,' Sally said. 'Perhaps they've gone for a walk. He's quite safe with his father.'

Somehow Angie managed a smile, although she felt sick and faint. If Dieter had seen them, he might think that he was about to lose his son. Was this her worst nightmare come true?

Rushing back indoors, she spun round to face Bob, who was right behind her. 'He saw us kissing and has taken Danny.' She tore up the stairs just to make sure, then tumbled back down again. 'He's taken him!'

'Calm down.' Bob spoke firmly. 'You don't know that for sure.'

'I do, I do! He would never take Danny anywhere without telling me first, unless he didn't want me to find them.' She was shaking so much it was difficult to talk. 'Have you got a car?'

'No, but –'

Angie was already running out the door and up the street.

In a few loping strides, Bob caught her up. 'Where are you going?'

'To the farm. We need John's truck in case Dieter is heading for the station.'

Bob caught her arm to stop her headlong flight of panic. 'He wouldn't take Danny away from you, and where the hell would he go?'

'To his sister in Germany.' Tears were flowing unheeded down her face. 'If he does, I'll never get Danny back. I can't let that happen!'

'It isn't that easy –'

But she wasn't listening. All she could think about was that she might have lost Danny. She was in a panic, incapable of being rational. Shaking herself free of his grip, she ran full pelt again, her hair flying in a bright mass around her head.

Not being so agile, Bob was a way behind when he reached the farmhouse.

'John, John.' She was calling frantically, running towards the large barn. 'John, I must have your truck!'

Her shouts had brought both John and Hetty into the yard. Badly out of breath, Bob joined them, bending over and gulping for air.

'My God, she can run,' he gasped.

'What's the panic?' Hetty looked alarmed.

Angie ran towards them. 'Dieter's taken Danny. Where's the truck? We've got to get to the station before he does.' She was spinning round and round. 'Where's the truck?'

'It's in the garage for repairs.' John caught hold of

her. 'What's all this nonsense about Dieter taking Danny?'

'I haven't got time to explain. Must get to the station.' She tried to run, but John held her firmly.

'Let go!'

'Angie!' Hetty stepped in front of her. 'Danny's here. He's upstairs with Dieter and quite safe.'

As the news penetrated her frantic mind, Angie went absolutely still. The fear inside turned to relief, and quickly to anger – blazing fury. With a growl of rage she went into the farmhouse and thundered up the stairs. Bob only just managed to stay with her and stop her at the top of the stairs.

'Easy. You'll frighten Danny if you go in there like this. Stop and think.'

But she was beyond thinking. After shoving him away, she stood with her head bowed and fought for control. Her hands were clenching and unclenching as if she needed to get them round someone's neck.

It took a couple of minutes before she lifted her head and spoke to Hetty, who was now next to Bob. 'Will you go in there and take Danny downstairs, please?'

'I could take him out to see the pigs,' Bob suggested.

The look she gave him would have withered a lesser man. 'You'll stay right where you are!'

Hetty knocked on Dieter's door, entered, and soon came out with Danny.

'Auntie, Uncle Bob.' The child was beaming. 'I've been looking at Daddy's badges. He's gonna teach me to talk like him.' He giggled as he took Hetty's hand. 'You won't know what I'm saying then, will you, Grandma?'

'No, I won't, but I don't always understand you now.'

Danny gazed up at Angie and held something out for her to see. 'Daddy's given me one of his badges. Look, Auntie.'

'That's lovely, darling.' Angie managed to control her voice only with extreme effort. 'Go and help Grandma with the tea and we'll be down in a minute.'

'Okay.' He went, oblivious of the row about to erupt.

Dieter was standing in the doorway. She pushed him back into the room, dragged Bob after her and kicked the door shut with her foot.

'Angie –'

'Don't say a word! You've just frightened the bloody life out of me. Didn't it enter your head I'd be worried sick? Didn't you realize that I would be frantic when I couldn't find him?' She bunched her hands into fists, knowing it wouldn't take much to make her lash out at someone in the room. 'How could you be so thoughtless? I trusted you. Damn you for putting me through this. Damn you!'

'Take it easy . . .' Bob stopped when she turned on him like a feral cat.

'Shut up! I'll deal with you later. First Dieter will tell me why he took Danny out of the garden without telling me. And it had better be good. Then I'm going to beat Dieter to a pulp,' she raged, stepping forward until she was toe to toe with him, tipping her head back to look up into his face. "Well, come on, I'm waiting.'

'He asked to see the badges . . . and as you were busy I didn't think you would miss him for an hour.' The expression on Dieter's face showed that he now regretted that decision very much. 'That was wrong of me. I am sorry.'

'You're sorry?' She fairly spat the words out. 'What did you think I was doing? Did you think I was going to jump into bed with Bob while the children played in the garden?'

She glared at the man in question, who was leaning against the door, arms folded and a wry twist to his mouth. When he looked as if he was going to say something, she snarled, 'Don't you say a word! I think you've enjoyed playing games with us and making Dieter jealous. I'm sick and tired of the pair of you. Ever since you came into my life, you've caused nothing but trouble.'

Dieter reached out to touch her arm.

She took one step away from him, breaking the contact. 'I told you time and time again that I would never take Danny away from you, but you didn't believe me, did you? You were still jealous of Bob, although there was no reason for it. I gave you my word, Dieter. I don't lie! You must have known I'd be out of my mind if Danny disappeared without a word. All you'd needed to say was that you were bringing him here. I wouldn't have objected. I trusted you. Now I'm changing the rules. You will not see Danny unless I am there. You can return my key, as you are no longer welcome in my house unless I invite you.' She held out her hand, not caring that it was shaking. 'The key!'

He unhooked the key from his ring and handed it back to her. 'Did you really believe I would take Danny away from you?'

'Yes, I did! God forgive me, but I did. I'll make sure you are never alone with him again.' The terror wouldn't leave her and she was completely out of control. She knew it, but could do nothing about it.

'He is my son. You cannot do that,' he protested.

'Just you watch me!' Having finished with Dieter, she rounded on Bob. 'You can't mess with people's affections and then laugh it off as a joke. It isn't a joke! I wish I'd never met either of you.'

Bob pushed away from the door at that remark, anger just under the surface. 'You've had your say, now drop it. No harm has been done.'

'No harm . . . ?' She couldn't believe he'd just said that. After giving him a contemptuous glance, she turned back to Dieter. Oh, how she longed to hammer some sense into the pair of them. 'Is that how you feel as well?'

When he began to speak, she stopped him. 'No, don't bother. I don't want to hear your excuses. But I'll tell you what harm has been done. I love that little boy with all my heart, and when Jane died I took him on willingly, even though the thought of bringing him up on my own was daunting and rather frightening.' Her voice faltered. 'You have just betrayed and destroyed my trust. That is the *harm* that has been done. But it's worse than that, Dieter. Not only did I trust you, but I also fell in love with you. That is what's tearing me apart.'

There was a stunned silence as he stared at her in disbelief. She knew she had said the wrong thing. Damn. Her blind fury had made her say things that should never have been said. Once she really calmed down she was going to regret some of this, but she couldn't think about that for the moment. They deserved to be on the receiving end of her fury.

She didn't fail to miss Bob mutter under his breath, 'At last we have the truth.'

Keeping her gaze fixed on Dieter, she spoke more reasonably now but still with firmness. 'Don't think that lets you off the hook, because it doesn't. The new rules stand.'

Then she turned and left the room before bursting into tears. Tears of fright and tears of crushing hurt that the man she had come to love had put her through this. She was still shaking, but the anger had burnt itself out.

'She loves me.' Dieter could hardly get the words out.

'Of course she does.' Bob, who was mopping his brow in mock relief, grinned. 'That was an explosive performance.'

'I must talk with her.' Dieter was on his feet and heading for the door when Bob caught his arm.

'Whoa there, I wouldn't go after her yet. Let her cool down first.'

'She was very angry, and rightly so. She didn't mean

half of what she said.' Dieter stuffed his hands into his pockets and hunched his shoulders, calling himself all kinds of names for being so stupid.

'She meant it when she said she was in love with you, but I thought she was never going to admit it. A fright and blazing anger finally brought it to the surface. I've had my suspicions since the New Year.'

'What do you mean?' Dieter frowned.

'I saw it in her eyes when she looked at you, but I think she feels that your affection for Jane is a shadow between you.'

'But that was quite different. My feelings for Angie are much deeper, stronger.' Dieter sat down again, as it didn't seem as if his legs would hold him. Oh, God, she loved him and he might have thrown away the chance of happiness with her.

'Thought so.' Bob nodded. 'So, do you love Angie?'

'Yes, of course I do, but I did not believe she could ever feel the same about me. That is why I have not said anything to her.' He eyed the Colonel with suspicion. 'You always were a devious bastard. Knowing this, you would have still claimed her for yourself?'

'Ah, you know me so well after your years in the camp.' Bob became serious and held Dieter's gaze. 'I want to make one thing clear, Dieter. I never set out to hurt you or Angie, whatever she may have said. I really was attracted to her, and did for a while seriously consider marrying her. She is a fine mother to Danny and would make a good wife. I'd have settled for affection and respect, but I'm not quite the bastard you

446

believe. There are too many involved in this charade, too many to get hurt, so I'll settle for friendship and being an uncle to Danny.'

'But I saw you kissing each other.' The picture was still vivid in his mind. Seeing the woman he loved in another man's arms had hurt.

'What you saw was us fooling around. I gave her a chaste kiss on the cheek.' Bob raised an eyebrow. 'As you would have seen if you'd stuck around.'

Dieter bowed his head. 'I cannot take this all in.'

Bob's shoulders shook as he laughed. 'Magnificent, wasn't she?'

'That is not the word I would choose. I would not have believed she could erupt like that.'

'Just a mother protecting her young. Puts you off, does it?'

'No.' Dieter stood up. 'I always knew she would guard my son with her life. I have hurt and frightened her, and do not think she will ever forgive me. How do I make her believe that I love her?'

'You're going to have to court her.' When Dieter still looked puzzled, Bob slapped him on the back. 'Give her flowers; things like that. If you play your cards right, you'll soon get her back.'

'What is this – play my cards?'

Laughing, Bob opened the door. 'Don't worry about it. Just convince her, and I'll expect an invitation to the wedding.'

When they reached the kitchen, everyone was waiting for them.

'Ah, you're here at last.' Hetty put the kettle on the stove. 'Tea's all ready, so sit yourselves down.'

'Have a good talk, did you?'

'Very enlightening.' Bob winked at Angie, then smiled at Danny. 'How is the swing going, young man?'

'Lovely, and we'd like a see-saw now.' Danny's hopeful gaze whipped from Bob to Dieter.

'Then we must see what we can do. I'm here for a couple of days.' Bob handed Dieter the butter. 'We'll build it together, shall we?'

He nodded. 'Should be easy enough.'

'Yippee.' Danny jiggled up and down in his chair. 'Wait till I tell Em.'

As Bob and Dieter began to discuss plans for the see-saw, Angie muttered under her breath. 'The best of pals now. Look at them, a picture of innocence.'

Dieter pulled a face at Bob. 'She's still furious with us.'

'Give her a couple of days.' He studied her expression for a moment. 'Perhaps three or four, Dieter.'

'Is that days or years?'

37

The next day Angie and Sally watched Dieter and Bob working hard in the garden to construct a see-saw. They had been at it for nearly three hours without a break. The children watched in fascination as it took shape.

Angie's gaze rested on Dieter and she cringed with embarrassment about the way she'd blurted out her feelings for him.

'That should be sturdy enough.' Sally gurgled with amusement when she saw Joe join them, rolling up his sleeves to help mix concrete to secure the main structure.

'Well, I hope they pack up soon, or our Sunday lunch will be overcooked.' Angie looked in the oven. 'I'll give them another half an hour.'

'Those two kids of ours can't wait to try it out.' She gave Angie a knowing smile. 'There will soon be three of them.'

'Hmm?' Angie was busy at the stove. 'Three of what?'

'Children.'

Angie spun round to face her friend. 'You're expecting again?'

'Yes, isn't it wonderful?' Sally did a little jig of delight. 'He's due early October.'

'He?' Angie laughed and hugged Sally. 'You're determined to have a boy.'

'Yep.' She patted her middle. 'I've told it to make itself into a boy.'

'I hope it does, but another girl wouldn't be so bad, would it?'

'No, of course it wouldn't.' Sally gazed at her pretty daughter in the garden. 'We'll be happy with either, but it would be nice to have one of each.'

The children suddenly sprang into action and tore into the kitchen.

'Daddy said they've nearly done, Auntie.'

'Good.' Angie turned on the tap for them. 'Wash your hands and sit at the table.'

There was a tussle between them for the soap as they stood on tiptoe to reach the running water.

'I'm starving.' Emma sat down next to Danny. It was becoming almost impossible to separate them.

Joe came in first and Angie reached up to kiss his cheek. 'Congratulations, Joe. Sally's just told me your wonderful news.'

'Thanks.' He couldn't have looked happier. 'We're very pleased.'

Bob arrived next, but there was no sign of Dieter. Angie looked out of the door and found him waiting outside.

'May I come in, please?'

She didn't know whether to laugh or cry. He was taking her at her word and not coming in unless she invited him. 'Oh, Dieter, you mustn't take what I said in the heat of anger seriously, of course you can come in.'

Danny hadn't missed the little charade and was frowning. 'Why does Daddy ask if he can come in, Auntie?'

As Dieter passed his son's chair, he smoothed his hand over the boy's hair. 'I did something bad and made your auntie angry. She told me off and I've got to be careful what I do until she forgives me.'

Danny was wide-eyed with disbelief. 'But Auntie's never angry.'

'She was yesterday.' Bob controlled a grin. 'She shouted at us.'

'Both of you?' When they nodded, Danny huffed out a breath. 'Did she shout loud?'

'Very.' Bob nodded. 'We were naughty and deserved a telling-off.'

He still seemed to be having trouble believing this astonishing piece of news. 'Auntie doesn't shout at me, and I'm naughty sometimes.' He swivelled round to look at Angie, who was dishing up the lunch. 'Do you, Auntie?'

'No, darling.' She didn't dare look round because she was nearly crying with laughter. All her anger had melted away during the night. The embarrassment of blurting out that she loved Dieter would take longer to disappear.

'That's because you're a little boy.' Bob winked at Danny. 'Just wait until you grow up.'

Danny gazed around at all the smiling faces and giggled. 'P'haps I'd better stay little.'

This produced roars of laughter and Angie joined

in, not being able to help herself. But the thought that she might have lost her darling boy still made her heart race in panic. Because she had fallen in love with Dieter, she had relaxed and become too trusting. Of course, she now knew that he had not been in any danger; that Dieter would never have kidnapped his son. And that is what she had accused him of doing. That had been unjust of her, but the only excuse she had was that fear had stopped her seeing the truth. Dieter had been in the wrong, though, for taking Danny without telling her. But Bob hadn't, and she must apologize to him before he left.

'Mummy's 'specting,' Emma announced to everyone. 'I'm gonna have a brother or sister.' She didn't seem to think that was a very good idea. 'If I don't like it, Mummy can take it back.'

'It won't be up to you, my girl,' Joe admonished. 'You'll be able to help Mummy look after it.'

Emma chased a pea around her plate. 'S'pose.' Successfully spearing the elusive pea, she popped it into her mouth, looked up and grinned. 'We can give it a go on our see-saw.'

'When's it coming?' Danny was much more interested in the thought of another playmate.

'Not until October,' Sally told them.

'That's a long time.' Danny leant towards Sally, who was on the other side of the table. 'Why's it gonna be that long?'

'We've had to put in an order.' Joe kept a perfectly straight face. 'And there's a long waiting list.'

'A big bird brings it in a bag.' Emma was proud of this knowledge. 'I've seen a picture in a book.'

'Cor.' Danny was impressed. 'We'll have to see that.'

'Yeah, Mummy'll tell us when it's coming.' Emma turned her attention to Dieter. 'When can we have a go on the see-saw?'

'Not until tomorrow. We have to wait for the concrete to dry.'

'Okay, thanks for building it. It looks smashing.'

'It was our pleasure, Princess.'

It began to rain in the afternoon, so the men rushed out to cover the concrete before it got too wet. Then they all crowded into Angie's small front room and listened to Dieter play. The time passed in a happy and relaxed atmosphere. This was just what Angie needed after the trauma of the day before.

Joe, Sally and Emma left around seven, and Bob and Dieter stayed until nine o'clock, when Danny was fast asleep.

'I'm catching an early train in the morning, Angie, so I'll say goodbye now.' Bob bent over her chair and kissed her cheek. 'It's been an interesting couple of days, and I'm sorry if I've made things difficult for you. That was not my intention.'

She grimaced and stood up. 'I must apologize for my behaviour yesterday. I took my fear out on you and that wasn't right.'

'Think nothing of it.' Then he said quietly, 'You can trust him, you know.'

She nodded, knowing full well that that was true, but yesterday her fear had overruled all common sense.

Bob turned to Dieter and held out his hand. 'When I go back I'll be stopping off in Frankfurt to meet my father – would you like me to give your sister a message?'

'Please, if you would.' Dieter shook his hand. 'Thank her for her letters – she has been writing twice a week – and tell her I'm pleased she is happy again.'

'I'll do that. Take care of Angie and Danny.'

'I will, and thank you, Colonel.'

'What for?' Bob raised an eyebrow in query.

'For everything you and your family have done for me.'

Bob slapped him on the back, smiled at Angie, and left.

Dieter remained on his feet after the front door had closed. 'I wish to apologize for my thoughtless actions yesterday. I can assure you that it will never happen again. It saddens me to know you thought me capable of doing such harm to you and Danny. I would *never* take him away from you. It would break his heart.'

She was touched by his sincerity and wanted to explain. 'I thought my worst nightmare had come true, and when I found he was missing I immediately assumed that you'd taken him. I'm sorry about that, but I wasn't the only one, was I? You saw me with Bob and also jumped to the wrong conclusion.'

'I admit that, and it clouded my judgement at the time.' He reached out tentatively for her hand. 'I beg your forgiveness.'

'We need to forgive each other.' Walking over to the fireplace, she picked up the key and held it out to him. 'I want you to have this back.'

'Thank you, Angie. That is gracious of you.' He curled his fingers round the key, then stepped back. 'May I see Danny on my way home from school tomorrow?'

'We will wait until you get here and then you must have tea with us.'

'Thank you. Good night, Angie.'

She watched him stride up the road and felt wretched. He was such a gentleman, and she had been unduly harsh with him. But in her anger she had blurted out her feelings for him, and that was embarrassing. What must he think of her? She had seen his expression. It had been one of disbelief and, yes, horror. Her outburst had complicated things further.

Resting her forehead on the window, she could have wept. After her unrestrained outburst, Dieter was keeping his distance. He was polite, as always, but had said nothing about her declaration that she loved him. She was making a terrible mess of everything, except of being a mother to Danny. When everything else around her was in shambles, she could be pleased with her efforts to see that her darling boy was happy.

The next day Dieter bought a bunch of daffodils at a shop near the station. He had wanted so much to kiss her yesterday, to tell her how overjoyed he was that she loved him, but the atmosphere between them was strained at the moment. She was embarrassed, he knew that, and it was up to him to put things right between them.

He knocked on the front door, clutching the flowers in both hands. When the door opened, he held them out to her, feeling like an awkward boy. 'I bought these for you. They were so lovely.' When he saw her startled expression, he thought he had done the wrong thing and felt a fool. He wasn't very good at this. During the years when he should have been dating girls and learning how to court, as the Colonel suggested, he had been locked in a POW camp.

She took the flowers from him. 'You're right; they are very pretty. Thank you.'

He breathed a silent sigh of relief as she stepped aside to allow him in.

'Danny's upstairs washing his hands and changing his trousers; he won't be long.' She gave a hesitant smile. 'I'll just go and put these in a vase.'

When she left the room he went over to the piano and examined the exercises Mrs Poulton had given Danny. He nodded in approval. She was a good teacher and taking it slowly. It wouldn't be right to rush a child of Danny's age. In another year he would take over the lessons himself.

Still standing, his fingers ran idly over the keys. His son would need a better piano too. He would start saving for that.

'Dieter.'

He looked up. 'I apologize; I did not hear you come back. Danny is doing well with his lessons, and shows

456

no sign of becoming tired of the discipline needed to learn to play well.'

'So Mrs Poulton tells me, and he does love it.' She put the vase of bright yellow flowers on the mantelpiece and stood back to admire them. 'Were you the same at his age?'

'Yes.' His smile was gentle. 'My mother said I could play almost before I could walk. But that was a mother's exaggeration, I expect. She was a fine musician and encouraged me, sending me to a school renowned for nurturing musical talent.'

'We must see that Danny has the same chance, if that is what he wants.' Spinning round suddenly to face him, her eyes wide with pain, she said, 'I'm sorry for losing my temper and saying such nasty things to you. I shouldn't have doubted you like that, but I was so very frightened, Dieter.'

'You had every right to be angry. What I did was wrong.' He stepped forward and drew her towards him. 'Angie –'

'Daddy!' Danny erupted into the room, all smiles. 'Our see-saw's smashing. Auntie had a go, as well, didn't you?'

Dieter released her and stepped back.

'I did, with you and Emma on one end and me on the other. It was fun.' Angie gazed lovingly at his animated face. 'Are your hands clean?'

He held them out for her to inspect, and when she nodded he showed them to Dieter. 'I got them very dirty and had to rub hard to get them clean. My fingers are growing, aren't they?'

'They most certainly are.' Dieter made a point of measuring his son's fingers against his own. 'You have a way to go yet, but you are growing all over.'

'Yeah.' He looked up at his tall father. 'I'm gonna be just like you.'

'He's grown almost two inches in the last few weeks,' Angie told Dieter, not hiding the pride in her voice. 'All the fresh air, exercise and good food have done wonders for him.'

'Yes.' Dieter spoke softly. 'Jane would have been proud to see what a fine boy he is growing into.'

'She loved him with every fibre of her being.' Angie's eyes clouded with sadness as she looked at Dieter. 'And she loved you.'

'I did not deserve such unselfish love after the way I allowed her to walk out of my life.' He knew the shame would always be with him, but he couldn't change the past.

Angie rested her hand on his arm. 'It's all done with now and we must move on. Jane would have expected us to do that.'

'You are right.' He covered her hand with his, holding it in place, and watched his son, who had gone over to the piano while they had been talking. 'The future is what matters now.'

She stood on tiptoe and kissed his cheek, smiling up at him, then she held her hand out to Danny. 'Come on, darling, time for tea. You can play for Daddy later.'

*

While Angie was washing up, Dieter and Danny were in the front room, talking about, and playing, music. Listening to his son showing him what he had learnt, Dieter smiled gently – not only at the delight of seeing Danny enthusiastic about music but because of Angie's changed attitude towards him. He knew he had been completely forgiven and was anxious to advance their relationship.

Angie came into the room and the next couple of hours passed quickly, with Danny taking up much of their attention. But it didn't stop him from curling his fingers around her small hand as they sat on the settee listening while Danny told them what he'd been doing at the church hall and with Emma.

She didn't try to pull her hand away but leant against him, smiling.

'*Ich liebe dich*', he murmured softly.

'That sounds lovely. What does it mean?' Angie gazed up at him.

'I will tell you when we are alone.' He pulled her closer, running his fingers through her hair, making his feelings quite clear to her.

'Tell us now, Daddy.' Danny picked up on it immediately and scrambled on to the settee, squeezing between them.

'It means, I love you,' he said, giving Angie a glance over his son's head, relieved to see her colour slightly and hold his gaze, her mouth turning up in a smile.

'Teach me to say it.' He was leaning on Dieter. 'Then I can say it to Auntie as well.'

There was much laughter as Danny struggled to say it just like his father. But it didn't take him long to make a passable attempt at the unfamiliar words.

Although Dieter treasured every moment with his son, just for once he wanted to be alone with Angie. He loved her so much and wanted her to know it.

When it was time for Danny to go to bed, he went without protest.

Alone at last, Dieter slipped his arm around Angie, looking at her earnestly. 'I really do love you, Angie.'

Then he kissed her, pouring out his feelings in the long embrace, talking to her in his own language. She didn't understand the words, but his meaning was clear.

'Oh, Dieter, I'm so very happy,' she said as the kiss ended and she settled in his arms. Her sigh, though, held a sad note.

'Something is worrying you, my darling.'

She laid her head on his shoulder. 'Danny's birthday will soon be here, and I don't want the bad memories to surface. Now it is so close, I can't get it out of my mind. Sally told me they've found Joe's magician's stuff and he's practising hard for the birthday party. He has to wait until Emma is in bed, otherwise she'd tell Danny, and that would spoil the surprise. I hope it's going to make it a special and happy day for him.'

This was the opening Dieter had been looking for and he decided to take a chance. There had been much wasted time in his life, and he was determined to change that now. 'There is a way we could make it a perfect day for him and us.'

'Oh?' She sat forward eagerly. 'How?'

'We could make his birthday our wedding day.' He waited, watching the play of emotions across her face. His heart thudded while she stared at him, absolutely still. It was almost as if she had stopped breathing.

He brought her hands to his lips and kissed them. 'When I saw how well you were caring for Danny, I could not help falling in love with you. However, I did not believe you could ever feel the same way about me. You must have hated me for leaving Jane.'

She pulled a face and tightened her grip on his hands. 'Once I'd met you and heard the whole story, I understood.'

'Then marry me, Angie,' he urged. 'Let us make a proper family for all of us and marry on his birthday. That would make him very happy. I would be a good husband to you, my dearest, for my love is great, and together we can face the future and leave the shadows behind us.'

He waited then, knowing she needed time to think, because this was a big step he was asking her to take. He could only pray she loved him enough to accept.

When she remained silent he knew there was one more thing he needed to clear up. He spoke clearly. 'My love for Jane was very different from my feelings for you. I had been a prisoner for years and freedom was a heady experience. Jane treated me like a normal human being and I grabbed at the chance of being a young man again. The letters from my family had stopped coming and I was dreadfully worried about them. Jane's love and laughter helped me, and I took advantage of her. I am not proud of that.'

Angie gazed at him, searching his face. 'But you loved her?'

'Yes, I did, as much as I was capable of at that troubled time. I would have stayed in touch, but she sent me away. I was hurt and puzzled, but of course now I understand why she did it.'

'They were confused times, but I'm glad you loved her.'

'I did, but my love for you is greater. I could never walk away from you, even if you ordered me to.'

Much to his relief she smiled.

'I wouldn't do that.' She pursed her lips. 'Danny's birthday is less than four weeks away. We can't possibly arrange a wedding in time, surely?'

Dieter surged to his feet, bringing her with him. 'Does that mean you will marry me?'

'Yes,' she laughed, throwing her arms around his neck.

He spun her round and around, lifting her off the floor. 'We shall see the Rector tomorrow and John and Hetty will help, so will Sally, I am sure. We will get it all done in time if we start at once.'

He drew her into his arms and arrangements were forgotten for quite some time.

38

The next day Angie's insides were still churning with excitement and happiness. The unbelievable had happened. Dieter loved her, not because she had adopted his son but for herself. He had explained his feeling for Jane and what had happened just after the war. She understood the turmoil in his life and could grasp, just a little, how he felt about being a prisoner for so many years. Wasted years of his youth. He had also shown how much he cared for her, leaving no room for doubt. Her smile was a touch self-conscious as she remembered his passion, and her response.

It was hard to concentrate as the children in the church hall claimed her attention. These mornings were always lively.

'Ah, Angie, my dear.' The Rector came in all smiles, and without the usual pile of papers he thrust at her a couple of times a week. 'Congratulations! Dieter came to see me early this morning. Wonderful news. Wonderful.'

'It's very short notice. Can it be arranged in time?'

'We'll do it.' He leant forward and whispered in her ear, laughter in his voice. 'I understand no one knows yet. We will start reading the banns this Sunday, and I've pencilled in your wedding date already. It will have to be at one o'clock, as that is the only space free.'

'Thank you, Geoff, that will be fine. We don't want Danny to hear about it until everything is arranged.'

'Understood, my dear. You must get a special licence.'

'Dieter's going to start dealing with the paperwork in his lunch hour today.'

'Good, good.' He beamed again, highly delighted. 'Splendid young man, and perfect that you will be a family.'

Angie gave him a questioning look. 'No typing today?'

'No, no, give you a rest today, but I shall have some at the end of the week. The Parish Newsletter, you know.' He wandered off, rubbing his hands together and still beaming.

'He looks pleased with himself.' Sally stood beside Angie and gave her a curious look. 'What's he planning?'

Making sure Danny was fully occupied, Angie whispered, 'My wedding.' Then she clamped her hand over her friend's mouth to stop her yelling out the good news.

Sally dragged her into the kitchen and shut the door. 'Tell me! Oh, Lord, I hope you're marrying Dieter. He's crazy about you.'

'I am.'

That was all she had a chance to say before she was caught and danced around the kitchen. 'When?'

'On Danny's birthday.'

'What?' Sally's mouth dropped open. 'But that's less than four weeks away.'

'I know, it's going to be a rush, but what better way could we make the day special for him – and us?'

'It's perfect. There won't be time for sad memories.'

'You can tell Joe, but no one else at the moment. And whatever you do, don't let Emma hear or she'll tell Danny. And I'm going to need your help.'

'A white dress.' Sally was now pacing the room. 'We must buy the material and I'll make you something beautiful.'

Angie looked at her aghast. 'But there isn't time. And I didn't know you could sew. I'll have to buy it ready-made because I can't put you to all that trouble.'

'It will be a joy, and I'm an experienced dressmaker. It's what I used to do before I was married and had Emma. Trust me, I'll have it ready in time.'

'That would be wonderful, Sally. Do you think I could have Emma as bridesmaid and Danny a pageboy?'

'If you want to live dangerously!' Sally roared and did a little jig, bursting with excitement. 'That's a wonderful idea, and very brave of you. I can't wait to tell Joe; he really likes Dieter. Oh, I'm so happy for you both. I was afraid there for a while that you were going to allow Bob to persuade you into an unwise marriage. He's a lovely man, but not for you, Angie.'

'I know it wouldn't have worked. I was drawn to him because he seemed like a safe, secure person to have in our lives, and he could have done a lot for Danny, but it wasn't love. I can see that now. He's a powerful, attractive man, but I couldn't take Danny away from his real father.' Angie's clear skin tinged with pink. 'And when I realized I was in love with Dieter, he was the only man I wanted to be with.'

'Thank heavens it's worked out right in the end. We guessed Dieter was in love with you by the way he used to watch you when you weren't looking. He has very expressive eyes, and I'm surprised you didn't see it as well.'

'No, I missed it completely. I spent my time fighting with shadows and not seeing what was in front of me.'

'Danny will be over the moon to have his daddy living with him.'

Angie grinned. 'I won't complain either.'

The door burst open and Emma tumbled in. 'Mummy, little Sammy's been sick!'

Both women shot back to the hall to deal with the crisis.

That evening it wasn't possible to talk until Danny was in bed. They didn't want to disappoint him if the wedding couldn't be arranged in time.

'How did you get on today?' she asked, sitting on the settee and resting in his arms.

'I've set everything in motion. There shouldn't be any problems getting the licence.'

'Oh, good. In that case what are we going to do about Joe? He's been practising his magic tricks for the party.'

'It will still be Danny's birthday, so go ahead with the party for the children. I don't think we should ignore the fact. We must give him presents and make a fuss of him, just as if it were a special day for him. He will have many more birthdays and we need to give him something happy to associate with the day.' Dieter pulled her close. 'There will be room in the church hall for everyone, and I'm sure a lot of the guests will enjoy the magic show as well.'

Angie couldn't help laughing. 'It will be an unusual wedding reception.'

Just then there was a knock on the front door and Angie went to see who it was.

'Joe, come in.'

'Congratulations you two,' he said, giving Angie a kiss on the cheek and then pumping Dieter's hand. 'This is wonderful news.'

'Thank you.' Dieter inclined his head. 'We have just been discussing your magic show.'

'You won't need that now.'

'But we will. Sit down, Joe.' Angie then explained their idea.

Joe chuckled. 'I'm game if you are.'

'There is one more thing, Joe. Would you be my best man?'

'I'd like that very much.' Joe turned to Angie. 'And who are you going to ask to give you away?'

'I'm hoping John will do it.'

Dieter nodded approval. 'I'm sure he would; he considers you their daughter. I haven't said anything to them yet, but I'll tell them tonight.'

'They don't know yet?' Joe said, surprised.

'No.' Angie smiled at Dieter. 'The only people who know at the moment are you, Sally and the Rector. Once the banns are read on Sunday the whole village will know, so we'll have to tell Danny before then.'

Joe stood up. 'I'll be off, then, to practise pulling a rabbit out of a hat.'

'Don't forget you will have a speech to prepare as well.' Dieter saw his friend to the door, and when he'd gone he pulled Angie into his arms. 'I must buy you an engagement ring. We shall go to the shops as soon as we can.'

She kissed him. 'That isn't necessary. We can leave it for a while, but we will need a wedding ring.'

'Two.'

'Are you going to wear one as well?' Angie was surprised, because not many men she knew wore a wedding ring.

'Of course. I shall be proud to wear a ring to show I am married to you.'

They sat down again and she snuggled up to him. She couldn't believe this was happening; she was so happy. 'This wedding is going to cost a lot, Dieter. The entire village will want to come.'

'I have a good job now and I want us to have a big, lively wedding. You must walk down the aisle in a white dress.' He leant back and gazed into her eyes. 'You are wearing a flowing dress with a long veil, aren't you?'

'You'll have to wait and see.' The teasing left her face and her expression sobered. 'There is something we must discuss. There are two houses in London: one belonged to Jane, which she left to Danny, and the other is mine. They are both rented out at the moment. Jane left instructions that I was to look after Danny's inheritance, and I think we should keep his house and let him decide, when he is older, what he wants to do with it.'

Dieter nodded agreement. 'A sensible idea.'

'But I think I'll sell mine and put the money aside for Danny's education.' She glanced hesitantly at Dieter to see his reaction. When he didn't say anything, she continued. 'I love this little cottage and would like to stay here. It's handy for your job and the farm and, anyway, I wouldn't want to go back to London again.'

'My darling, you must do whatever makes you happy. I am now in a position to support you and make a good life for us here.'

She laid her head on his chest and sighed contentedly. 'We must buy a new bed; mine is only a single.'

'We shall see to that as a priority.' He turned her to face him and kissed her.

The embrace went on and on as he began to explore her soft curves, moulding her closely to him, until she could feel the thud of his heart. She was completely lost in the sensations he was creating in her. Suddenly he stopped and leant back away from her, his breathing erratic, and she felt a sense of loss, wanting him to continue loving her.

'No, no, my darling. If I do not leave now, we will

go too far. It is only a short time before we are married and I want us to wait until then.'

With one final kiss, he left.

The next few days raced by in a flurry of activity. Hetty and John were thrilled to bits, and Hetty was already planning the food for the reception, and the cake. Everyone was pitching in to get it all ready in time. Angie had bought the material for her dress – a lovely satin that shimmered in the light – and Sally was hard at work. Angie was borrowing her friend's pearl tiara and billowing veil. Sally's generosity had saved her money and enabled her to buy a good-quality satin.

Dieter had also been busy dealing with all the legal aspects of getting married, and was absolutely determined to have everything settled so they could marry on the day they had chosen: Danny's birthday, Saturday, 27 May.

And now it was time to tell Danny before the banns were read tomorrow in church.

'Daddy's here.' Danny ran to open the door before Dieter could let himself in.

He swung his son up high, laughing. 'My, but you are getting too big for me to do this now.' With Danny still in his arms he kissed Angie, his lips lingering on hers. Then he sat Danny on a chair.

She watched the rapport between father and son with joy. It had been a rocky path reaching this stage, but once she was married to Dieter their family would be secure.

Dieter crouched in front of Danny. 'Before we go to the farm, your auntie and I have something to tell you.'

'You're not going away.' He looked alarmed.

'No, it is nothing like that. This is wonderful news and we hope it will make you very happy.'

Danny smiled then and his dimples flashed in anticipation.

'In three weeks' time I am going to marry your Auntie Angel, and after that we shall all be living here together.'

'You won't have to go away no more?' Danny was looking from one to the other, questioning. This seemed to be a very real fear to him.

Seeing that he was having difficulty understanding, Angie sat on the arm of the chair. 'You know how Emma's mummy and daddy live with her all the time?'

Danny nodded, eyes wide.

'Well, after we are married, your daddy will be living with us. He won't have to go back to the farm every evening. Will you like that?'

He nodded again, kicking his legs in excitement. 'Will you be my Mummy Angel then?'

'Yes, darling.' Angie's eyes misted with emotion. He was never going to forget that Jane had been the mother he had adored, and it was right he shouldn't, but this was more than she could have hoped for. Mummy Angel sounded wonderful to her.

'Right, let us go and see Grandma and Grandpa, shall we?' Dieter lifted Danny off the chair and set him on his feet. 'They are very excited about the wedding.'

'And so are we,' Angie murmured softly as they closed the front door and set off towards the farm.

With Danny trotting along between them, they smiled at each other, feeling as excited as he looked.

It would be nice when Daddy didn't have to go away all the time. He'd like that. Em said hers was there all the time, 'cept when he was working. Danny skipped along. He'd ask her what a wedding was. She knew a lot, for a girl.

Grandma and Grandpa were waiting in the yard for them, so he ran to see them. 'Daddy's gonna live with us!'

'We know,' Grandma laughed. 'Isn't that wonderful?'

'Yeah.' He watched them all talking and laughing. That made him all pleased inside.

'We've got something for you to see.' Grandpa held out his hand. 'She's in the next field.'

Danny reached up and caught hold of his hand. Everyone came to see what was in the field.

When they reached the gate, Danny climbed on the bars so he could see better. He was quite safe because Daddy was holding him.

'Ow, she's pretty!' A small brown and cream pony stared at them, and then came closer. 'Can I touch her, Grandpa?'

'Not just yet, she's only just arrived and hasn't settled in, but when she has you'll be able to ride her.'

What a lovely day this was! Now he'd go to see his pigs.

*

Angie walked back to the farmhouse with Hetty while the men took Danny to see his favourite animals.

'The little lad is happy with the news, then?'

'Yes, but I don't think he understands what it means.' Angie filled the kettle and put it on the stove, then laid out the cups. 'But he's pleased Dieter will be with us all the time.'

'Are you going to tell him you're marrying on his birthday?'

'Yes, we've decided he should have a proper birthday and hope this one gives him happier memories.' Angie gave a worried sigh. 'It was such a terrible day.'

'I know, my dear, but this one will be very different. It will be a day filled with happiness. He lost a mother on his last birthday, but he's gaining a father on this one. And with you as his mother now, he will have a complete family for the first time.'

'Yes, of course. It's been a difficult year, but things have turned out better than I could ever have hoped. I'm so glad we came here.'

'So are we, Angie. You have made our lives complete as well.' Hetty placed a pad and pen on the table and sat down. 'Now, while the men are out of the way, let's make a list of guests, so I know how much food to prepare.'

It was Sunday morning and they had all been to church to hear the banns read. When they eventually arrived back at the cottage, Angie checked the roast she had left cooking slowly in the oven and lit the gas under the vegetables.

John and Hetty stayed for lunch and it was a real squeeze to get everyone round the table. The children thought this was great fun, and it was a lively meal.

Work at the farm never stopped for anything, so John and Hetty left immediately after lunch. Joe and Dieter disappeared into the garden with the children, leaving Sally and Angie on their own for a bit of peace and quiet.

'Um . . .' Angie hesitated. 'Can I ask you something?'

'Of course.'

'Er . . . I was wondering how you manage to . . . make love with a young child in the next room?'

Sally chuckled. 'Very quietly, or else Emma would come into our room wanting to know what we were doing.'

'I bet she would.' Angie couldn't help grinning as she imagined the little girl demanding an explanation. Then she shook her head. 'We're not going to start out like most newly married couples, but Danny is such a blessing. A demanding one, but a blessing none the less, and I wouldn't have it any other way. Neither would Dieter.'

'Of course you wouldn't.' Sally cupped her chin in her hands, elbows on the table, giving Angie a speculative look. 'I take it you haven't made love properly yet.'

'No, Dieter always stops. He says we have all of our lives together and he wants to wait until we're married.'

'Joe was the same.' Sally snorted in amusement. 'Damned frustrating for both of us, but I'm glad we waited. Made our first night all the more exciting and special.'

'Yes, you're right. I know that since the war some couples don't wait, but it is the right way to start a marriage.'

'Phew, what a day!' Later that evening Dieter sat on the settee beside Angie and drew her into his arms for a long, much needed kiss. 'That's better. I have wanted to do that all day.' He ran his long fingers through her hair, admiring the colour as the light caught it, making it shine with red, gold, brown. 'Chestnut is the right name for this shade. I hope we have a girl with your colouring.'

'Would you like more children?' They hadn't discussed this before.

'Oh, yes, if you do also.'

'I'd love one or two.'

'Perfect.' Dieter held her away so he could look into her eyes. 'We must have a honeymoon. I would only be able to take two days off, but we could go to the seaside. Yes?'

'How can we do that, Dieter? We can't leave Danny. It would upset him even if Sally agreed to look after him.'

'I did not mean we should go on our own. Our son must come with us, of course.'

Angie kissed him lovingly for saying 'our son' and being so understanding.

'Does that mean you agree?'

She nodded, laughing softly. 'It will be a strange honeymoon with a four-year-old in our room.'

'We shall have to be very, very quiet.' Dieter put a finger to his lips.

'That's just what Sally said.' Angie was pleased they had talked in this way. It was right to discuss things that would touch their lives together. And it was also comforting to know that she was no longer alone. It would be wonderful to have someone to share the ups and downs of life with.

'I shall write to Gerda and ask if she will come for the wedding. I would very much like her to be there.'

'Oh, she must come.' She knew how much this would mean to him. 'Why don't we invite the Mansteins as well? I'm sure your sister will come if they do.'

'That is an excellent idea and I shall write and ask them. We should also invite the Colonel and his parents.'

'Are you sure you want Bob to come?' Her smile was teasing.

'Quite sure. I quite like him now you are going to marry me. I will write to the Colonel in the morning as well.'

'You never call him Bob, Dieter. Why is that?'

He lifted his hands in horror. 'The man was my gaoler and then he tries to take from me the girl I love. No, no, I admire the man, but could not be that familiar with him.'

'Did I make you jealous?'

'You did indeed. Very jealous.'

He tipped her back on the settee until she was

laughing with glee at his expression. The attempt at appearing stern just did not work. His eyes were so expressive, and they were glinting with amusement.

He put a finger to his lips. 'Shush, you will wake Danny and he will believe I am attacking you. He is happy now that I am his father, but he will not allow anyone to lay hands on his Auntie Angel.'

That caused them both to shake with silent laughter.

A week before the wedding, and it was chaos. There was still so much to do, and Angie was close to panic. Dieter had worked tirelessly to see that all the necessary paperwork was in order, but everything else had been left to her and Hetty.

'Keep still!' Sally ordered as she tried to get the hem on the dress right. 'If you keep fidgeting I'll never be able to make it hang properly.'

Angie forced herself to stop shifting about. 'It's a beautiful dress, Sally. You're really clever to make it without a pattern.'

'I had the drawing you did, and that was all I needed. You were right to keep it plain and simple. Get off the chair and turn around slowly so I can see what the train is like. Don't want you tripping up on your way down the aisle.'

Holding on to Sally's hand and being careful not to fall, Angie got down and walked across the floor, turning as ordered.

After another walk around the room, she faced her friend. 'It feels perfect.'

Sally was nodding. 'The extra money you spent on the material was well worth it. The skirt hangs beautifully. Okay, let's get you out of it and I'll finish the hem this evening. That's the last job.'

'Oh, good.' Angie breathed a sigh of relief. 'At least the dress is ready on time, and the cake, of course. You wait until you see it, Sally. Hetty's made a wonderful job of it.'

She got dressed again as Sally laid the beautiful creation on the bed.

'Let's have some tea; I'm gasping.' Sally made sure the bedroom door was locked so her daughter couldn't get at the dress, and they went downstairs.

It had been a rush, but it looked as if everything was going to be ready in time.

39

The day had arrived, and Angie's insides were in a tight knot as Sally adjusted the veil.

'I'm so nervous,' she groaned. 'My legs are shaking badly and I'll never be able to walk down the aisle. I should never have bought such high heels, but I wanted to look taller. I'll fall over.'

'No, you won't.' Sally stood back to admire the bride. 'You look absolutely beautiful.'

Angie gazed in the full-length mirror, hardly able to believe her eyes. The dress had a heart-shaped neckline and long sleeves; the skirt fell straight at the front and then fanned out at the back into a short train. Her hair had been piled up on top, with the lovely tiara nestling in the curls and the pearls glinting in her chestnut hair. The finished effect was one of simple elegance.

'We gave Danny his presents this morning and he smiled politely as he took them.' Sally fussed with the veil. 'How is he taking the anniversary of his mother's death?'

'He was a bit tearful early this morning when he opened his presents and cards, but I sat on the bed with him and talked about the wedding, and what a lovely day it was going to be. He looked at me with those big grey eyes swimming with tears, and then smiled. He's such a brave boy.'

'He is.' Sally nodded in agreement. 'Once he gets caught up in the excitement of the wedding, the dark memories of a year ago will fade, but they'll never be forgotten, Angie.'

'They certainly won't. I'll never forget the horror of that day either. Choosing this day to marry might seem strange and unfeeling to some people, but we've done it in the hope it will give Danny happy memories of his birthday. Instead of saying this is the day my mum died, he will hopefully say this is the day my daddy married my auntie.'

'Well, you wanted something special and this couldn't be more special.' Sally smiled sympathetically.

Angie's frown disappeared when Danny, Emma and Hetty came in the bedroom.

Emma was in a pink dress with a circle of pink and white flowers in her hair; she carried a little basket overflowing with the same flowers. She looked a picture. And when Angie saw Danny her eyes shone with pride. He was wearing long trousers and jacket in dark royal blue, a white satin shirt and blue bow tie. In his buttonhole was a pink rose the same colour as Emma's dress. But even more pleasing was the bright smile on his face, and she knew everything was going to be all right.

She bent and kissed them. 'Oh, my, don't you both look gorgeous.'

'Ooh, Auntie!' Danny ran round her, looking at the

dress from all angles. 'I've never seen you dressed like that before.'

'You look like a fairy princess.' Emma couldn't take her eyes off the vision in front of her. 'Are you going to have a basket like mine?'

'No, I have a bouquet.' Angie pointed to the flowers on the bed. It was a profusion of pastel-coloured roses with trailing ferns. 'You will have to look after that for me when the service begins.'

Emma nodded. 'Mummy told me.'

Angie then reached out and straightened Danny's tie. 'And you must stay near your father in case he needs you.' She wanted him to feel he had an important part to play in the wedding.

'Emma!' Sally spoke firmly as her daughter reached out to touch the flowing veil. 'Don't touch.'

'I'm only looking.' Her hand shot back down again, and she scowled at the reprimand. She held out her hands. 'I'm clean, look.'

General Strachan strode in then and stopped suddenly. 'My word, but the bride does look exquisite. Just wait until Dieter sees you. I'll take the children to the church now and then come back for you and John.'

'She's dressed like that because it's a special day.' Danny beamed proudly. 'Are we going in your big car?'

'Of course. We can't have you walking along the street in all your finery, can we? Off we go, then.' He held out a hand to each of the children.

Having been well schooled by Sally and Hetty in what they had to do, they left eagerly.

Soon the cottage was empty except for John and Angie.

John appeared quite overcome. 'I'm so proud to be standing in for your father.'

'Thank you for doing it. I wouldn't have asked anyone else.'

The General soon arrived back, and, with John's help, Angie was settled in the back of the car. When he'd heard about the wedding he had insisted on being their chauffeur and using the Rolls-Royce as the wedding car. He drove very slowly so they would arrive right on time.

'Robert got home in the early hours of this morning and he's at the church helping with the ushering. That was a wise move, inviting Gerda's German family as well. They are happy to be here and looking forward to the wedding.' The General chuckled. 'Robert's come in full uniform, much to the delight of the children. There was much saluting going on when I took them inside the door.'

'Oh, Danny will love that. I'm so pleased Bob was able to make it after all.'

There wasn't time to say anything else, as the car pulled up outside the church. Hetty and Sally came forward to help her out and make sure the dress was hanging properly. The sun was shining, bells were ringing, and the children were waiting in the porch. She walked towards them, smiling through the thin veil.

Once they were all together, Sally fussed, getting everyone in their right place. 'Now you must be careful not to step on the dress,' she reminded Emma and Danny.

They both nodded, wide-eyed with excitement.

'Mrs Poulton's playing the organ,' Danny told Angie. 'She's doing it special for you and Daddy.'

Angie smiled, too nervous to speak, and turned to gaze round the crowded church.

'Stop it!'

Angie turned her head and saw Danny pulling his hand away from Emma.

The little girl grabbed at him again. 'You've got to hold my hand.'

'Stop arguing, you two,' John scolded in a whisper. 'No squabbling here.'

'Danny's got to hold my hand,' Emma hissed. 'He might walk too fast and step on the dress. And it's a wedding, so we've got to hold hands.' She gave everyone a 'so there' look.

They were causing people to look round and smile, so Danny let her take his hand, muttering, 'Daft girl.'

With that little disagreement settled, John held out his arm, and at the sound of the wedding march they started down the aisle, where Dieter was waiting with Joe.

How handsome they both looked in their new suits, Angie thought, especially Dieter.

He never took his eyes off her, and when she was near him he reached out for her hand and grasped it tightly, as if he was afraid she would disappear. Then he brought her hand to his lips and kissed it gently. It was such a loving gesture that she was sure her voice would fail her.

But it didn't. She spoke clearly, confidently, as did Dieter. The service was lovely and the music glorious. Dieter had chosen it all himself and Mrs Poulton played with much skill.

In what seemed no time at all they were signing the register. Their kiss told them just how delighted and happy they were.

The sun was still blazing down as the photographs were taken. It was chaos trying to usher everyone into the right places and keep the children still for the pictures. Bob stepped in and, with true military discipline, sorted it out. Dieter had one taken on his own with his sister, who smiled up at him. There was no sign of the troubled girl who had come to England. Gerda was quite happy to be here with her other family, knowing she would be going back with them to her home the next day.

Once the photographer was satisfied, they all made their way to the church hall. There was a long table by the stage with a splendid cake as the centrepiece, and a buffet laid out for guests to help themselves. There were even a few bottles of wine for the toasts. Hetty had insisted on providing the food and had done a wonderful job, considering that rationing was still in place. Living on a farm had its advantages at a time like this.

Angie held on to Dieter's arm as they received their guests and, for a moment, her thoughts turned to Jane.

Her silent prayer asked, 'Would this please you?' A warm feeling spread through her, as if her cousin had answered with an emphatic 'Yes!'

After the cutting of the cake, Joe made his speech, amusing everyone with his dry sense of humour. Then John spoke for a few minutes in his role as father of the bride.

Bob stood up. 'I would like to say a few words about my friends. I have known Dieter for some years. He was one of the least troublesome of my charges, but I had to keep a sharp eye on all of them. I was never sure if they were tunnelling or planning many other ways of escape from me. They were just a bunch of young men and most of them I liked, but Dieter stood out from the crowd. He is a talented man, and those years of captivity must have been hell for him. I know he endeared himself to everyone in this village, and I am delighted he has found happiness here with Angie. She is a fine girl and will make him a wonderful wife.' He raised his glass. 'I wish you many years of bliss together.'

The speech was greeted with thunderous applause, as they all raised their glasses in salute to the bride and groom.

'I never realized Bob would be so gracious in defeat,' Dieter smirked.

Angie looked at her new husband in surprise. 'Oh, it's Bob at last, is it?'

The only reply was a deep amused chuckle.

It was then time for the magic show, and Sally

rounded up all the children. Joe popped behind a door and came back wearing his cape and pointed hat, making the youngsters yell in delight. Danny and Emma were right in the front. The show turned out to be as popular with the grown-ups as with the children; everyone joined in and gave Joe advice when things didn't go quite to plan.

After that Mrs Poulton played music for them so they could dance.

By six o'clock Emma and Danny were exhausted, and Sally needed a rest. 'I'll take them back with me,' she told Angie. 'There are two beds in Emma's room, and Danny can sleep there. You can have at least one night to yourselves.'

'We can't put you to all that trouble, Sally.'

'It's no bother. The little things are so tired I don't think there will be any argument at all.' She kissed Angie's cheek and stood on tiptoe to reach Dieter. 'Take this chance to be alone for a while.'

Joe and Dieter helped Sally home with the two very sleepy children, and in less than half an hour the men were back.

'Is Danny all right?' Angie asked anxiously.

'He is already sound asleep.' Dieter placed an arm around her. 'We can safely leave him for tonight.'

There was no sign of the party ending, so Angie and Dieter slipped away at nine o'clock. She was a little nervous about their first night together and put the kettle on as soon as they got back to the cottage.

Dieter turned off the gas and led her upstairs. 'We don't need tea, darling.'

Once in their room he helped her remove the wedding dress, and when he began to make slow, passionate love to her, all her nervousness disappeared. It was a time of mutual pleasure, and she knew just how lucky she was to have married this wonderful man.

She slept curled around him and woke in the morning to his gentle caresses. They made love again just as it was getting light.

Dieter propped himself up and gazed down at her. 'That will have to last us for a couple of days. After breakfast we are going to Burnham-on-Sea, and Danny will have a bed in our room at the guest house.'

It was when she was washed and dressed and in the kitchen that Angie realized just how hungry she was. She had been too excited to eat much at the reception, so she set about cooking a large fry-up.

There was a knock on the back door and Sally peered in. 'Ah, good, you're up.'

'Hello, Sally.' Dieter smiled. 'How has Danny been?'

'Fine. Never woke up once in the night, but he wants to come back now. He's had his breakfast.'

'Send him back, Sally. We're going away as soon as we've eaten.' Angie put a plate of bacon and eggs in front of Dieter.

'Okay.' Sally grinned. 'Have fun at the seaside. Danny's very excited about going.'

No more than five minutes after she left Danny tore

in, still wearing his wedding suit, and hugged them both. 'When we going to the sea?'

'As soon as we've washed the dishes and you've changed into different clothes.' Angie ruffled Danny's hair. 'I've already packed your things.'

By the afternoon Dieter and Angie were walking along the beach hand in hand, watching Danny rummaging along the edge of the water looking for shells.

He ran back towards them, holding out something he'd found. 'Look at this, Mummy Angel. Isn't it pretty? I'll give it to Emma when we get back.' He gave it to her for safekeeping.

'You are getting all wet.' Dieter stooped down and unlaced Danny's shoes. 'Take these off and you can paddle.'

As soon as his shoes and socks were off, he was tearing towards the sea again, laughing and squealing when the gentle waves lapped around his bare feet. He was loving every minute of it.

Dieter and Angie went and stood next to him. Danny pushed between them and reached out for their hands, his eyes clear and happy as he grinned up at them.

There wasn't a cloud in the sky. The sun was blazing down, turning the sea many shades, from blue to green, with flashes of light as it caught the tops of waves. Even the sandy beach sparkled.

And there wasn't a shadow in sight.

ALSO BY
BERYL MATTHEWS

What will one girl do to follow her dreams?

Her Mother's Daughter

BERYL
MATTHEWS

WHICH BOOK WILL YOU READ NEXT?

ALSO BY
BERYL MATTHEWS

WHICH BOOK WILL YOU READ NEXT?